BOURBON STREET Nights

Volume One of CRESCENT CITY

JACK CALDWELL

WHITE SOUP PRESS

BOURBON STREET NIGHTS: VOLUME ONE OF CRESCENT CITY

Copyright © 2015 by Jack Caldwell.

White Soup Press, c/o Jack Caldwell, 3140 Sunset Beach Drive, Venice, FL, 34293.

info@cajuncheesehead.com
https://cajuncheesehead.com/
http://whitesouppress.com/
http://austenvariations.com/

ISBN: 978-0-9891080-3-4

Back cover Superdome: David Grunfeld, *The Times-Picayune*
Back cover beads: copyright © 2013 Arina Habich
Book layout & design by Ellen Pickels

Dedication

For Barbara

For those who are gone and for those who remain.
May America never forget.

I'm not going to lay down in words the lure of this place. Every great writer in the land, from Faulkner to Twain to Rice to Ford, has tried to do it and fallen short. It is impossible to capture the essence, tolerance, and spirit of south Louisiana in words, and to try is to roll down a road of clichés, bouncing over beignets and beads and brass bands, and it just is what it is.

It is home.

— Chris Rose, *1 Dead in Attic*

Crescent City

Prologue

O nce upon a time, there was a grand city on the banks of a mighty river. That the city existed at all was a mistake. The land was poor, low, and prone to flooding. René-Robert Cavelier, Sieur de La Salle, was looking for the Holy Grail of explorers: the Northwest Passage, the waterborne route through the Americas to the Far East. Even though the newly discovered territory was less than ideal, La Salle claimed the swampy land anyway for Louis, his king. Later, the Le Moyne brothers, Iberville and Bienville, found the closest high point of land along the river to the ocean. The younger brother would name it for the regent of France.

The city had always been considered French, and yet the Spanish owned it for decades. A great emperor reclaimed it, only to sell it to an upstart democracy because of a slave revolt in the Caribbean. So valuable was the city, that an epic and bloody struggle was fought over it after the war was over. Only Gettysburg would replace it as the greatest battle in American history.

The city, the largest in the South, was the first target of Abraham Lincoln's Union in its life-and-death struggle against Jefferson Davis's Confederacy. With its fall, the Confederate States of America was doomed. The city and its state were among the last to be released from the yoke of Reconstruction. Left to its own devices, the city looked inward and allowed others to replace it as the leading metropolis in the South. This isolation also allowed it to develop one of the most unique cultures in the United States.

The city was a powerhouse in petroleum and chemicals. It boasted the largest port in the nation. Millions of people from all over the world spent billions of dollars just to walk its streets. Its music changed entertainment forever.

This story is about three women: one a Cajun from the swamps, one an Uptown Jew, and one a Mississippi girl. It is about their trials and tribulations, the men who loved them, and the men who broke their hearts.

But it is also about a fourth lady, one known by many names. *Isle d'Orleans. The Paris of the Americas. Queen City of the South. The City that Care Forgot. Birthplace of Jazz. The Big Easy. Crescent City. New Orleans*—what she was, and what she may be again.

This is their story.

Volume One

Bourbon Street Nights

Dramatis Personae

Tommy Bertram Sophomore at Tulane University and member of Alpha Iota, roommate of John Waguespack.

Charles "Chuck" Bingley Son of Catherine, senior business major at Tulane University, chapter president of Alpha Iota fraternity.

Carrie Bingley Daughter of Catherine, junior at Louisiana State University, member of the Golden Girls dance squad.

Catherine Bingley Wealthy widow, lives in Baton Rouge.

Elizabeth Boudreaux Second daughter of T.B. Boudreaux, sophomore English Writing major at Loyola University of New Orleans.

Jane Boudreaux Eldest daughter of T.B. Boudreaux, senior Nursing major at Southeastern Louisiana University in Hammond.

Chris Breaux Second-year medical student at Tulane School of Medicine, alumnus of Alpha Iota.

John Buford Lawyer in Baton Rouge and captain in the Louisiana National Guard.

Marianne "Mari" Dashwood Sophomore Vocal Music major at Loyola from Jackson, MS.

William Darcy Son of George Darcy, second year MBA student at AB Freeman School of Business at Tulane University, past chapter president of Alpha Iota.

George Darcy CEO and majority stockholder in Delta Global Shipping Inc. (DGS) of New Orleans, widowed, lives at Dansereau Plantation in St. Charles Parish, LA.

Gina Darcy Daughter of George Darcy.

Anna Elliot Member of the Golden Girls dance squad, best friend of Carrie Bingley.

Richard Fitzwilliam Lieutenant in the New Orleans Police Department assigned to the Second District, cousin of William Darcy.

Olivia Fitzwilliam Wife of Richard Fitzwilliam.

Dr. Jennings English professor and faculty advisor of the *Loyola VOICE.*

Dr. George Katz Surgeon and instructor at Tulane University Medical Center and Medical School, alumni advisor for Alpha Iota.

Justin Middleton Student editor of the *Loyola VOICE.*

Catherine Morland Student at Tulane University and Alpha Iota Sweetheart, dates Henry Tilney.

Nikhil "Nick" Patel Student at Tulane University and a member of Alpha Iota.

Henry Tilney Junior at Tulane University and vice president of the Alpha Iota Chapter.

John Waguespack Sophomore Marketing major at Tulane University, member of Alpha Iota.

Emma Weinberg Second daughter of Abe Weinberg, sophomore Fine Arts major at Newcomb College, Tulane University.

Abe Weinberg Partner in an architectural firm, widower, lives in the Garden District neighborhood of New Orleans.

Gregory Wickham Unemployed, small-time drug dealer in New Orleans, specializing in sales to the college crowd.

Part One

America has only three cities: New York, San Francisco, and New Orleans. Everywhere else is Cleveland.

—Tennessee Williams

Way down yonder in New Orleans
in the land of the dreamy scenes
there's a garden of Eden.
You know what I mean.
Creole babies with flashin' eyes
softly whisper their tender sighs.
And then you stop.
Won't you give your lady fair a little smile?
Stop.
You bet your life you'll linger there a little while.
We've got heaven right here on earth
with those beautiful queens.
Way down yonder in New Orleans.

"Way Down Yonder in New Orleans"
by Henry Creamer and Turner Layton

Chapter 1

Elizabeth Boudreaux, a new sophomore at Loyola University of New Orleans, waited for the elevator in the twelve-story Buddig Hall dormitory, her arms full of hanging clothes, rumpled from the hatch of her old Civic. After a wait that seemed to last forever, the car arrived and the doors opened. Fortunately, no students came barreling out of it to knock her down. The curvy brunette, her curly hair pulled back in a ponytail, entered the car and pressed the button for the fifth floor. A creaking minute later, she walked down the hallway to her new room—and new roommate.

She's got to be better than Louisa the Loser!

Elizabeth had asked Housing to assign her a new roommate for the fall term. All of her friends were settled, so there was no solution there. Elizabeth hoped "roommate roulette" would work better this time.

Her large brown eyes scanned the descending numbers. Reaching her door at the end of the hall, Elizabeth realized she had a dilemma. With her arms full, she could not pull out the room key, wedged securely in the front pocket of her Levis. She wondered whether she should drop the clothes or knock on the door.

While she tried to make up her mind, the door opened. "Oh... Hi!" cried a slim girl with straight black hair and blue eyes. "Can I help you?"

"Umm, yeah. This is my room."

"Oh, you must be Elizabeth!" the girl cried in a southern accent. She stuck out her hand. "I'm Marianne Dashwood, but my friends call me 'Mari.'"

With no other choice, Elizabeth took the offered hand. "Hello, Mari. Can I come in now?"

Marianne started to laugh. "Oh, I am so stupid! I'm sorry. Come in, come in!" She backed up, allowing Elizabeth to move into the room. She looked around and found Marianne had taken the bed on the right side of the room.

Good, things are already looking better. At least this ditz didn't take my bed. Where is she from—Mississippi? Elizabeth preferred to sleep on her left side, and because Louisa had claimed the left bed the year before, Elizabeth slept facing the wall for nine months. She dropped her burden on the unclaimed bed.

"There! Now I can greet you properly. I'm Elizabeth Boudreaux."

"Do you go by Elizabeth?"

"I'm called 'Elizabeth' or 'Liz,' too."

"So, tell me about yourself. Where are you from?" Marianne sat on her bed, pulling one foot underneath her.

"Chackbay, Louisiana. It's a little town outside of Thibodaux."

"I'm from Jackson, Mississippi—as though you couldn't tell from my accent."

Nailed it, Elizabeth thought.

"You got any family?"

"Four sisters. Umm, Mari, can we hold off on twenty questions for a bit? I've got to get the rest of my stuff out of my car."

"Oh, you want some help?"

Things were definitely looking up! Louisa wouldn't pick up after herself, much less volunteer to help a stranger move in.

"Sure. Come on."

AN HOUR LATER, ALL OF Elizabeth's possessions were moved from the car into her room. Marianne insisted on helping Elizabeth put her things away. While working together happily, Elizabeth learned that Marianne was a sophomore like herself, majoring in vocal music. She had one sister at home with her divorced mother. Her father was an oil field worker in Saudi Arabia.

"Yeah, ol' Dad thought getting out of the country would save him money. He didn't figure on the company docking his pay for Mom's child support. He was mad at first, but it's all cool now."

"Are you still in touch?"

"I haven't seen him in seven years. Just a couple of cards a year and a phone call on my birthday—his loss."

"I don't know what I would do without my dad. He's my best friend."

"I feel the same way about Mom." Marianne clasped her hands against her heart. "What's your mother like?"

"Don't ask."

"Is she mean?"

"Oh, no. It's just…well, she swallows you, you know?"

"I understand. Four sisters, huh?"

Elizabeth nodded. "Jane's at Southeastern Louisiana in the nursing program. Mary and Kit are still in high school—Mary graduates this year. Lydia starts high school next year."

"Does Mary know what she wants to do?"

"Teaching. Mom gave us a love of reading, but Mary's the family bookworm."

"What are you majoring in?"

"English writing. I want to go into journalism."

"Awesome. Will you write for *The Maroon*?" Marianne asked about the Loyola student newspaper.

"I did that last year. I'm thinking of joining the staff of a new paper, the *Loyola VOICE*. It's supposed to be innovative and hard-hitting. Oh, and I'll submit some stuff for *ReVisions*, the literary arts journal."

"I wish I could write."

"I wish I could sing. I'll bet you're good."

"I'm okay."

"Okay? Didn't you say you've got a scholarship?"

"*Partial* scholarship. And that was for my voice. You got one for your brain."

"*Partial* scholarship, Mari," Elizabeth replied with a grin.

"Well, us two *partials* are gonna have a great year, Elizabeth! I love this room. It's a lot better than the one I had at Biever Hall last term." She sighed. "A bathroom of my very own."

"Mari, in case you didn't notice, we share it with the girls next door."

"Don't disrupt my groove, Elizabeth. At Biever, I had to go all the way down the hall." Elizabeth shuddered. At that moment, Marianne's cell phone rang.

"Hello? Emma, darling! How're you, sista? Where? Okay, can I bring my new roomie? Lemme ask." Marianne put her hand over the phone. "Elizabeth, got any plans for dinner? I'm meeting my friend, Emma, at Fat Harry's. She's real nice. You'll like her. Say you'll come, please?"

Elizabeth shrugged. "Sure, I'd love to go."

"Awesome!" She returned to the phone. "She's in. Her name's Elizabeth, and she's a sweetheart. We'll see ya there at seven. Okay. TTFN!" She switched off the phone. "This is gonna be so much fun! My friend's name's Emma Weinberg; she's at Newcomb. I met her at Summer Lyric. We were doing *Man of La Mancha*, and she was helping out with set design."

"I love that musical! Did you play Aldonza?"

"I was the understudy, but I got one performance. Anyway, with all the time backstage, I got to be friends with Em. That's what a lot of us call her—Em. Em's real cool, and she knows *everybody*. She lives at home in this big ol' house off St. Charles Avenue. Her dad's a widower. Oh, and she's Jewish—you're cool with that, right?"

"Of course." Elizabeth wondered where Marianne was going.

"Oh, good. Some people are funny that way. Back home, a couple of the matrons at the New Antioch Baptist Church—woo! Jesus is gonna come back and smite them, just wait and see. You're Catholic, right? I mean, that is a crucifix, right?"

Elizabeth looked at the small crucifix she had placed on her desk.

"Yes, it is, and yes, I am."

"I'm Methodist, myself. People ask me why I came to a Catholic college, as if I was going to a seminary. Hello! Notre Dame is a Catholic college! Stupid people just give me the red ass. Anyway, Catholics don't have any problems with Jews, right?"

Elizabeth just shook her head at Marianne's steady stream of consciousness. "No, we don't. At least, we shouldn't."

"Hate just sucks, you know? So, we'll meet Em at Fat Harry's at seven. That will give us some time to get to the bookstore."

"Why are we going to the bookstore?"

"Roomie, get with it! These walls are too bare! We gotta get some posters!"

Elizabeth smiled. *I think I'm gonna like this semester.*

New Orleans's very reason for existence is the Mississippi River, the longest river in North America. Starting in Minnesota, the Father of Waters (as the natives called it) snakes south, cutting the United States in half. Joined by first the Missouri River and then the Ohio, the Big Muddy flows down through Dixie until it reaches present-day Baton Rouge. The river then turns east, flowing for over fifty miles before turning southeast again just past Chalmette to empty into the Gulf of Mexico. Therefore, for some distance, the East Bank of the Mississippi is north of the river, and the West Bank is south.

In New Orleans, north, south, east, and west—as with so many other rules and terms—have no meaning.

If you are in the city and moving in an eastwardly direction, you are moving downriver, towards St. Bernard Parish, known to locals as "Da Parish." If the journey is started near Tulane in the heart of the

Uptown district, you are also considered to be traveling Downtown, towards the downtown Central Business district (CBD) and the French Quarter. Heading north, you are going towards the Lake, referring to Lake Pontchartrain. Going west means heading towards the state's second most populated parish, Jefferson, and the large, unincorporated area called Metairie. So when traveling, one is said to be going towards Jefferson, Metairie, or upriver.

Crossing over the river, meant one was going to the West Bank, which is south of the city as the crow flies. The North Shore is the north shore of Lake Pontchartrain (the Lake)—St. Tammany Parish.

Confused? It does take a bit of time for new residents and college students to figure it out. For tourists, it's best to take taxis.

Located on famous St. Charles Avenue between the Uptown and Riverbend neighborhoods of New Orleans, Loyola stood next door to the much larger Tulane University and across the street from Audubon Park. Many people took advantage of the streetcar stop right in front of the two schools, but Marianne and Elizabeth hopped into Marianne's rusty, used Corolla and drove down the majestic live oak-lined avenue to the corner of St. Charles and Napoleon. Parking on Napoleon Avenue, the two girls walked to a dark wood storefront that was the entrance to Fat Harry's.

In a town renowned for its neighborhood joints, bars, and pubs, Fat Harry's was an institution with the college-aged crowd. Dark, crowded, and smelling slightly of stale beer, it was the stomping ground of generations of the Uptown university types. Students consumed burgers and quaffed beer while listening to the same Motown music their parents rocked out to. If New Orleans ever passed a law against polo shirts and khaki pants, half the men in the city would be naked.

Marianne and Elizabeth squeezed their way in. It took only moments for Marianne to spot her quarry. The two girls made their way to a tall bottled-blonde sitting at a high table.

"*Emmm!*" screamed Marianne.

"*Mar-eee!*" The blonde returned the greeting, and the two hugged and blew air kisses.

"Emma Weinberg," said Marianne, "this is my new roommate, Elizabeth Boudreaux."

Emma shook Elizabeth's hand. "Nice to meet you. Where did you go to school?"

Elizabeth understood her question to be New Orleans code for *Where did you go to high school?* "E.D. White in Thibodaux. You?"

"Newman," Emma answered, naming one of the more prestigious private schools in the area. She was a slender girl with three prominent features: a slightly long nose and one of the most impressive chests Elizabeth had ever seen on a woman of her slim frame. It wasn't anywhere near Pamela Anderson big, but it was impossible to ignore. Emma wore designer clothes—Manolo Blahnik pumps and a Prada bag sat on the table—but Elizabeth found her smile to be genuine.

"Sit down," she said with a wave of her hand. "Why don't y'all look over the menu while I get us something to drink? What can I bring you?"

Before Elizabeth could answer, Marianne chimed in. "A Miller Lite. How 'bout you, Elizabeth?" At Elizabeth's questioning look —they were all sophomores, at least a year too young to buy alcohol —she continued. "You want a beer?"

Elizabeth shrugged. It was Emma's neck for buying beer underage. "Abita Amber."

Emma smiled and moved to the bar. Once there, she caught the eye of one of the younger bartenders.

"Yeah, Em?"

"Jimmy, I need a Lite, an Abita, and a Zima."

"Aww, Em, I don't know—"

"C'mon, Jimmy, this is for your Emma. Please?"

"Jeez, you'll be the death of me. If I get busted—"

"You won't, Jimmy," Emma assured him.

The bartender capitulated and soon returned with the drinks. "Run a tab?"

"You're a sweetheart. I'll settle up before we leave. Bye-bye." Jimmy grinned and his eyes followed Emma as she returned to the table.

"Here we are, ladies. A toast to a new semester."

After drinking to the new school year, Marianne asked, "So what you gonna order?" as the waitress approached.

"Small burger," said Elizabeth.

"I'm gonna get some cheese fries. Y'all want to share?"

"Ooooh, cheese fries! I'm in," said Emma.

Elizabeth smiled. "I tell you what. Forget the burger. I'll take nachos."

"With extra jalapeños?" asked Marianne.

"You bet."

"Yeah!" Marianne turned to the waitress and ordered the nachos and cheese fries. After the waitress left, the girls continued their conversation. Responding to Emma's question, Elizabeth told her she was studying to be a journalist.

"So what are you studying, Emma?" asked Elizabeth.

"Oooo…that's a good question!" Marianne laughed.

"Oh, shut your mouth, you redneck!" Emma teased back. "Well, Elizabeth, I started out as a psychology major, but I didn't enjoy it, so I switched in my second semester to sociology. Now I'm in fine arts." She smiled. "I'm experiencing all college can offer."

"She's really working on her M-R-S, if you ask me!" said Marianne.

"Oh?" said Elizabeth at Emma's frown. "Any prospects?"

"No," Emma admitted. "How about you?"

"No. There was a boy back home, but that's history."

Emma sighed. "Long distance romances never work."

Elizabeth grimaced. "It would if the asshole in question would stop rodayin' around behind my back."

Everybody laughed. Emma turned toward a flash of sandy hair. "Hey, there's Chuck. Chuck! Over here!"

A good-looking, tall man with a friendly grin approached the table, a Bud in his hand. "Emma! Good to see you, lady! How was your summer?"

"Not bad. All ready for your senior year?"

"Can't wait."

Emma turned to the others. "Girls, this is my friend Chuck Bingley from Tulane."

"Howdy do, ladies?"

"Chuck, this is Marianne Dashwood and Elizabeth Boudreaux, both from Loyola."

Chuck grinned. "Loyola, huh? You gals know why Jesus has his hands raised in front of the school?" He was referring to a large statue of Christ at the entrance to Loyola.

Both had heard the old joke before—countless times. "Yeah, we know. 'I can't help it if Loyola is a better school than the one next door!'" they cried in unison.

"No, no, that's not it." Chuck laughed. "It's the other way 'round!"

"Give it up, sugar," advised Emma, "or you'll never get a date." Chuck's face fell. "You heard?"

"What?" asked Emma.

"Jennifer and I—we broke up over the summer."

"Oh, Chuck, I'm so sorry."

"Ah, well, water under the bridge. Hey, I've got to join my buddies, but I've got an invitation for y'all. First night of Rush we're throwing a big party, and you're invited—all of you."

Emma turned to the others. "Chuck is president of the Alpha Iota fraternity chapter at Tulane."

"It'll be dry—college rules—but it'll be fun."

"It sounds great. Hey, is that William over there?" Emma pointed to the crowd in the back.

"Yeah, and Chris, too."

"Tell them 'hi' for me."

"Sure. It was great seeing you, Em. And nice meeting you ladies. Don't forget, first night of Rush! AI House! Be there!" he said as he moved away.

"Cute guy," said Marianne after Chuck was out of earshot.

"Yeah, he's really nice. Too good for that bitch Jennifer," Emma growled.

"Whoa," remarked Elizabeth. "Sounds like history there."

"I watch out for my friends, Elizabeth. Jennifer treated Chuck like shit. She was a real user, you know?"

"And now he's free," Marianne said with a grin. "You're going after him?"

"Maybe," Emma said with a smile.

"Aww, looks like Chuckie's gonna get some TLC for that broken heart." Elizabeth laughed.

"Chuck E's in love," Marianne sang.

"Mari!" Emma laughed. "Stop it, you redneck!"

Elizabeth basked in the good humor of her new friends. She was relieved she had found some friends at school at last.

"AHH, CHEESE FRIES." WITHOUT WAITING for permission, Chuck took a handful out of the basket. No "processed cheese product" here, the hot French fries were topped with piles of grated cheddar, and the heat of the fries melted the cheese into gooey strings of addictive, cholesterol-filled goodness.

"Leave some for us, Chuck," warned Chris Breaux.

"Nope," he mumbled with a filled mouth.

"That's the way with those Baton Rouge guys," remarked William Darcy. "If it wasn't for low class, they would have no class at all."

"Hey, I resemble the remark!"

"You're going to resemble a whale if you keep stuffing down those fries," said the fourth member of the group.

"Aw, who invited the cop?"

"Someone's got to keep an eye on you guys," responded Lt. Richard Fitzwilliam of the New Orleans Police Department and Darcy's cousin. Unlike the rest of the family, Richard felt a calling for law enforcement. He had earned his Criminal Justice degree at UNO before joining the NOPD. His parents, while proud of him, did not know what to make of their boy in blue. Still, he remained good friends with his younger, wealthy cousin. "Was that Emma Weinberg you were talkin' to?"

"Yeah, and a couple of babes from Loyola."

"Babes is right," said Chris. "You get some introductions?"

"Down, boy," advised William. "They've got be sophomores, at most. Too young for my blood."

"Willie, you are *way* too picky for your age," said Richard.

William frowned. He hated being called Willie, but there was nothing he could do about it. Richard knew it bugged him, and he lived to see William get upset. William would not give him the satisfaction.

"You got that right," agreed Chuck. "Their names are Marianne and Elizabeth. I invited 'em to the big Rush party in a couple weeks." He turned to Richard. "Don't hassle them about their beers, okay?"

"Not my problem. Let the alcohol boys handle that," Richard said as he took a pull on his longneck.

"So, is the chapter ready for the semester?" asked William.

"Yeah, I got a good crop of officers. The house is in good shape. There's money in the bank. It's all good." Chuck sipped his beer.

William lowered his Heineken. "Being president all you thought it would be?"

"It's a pain in the ass. You should have told me. I worry every day."

"I did tell you, *pledge*." William was Pledge Director when Chuck joined AI, and he reminded his friend of that fact every now and then. "You didn't listen."

"Remember the time you were trying to show his pledge class how to run the floor buffer?" Chris chuckled. "I thought I'd die laughing."

"Damn, those were the days," said Chuck with a smile. "We drove Will absolutely nuts. It was great."

"Chuck, if I die young, you'll be happy to know it was all your fault."

"Young?" Richard snorted. "Willie, you were NEVER young!"
Everyone else broke up at that. "What is this—pick on Darcy day?"

"Whatsamatter, Mr. Perfect?" Chuck teased. "Can't take it?"

"Better than you, *pledge*—or should I remind you of the peanut butter and mayonnaise incident?"

"Man, that's cold, Will," said Chris.

"All right, enough of this fraternity bullshit," Richard broke in. "I gotta get home to Olivia soon. How do you think the Greenies are gonna do this year?" This got them into one of their favorite subjects: Tulane Green Wave football.

The group fell into a discussion of the quality of the receiver corps and the chances of the coach being lured away that season. Richard was enjoying the conversation when, glancing around, he spied a familiar face. Only his years of training prevented his beer from going down the wrong way. He carefully placed his bottle on the table.

"Guys, I gotta run, or the wife'll have my hide. Chris, Chuck, Will—have a good evening." The group exchanged good-byes, and Richard moved towards the door.

They were still so busy arguing over football, they didn't notice Richard hadn't yet left the bar.

Richard approached a young man with blonde spiky hair. "Well, well, well. If it isn't my favorite reprobate, Greg Wickham."

The man whirred around. "Lieutenant!" he cried, eyes bugging out. "What do you want?" He nervously wiped the back of his hand across his mouth.

Richard leaned closer. "Why don't you tell me what you're up to?"

"Fuck off. You're off duty." Greg turned back towards the bar.

Richard grabbed Greg's arm in an iron grip. "Wrong answer, punk. I'm never off duty. Outside or I break your arm."

Greg must have seen the seriousness in Fitzwilliam's eyes because he put down his drink and allowed himself to be escorted out of the bar. Once on the sidewalk, Richard guided Greg to his un-marked police car and threw him against the hood.

"Assume the position, punk," growled Richard. With a groan,

Greg turned around and leaned over the hood, his arms spread wide and his legs apart. Richard quickly patted him down.

"Any guns or sharp objects, Wick—? Hello! What have we here?" Richard extracted a wad of cash from Greg's front pocket. "My, my, my. You have been a busy boy, haven't you? What's in here—a couple thousand?"

"My inheritance from my aunt twice removed, officer."

Richard counted the cash. "All in twenties? Yeah, right. Don't get smart, punk, or I might just hold this as evidence. How did you earn it? Selling crack to kids?"

"I don't do that shit—"

Richard slammed him against the car hood. "Watch your language, Wickham. You'll hurt my little ears. Now, again—where did you get this money?"

"I'm tellin' you, I just got an inheritance!"

Richard pulled out his handcuffs. "This is just for your protection. Let's go check out your car, Greggie-boy." Once Greg's hands were secured behind his back, the two walked over to where Wickham's Camaro was parked. "You got any problem with me searching this thing? Just asking. Remember, I got probable cause."

"Go ahead. I got nothin' to hide."

"We'll just see." Richard quickly and expertly searched the vehicle. As Wickham was being cooperative, he expected he would find nothing, and he was right. Richard returned to his prisoner and released the handcuffs. Greg rubbed his sore wrists, glaring at the policeman.

"How about my money?" Just as he finished mouthing the words, the roll hit him in the chest. Greg quickly picked up the money and stuffed it in his pants. "I ought to sue you for false arrest—"

Greg was slammed backwards against the roof of his car. "Oh, please do that, *sir*." Richard gripped Greg by his shirtfront. "I would love to have you explain that money in court. The IRS would be on your ass so fast it would make your head spin. I *know* you're still dirty, Wickham. The word's out about you on the street. Coke and weed—you're the man. The only reason you're walking away tonight is because business is tight…*this* time."

Greg remained silent.

"Uptown is *my* town, punk. I *hate* drug dealers in my town, *especially* ones who sell to high school kids. I busted you once—"

"I don't do that anymore!"

"Shut it! And I *will* bust you again! You're too stupid not to make a mistake. It's just a matter of time. And next time it won't be probation. It will be a nice little cell in Angola. They *love* pretty little white boys in Angola. By the time they get finished with you, you won't be able to sit down for a year." He leaned very close. "Stay. Out. Of. Uptown. Got it?"

"I hear you."

"Good." Richard shoved Greg against the car one last time. "Drive safe, Wickham. And remember—I'm *always* looking out for you."

Greg dusted himself off, walked around to the driver's side, and let himself in. A moment later, Greg fired up the Camaro and pulled away.

Richard sighed. He hoped, rather than expected, his warning would do some good. The drug war was never-ending with a steady supply of fools and the curious willing to escape reality for a while. With that depressing thought, Richard returned to his car and went home to his wife.

Greg Wickham was still shaking as he drove up Napoleon towards Claiborne. He knew he had been lucky—lucky and stupid. It was only good fortune that he completed his last delivery of cocaine just before he stopped by Fat Harry's to grab a bite to eat and perhaps run into one of his customers. Instead, he ran into the cop who had arrested him. He was stupid not to put his earnings into safekeeping before he went to the bar. *Lazy! Lazy will get you killed, dude!*

He drove around in circles, taking turns at odd intervals and making sure he wasn't being followed.

Greg had changed his *modus operandi* since getting out of jail. Instead of hanging out on street corners waiting for whoever showed up, he now cultivated a clientele of college students and young professionals—white kids who were scared of driving into the projects yet willing to pay top dollar for quality product. As long as he was careful and not greedy, Greg figured he would make a fortune and live to spend it.

Tonight, he was lucky—lucky it was Fitzwilliam he bumped up against. He might hate him, but the cop was squeaky clean. Fitzwilliam wouldn't steal his money. Another cop might not have been so honest.

Finally assured he was clear, Greg turned his car towards the West Bank. His crib was nice and quiet. No gang-bangers hung at the street corners, and the Benjamins would be safe in his vault under the floorboards of the place. He didn't live large and never had any of his customers there. No land line phone. A private company post office box. He was as invisible as he could be. And as long as he never did business in Jefferson Parish, the sheriff's office wouldn't be hassling him.

Greg beat his steering wheel in frustration. He had a good thing going, and he almost blew it! Two big ones! Focus! He had to focus. If Fitzwilliam could find him, so could a potential competitor. He needed to blend in better yet stay out of sight. Hit and move—make your appointments and leave. Don't stick around.

He needed a cover. He needed a "friend" at school. Tulane would be best. Lots of money at Tulane. Those rich assholes were loaded. Lots of potential customers. All he needed was a fool.

Who among his current customers was a fool? Someone who *thought* he was bright? Somebody too damn clever for his own good?

Greg Wickham smiled. He knew his man.

Chapter 2

Elizabeth walked down the hall of the student center. Now that school had been up and running for the past few weeks, it was time to sign up with the *VOICE*.

Near the end of the hallway, she came upon a door with a paper sign taped to it. The name "Loyola VOICE" was written in blue Marks-a-Lot across it. She tapped on the door as she opened it.

"Hi," she said to the lone occupant, "I'm here to sign up. Are you Justin?"

A shaggy-haired male rose from the PC he'd been typing on. "Yeah, I'm Justin Middleton, editor of the *VOICE*. And you are…?"

"Elizabeth Boudreaux," Elizabeth said as she extended her hand. "Dr. Jennings sent me."

"Oh, yeah. She said somebody would be coming by." Justin shook her hand. "Welcome aboard, Elizabeth. Welcome to the future of journalism—the *VOICE*." He gestured around the room. "What do you think?"

She didn't think much of it. It was a small room with four computer workstations scattered about it. Wires were going every which-way, a printer/scanner was on one wall, a fax machine on another, and a couple of beat-up file cabinets were near the door. A small refrigerator was next to the desk Justin had been using.

"It's…different."

"Yeah, we're completely electronic. No paper. Everything is done right here and in the server. I was just working on an environmental justice story. Want to see it?"

Justin sat down, pulling another chair next to him. Once Elizabeth took a seat, he began showing her what he had written.

"We do everything in Word, and then we send it to the layout folder in the server. Julia—you'll meet her later—Julia then cut-and-pastes the stories in Quark and posts it on the website. It's fast and cheap except for the equipment and the bandwidth. We can even do this off-site. Just write your stuff and shoot it over in an email."

"They're doing some of this stuff over at the *Maroon*."

Justin snorted. "Yeah, but it's still Stone Age. Typesetting and printing, we've blown that off. And we're more aggressive. We don't give a shit about what's being served at the cafeteria or what the new parking regulations are going to be. We're about what's going on in the world. We're trying to get the kids fired up about changing things."

"How many people read the *VOICE*?"

Justin ran his hand through his hair. "We're averaging about two hundred hits a week right now, but we're planning a big email campaign to up readership. We're still new, you know. A couple of big stories and we'll be set."

"The funding is okay?"

"For the rest of the school year, yeah. The Student Senate okayed our request." Like many clubs and activities, the *VOICE* was funded through the mandatory student activity fee charged every semester.

Elizabeth sat back. The *VOICE*, for all its claims of being cutting edge, was still an amateur outfit. But she didn't go into journalism to attend Student Senate meetings and take notes like a glorified court reporter. She wanted to write important stories that would make a difference or right injustices. The *Maroon* wasn't doing that, she reasoned. And Dr. Jennings, the *VOICE*'s faculty advisor, was very enthusiastic about the promise of New Journalism. Elizabeth could be at the beginning of something great. She made up her mind.

"Okay, boss. What's my first assignment?"

"Great. We'd like something about co-ed safety. I know it's going to take a lot of research, so until you can come up with something, you'll get a column where you can give advice and guidelines and whatever. Will that work for you?"

"Sure. What's my deadline for the column?"

"Once a week on Wednesdays. You'll run on Fridays."

Elizabeth grinned. She was already a columnist!

WILLIAM DARCY PICKED UP HIS phone. "Hello?"

"Hi, Will."

"Dad! Where are you? It sounds like you're in your car."

"I am. I'm on the I-10 trying to get to Dansereau, so I thought I'd spend the time talking to my boy. How are you?"

"I'm good. Classes are going fine. I got re-elected to the Business School Senate."

"That's great, Son! Congratulations."

"Thanks. How's the traffic?"

"Not bad for a Friday. Just passed Causeway, it ought to ease up a bit now."

"Any plans for the weekend?"

"Just going to the Destrehan High game tonight, and a little golf at Ormond tomorrow. How about you?"

"Chris wants me to go to the AI Rush Party tonight, but I don't know."

"Go ahead and go. You work too hard. Take this time and enjoy yourself. You've got the rest of your life to worry about things."

"Maybe I will, Dad. How's Gina?"

"She's fine. She settled right back into school. You know how she is —one moment she's pouting that school is starting again, and the next she's happily babbling about all of her friends and what they're wearing."

"That's our Gina."

"Your mother, God rest her soul, would be so proud of you two."

"Thanks, Dad. That means a lot. Anything new at work?"

"Nope. We made up the deliveries that were delayed by Hurricane Earl, and Tropical Storm Francis only cost us twenty-four hours at our facility in the Houston Ship Canal. There might be another storm in the Gulf. We'll have to wait and see."

"I sure hope we don't get hit."

"Don't worry about that. It's a Friday in Louisiana, it's not rain-ing, the tropical storm went into Texas and didn't hurt anybody, and football's on deck for tonight. Life is good, William. Never forget it. Laissez les bon temps roule! [1] *"*

"Okay, Dad. I love you. Talk to you Sunday."

"I love you, too. Bye."

As William hung up the phone, Chris came out of his bedroom. "Will, are you gonna come tonight?"

"I guess so. Let me go clean up." William moved into his half of the two-bedroom apartment he shared with Chris Breaux. Each bedroom had its own small bath, and William went into his. He washed his face in the sink and spread on shaving foam. He looked in the mirror as the sink filled with hot water.

Staring back at him was a dark-eyed, black-haired man in his mid-twenties, six feet two inches tall. Fastidious about his dress and appearance, he knew women found him attractive. Some, like Chuck's sister Carrie, constantly plagued him with their attentions. It was a royal pain.

While he shaved over the sink, he reflected over the changes in his life. Losing his mother at a relatively young age had made William Darcy very close to his family. Graduating with top grades from high school, he had received academic and baseball scholarships from universities across the nation, but he was a hometown boy. He enrolled at Tulane and walked on to the Green Wave golf team. A legacy, he was immediately pledged by Alpha Iota. His father insisted that he not commute from Dansereau but live on campus in New Orleans. In that way, he could see his beloved father and sister as often as he wished yet still experience the life of a college student.

Just as in high school, William was Big Man on Campus at Tulane. He received top honors in his business classes. He served for two years on the Associated Student Congress, and he had been an officer of his fraternity chapter since he was initiated, as well as two years as president.

---

1 Let the good times roll!

At first, it was fun, but as his responsibilities grew, so did the attention of the shallower members of the opposite sex. Tulane had its share of husband hunters, and they all seemed to have their caps set on him. The novelty of having women throwing themselves at him soon grew to be a bore. It also gave him a rather jaded view of females. He didn't mind dating them; he just didn't want to have to raise them. Always a bit more mature than his buddies, William became a bit of a hermit in his senior year, tired of playing the game.

Tonight will be the same as always—girls who think they are women acting…well, acting immature. I'm done with fooling around. I want to find somebody who's got a brain and character as well as a body. They are out there, even at Tulane, but…how come I never seem to meet them? Hell, I sure won't tonight! If it weren't for Chuck and Chris…

William sighed. Of his numerous friends and acquaintances, the four men he was closest to were his father, his cousin Richard, Chris Breaux, and Charles Bingley. Chris, a pledge brother, had a similar serious demeanor, but unlike William, he was no athlete. Instead, he was the musician of the chapter. A superb judge of character and a generous listener, Chris was what William needed in a confidant. Together, they had run the chapter. Chuck, two years their junior, was different still. Gregarious and talkative, his unbreakable moral code attracted William. It was no secret that William groomed Chuck to take the reins of the chapter. However, it was Chuck's hard work and popularity that enabled him to ascend to the presidency the year after William and Chris graduated.

William and Chris were alumni of Alpha Iota. They would always be members, but it wasn't *their* chapter anymore. It belonged to the undergraduates, and they, like Dr. George Katz, were merely honored guests. George was another good friend. He had graduated years before, but in his role as Alumni Advisor, he and William had grown to like each other.

"Les bon temps roule!" Dad had said. He's right. I should suck it up and enjoy myself.

William splashed hot water on his clean-shaven face. After a moment's reflection, he used a bit of after-shave, changed his shirt, and walked out to the living room. Chris looked up from reading the sports page.

"Ready to go, Will?"

"Let's get it done, partner."

MARIANNE AND ELIZABETH MET EMMA in the lobby of Buddig Hall. The girls wore their usual jeans, but Elizabeth had on a cami-top and heels while Marianne settled for a T-shirt and western boots. Emma had on a Betsy Johnson dress and heels, which drew a lot of admiration from the others. They left the dorm and walked along Freret Street towards Broadway. Within moments, they were on the campus of Tulane. They passed Fogelman Arena, the home of the basketball and volleyball teams, and Percival Stern Hall, the 120,000-square-foot science building shaped like an old-styled computer punch card. Three blocks later, they were on Broadway, the upriver border of the university and the home of most of the fraternity and sorority houses. It was also the location of The Boot, a bar well used by Tulane and Loyola students.

The street was filled with students of both genders moving between the houses. The sororities were decked out with paper streamers in their colors. The frats were clean and welcoming. It was not long before the trio reached the AI house.

The place was a large, wooden, two-story building, built in an earlier era, painted light blue with black trim. A blue flag with a black crest in a white circle flew from a large flagpole between the house and the sidewalk. A narrow driveway was taken up by three cars. A porch spanned the entire length of the front of the house. The Greek letters "AI" were on a plaque beside the open front door. The house was lit up on this muggy, late summer's evening, and music was heard from within. With a smile, Emma led the girls inside.

Elizabeth wasn't sure what to expect. She had heard about fraternities, usually stories bandied about describing the trouble this one or that one had gotten into. She figured she would see either a group of loud guys in jeans and sandals sitting around a keg, or a bunch of uptight Uptown types in blazers and striped rep ties with button-down shirts.

What she saw was a house full of young men and women in a large, brightly lit room. Couches and tables were against the walls, and above them were numerous identically framed collections of photographs. Many of the guys were dressed in light blue polo shirts with a crest and black slacks. They appeared clean-cut and friendly. Before Elizabeth could take in any more, Chuck Bingley was welcoming them. Emma was especially enthusiastic in her greeting, which brought smiles to her two companions.

Chuck walked them through the room, Emma taking a position by his side, and pointed out a large framed document, which was the charter of the fraternity. He explained that the other decorations were chapter photos from years gone by. "We've got about twenty years' worth here," he said. "The rest are in storage."

"How many do you have?" asked Elizabeth.

"A bunch. The chapter's been here for over eighty years."

Chuck introduced the girls to several people. Many were members of the chapter or their girlfriends. There were several potential members, shy men with name tags on. A moment later, they were at the far side of the room where two men stood. They were both tall and dark haired, one with dark eyes, the other with blue. They wore neither the blue polos nor name tags.

"William! Chris! How are you?" cried Emma.

"I'm fine, Emma," replied William as he received a peck on the cheek.

Chris grinned. "I need more than that, lady!" He gave her a big hug. "You're looking wonderful, isn't she, Chuck?"

"Yeah, she is," Chuck said with a slightly goofy smile.

"Guys, these are my friends, Elizabeth Boudreaux and Marianne Dashwood. Mari, Lizzy, this gorgeous man is Christopher Breaux. And this ol' stick-in-the-mud is William Darcy. C'mon, Will, show off those devastating dimples of yours."

William rolled his eyes. "'Devastating dimples?' I didn't know I had that effect on you, Em."

Emma gave him a cheeky smile. "Don't you wish." She stepped closer to Chuck.

"Ladies," said Chris, "I'm very glad to meet you."

After exchanging pleasantries, Elizabeth pointed out they weren't wearing polos. "Is there a penalty for being out of uniform, Chuck?"

Chuck and Chris laughed, while William looked at her with an amused expression.

"There is," said Chuck, "but not for these guys."

"We're alumni, Elizabeth," said William. "Chris and I graduated last year."

"Oh! I'm sorry."

"Don't be," assured Chris. "I, for one, am glad to be mistaken for an undergraduate!"

"Speak for yourself, Chris."

"Can we get y'all something to drink?" asked Chuck. "Soft drink? Water? We've got some punch."

Marianne and Elizabeth requested diet colas. "I'll go with you to get the drinks, Chuck," volunteered Emma. "You two just stay here and get acquainted."

The two of them moved away, and Marianne and Chris fell into conversation. William looked on. Elizabeth listened for a moment then allowed her eyes to roam over the chapter pictures hanging on the wall. She noticed they were from the last few years. She began to look closely at them.

"Something interests you, Elizabeth?" asked William.

"I was looking at the photos." She paused. "You were quite the leader of this place."

"Yes, president for two years."

"Is that usual?"

Chris heard her question. "Nope. First time that's happened in ten years." He thought for a moment. "Now that I think on it, wasn't your dad president, too?"

"Yes."

Elizabeth turned to William. "Your dad was a member of this fraternity?"

"Yep, I'm a legacy."

"How you think he got in?" laughed a newcomer, his voice giving away his New Jersey roots. A redheaded man of medium height, he had a pretty blonde girl on his arm.

"I knew it was a mistake to pledge you, Tilney," said William good-naturedly. "Why you put up with him, Cathy, I'll never know. Ladies, let me introduce this loudmouthed Yankee, Henry Tilney, vice-president of the chapter, and our beautiful Chapter Sweetheart, Catherine Moreland."

"Who has the incredibly bad taste to date Henry!" cried Chris.

"Oh, don't listen to them! Please call me Cathy," the girl said in a soft Southern drawl as she shook the girls' hands. They were just getting acquainted when Chuck and Emma returned with the soft drinks.

After some more conversation, Henry tapped Chuck on the arm and pointed at the door. "Right," Chuck mumbled. "Ah, duty calls, folks. Time to get to work. We've got potential pledges to impress."

"Girls, why don't y'all come with me?" Cathy said. "I'll introduce y'all to everybody."

"Chuck, Will, it was nice to meet you," said Marianne. Elizabeth nodded her agreement, and the group moved towards the center of the now-crowded room. They split up, Chuck and Emma taking positions near the front door and greeting the guests while the others worked the room.

"Lizzy and Mari," said Henry, "this is John Waguespack and Tommy Bertram. They're a couple of our newer members, initiated last spring."

Elizabeth felt much more at ease with these guys as they more fit her expectations. Tommy was a tall, lanky, laid-back fellow whose shirttail was outside of his black jeans. John was not as tall but had an easy smile and an open manner.

"Dude," drawled Tommy, "thanks for introducing us to such awesome babes! You are truly a gentleman an' a scholar."

"Cool it, Tom," said John with a smile. "Ladies, welcome to Alpha Iota house. Are you going to Tulane?" Told they were Loyola coeds, he continued. "I must thank our dear neighbor for enrolling you. I hope you won't be a stranger, will you, Marianne?" John was clearly taken with the slim brunette.

Marianne chatted with John, while Elizabeth talked with Tommy. Assured the ladies were engaged, Henry and Cathy excused themselves. A few moments later a young man with spiky hair approached.

"Greg! You made it, dude!" cried Tommy.

WILLIAM AND CHRIS, JOINED BY a third slightly older man, were watching from across the room. "Another year, another smoker. Glad those days are over, Will?" asked Chris.

"Yep. Emma's really putting a full-court press on Chuck, isn't she?"

"Yeah, it's kinda funny. Think Chuck realizes it yet?"

"If he doesn't by the end of the night, I'm sure Cathy will cue him in. Emma's a nice girl. Hope it works out better than Jennifer."

"Emma and Chuck?" asked the third man. "Really?"

"Yeah, Doc. Something wrong?"

"No," said Dr. George Katz, alumni advisor to AI. "I know her family. My folks were close to her father and grandfather. Don't get me wrong; Emma's a nice girl. I just never figured her for somebody like Chuck."

George, a tall man in his late twenties whose curly hair had begun to thin in front, had just finished his surgical residency at Tulane University Medical Center. He had been presented with the extraordinary honor of an offer of an instructor/practitioner, a position almost never offered to a new physician.

"What do you mean?" asked Chris.

"You know how Chuck is—real easygoing. Now, I'm not saying Emma's high-maintenance, but…"

"Yeah," Chris laughed. "We'll see." He looked over at William to see him frowning. "Will, something bothering you?"

"What? No. I just noticed Emma's friends are talking to John and Tommy."

The other two men glanced over. Chris turned to his friend. "What is it with you and Waguespack? You've never gotten along with him. He ever do something to you?"

"No. It's just...I don't know. I guess we're oil and water. I just can't warm up to the guy—or Bertram, either. Don't trust them."

"John and Tommy are fraternity brothers. If you can't get along with them, just avoid them." George paused. "Why does it bother you that those girls are talking to them?"

William shook his head. "It doesn't. Forget about it."

ABOUT AN HOUR LATER, ELIZABETH felt she needed air. She looked at Marianne, but she was still engrossed in conversation with John, and Emma was on the other side of the room, glued to Chuck's side. Elizabeth smiled. It looked as though Emma's plot to capture Chuck was succeeding.

Tommy had disappeared with Greg Wickham, a spiky-haired blonde guy, and she hadn't seen them for about twenty minutes. Feeling like a third wheel, she caught Marianne's eye, pointed at the front porch, and walked out the door.

Leaning on the railing, Elizabeth drew in a deep breath of the warm, humid, night air. She watched the traffic, both pedestrian and automotive, pass by. She didn't notice someone had joined her.

"Elizabeth, are you all right?"

Startled, she turned to see William Darcy looking at her. Her breath caught in her throat. Darcy, backlit by the light from the house, was a tall, dark statue of masculine perfection. She could feel his dark eyes staring at her.

"I'm fine. I just wanted some air."

"It does get a little close in there. I was just coming out for the same reason. Mind if I join you?"

"It's a free county."

William frowned. "Have I offended you?"

Elizabeth gasped. "Oh, no. I'm sorry. I get a little flippant, sometimes. My dad is always on my case about it. He says I sometimes talk before I think."

"He's really important to you." He moved over to the railing, a little way from her.

"How did you know that?"

"The way you speak about him. I feel the same way about my dad."

She nodded, having no response to that. She was a little disconcerted that he had read her so easily.

"Are you having a good time?" he asked, leaning against the railing.

"Yes. Though not as good as Emma."

He nodded. "Chuck's a nice guy and a good friend."

They fell into silence. Elizabeth could not help but consider the man next to her. He was certainly handsome and well spoken —when he chose to speak. Yet she was uncomfortable with him. His age, his self-assured manor, his silence, his tendency to stare a hole through her, all made her feel unexpectedly inadequate. She felt as though she were being weighed, judged. And it *really* irritated her.

William started talking again. "Have you always wanted to be a journalist?"

Elizabeth was surprised he remembered her major. "I guess so. I've always enjoyed writing. I like to know what's going on, and I like telling stories. I want to make a difference."

"And you can do that through journalism?"

Elizabeth frowned. "You sound as though you disagree."

"A bit." He turned towards her, leaning on the rail. "After all, aren't reporters supposed to just tell us the facts? Who, what, where, when and how? How is that making a difference?"

Her eyes flashed. "By bringing stories to people's attention. Stories they need to hear. Let them know how the other half lives."

William smiled. "And who picks the stories?"

Elizabeth opened her mouth to reply and stuttered. She had no answer. She glared. "You're just one of those people who hate the press!"

William laughed. "Now, Miss Boudreaux, if you're going to be a journalist, you'll have to defend your position better than that! Name-calling is a sure sign of losing."

"Great. You were probably in the debate club."

"My high school team went to the state finals three years in a row."

"Handsome *and* modest, too," she blurted before she could catch herself. She was glad the darkness prevented William from seeing the blush on her face.

"It's not bragging if it's the truth. You asked, I answered. Look, Elizabeth, I'm not trying to put you down. Journalism is a worthy profession. Benjamin Franklin was one, and he was one of our Founding Fathers. I hope I didn't hurt your feelings. I wish you good luck."

Elizabeth wasn't completely satisfied. "And what about you? Business school, running a corporation? How is that helping the world?"

William shrugged. "I don't know. Maybe providing jobs? Bringing or making goods for people? Providing a needed service like printing a newspaper? Say all you want about the government, true prosperity comes from gainful employment. That's where most people's income and health benefits come from."

"You're right, but how do you justify CEO salaries?"

"Some aren't justifiable. But the same can be said of what entertainers, sport figures, or network news anchors make. Where do you start? Who makes that choice?"

"All right, I'll ask you. Who *should* make that choice?"

"I don't trust the government to do it. That's socialism, and you can see what that's done to the world. It should be personal conscience, but as we know, not everyone listens to their conscience. So in the absence of anything else, I'd have to say the market."

"What if the market's skewed, like oil prices?"

"That's not the market—that's monopoly and collusion. Different from true competition."

"And jobs going overseas?"

William paused. "That's hard on the people involved. Losing their jobs. But, if everyone else can buy the same goods at a cheaper price, who is to say they shouldn't? What about the people in those foreign countries? Don't they deserve the chance to support their families? There's no easy answer."

"How can people buy goods if they have no jobs?"

"That's not quite true. I know there are jobs out there—"

"Yeah." Elizabeth smirked. "Minimum wage jobs."

"Not really. Did you know there's a shortage of nurses? Of engineers? Blue-collar jobs of every kind are going unfilled. Dad tells me he could hire twenty people tomorrow if he could find them."

Elizabeth blinked. Her own father was complaining about the same thing only a few weeks ago. "What kind of work does your father do?"

"Delta Global Shipping. It's an international shipping company."

"I've heard of it. What does he do there?"

"Umm…he owns it."

Elizabeth was stunned. She knew a lot of the students at Tulane came from well-to-do families, and she had assumed Darcy had money, but she had no idea he had *that* much. It didn't help her stomach that he finally showed those dimples Emma had referred to earlier. If he was a nine-and-a-half before, he was an eleven now. An eleven, at least. And super-rich. He was way out of her league.

William noticed her reaction. "Look, it's no big deal."

"Oh! Oh, no, no. I'm sorry for zoning out like that. I guess I'm a little tired."

"Yeah, me too. Do you want to sit down? Or leave? Do you want me to get Marianne or Emma?"

"No, don't trouble yourself."

"There you are!" cried Chris from the doorway. "I wondered where you got off to. Keeping our boy company, Elizabeth?"

"We were having a conversation, yes."

"Elizabeth is tired," William stated. "Can you get Emma and Marianne?"

"No, wait! Please don't go through all that trouble."

"It's no trouble," said Chris.

"They're having fun and I'm fine."

"Then, can we give you a lift back to your dorm?" asked William.

Elizabeth turned to him again in amazement. He was full of surprises. "No, that's not necessary."

"It's not out of our way," said Chris. "You live at Loyola, right? We can pass by your place on the way to our apartment. We'd be glad to help."

"Please, you both are very kind to offer, but I'm not ready to leave. Thank you, though."

"All right. You ready to go, Will?"

"Yeah." He turned to Elizabeth. "I enjoyed our conversation, Elizabeth. I hope you enjoy the rest of your evening."

"I enjoyed it too," she was surprised to admit. "And please, I'm 'Lizzy' or 'Liz.' Good night."

William smiled. "Good night, Lizzy."

CHRIS DROVE BACK TO THEIR apartment while William thought about the evening. He had not sought out Elizabeth Boudreaux when he walked onto the front porch of the AI house. He had always disliked being in the middle of a closely pressed crowd. It was a weakness, he knew, one he constantly fought against. Tonight was just too much.

The conversation he shared with Elizabeth was an unanticipated pleasure. She had that pretty, girl-next-door look he was a sucker for. That she had a brain was a big plus. She had her opinions and defended them admirably, and he respected that, even when they disagreed. Their banter had been fun.

"Nice party, eh, Will?" Chris said off-handedly.

"It was okay. What do you think of the prospects?"

Chris chuckled. "It was a respectable group, but I wasn't talking about that! I meant Emma's friends. Cute girls, weren't they?"

"Yeah, I guess so."

Chris glanced at him. "You *guess* so? You were on the porch talking to Elizabeth for how long? Twenty minutes? Will, you never talk to a girl that long unless you're interested!"

"Oh, yeah, right. I don't even know her."

"Looked like you were on your way, partner."

William, an intensely reserved man, grew irritated. He hated when Chris started poking around his private life, especially because his friend was good at it. "Chris, drop it. I was just talking to a girl, all right? I doubt I'll see her again."

"Sure, William. Sorry."

William appreciated that Chris knew when to back off. Meanwhile, he tried to push all thought of Elizabeth Boudreaux out of his mind. What good would it do him to admire the way she filled her jeans, the graceful way she walked in her heels, her quick wit, or her expressive eyes? She was too blasted young! She was at least four years younger than he was. An immature babe was trouble. He had learned that the hard way.

He wanted intelligence and maturity, not just a great rack. And Elizabeth did have a great rack—

Oh, cut it out, Darcy!

He needed someone he could respect, someone he could confide in. A partner. Like his father had with his late mother. Why waste time with bimbos?

Garden District

THE GIRLS LEFT THE PARTY about a half hour later. Marianne spent the entire walk back to Loyola rehashing the party. She seemed to be taken by John Waguespack. Elizabeth was quiet, encouraging the others to talk. She was still trying to decide whether a certain MBA student was interesting or not. After exchanging farewells, Emma climbed into her black Saab and drove back to her home in Uptown.

Within minutes, she pulled into the two-story house off St. Charles Avenue. It was not the home Emma had been born in. Her father, a partner in Weinberg & Larson, one of the more prestigious architectural firms in New Orleans, had always wanted to restore one of the old mansions in Uptown. Ten years ago he had finally found the right house. He moved his family from Lakeview, and with the help of his decorator wife, returned the house to its former glory. It was the last thing Emma's mother ever did. Within three years of completion, Ruth Weinberg was dead of breast cancer.

Quietly, Emma let herself into the house. Locking the door behind her, she saw there was a flickering light coming from the den.

"Papa?"

"Emma," called out Abe Weinberg, "you're home."

Emma walked into the den. Her father was sitting in his favorite La-Z-Boy recliner, the room lit only by the light from the television set. "Papa, you shouldn't wait up for me. It's late. You should be in bed."

Abe shook his head, his eyes never leaving the TV screen. "I can't sleep when you're out, princess. Did you have a good time?"

Emma knelt at the side of his chair and looked at the set. Conan O'Brian was just finishing his show. "Yes, Papa. We had a nice time. I'll have to have Mari and Lizzy over. You'll like them." She didn't tell him Chuck had invited her to catch a movie Sunday night. She would do that tomorrow.

"Irene called."

Irene, Emma's older sister, was attending Vanderbilt University in Nashville when their mother died. A year later, she married her gentile boyfriend and, after graduation, moved to the Washington DC area. Irene now worked in the HR department of a large defense electronics manufacturer in Maryland while her husband was a mid-level staffer in the State Department.

"How are Irene and Tyler?"

"Good. Irene's expecting."

"Papa, that's wonderful! When is she due?"

"She said, but I don't remember." He changed to the Weather Channel. "Call her tomorrow, Emma."

"I will." She looked at him. He was so much stronger, so much livelier when Mama was still alive. When Irene married, his joy at his oldest finding love was tempered by the knowledge she had married outside the faith and was moving a thousand miles away. Tyler was a *mensch*, but he was still a *goy*. Abe continued to ride the streetcar ever day to his office Downtown, but much of his energy seemed to have been drained away. Emma gave him a kiss on the side of his forehead.

"Rosh Hashanah's coming up. I invited George Katz. He's all by himself, his folks being in Fort Lauderdale now."

"You did? I saw him tonight at the AI house. It will be good to have Dr. George here. Did you eat?"

"Yep. It was good."

"Do you want anything else?"

"No, princess."

Emma stood. "I'm going to bed now. Are you staying up?"

"Just for a little while. Good night."

"Good night, Papa."

As she was leaving the room, her father called out. "Emma! It looks like there's a tropical storm in the Gulf."

"Is it coming here?"

"We're in the cone of probability."

"How strong is it?"

"Minimal. We'll know more tomorrow."

"Okay, Papa. Keep track of it for me."

Emma went up the stairs to her room as Abe Weinberg kept vigil before the TV set.

Chapter 3

This is the Tropical Storm 1998 Wrap-up from Weather TV. "By about ten p.m. on Saturday, Sept. 19, 1998, minimal Tropical Storm Hermine, with top winds of forty-five miles per hour, passed over Cocodrie, Louisiana about seventy miles southwest of New Orleans. It drifted north-northeast with wind gusts of forty miles per hour, passing within fifty miles of New Orleans. The National Hurricane Center in Miami downgraded Hermine to a tropical depression the next morning as the disorganized center spun farther from the warm, nurturing waters of the Gulf of Mexico."

SEPTEMBER 26 (AP): THE TULANE Green Wave won its home opener in the Superdome tonight, defeating Navy 42 to 24. It was a costly victory, as senior starting quarterback Shaun King broke his hand during the game. The Green Wave is now 3-0 for the season, after beating Cincinnati 52-34 and SMU 31-21 on the road. Only 19,000 were in attendance, as a hurricane neared the Gulf coast.

"WELCOME BACK TO TROPICAL STORM 1998 Wrap-up from Weather TV.

"On September 21, Hurricane Georges began ravishing the Caribbean, killing over six hundred, before sweeping over the Florida Keys and entering the Gulf of Mexico. Georges made final landfall as a Category 2 storm, with winds of 105 miles per hour and a storm surge of ten feet, near Biloxi, Mississippi, on September 28. In New

Orleans, 14,000 took shelter in the Superdome. About one million people lost power on the Gulf Coast."

EMMA COULD FEEL THE EXCITEMENT as she walked into her drafting class. Tommy Bertram waved her over.

"Em, we gotta model posing today, right?"

Emma smiled at her classmate. Tommy, like many of the non-art major guys who had signed up for the class, was interested in only one thing: models. Nude models. "That's right, Tom."

"Righteous!" Tom turned to his fellows, all high-fiving.

Emma made her way to her table, setting out her charcoal and paper and shaking her head. The instructor entered only a moment later.

"Class, today we will be doing quick studies of the human form. As I mentioned last class, we will be using charcoal. I am not looking for any detail work. Instead, I want you the see the lines and curves, the light and the shadow."

"Yeah," Emma heard Tom whisper with glee.

"Be quick! Dash off what you see in as few lines as possible. I expect at least—oh, here is our model now."

The class turned. A slim young man wearing a terry cloth robe came into the classroom from a back door. His graceful movements gave Emma the impression he could be a dancer of some kind, perhaps ballet. A couple of groans could be heard in the classroom. Emma glanced around, but the sounds ceased.

Unperturbed, the model climbed up on a low platform in the middle of the room. The students surrounded the platform.

"All right, no talking," the instructor demanded. "You have one hour. Begin."

With that, the young man's robe hit the floor. He was, of course, nude.

"Aw, shit!" mumbled Tommy.

Emma grinned and got down to work.

Friday, October 16

"EXCELLENT PRESENTATION, MR. DARCY. YOUR team's presentation was a first-rate job."

William and the other members of his project team thanked the management professor and took their seats. The professor glanced at the wall clock.

"No time for any more presentations today. The remaining teams will give their presentations Friday. That is all. Dismissed."

William spent a few minutes talking to his teammates and some of the other members of the class. One of them asked how William's team came up with their plan of dealing with the hypothetical hostile takeover case study that was the assignment for the class. As the other student's team had already given their presentation, William walked out with him, outlining his team's thought process.

The two men strolled through the high-tech corridors of Goldring/Woldenberg Hall, the home of the graduate and undergraduate business programs at Tulane University. As they descended the stairs, William heard his name called out. Turning around, he saw John Waguespack waving at him. William frowned.

"You got a minute, Will?"

William turned to his companion. "Thanks for the insight, Will," said the other man. "Wish you'd been on our team."

"It wasn't just me. It was a team effort," William insisted.

His fellow MBA candidate grinned. "Yeah, well, somebody got it out of 'em. Good job. See ya." He waved at William and John and continued down the stairs.

"What's up, John?"

"I need your help, bro; I'm taking Intermediate Accounting. It's a real bitch."

"Yeah, I remember," William said, not comfortable with being referred to as John's fraternity brother even though it was true. "What can I do?"

"It's the professor—that Arab."

"He's not an Arab; he's Egyptian-American, and he's damned good."

"Yeah, maybe, but I can't understand half of what he says!"

William nodded. "His accent does take some getting used to. Hang in there; you'll catch on. And everything he teaches is right in the textbook. What's the problem?"

"I'm a little behind, and there's this test on Friday."

"Talk to him."

John laughed. "I'd rather go walkin' through the Iberville Housing Project wearing a KKK shirt. C'mon, dude; cut me some slack. You took him. You've got some of his old tests, right?"

William did, but he wouldn't admit it. "I think some of his stuff's in the house's test files. Go check there. I think Henry's in charge of it."

"Henry's pissed at me."

"What did you do now?"

"I blew off the Active Work Day last weekend—me and Tommy. Henry was in charge."

William shook his head. "Stupid, John."

"Yeah, I know. Can you help me out?"

William didn't want to save Waguespack's bacon, but the guy was a fraternity brother. "Go talk to Chuck. He'll smooth things over. You'll have to make up the work day, though."

John grinned. "Yeah, I know. You'll give Chuck a call? Tell him I'm coming?"

Shit. I walked right into that one. "Yeah, no problem."

John slapped him on the shoulder. "Thanks, bro! Catch you later!" John ran back up the stairs.

William watched him go before checking his watch. He had several hours before his next class. Sighing, he pulled out his cell phone and dialed Chuck's number. *I'm going to need a Camellia Grill pecan waffle after this one,* he thought as Chuck answered.

"Chuck? Will. Listen buddy, John Waguespack's in a jam."

WILLIAM CAUGHT THE STREETCAR RIGHT in front of the school on St. Charles and rode upriver to the Riverbend neighborhood where St. Charles and Carrolton intersected. Jumping off, he was right in front of a little white clapboard lunch counter named The Camellia Grill. Crossing the street, he entered the light pink and white walled diner to find only one stool open at the double-U shaped counter. Easing down he glanced at his neighbor.

"Elizabeth Boudreaux?"

Elizabeth turned towards him. "Will Darcy!"

He gave her a short laugh. "Small world. How's things at Loyola?"

"Good, good. And you? You're at…err…business school, right?"

"Yeah." Before he could say anything else, a tall, black waiter in a white jacket on the inside of the counter placed a menu and receipt ticket in front of him.

"Getcha somethin' ta drink?" he asked William as he filled a water glass.

"Don't need the menu. Pecan waffle and a Coke."

"Right, my man," the waiter said as he wrote the order on the ticket. "Coke comin' up." He turned to Elizabeth. "Food's almost done. Refill the coffee?"

"Yes, please."

The waiter turned to get the coffee pot and yelled William's order to one of the two line cooks at the flat grills along the back wall. The cook poured some batter into one of the waffle machines as he kept an eye on three hamburgers and a Western omelet on his grill. The waiter refilled Elizabeth's coffee and placed a glass of cola before William. In a bit of showmanship the Camellia Grill was known for, the waiter extracted a paper-covered straw from a bowl behind the counter and, with a twist of his fingers, presented the straw to William, half of the paper wrapper suddenly missing. It was a performance regulars had been enjoying for generations, but it tickled the young children and tourists. William pulled the straw out of the wrapper, which remained in the waiter's hand, and placed it in his drink. The waiter nodded, disposed of the wrapper and moved on to his other customers.

Elizabeth said, "You often get the waffle?"

"Yeah, sometimes I get it for desert, but I like the burgers, too."

"Yeah, cheeseburgers are great."

"Good fries, too. Not as good as Fat Harry's, though, huh?"

Elizabeth looked at William. "What? What do you mean?"

"Weren't you with Emma and Mari at Fat Harry's having cheese fries?"

Elizabeth's eyes grew big. "That was almost two months ago!"

"Really?" William became embarrassed. "Umm…I guess it was. Funny what you remember sometimes."

"Yeah, funny."

Further conversation was interrupted by the arrival of Elizabeth's order: cheeseburger, dressed, with French fries. Elizabeth eyed the fries, then William.

"Don't mind me," William said as he turned slightly on his stool.

Elizabeth reached for the ketchup as William recalled the night at Fat Harry's. He had told his buddies Emma's friends were too young, but he saw how the curly-haired girl enjoyed the cheese fries at the table. He would not know her name until the AI party two weeks later, but he would never forget the sight. He could see her clearly from across the bar. Backlit from the streetlight outside, she picked up each fry, oozing with melted cheese, and delicately placed it in her mouth, sucking on her fingers.

No wonder he remembered. It was downright erotic.

"Want some?"

William was jolted out of his thoughts. "Huh?"

Elizabeth indicated her plate. "The fries, you want some? The way you were staring at them, you must be hungry."

"I don't want to take your food." William was mortified; he didn't realize he had been staring at her fries again.

"It's all right. I've got more than I can eat." She picked up her burger.

"Okay, but only if you have a bite of my waffle."

Elizabeth nodded with a small smile, and William grabbed a couple of fries. By the time he popped them into his mouth, his waffle arrived. He smiled as the smell of fresh, hot waffle with the aroma of toasted pecans rose from the plate. Syrup and butter were placed before him. Fixing the waffle the way he liked it—heavy on butter and light on syrup—he prepared to dig in before he remembered his manners.

"You first."

"No, it's okay."

"C'mon, I've got to return the favor. You ever have the pecan waffle?"

Elizabeth shook her head. William gave her a smile that showed his dimples. Giving up, she picked up her knife and fork and cut a bite out of the most syrupy part. Clearly, Elizabeth liked syrup.

"Oh, wow," she said after she tasted it. "That's good!"

"Isn't it? Best thing in the house."

"Thank you," she said as she returned to her burger. The two ate their food in silence.

Finishing at the same time, they got up, grabbed their tickets, and stood in line at the cash register at the door. Paying the bill, both returned to their stools, now occupied by others and left tips. "Thanks, cap!" the waiter cried as they left.

"So," William said as he looked about, "you going back to campus?"

"Umm…yeah."

"You want to jump on the streetcar, or did you bring your car?"

"I walked. It's not that far."

William looked up. It was a fine October day in the low 80s with no humidly to speak of. "I'll walk back with you."

Elizabeth eyed him. "I can get back on my own. I know where school is."

"It's a nice day, Boudreaux—I don't mind." William thought using her last name would make her more comfortable. *I'm not trying to pick you up, lady, just trying to be nice.*

"All right, Darcy, come on."

The two crossed Carrollton and walked on the sidewalk along St. Charles, the green streetcars rolling past. They walked in silence. The only sounds were the rumbling of the streetcars, the noise of the car traffic, and the click of Elizabeth's heels.

William tried not to stare at the very pretty girl beside him. He had been caught before, and he wasn't going to make that mistake again. But it was difficult. Not many girls looked as nice in a trim T-shirt and well-fitting jeans.

Too many girls are into that silly baggy-pants urban look, he considered. *I don't get it. What's nicer than a gorgeous ass in a snug pair of jeans?* His eyes traveled down. *Like that one.*

He closed his eyes momentarily. *Stop it, Will! She's too young for you!*

Soon they were before the main entrance to Tulane. William glanced at the imposing, grey buildings. "I guess this is my stop. I enjoyed the company."

Elizabeth looked at the red brick buildings of Loyola right next door. "Do you think I can safely see my way back home all by myself, kind sir?" She gave him a grin to show it was all in good fun.

"I think even *you* could find your way to Loyola from here, Boudreaux." He returned the grin.

"See you around, Darcy." She waved and continued down the street.

William tried not to watch her as he turned to stroll to the business school building a block and a half away.

ELIZABETH COULD NOT UNDERSTAND WHAT the hell William Darcy was about. He was the last person she thought she would run into at the Camellia Grill. She thought rich kids ate better than that.

In the next instant, she berated herself. Camellia Grill was an institution around the campuses. It was a place where all classes of people rubbed shoulders. Of course a guy like William Darcy would eat there.

The real surprise was that he talked to her. She had enjoyed their conversation on the porch of the AI house, but that was over a month ago, and she had not seen him since, either around campus or at the fraternity house. She doubted he'd remember her. She had not known he was at Fat Harry's in August and was astonished he had seen and remembered her.

Was this guy some sort of stalker?

Elizabeth laughed at herself. Darcy was harmless, even if he was too darn handsome for his own good. Anyone with those dimples could prove to be *very* dangerous. *Maybe*, she considered, *I'm reading too much into this? Maybe he's just a nice guy with a great memory.*

Saturday, October 24: Carrolton, New Orleans
THE GREEN WAVE WAS PLAYING in New Jersey that week , so what better way was there to pass a good time on a hot Saturday night than to go bowling New Orleans style at the Mid-City Lanes Rock 'N' Bowl on Carrollton?

At least that was the argument Marianne gave Elizabeth as she talked her into accompanying her to the joint. Elizabeth thought it might have something more to do with certain Alpha Iotas who might be there, but she was willing to tag along. But she was not willing to ride in Marianne's rusty Corolla again. They took Elizabeth's Civic instead.

Arguably one of the most unusual clubs in New Orleans, or anywhere for that matter, Mid-City Lanes threw a New Orleans party like no one else. Where else could you find college students, local working folks, seniors, and trendy club-goers dancing and going for the 7-10 split at the same time? The place was a combination dance hall and bowling alley. This unlikely live music venue attracted all kinds. Locals of all ages came to Cajun two-step on the large, wooden dance floor. Tourists generally stood at the protruding half-circle bar and eyed the dancers. Some patrons just came to bowl with great background music, not the usual repetitious drone heard in more traditional alleys. Rock 'N' Bowl focused on regional roots styles, from Cajun and Zydeco to swing and rockabilly, blues, rock and R&B.

Elizabeth pulled into the parking lot of a strip shopping center that had seen better days. Already, the lot was almost filled with cars, trucks, and SUVs as the crowd streamed towards the door. Entering, they paid the cover charge and walked up the stairs to the bowling alley. A downstairs performance space, cheekily named Bowl Me Under, hosted special events and local acts during busy times such as Mardi Gras and Jazz Fest.

Making their way through the Saturday evening crowd, rock and blues music blaring, the girls saw a large group of AIs and Emma as she waved her arms.

"Elizabeth! Mari! Over here!" Chuck was seated next to her, waving as well. To his left was John Waguespack.

"Hi, everybody!" said Marianne as she hugged Emma. Her eyes were on John.

After exchanging greetings, Cathy Moreland grabbed their hands. "C'mon, let's get your bowling shoes."

Elizabeth was hesitant. "Uhh, I don't bowl."

"Scared, Boudreaux?" asked a deep voice behind her. She turned around and saw William Darcy.

Elizabeth's eyes flashed at the challenge. She wasn't used to being teased. She usually dished it out; it was a new experience for her to be on the receiving end.

"Are you bowling?" she demanded.

William grinned and pointed at his shoes. She saw the ugly two-tone things on his feet. With a snort, she followed the other girls to the counter. Minutes later, they were back with the god-awful footwear.

"Okay," said Emma, "it's just for fun. Girls versus guys. Y'all have your balls? They're over there," she pointed.

"I hope you mean *bowling* balls, Em," quipped Chuck.

"Chuuuck!" cried Emma was she swatted him.

The girls laughed as they walked to the counter and got their shoes. When they returned, Chuck started writing on the score sheet. This was no high-tech bowling palace with automatic scoring machines. This was an old score-sheet-and-pencil kind of alley.

Chuck's work was interrupted by William's muttered oath, "Aw, crap!" He looked at his friend's pained expression and then turned in the direction of his stare. He blanched.

"Sorry, dude," he whispered.

"What's wrong?" asked Emma.

Elizabeth turned. All she could see were two tall, fashionably dressed women walking through the crowd towards them. One was black, the other a redhead. The redhead was waving at Chuck. "Who are they?"

"My sister and her best friend," moaned Chuck.

"Why didn't you tell me she was coming?" demanded William in a low voice.

"It's news to me, man!"

Elizabeth looked blankly at both men as the newcomers joined them.

"Hey, Charles! Surprise!" cried the redhead.

"Hi, Carrie. I didn't know you were in town." He got up and hugged her, her eyes never leaving William's body. "How did you find us?"

"I called the AI house. William! It's *so* good to see you again," she cooed.

"Carrie," he said in a neutral voice.

Carrie gestured to her companion, a tall light-skinned black woman. "Everybody, let me introduce my friend, Anna Elliot. She's on the Golden Girls with me." Both were dressed in tight tops and hip-hugging jeans, exposing their well-defined abs. "Anna, you know my brother, Charles. This handsome man is his friend, William, and this is...Emma?"

Elizabeth picked up on Carrie's vibe right away. Emma smiled. "Hi, Carrie. I'm with Chuck." She stepped closer to Chuck.

Carrie's smile grew frosty. "Well, Emma, I'm glad to see you." She turned to her brother as the other girls returned. "This is certainly news. Does Mom know you're dating again?"

"I don't tell her everything, Carrie."

"Of course you don't." She turned to the others. "Henry, Cathy, and umm...John, right?" she named some of the other AIs before she turned to the two girls from Loyola. "And, oh, I don't know y'all."

Elizabeth and Marianne introduced themselves. Anna acknowledged the greetings and stood around, bored.

"Where are you staying, Carrie?" asked her brother.

"We're staying with Anna's folks in town. So, William, are you ready to hear some blues?"

"We're bowling, Carrie."

Carrie and Anna looked on with astonishment then shared a look. "Wait—do you mind if we join you?" Carrie asked.

Chuck shrugged. "Shoes are that-a-way," he pointed.

As the two dancers scurried towards the counter, Marianne sided up to John. "What's up with her?"

"Chuck's sister from LSU? Word is she's hot for Darcy."

Elizabeth flashed an impertinent smile at William, who just shrugged.

Marianne asked, "Golden Girl? What's that?"

"LSU dance squad. Very competitive." Elizabeth turned to William again. "Looks like you're the hunted tonight."

"Hey," said Cathy. "Are we bowling or what?"

"Go get it started," said William.

Cathy gave Henry a kiss, retrieved her ball and took her stance. As the game commenced, William moved close to Elizabeth.

"Looks can be deceiving, Boudreaux."

"Oh, I don't know." She returned as she watched Carrie and Anna rent their shoes. "It looks like she's loaded for bear."

"Maybe so, but that won't help to catch a coyote, will it?"

Elizabeth looked at him and giggled. "So that's how you see yourself? As a coyote?"

"You tell me, Boudreaux."

She looked at him closely and shook her head. His dark look was disconcerting. "No, definitely not a coyote. A big, bad timber wolf, maybe. Poor Carrie."

"She should be used to disappointment." William saw the two returning. "I think you're up."

She turned to see Marianne make a 7-10 split. High-fiving her teammate, Elizabeth took her turn and promptly rolled a gutter ball. Her second ball knocked down four pins.

"You've played before," she said to Marianne as she took her seat.

"We do more than gig frogs in Mississippi, darlin'," she drawled. They watched Carrie make a valiant attempt, scoring seven pins, and Anna put two in the gutter.

It was now the men's turn. John was first. "Now I'll show y'all how it's done," he bragged. He eyed the lane before hurling a mighty roll—right into the gutter.

"Yeah, that's how's it's done!" Marianne laughed as the girls hooted. John retrieved his ball and rolled an easier ball that got seven pins.

Carrie had taken the seat next to Elizabeth. They sat quietly until it was William's turn. He confidently took his position and rolled a strike. Carrie cheered almost as loudly as the men. As he prepared to bowl his second ball, Elizabeth noticed Carrie eying William's tight jeans. She couldn't blame her. William did have a world-class ass. He threw another strike.

"No fair!" cried Marianne. "He's a ringer!"

"All's fair in love, war, and bowling, Mari." Chuck laughed. William accepted high-fives from his teammates.

"Will's a natural athlete," added Emma.

"You got that right," agreed Chuck as he got up to bowl. "I remember the first time I took him bowling. He never touched a ball before in his life, and he bowls a 205. Pissed me right off! Never bowled against him again."

He then proceeded to show why. While William's form was flawless, Chuck's was not. Only the force of his throws allowed him to score at all. He returned to the scorer's table, sat next to Emma, and marked his six pins.

"Okay, the guys are up by ten pins in the first frame. Bowl on!"

As the contest continued, hunger made its appearance. This was no ordinary bowling alley when it came to the food—no pizza at all. The kitchen offered po'boys as well as the Cajun standards of gumbo, jambalaya, and alligator sausage. The female bartenders were an entertainment all by themselves.

Munching on half of an oyster loaf she was sharing with Marianne, Elizabeth found herself sitting next to Carrie Bingley again. They watched the bowling, waiting for their turn. Elizabeth decided to start a conversation.

"So, what are you studying at LSU?"

Carrie looked at her as though she had grown two heads. "Political science." Remembering her manners, she added, "And you?"

"Journalism."

"And where did you say you were from?"

"Chackbay. I went to school at E.D. White."

Carrie thought for a moment. Her eyebrows went up. "Do you know Ashley Robichaux?"

Elizabeth nodded, surprised at the warmth in Carrie's voice. "Yes, she was a couple of years ahead of me in high school."

"I know Ashley real well. She's one of my best friends. She's one of the captains on the Golden Girls!" Carrie smiled at her companion. It was as though Elizabeth had passed a test and was deemed worthy of having a conversation with her. Carrie leaned back. "So, how did you meet up with these guys since you're attending Loyola?"

Elizabeth was amused at Carrie's change of demeanor but decided to go along. "My roomie, Mari, knows Emma." She pointed to where Marianne was sitting next to John.

Carrie laughed. "And Emma knows *everybody*." As her gaze fell on Emma and Chuck, her look became thoughtful. "I didn't know Chuck was dating Emma. How long has that been going on?"

"Maybe a month."

"Mom'll *love* that," Carrie mumbled.

"Pardon me?" It was automatic. Elizabeth had overheard Carrie's comment, and she was confused.

"Oh! Umm." Carrie sat flustered. "Look, I've got nothing against Emma. It's just," she whispered in Elizabeth's ear, "not everyone's *tolerant*, you know? Different generation, different expectations."

"I see," Elizabeth whispered back. "Your mom wouldn't be too fired up about having a Jew in the family, huh?"

"Is it *that* serious?" Carrie's eyes grew wide.

"No, no. They just started dating."

"Good. Chuck falls in love at the drop of a hat. He was dating this one girl—well, never mind. I hope you're right. I don't need any more crap from Mom right now."

Their attention was drawn to the ball return as William prepared to bowl again. Carrie leaned in. "He's gorgeous, isn't he?"

"He's best friends with your brother, so you must have known him for a while."

"Ever since Chuck pledged AI."

And you've been chasing him ever since. "Any family rivalry with you at LSU and Chuck at Tulane?"

"Not since we kick their ass every year."

"Not in baseball."

Carrie gave Elizabeth a pitying look. "Baseball doesn't count."

"Why is a Baton Rouge boy at Tulane, anyhow?"

"He said it was because Tulane had a better business program, but that's just talk. Getting out from under Mommy-dear's wings —that's the real reason."

"Your mother sounds like something else."

Carrie rolled her eyes. "You have *no* idea."

"So how do you deal with her?"

Carrie grinned. "I just smile and listen and say, 'Yes, Mother,' and do what the hell I want." Her attention went back to her brother and his date.

Emma giggled as she watched Chuck add up the score. "Hey, stop it! I can't write if you keep tickling me!" he cried.

"Just trying to win, Chuck! All's fair in love, war, and bowling, you said!"

"Well, you can do all you want, we're still kicking your asses!"

Emma looked at the scorecard. It was ugly. "Okay, that's enough!" She stood up. "Bowling's over! Let's go dance!"

THE CROWD WAS GROOVING TO a rock & blues band. Marianne was swaying to the sounds when John leaned in close.

"Having a good time, Mari?"

"Yeah," she shouted over the music. "The band's great."

"Wanna go take the edge off?"

"What?"

John pantomimed taking a hit on a joint.

"Ummm…no thanks, John. I don't do that. It's bad for my throat."

"What is?"

"The smoke. You go ahead if you want. It's cool."

Before he could answer, Emma parted the crowd and grabbed John with one hand, her other one in Chuck's. "C'mon, let's get this party going! Dance!" She released him and began two-stepping with Chuck. The other couples joined right in. Carrie saw her chance and grabbed William for herself. A new pledge, Nick Patel, claimed Elizabeth.

Elizabeth was amused at Carrie's determined pursuit of Darcy. She could see William was not happy, but he was being a good sport. Elizabeth actually felt a little sorry for the aggressive Carrie. The girl couldn't see that William just wasn't into her. Elizabeth wondered how Darcy was going to get out of it.

Chuck whispered in Emma's ear. She looked at William and Carrie and grinned. She nodded and moved towards Carrie.

"Time to change partners!" she cried.

Before Carrie could react, Emma cut in and danced away with William. Chuck began dancing with his sister in the opposite direction. As Carrie tried to break away, Chuck exchanged partners with Patel. Now she was with Nick, and Chuck was with Elizabeth. Emma was with John, and William was nowhere to be seen.

"That was pretty slick, Chuck," said Elizabeth.

"I'll deny it to my dying day."

A minute later, partners were exchanged again, and Elizabeth found herself with William.

"Well, hello there, Boudreaux."

Elizabeth saw him look away and followed where he was looking —Carrie on the other side of the floor with Henry.

"Shall we drift over there, Darcy?"

William blanched for a moment. "I'm fine right here if you don't mind."

Elizabeth laughed. "I can handle you as long as we aren't bowling. You don't scare me."

"Somehow, I get the impression you don't scare easily."

"Nope, but I think you're a bit wary of a certain redhead."

William shook his head. "If she weren't Chuck's sister, I would have blown her off. She's not a bad person; she just tries too hard. I wish her well, really."

The song ended, and the crowd cheered. "Thanks for the assist, Boudreaux. If you ever need the favor returned, let me know."

Elizabeth caught the finality in William's voice. "You're leaving?"

"Yeah, I got family business early tomorrow. Good night, Elizabeth."

Elizabeth was faintly disappointed William was leaving, and had no idea why she felt that way. "See you around, Darcy." She watched him leave, waving to his friends. Her observation was disturbed by Marianne jostling her.

"Hey, Elizabeth. Where's William going?"

"Home. Said he wanted to make it an early night."

"Loser. Hey, have you seen John?"

John Waguespack looked at the amount of weed he had just scored. "What the fuck is this, man?"

Greg Wickham looked across the front seat of his red Camaro, his Glock nine-millimeter under the driver's seat within easy reach. "That, dude, is your merchandise."

"You told me I'd get a discount!"

Greg looked around the parking lot of the Rock 'N' Bowl, making sure there weren't any guards or cops prowling around. "Look, I said I would do something with the price *if* there was an increase in my market share. So far, I ain't seen shit." He leaned closer. "Where's all the customers you promised, dude?"

"I'm workin' on it, man, but it takes time."

Greg's hand whipped across John's windpipe. "I ain't got time, fucker! I make a business proposition; I expect to see some sugar. I need more than your brain-dead roommate! You come through, or things get ugly."

John gasped as Greg tightened his hand on his throat. "Be... be cool, man."

Greg, satisfied he had gotten his point across, changed tactics.

He released his hold. "It's all copacetic, dude. Here." Greg tossed a little baggie to him. "On the house for my main man."

John picked up the bag. "Wh…(cough) What is it?" he asked as he rubbed his throat.

"Just a little coke." Little was right. It was so cut there was hardly anything in it.

"Th…thanks."

"Forgetaboutit. Go back in there to your woman."

John grimaced. "She ain't my woman, yet."

Greg frowned. Was this asshole such a fuck-up he couldn't get laid? "She puttin' the freeze on ya, dude? I got somethin' for that."

John glanced at Greg. "I don't need that shit."

"Whatever. Ya need it; I got it. You get the word out. You'll be everybody's friend."

John nodded as he opened the door. "See ya 'round, Greg."

Greg started up the car and smiled a smile that didn't reach his eyes. He pointed two fingers at him. "Damn right ya will." With that, he sped out of the parking lot, leaving a frightened John Waguespack in his dust.

Chapter 4

Sunday, October 25: St. Charles Parish, Louisiana

William pulled his BMW into the driveway of his family's home in St. Charles Parish, upriver from New Orleans, early on Sunday morning. He entered the house from the back door—only company used the front one—and he was attacked by a blond whirlwind.

"William, I missed you so!" the teenaged girl cried.

He hugged his sister back. "Same here, Gina. You're growin' as fast as the sugarcane. How's school?"

"Aw, it's okay. How long are you here for?"

"I've got to get back to the city tonight." At Gina's pout he said, "It's only New Orleans. I'm not on the moon, you know."

"But you're not *here*," she said, as though it explained everything.

"Sorry, Sis. School is school. Where's Dad?"

She pointed down a hallway. "He's in his office, taking a phone call. You want some breakfast? We've got cinnamon rolls."

"Mmm...yeah. Let me go see Dad first." William walked down a hallway to his father's home office. He opened the door to what was at one time a small parlor and heard George Darcy on the telephone.

"All right, you've got all of our ships rerouted? ... Good." He looked up and saw his son. He waved William in as he continued. "What do we have unused? ... *Matthew Darcy*—she's in refit, right? Can she go? ... Good, how about Houston? How soon can *Philip Fitzwilliam* get underway? ... Good deal, Terry. I'll call for an update at 1800 Central time. Keep up the good work." He hung up as he greeted William.

"Dad, what's going on?"

"Look here," George Darcy pointed at his computer screen. "There's a bitch of a storm in the Caribbean. Name of Mitch. We're getting all of our ships out of there."

"Is it coming here?"

"The weather forecasting company we contract with says no. But they're real worried about the steering currents near Central America."

William peered at the screen. "Why?"

"There aren't any."

William turned to his father, his face pale. "Dad, this program forecasts the storm to intensify to a Category 5. Is it going to hit them?"

"Worse, it might just take its sweet time getting there. Pound them for a couple of days or more."

William had been to the mountainous countries of Honduras and Costa Rica. "Floods, mud slides. Oh man, that's gonna be bad."

George Darcy shook his head. "No way to warn those poor people in the hills. That's what I was on the phone about. We're gearing up to help in the relief effort, if needed. *Matthew Darcy* in New Orleans and *Philip Fitzwilliam* in Houston will be ready to carry anything that can fit in a container."

"Has the government called yet?"

"No, but they will. The Red Cross, too."

A pale William and his grim father stared at the screen. Mitch could be a Camille-class storm, with winds of 150 miles per hour or more, enormous storm surge and torrential rain. In the hundreds of isolated villages in Central America, hundreds could die.

"Son, we could be wrong. The National Weather Service says it just might miss them and stay out to sea."

"Yeah, but what do our people say?"

"Pray."

Monday, October 26: Uptown

THE TROOPS OF THE AFTERNOON shift filed into the main room at the NOPD Second District office, Richard Fitzwilliam among them. Some had coffees, most had water, and all were joking around. Richard was discussing the Monday Night Football game with a couple of comrades when a big black captain of police took the microphone at a podium in the front of the room.

"Take a seat, take a seat," the supervisor advised them in a deep, gravelly voice. He began with a rough listing of what had happened since their last shift. Richard heard nothing new.

"All right, I want to meet with Narcotics. Everybody else is dismissed." The room exploded with the sound of chairs moving as the officers stood up and left the room. A few minutes later, the supervisor closed the door and turned to the seven men and two women remaining.

"Listen up. We've got a spike of narcotics trafficking around the university section." He outlined what had been gathered from informants and evidence of robberies.

Richard reviewed his notes. "No names yet?"

"It doesn't seem to be the usual suspects. Might be somebody new. Since it's this quiet, he's gotta be experienced."

"Or *she*," added a female narc.

The supervisor chuckled. "Just like you to keep us politically correct, Jones."

"Just tryin' to keep our eyes open to anything, Captain."

"Yeah, 'cept the only name we've heard is G-Daddy. That don't sound too female, do it?"

"Thanks, boss. Just when were you gonna tell us that?"

"Patience, Jonesy, patience."

"You just like ridin' my ass, sir."

"We all get our fun somehow, Officer Jones. Take Fitz here...*please*."

Richard chuckled. "You're a real comedian, boss."

"Gotta do somethin' to survive. All right—any questions?"

The officers shook their heads. "G-Daddy—I haven't heard that one before," said Richard.

"Like I said, it might be somebody new. *Might* be. Stay with your informants. He just might be somebody we know with a new name. Now get outta here and do some good."

As the others left for their desks or squad cars, Richard walked over to his supervisor. "Heard anything about Hurricane Mitch?"

The man shrugged. "That storm's kickin' their asses down there."

MARIANNE WALKED TOWARDS THE LOYOLA library with purpose. She was on a mission. It took her only a couple of minutes to find her quarry.

"There you are, Elizabeth!"

"Shhh, Mari!" Elizabeth corrected her. "People are studying."

Marianne propped herself on a corner of Elizabeth's desk. "You do too much of that. You need to cut loose."

"I have fun."

"Right. Come on to Tulane's Homecoming with me. It's a party —it's on Halloween night!"

"I thought you were going with John."

"I am. But I can't have any fun if I know you'll be at home all by yourself watching *Saturday Night Live*."

Elizabeth returned to her book. "Who would I go with?"

"Hmmm…leave it to me."

Elizabeth closed her book and looked at her roommate. "Are you setting me up?"

"Sure, why not?"

"Oh, great! I'm such a loser; I have to have my roomie get me a date."

"You are SO not a loser, Liz!"

"Lower, Mari! So, who do you have in mind?"

"Tommy?"

"No, thanks. I could get stoned just from his secondhand smoke."

"It's just a football game and a dance at the Hyatt." At Elizabeth's glare, she threw up her hands. "Okay, no potheads! I'll surprise you. C'mon, let's go get something to eat."

"The cafeteria?"

"Yuck! I can't do mystery meat tonight. I want some real food."

"How 'bout Ye Olde College Inn?"

"Righteous! I love their meatloaf!"

Minutes later, they were in Marianne's rusty Corolla rolling up Broadway. They made their way to Carrolton, and within a few blocks, they pulled into the lot next to a neighborhood joint near Earhart. The place had a muddy yellow exterior with its name painted on one side. The girls walked through the side door, the bar's entrance, and crossed the dark room to the better-lit restaurant half of the building. They were shown to a table in the raised room in the far side of the place, and they saw a familiar face.

"Hey, Chris!" Marianne cried. "Are you alone tonight? C'mon and join us!"

Chris Breaux picked up his iced tea and took a chair at their table. "I haven't seen you girls in a while."

Marianne pouted. "We missed you at the Rock 'N' Bowl."

"I had a clinical I had to study for. What are y'all up to?"

Before Elizabeth could say anything, Marianne said, "Just getting something to eat and finding a date for Lizzy."

"Mari!"

Marianne was unrepentant. "I want her to come to Tulane's Homecoming, 'cause Loyola's isn't until the spring, an' it's gonna be lots of fun, but she won't go unless I get her a date."

Chris gave Elizabeth a kind look. "I'm sure that won't be hard."

Elizabeth covered her face with her hands. "Thank you, Chris, now that I'm embarrassed to death."

Further conversation was interrupted by an elderly waitress. Marianne ordered the Blue Plate Special, roasted chicken with stuffing and peas, while Elizabeth asked for a chicken Caesar salad. Elizabeth and Chris began talking about their classes and instructors while Marianne fiddled with the straw in her tea. This went on for several minutes.

Just when the waitress brought Chris his cheeseburger po'boy, Marianne stared hard at Chris.

"Chris!" she cried. "Are you doing anything for Homecoming?"

"Nope."

Elizabeth realized what her friend was getting at. "Mari!"

"Why don't you take Lizzy?"

"Marianne!"

Chris had a vacant look on his face. "Me?"

"Don't pay attention to her, Chris—she's insane!"

Chris looked at her. "No, it's okay. Sure…I mean, yeah, I'd be glad to take you."

Elizabeth's face couldn't turn redder. "Chris, don't. You don't have—"

"Do you want to go, Lizzy?"

She looked into his kind, sincere face. "Are you sure?"

Chris smiled. "Yeah, it sounds like fun."

"All right!" cried Marianne. "Woo hoo! Lizzy's gonna party!"

Elizabeth held her chin in her hand, an amazed look on her face. "Okay, I guess it's a date."

LATER THAT EVENING, ELIZABETH CALLED Chris.

"I want you to know you don't have to take me to Homecoming. I think Mari kinda trapped you into it, and I don't want you to feel you have to do this."

"Lizzy, it's fine. I'd be happy to bring you to the game and dance."

William, sitting across the room, looked up at Chris's words.

"All right, then, but it's Dutch treat, okay?"

"All right."

"Are you wearing a costume?"

"I wasn't planning on it. Are you?"

"No! I mean, that's fine. Regular clothes."

Chris chuckled. "Relax, Elizabeth. It's just two friends going to a game and a dance."

"Right—friends."

They spent the rest of the short conversation arranging the time Chris was to pick her up. Hanging up the phone, Chris noticed William's attention to his phone call.

"I'm taking Elizabeth Boudreaux to the USL game," he explained.

"Really? I didn't know y'all were dating."

Chris was taken aback. "It's not a *date*-date. Mari arranged it. We're just going together." He was curious over William's reaction.

"Oh. She's a nice girl." He returned to his economics text.

"Yeah." *Is Will interested in Lizzy?* "You want to come with us?"

"What? Oh, no thanks. Dad wants me to join him in the DGS box."

"Maybe you can go to the dance afterwards."

"Maybe. We'll see."

Chris smiled to himself. *Yeah, we'll see.*

Saturday, October 31

"Well? Whatdaya think?" Marianne demanded. She was dressed as Morticia Addams.

"You look like a Goth nightmare."

"Great," Marianne smiled. "You're not going like *that*, are you?"

Elizabeth wore a T-shirt and jeans. "Why not? It's a Tulane T-shirt."

Marianne was berating Elizabeth for her lack of a sense of adventure when her cell phone rang. "It's John! Gotta go! See ya there!" she cried as she left the dorm room.

Elizabeth looked critically in the mirror at herself. *Am I a coward?* With new determination, she stripped off the T-shirt and donned a tight scooped-necked shell in dark green. She rummaged through Marianne's jewelry for a chunky black and blue stone necklace. As she fastened it around her neck, her phone rang.

"Lizzy? I'm here in the lobby."

"Be right there!" Giving in to a last minute impulse, she spritzed herself with her favorite cologne before leaving the dorm room.

Elizabeth immediately saw Chris on one of the couches in the lobby as she exited the elevator. He was wearing a white buttoned-down shirt with a blue & green striped tie.

"Hi, Lizzy. Ready to go?" At her acknowledgement, they left the dorm and walked to Chris's truck—a white Chevy Silverado 2500 extended-cab with flared sides.

"That's a big truck, Paw Paw!" Elizabeth imitated a local car commercial.

"Yeah, it comes in handy in the country."

Elizabeth noticed the trailer hitch. "You do any fishing?"

"Fishin' an' huntin' too, cher," Chris said in a fake thick Cajun accent as they climbed in. "There's some good stuff in that there swamp, I *gar-ron-tee*."

"Where's home?"

Chris pulled out into the traffic on St. Charles. "Just outside of Lafayette."

"We're playing the University of Southwest Louisiana—they're from Lafayette. How's that gonna be?"

Chris grinned. "I might be a Cajun, but I ain't no Ragin' Cajun," he quipped, using USL's nickname.

Louisiana Superdome, Downtown, New Orleans
A FEW MINUTES LATER, CHRIS parked his truck in one of the surface lots next to the Superdome. The two crossed over Girod Street and made their way to the crowded student entrance. About half of the students were in Halloween costumes. By pure luck, they met up with Marianne and John, who was dressed as Gomez Addams, of course.

"Long time, no see, roomie." Elizabeth laughed.

The group showed their passes or handed over their tickets to the ticket-takers. The entrance was flanked by ramps and escalators to each side, leading to the upper sections. Walking forward with the crowd into the main concession walkway, the students continued to the section of seats reserved for them.

This was Marianne's first time in the Louisiana Superdome, and she was amazed at the size of the place. Multi-colored upholstered seats with armrests for 70,000 souls were arranged in three sections. The upper level, the Terrace, flowed in a curve like the Mississippi River against the ceiling, two hundred feet above the field. Large screens, the Jumbotrons, were hung on either end of the Dome. A huge American flag was at one end; the Louisiana state flag was at the other. Banners of honor for the Saints, Tulane, and the long-gone NBA Jazz players circled the ceiling. The enormous climate system chilled the air to such an extent that it was almost too cool. The lights were as bright as daytime.

The football field was made of artificial grass, and great care and millions of dollars were spent to provide the most advanced playing surface available. TULANE was written in one end zone, SAINTS in the other, and a giant *fleur-de-lis*, the symbol of the Saints and the city, was at mid-field.

"Wow, this place is big!" she cried.

It was Chris who answered. "Yeah, it's one of the biggest buildings in the world. They built it for the Saints and the Sugar Bowl, so that's why Tulane plays here. We're the hosts for the Sugar Bowl. The NFL just loves the place. That's why more Super Bowls have been played here than anywhere else.

"It's used for other stuff besides sporting events: conventions, concerts, even home shows. And since its designed to withstand a Cat 5 Hurricane, it's the city's shelter of last resort."

Marianne looked around the arena. "This place seems less than half-full. Where is everybody?" she asked John.

"Not here. Ten years of losing seasons will do that to a program."

"Yeah," agreed Chris. "Back in the seventies, Tulane used to draw over 40,000. The team lost a generation of fans because of bad coaches and bad teams."

"But the team is playing so well! The Wave's undefeated, isn't it?"

Chris shrugged, and Elizabeth joined in. "People are fickle, Mari. But look around—these are the die-hard fans. I'd rather be with them than a bunch of fair-weather friends."

Chris asked, "Do you want anything, Lizzy? I'm going to get something to drink."

"A Coke, please." Chris nodded and turned to the others. No one requested anything, and Chris left to get their soft drinks.

"Do you want anything with that, Liz?" asked Greg Wickham. Elizabeth hadn't noticed he was there before he spoke. Greg pulled a flask from his boot. "Ol' college trick." He laughed at his own joke.

Elizabeth couldn't have known Greg had borrowed John's student ID to make a counterfeit. As far as most of Tulane's security was concerned, Greg Wickham was a student.

"High school, Greg. We did that in high school," Elizabeth dismissed him. "By the way, where's Darcy? I figured a rah-rah guy like him would be here."

"Probably in his dad's box," said John.

"His dad has one of those suites?"

"Yeah, too good to sit with the peons like us," said Greg.

"Hey," cried Marianne, "that's not like Will!"

Elizabeth didn't quite buy Greg's reasoning either, though she could see how someone like him could get that impression. William Darcy was a rather formal guy for his age, and it put some people off. No, she couldn't blame William for using his father's luxury suite; she sure would, if given the chance. *Those things have their own bathrooms!* But it did remind her of the difference in their situations. She was a scholarship student from the swamps, while he was the heir to a fortune. *Out of your league, Lizzy.*

Chris made it back to their seats as the band took the field. It wasn't the Tulane band—there wasn't one. Instead, the university hired a local high school band to play for the home team. It looked bad, especially tonight, as USL brought their large marching band to perform.

It was a Tulane tradition that the Alma Mater be played before the game, and Marianne thought the lyrics beautiful. After a bizarre cheer called "The Hullabaloo," the teams got ready for the kickoff.

"PARKER, THIS IS MY SON, William." George Darcy introduced his son to one of the members of the Delta Global Shipping Board of Directors.

"Pleased to meet you, sir," William said as he shook the older man's hand.

"I've heard a lot about you, young man," Mr. Parker said. "You'll be joining the company soon, I trust?"

"Yes, sir. Right after graduation." George Darcy had invited

William and Gina to sit in the DGS suite in order for his son to meet some of the board members.

"And this is my daughter, Gina," continued George. As the two were getting acquainted, William moved towards the open balcony where the seats were. The vice president of operations, a man William already knew, engaged him in a conversation over the upcoming game as the teams took their places for the kickoff.

"So, do you think your Cajuns can keep up with us?" William asked the USL graduate.

"You're not so tough. Just watch, Will."

"Ten dollars says we cover the point spread."

"You're on."

William looked out onto the field as the game began. His eyes couldn't help but glance at the student section on the other side of the arena.

Downtown

"OH MY GOD, I'M STILL dizzy." Marianne laughed as everyone filed out of the stadium. "I can't believe Tulane could score so many touchdowns! Seventy-two to twenty? It was like a basketball game!"

"That was something, wasn't it?" John agreed. "I've never seen anything like it."

"It's a new type of offense," explained Chris. "It's called the spread. We run it like that; it's hard to stop. And the defense uses the Cover-2. You see, the two safeties are responsible for two deep zones—"

"Enough, professor!" cried Marianne. "I'd forget everything you said by tomorrow. The game was a lot of fun, but now it's time to dance!"

The crowd of students and younger alumni made their way across a walkway that connected the Superdome with the Hyatt Regency Hotel. Signs directed the horde to a large ballroom where the student government hosted an after-game dance. As the Wave had built up a huge lead, the ballroom was already filled with fans that had left the game early.

As with all university-supported student activities, it was an officially "dry" event. That didn't stop the drinking. What was a girl's purse for if not to haul a bottle of booze? The Cokes and 7-Ups were going fast as people mixed their rum and bourbon with varying degrees of discretion.

The cover band was jamming the hit songs of the day by Alanis Morissette, Smash Mouth, Dave Mathews, Faith Hill, No Doubt, Barenaked Ladies, Shania Twain, and Celine Dion. They also played some Motown classics for the older folks. "Tubthumping" was blasting out of the speakers when Marianne and John hit the floor. Her blue eyes flashed as she moved with the music, and John came close for some dirty dancing.

Elizabeth and Chris watched from the sidelines, sipping their unadulterated Cokes.

"Are you having a good time?"

"Yeah, it's great." Elizabeth looked around. "I think we'll need a crowbar to separate Emma and Chuck!"

Chris gave a short snort of laughter, which died as his eyes returned to Marianne and John.

"How come Darcy's not here?"

Chris asked her to repeat her question over the noise. "I don't know. He said he was with his dad and sister for the game, but he might drop in. Why do you ask?"

"No reason. Wanna dance?"

"Sure."

WILLIAM WALKED INTO THE BALLROOM, taking in the crowd and music. He wasn't sure why he came as he didn't have a date. He had wandered over to a refreshment table to grab a Coke when he spied some AIs.

"Tommy. How're ya doing?"

"Whatzupp, William! Dude, I'm psyched you made it! This is one bitchin' party!" Tommy had on a glittery green wig.

"Yeah, it's cool."

"Dude, do you know Greg Wickham here?"

The two shook hands. "What're you studying, Greg?"

William asked.

"General studies."

"Yeah, he's general, all right!" Tommy cackled. William looked hard at the younger man. His behavior seemed out there, even for Tommy.

A couple joined them from the dance floor. "William!" cried Emma. She had on a black wig, a ton of make-up, and a dress cut down to *there*. "Look, Chuck—Will's here."

The group fell into conversation as Greg slipped away. Time was burning, and he needed to make some contacts.

A few minutes later, William pulled Chuck and Henry over to the side. "Tommy's pretty out of control, Chuck. Who did he come with?"

Henry said, "I think he rode with that Greg guy."

"Who is he? A new pledge?"

"Nah," said Chuck. "Just some friend of Tommy's and John's who's been hangin' around."

"I know there's no rule against it, but I just don't like non-members around the house," Darcy said.

"C'mon, William. Half the basketball team's at the house most weekends," Chuck pointed out.

"That's different."

"No, it's not. Look, if it gets to be a problem, we'll just tell Wickham to get lost. We've done it before."

William held up his hands. "You're the boss."

Henry glanced at Tommy. "I'll let John know to keep an eye on his roommate."

"Good," said Chuck. "Let's get back to the party. You dancing, Will?"

"Didn't bring a date."

"Heard that, Em? Will's solo."

Emma grinned. "Is that so? C'mon, big boy." She tugged on one of his arms, only to find she had competition.

"Hey!" cried Cathy dressed as Raggedy Anne. "I saw him first!"

"Let's share him!"

"Yeah! See ya, Henry!"

Chuck and Henry watched as a helpless William was forced to dance with Raggedy Anne and Elvira, Mistress of the Dark, to "Smells like Teen Spirit."

"I didn't think William could dance," remarked Henry.

"He can't," quipped Chuck.

Soon, William's torture was over. Not only were Henry and Chuck giving him a hard time, Elizabeth, Chris, Marianne, and John had made an appearance. The joking died down, and Henry pulled John aside to talk to him about Tommy.

Elizabeth fell into conversation with the girls, and Chris excused himself to fight his way through the crowd to the restroom. The line wasn't too bad, and it was only a few minutes later that he was washing his hands.

Try as he could, the image of a beautiful Goth gal from Mississippi was stuck in his head. His guilty musings were interrupted by a bloodcurdling scream. Spinning around, he saw a tall, green-haired man completely out of control and banging against the other occupants of the rest room. Chris moved quickly to the man before things got out of hand and was shocked to find it was Tommy Bertram.

"Tommy! Tommy! It's Chris! Tommy!" He seized Tommy's arms.

Tommy struggled in Chris's grip. "Get away from me! You're trying to kill me!" He broke away and ran full force into a baseball player. Before Chris could move, the man had decked Tommy.

"Stop it!" Chris cried, pulling the other man away from his prone fraternity brother. "Can't you see he's messed up?"

"Dude! *He* attacked *me*!" the man defended himself. "Talk to your boy there!"

Chris shoved him away. "Just get outta here! Now!" Chris bent down to examine Tommy.

"What's wrong with Tommy?"

Chris turned to the sound of the voice and saw John standing in the doorway looking scared. "He's on something. Do you know what it is?"

"No. Is he gonna be all right?"

"I don't know. Get some help."

John nodded and left the bathroom. He knew right where to go.

"Greg!" John grabbed his shoulder. "I gotta talk to you!" Greg excused himself from the girl he was trying to pick up and withdrew to a corner.

"What do you want?"

John leaned in close. "Tommy—he's messed up. He's on the floor of the bathroom."

"Yeah, so?"

"Did you give him anything?"

"Just a little angel dust in his fatty."

"Angel dust—PCP! Crap! What did you do *that* for?"

Greg grinned. "A reward for rounding up some new customers. He'll get over it."

"Greg, I gotta get him to a hospital. There's something wrong!"

"No!" Greg seized John's shirt. "You go to Charity; they'll call the Five-O. Get him back to your crib. He'll be all right."

"But—"

"Just do it! Get him home!"

"You gonna help me?"

Greg looked around. "I can't get mixed up in this. I gotta take off."

"What?"

"Shut up!" Greg hissed. "I can't call attention to myself! Get him home and call me." With that, Greg shoved John out of his way and headed for the exit.

John was stunned for a moment. *Shit! I can't get the cops involved. There's no telling what Greg'll do. I gotta get Tommy outta here, like he said.* He saw William walking over to the refreshment stand. He ran over to intercept him.

"Will, I need your help, man! Tommy's sick." William nodded and followed John to the men's room.

"Chris, is Tommy any better?" John asked as William looked on.

"He's breathing okay, but I don't like how his eyes are dancing. You find out what he took?"

John claimed Tommy had only smoked marijuana before going

to the game. "He drank some tequila at the game, too. That's all I know."

"John—"

"Look, I'll get him home and sober him up. I'll take care of it."

"He needs to go to the emergency room," injected William.

"No!" John cried. "He might get into trouble. His dad—his dad's real strict. He might pull him out of school."

William turned to Chris. "What do you think?"

Chris looked concerned, but just then, Tommy groaned as he started to come around. "I don't see any evidence of a concussion. Let's get him to bed. I'll help you."

"No, that's all right! I got it. You make sure Mari gets home okay. I don't wanna ruin her night." He bent down to help Tommy to his feet. "C'mon, buddy."

Tommy was extremely woozy. "D-dude…what the fuck hit me?"

John chuckled. "Somebody's fist. I'll getcha home. Chris, tell Mari I'll call her tomorrow."

"You sure you don't want our help?" asked William.

John tried hard to hide his fear. "I'm sure. Y'all have a good night."

William and Chris watched helplessly as John maneuvered Tommy out of the bathroom. They looked at each other before returning to the group.

"What do you mean, John's gone?" Marianne cried.

"Tommy got sick, so John took him home," replied Chris.

Marianne looked towards the door. "Why didn't he get me? I could've helped."

Chris talked to her kindly. "He didn't want you to have to leave early. He asked me to make sure you got home."

"Oh, that's so sweet!" Marianne said. Chris disagreed, but kept his opinion to himself.

William spoke up. "Can I get you something to drink, Mari?" She requested a diet drink, and Elizabeth offered to go with William. Once they got out of earshot, she began to question him.

"Darcy, what's going on?"

"It's like Chris said: Tommy got sick, and John took him home. He asked Chris to look after Mari."

"Is that it?"

You're a smart one, Lizzy. "That's all he said, Boudreaux."

"Tommy was on something, wasn't he? I saw him earlier."

"Look, I don't know that and neither do you. Chris says Tommy'll be okay, so why don't you let me buy you a drink?" They had arrived at the counter.

"You're not going to distract me, Darcy. I'll take a diet."

Darcy ordered the soft drinks. "Great top, by the way," he said in a low voice as he watched the attendant pour the drinks.

"What?"

William grinned as he handed her two diets. "I thought you said I couldn't distract you, Boudreaux." As Elizabeth sputtered, he picked up a holder with four cups and left her in his wake.

By the time she caught up with him, they had reached the group. Everyone was commiserating with Marianne, who was proclaiming how noble John had been. William and Chris shared a look.

The band came back from a break. "We've got a slow one for you old fogies," claimed the lead singer. The keyboard started a familiar riff.

"Oh, this is a good one!" cried Emma as she hauled Chuck towards the dance floor.

"I love 'New Orleans Ladies'," moaned Marianne.

"Chris, why don't you dance with her?" suggested Elizabeth.

Chris looked first at her, then at Marianne. "Shall we?" He gestured at the floor.

Marianne nodded and turned to William. "Don't stand there like a rock, Will. Dance with Lizzy," she said as Chris took her into his arms.

William smiled. "Scared, Boudreaux?"

She took his hand in hers. "Of you? Ha!" They began to dance.

Marianne and Chris sang along with the song as they danced. Meanwhile, William and Elizabeth swayed in each other's arms.

"You like my top, huh?"

"Yep."

She shook her head. "You're a bad one, Darcy."

"I sure am."

Carrolton

"C'MON, YOU ASSHOLE," JOHN SAID between his clenched teeth as he half-walked, half-dragged Tommy up the stairs to their second floor apartment off Magazine Street. Tommy was babbling, but at least he hadn't tossed his cookies yet.

"Duuuude," mumbled the stoned sophomore.

John had to prop Tommy by the door as he dug into his pocket for his keys. Soon they were inside and moving towards Tommy's bedroom.

"Keep going, buddy. Just a few steps more."

Finally, John was able to let Tommy fall onto his bed. John took a breath before bending over to lift his roommate's feet onto the bed. John then collapsed into a nearby armchair, covered in discarded clothes, and thought about how his life had gotten so fouled up. His dark musings were interrupted by his cell phone ringing.

"Hey," said Greg, *"you get back okay?"*

"Yeah," John said. *No thanks to you.*

"Cool. Go look in your mailbox."

John did as he was told and found an envelope inside. "What is this?"

"Open it."

Inside were ten one-hundred-dollar bills.

"Just lookin' out for my peeps. Later." The phone went dead.

John wandered back into Tommy's bedroom, the envelope still in his hand.

"J-John?" moaned Tommy.

"Yeah?"

"T-thanks, Brother," he said as he fell asleep.

John sat in the chair again, his gaze moving between the money and his friend. With a groan, he buried his face in his hands.

Downtown

AT THE NEXT BAND BREAK, Marianne and Elizabeth expressed their desire to call it a night. Chris agreed and William offered to walk out with them. The four took leave of their friends and left the ballroom.

"Where'd you park?" William asked as they crossed the walkway to the Dome, the warm dark sky threatening rain.

"I'm in a surface lot on Girod," answered Chris. "You?"

"Right here in the garage. I'll walk you to your truck."

"Will, you don't have to do that," Elizabeth pointed out.

"Yeah, we'll be all right," agreed Marianne.

"It's no trouble, ladies." *You never know what's waiting in a parking lot downtown*, his look said to Chris.

A few minutes later, the group made it safely to Chris's Chevy. William held the two passenger-side doors for the girls. Marianne climbed into the front while Elizabeth took the back.

William gave them a smile. "Ladies, I hope you had fun. Mari, I'm sorry about John."

"Me, too."

"Lizzy, nice to see you again." Elizabeth nodded. "Chris, see you later. Drive safe."

"You, too, partner. Later." He turned the ignition as Darcy shut the doors.

Chris idled, his headlights on bright, as his roommate made his way into the Dome parking structure. Elizabeth watched him go, struck by how lonely he looked.

Chapter 5

Loyola VOICE
Elizabeth's Journal

So, I'm sitting on a bench in Audubon Park watching the young joggers and elderly golfers on this bright fall morning. I'm alive; they're alive; the Live Oaks are still green. And I am so thankful for it as I think back to a story I saw in the *Times-Picayune*:

"Hurricane Mitch was one of the deadliest and most powerful hurricanes ever observed, with maximum sustained winds of 180 mph. Its lowest barometric pressure of 905 millibars equaled that of 1969's Camille.

"Mitch formed in the western Caribbean Sea on October 22, and after drifting through extremely favorable conditions, it rapidly strengthened to peak at Category 5 status, the highest possible rating on the Saffir-Simpson Hurricane Scale. Due to its slow movement from October 29 to November 3, Hurricane Mitch dropped historic amounts of rainfall in Honduras and Nicaragua, with unofficial reports of up to seventy-five inches. After drifting southwest and weakening, it hit Honduras as a minimal hurricane. Peak storm surge was twelve feet.

"It drifted through Central America, reformed in the Bay of

Campeche, and ultimately struck Florida on November 5 as a strong tropical storm. Mitch became extra-tropical later that day, but it continued for several more days before losing its identity north of Great Britain on November 9.

"Deaths due to catastrophic flooding are estimated at over 10,000 with more than 10,000 missing. The flooding caused extreme damage, likely over $5 billion."

Ten to twenty thousand people dead? I don't understand how such a thing could happen at the end of the twentieth century. Was there no radio, no TV? Was there no warning?

Then I remember where it happened. Even if the people knew what was coming, where would they go?

I look around again at this lovely spot in a city that's below sea level in some areas. What if a Mitch-strength hurricane came here. I shudder and think no more about it.

Except I cannot forget all those Hondurans and Nicaraguans no longer in this world. And the hundreds of thousands without homes or employment. The children with no parents or schools or food.

I get up off my comfortable bench and go look for the nearest relief center. For if there is one thing Louisianans know, it's the results of a hurricane.   (Published November 13)

Sunday, November 15: Uptown

THE MEN OF ALPHA IOTA sat on chairs against the walls of the main chapter room, forming a large circle, for a rare evening meeting. The room was dimly lit as the overhead lights were not sufficient to illuminate the space, and the window drapes had been drawn closed. The three main officers of the chapter sat before a candle-lit table at one end of the room, the medals of their office hanging from blue ribbons around their necks. The recording secretary sat poised over his notebook. Sitting next to the table was Dr. George Katz, the chapter's alumni advisor, and two alumni. A single chair was placed in the middle of the room, facing the table.

Chapter President, Charles Bingley, gaveled the meeting to order. "Brother Vice President, please read to the brothers assembled the letter we received today."

Henry Tilney rose from his place at Chuck's right. "Aye, your honor. Brothers, I have a letter from Brother Thomas Bertram.

"*To all my brothers of Alpha Iota,*

"*As of today, I am withdrawing from Tulane University to seek medical attention. I expect this will take some weeks. Hopefully I will be able to return to Tulane next fall.*

"*I want all of you to know how much AI means to me. You have all been my friends, and I'm sorry to have to leave you at this time. I will be thinking of you, and I look forward to returning as soon as my health permits it.*

"*Fraternally,*

"*Thomas Bertram, AI-1998.*"

Chuck looked at his fellow officers before turning to the man standing by a doorway. "Brother Sergeant-at-Arms, bring in Brother Waguespack." A minute later, John found himself directed to the chair before the chapter table.

Chuck began. "Brother Waguespack, this meeting has been called to investigate the incident of October 31 at the Homecoming Dance. Before we continue, I ask if you are aware Brother Bertram has withdrawn from school."

John nervously looked around before answering. "Yes, I know. I mean, aye, your honor. He's going to a rehab facility."

Chuck turned to the side. "Brother George Katz."

"Aye, your honor."

"You have been charged with an important task," Chuck read from a book before him, the metal of his medallion of office gleaming in the candlelight. "Do thy duty well, Honored Interrogator, and bring credit to thy chapter and thyself."

George bowed. "I will." He then turned to John. "Brother Waguespack, it is the significance of this infraction that has initiated this investigation. His honor, Brother President, has empowered me as Interrogator to ask you certain questions." He paused. "This is serious, John, but remember, we are all brothers here. Just relax and tell us everything."

John nodded. "Aye, Brother Katz."

"Brother Waguespack, do you know what Brother Bertram consumed before the dance?"

"He smoked some marijuana, I believe."

"Is that all?"

"I saw him take nothing else," John dissembled. "I think he did take something else, based on his actions. What it was, I don't know."

"Do you know where he got the drugs?"

"No, Brother."

Katz turned to Chris Breaux, who was sitting next to William Darcy. "Brother Breaux, you were the first to find Brother Bertram in the men's room, were you not? Please tell us what you saw."

Chris relayed what happened that night. "When Brother Waguespack returned with Brother Darcy, he volunteered to bring Brother Bertram home."

"You're a medical student. Were you comfortable with that?"

"Tom—Brother Bertram was coming around. Brother Waguespack said he would watch over him. I was satisfied with that."

"Brother Darcy, do you have anything to add?"

William refused to look at John. "No, Brother."

George returned to John. "Brother Waguespack, did you take Brother Bertram to the emergency room?"

"I didn't think it was necessary. Brother Bertram slept most of the night and much of the next day. He was pretty hung over."

A few AIs chuckled, which drew a glare from Darcy.

John began laying out the lie he had prepared in advance. "We talked that Sunday. I told Tom…Brother Bertram he needed to get some help. He didn't want to go, but I got in touch with his dad. Together, we got Tommy to change his mind. That's when he was checked into Greenleaves Rehab."

Actually, John was terrified Greg would think Tommy was a liability. He wanted Tommy to stay, to sober up, and get back into Greg's good graces, but his plans were overthrown when Mr. Bertram paid a surprise visit. It was he who dragged Tommy to Greenleaves. The grand that Greg had given him came in handy.

John had lost a rent-paying roommate.

George cleared his throat. "Brother Waguespack, do you use illegal drugs yourself?"

John was ready for that one. "I've smoked marijuana occasionally on a recreational basis. But never on school grounds or in the fraternity house." Only the last part was true.

"Anything else?"

"No, Brother."

"You understand the use of illegal drugs could lead, ultimately, to your expulsion from Alpha Iota?"

"Yes, Brother. While it is my opinion marijuana should be legal, I know I could be thrown out of the chapter." He paused dramatically. "I've chosen to refrain from using marijuana in the future."

"Very good, John." George smiled and turned to Chuck. "I have no further questions, your honor."

"Thank you, Brother Katz," Chuck said as George took his seat. "Does the chapter have any questions for our brother?"

William almost opened his mouth, but paused at Chuck's use of the word "brother." Yes, John was his fraternity brother, but William had never liked him. William knew his power. He had been a very popular and respected leader of the fraternity. He knew a five-minute speech from him would result in John's expulsion from Alpha Iota.

He looked around the room and saw John had a lot of friends there. *Maybe the problem is with me. Maybe I've got the hang-up. Aren't we supposed to help our brothers grow? Maybe we need to give him another chance.*

And so the only man who could have gotten Waguespack thrown out with a few words kept silent.

"Very well," continued Chuck. "Brother Waguespack, the chapter shall deliberate now. I charge you to leave the room until you are recalled." Chuck smiled, and John nodded and left the room with the Sergeant-at-Arms with a lighter step than when he entered.

Chuck banged his gavel. "We will begin deliberations. I remind you that only current members of the fraternity in good standing may cast a vote. So if you are behind in your dues, pay the treasurer now!"

The laugh his comment drew dissipated any remaining tension in the room. William, Chris, and George watched as the men of AI put John on probation, the lightest sentence possible.

Tuesday, November 17: Uptown
EMMA PARKED HER SAAB IN the parking lot of the National Council-Jewish Women on St. Charles Avenue and entered through the front door. She made her way through familiar halls toward a large room in the rear.

As she walked, she remembered how, in years past, her mother had dragged her and her sister, Irene, down these same halls when they were children as she volunteered for yet another relief effort —Africa, AIDS, Hurricanes Hugo in South Carolina and Andrew in Florida. Now, in the aftermath of Hurricane Mitch, Emma would volunteer to help at the same place, the NCJW. , She felt the warmth of her mother's presence all around her here.

"Ah, Emma! Hello, dear," greeted one of her late mother's friends, Mrs. Rosen. She rose from a table and took her hands. "Thank you for volunteering, dear. Edna! Emma's here!"

"Who?"

"Emma Weinberg, Ruth Weinberg's daughter!"

"Ruth's daughter?" repeated Edna Copeland. "Oh, yes! Look at you!" The elderly woman shuffled over. "I haven't seen you in years. Let me get a good look at you." She cupped Emma's face with her wrinkled hands. "So lovely. What a *shayna punim*! Such a pretty face! Ruthie would have been so proud."

"Thank you, Miz Edna."

Edna looked over her reading glasses. "So, are you married yet?"

Emma turned red. "Umm...no, Miz Edna. I'm still in school."

"That didn't stop me, child," Mrs. Copeland cackled.

Mrs. Rosen saved Emma future embarrassment. "That's enough, Edna; we've got loads of work to do. Come along, Emma." The two walked through the room piled high with sealed boxes to a bank of phones set on folding tables against the far wall where three women sat, talking quietly and taking notes.

"Here," Mrs. Rosen indicated a chair, "how much time can you give us, dear?"

"Just a couple hours. My boyfriend is coming over for dinner."

"That's lovely. I'll be sure and tell Edna." She handed Emma a paper. "Here is a list of potential contributors. We're looking for dry goods only—blankets, towels, clothes, bedding, that sort of stuff. These ladies," she waved at the others, "are collecting canned food and power equipment."

Emma studied the list. "When is the deadline?"

"Delta Global Shipping wants the ship to leave for Honduras by the end of the week. They will take as many containers as we can fill. We understand the Hispanic Chamber and Catholic Charities are gathering goods, as well. Just remember, there's no refrigeration. So no fresh or frozen foods. And no toys. We need things that will help keep the people alive. We'll collect books, paper goods, and toys for the next shipload." Mrs. Rosen pointed at another table. "We have coffee and water. There were some goodies—doughnuts and Danishes—but they're a bit picked over by now."

"That's okay."

"Emma, you're a sweetheart. Just dial nine before the number. Any questions, come find me."

Emma smiled as Mrs. Rosen moved on to check on the other ladies. She dialed her first number. "Hello, I'm calling from National Council-Jewish Women," she recited the prepared speech. "We're calling to ask for your support for the Hurricane Mitch relief effort."

Friday, November 20: Garden District
EMMA WAS PUTTING THE FINISHING touches on her make-up when the doorbell rang. "I'll get it, Papa!" she called as she hurried down the stairs, the skirt of her black dress dancing along her thighs. She threw open the door and found a man standing outside—the wrong man.

"Doctor George?"

George Katz smiled. "Good evening to you, too, Emma." As she continued to gawk at him, he asked, "May I come in?"

Emma stepped aside to let the family friend enter. "Sure…but what are you doing here?"

George answered her quizzical look with one of his own. "Dinner? Your father invited me."

"Papa? Papa invited you?" She closed the door and marched directly into the den, a puzzled George following behind. "Papa, did you ask Doctor George over tonight?"

Abe Weinberg climbed out of his La-Z-Boy and extended his hand to their guest. "George, good to see you, son." As they shook hands, Abe said to his irritated daughter, "Yes, I invited him over since we're making dinner anyway."

Emma's eyes grew wide. "Papa, you *knew* I invited—" Emma's sotto voce was cut off by the doorbell. "There he is!" She gave Abe one last glare and returned to the front door.

"Umm, Abe, I seem to have intruded. We can make it another night."

"No, no, you're *my* guest, George. Emma's guest has just shown up."

George's eyebrow went up. "What are you playing at, Abe?"

Further conversation was impossible as Emma returned to the room with a young man. "Papa, I want to introduce Charles Bingley, my *friend*. Chuck, this is my father, Abe Weinberg."

Chuck gave him a hearty handshake. "*Shalom!* Glad to make your acquaintance, Mr. Weinberg!"

Abe nodded in return. Mirth mingled with skepticism curled his lip.

"Chuck," Emma said, "you know Doctor George, right?"

"*Shalom*, Chuck." George started to get a clue.

"George? I didn't expect to see you here, but hey, the more the merrier!" Chuck turned back to Emma's father. "Thank you for having me over to dinner." He eagerly handed Abe a paper bag.

Abe withdrew the bottle within and lifted his bushy brows. "Manischewitz? How…nice—Chuck, is it? Yes, very kind." He let the wine slip unceremoniously back into the sack. "I'll just put this aside for later."

George worked hard not to explode in laughter. *Manischewitz —the cough syrup of table wines? Did the fool think Friday night dinner at Emma's was a full-blown Shabbat meal? I should have warned him about Abe's teasing nature, but...oh, what the hell! This is too good.*

"What can I get you to drink, Chuck?" asked Abe. "I've got this wonderful Pinot Noir from a little winery I visited in Napa a couple years back. Can I interest you in a glass?"

"Pinot is kosher?"

"No, but that's not going to be problem for you, is it?"

"Umm, no, of course not. I'd love some, sir."

Emma blanched. "I'll help you, Papa. Can I get you a glass, Doctor George?" He nodded. "You two just make yourselves comfortable," she said through a tight smile. "We'll be right back."

Seeing the uneasiness in Chuck's eyes, George thought, *At least, we'll be more comfortable than Abe at the moment; that's for sure!*

"Papa, how could you?" Emma hissed at him, as soon as the kitchen door swung closed.

Abe eyed the cook stirring the contents of a boiling pot. "Emma, we're not alone."

"Don't try to change the subject! Miz Taylor's chewed you a new one more times than I have! You're not going to get away with this!"

Abe began to open the wine bottle. "Pass me down some glasses, princess. Get away with what?" Abe moved in slow, deliberate, and —to the livid Emma—infuriatingly calm gestures as he twisted the cork from the bottle.

"Interfering with my dinner! I wanted you to get to know Chuck," she said as she passed him the glasses. "And now—why did you invite Doctor George?"

"I thought he'd be a nice addition to the party," Abe said as he poured the wine. "I thought you liked George?"

"Of course, I like him. He's like a big brother. That's not the point. Try to be nice to Chuck—*please?*"

"I'm nice to everybody, princess. Aren't I, Miz Taylor?"

The black cook rolled her eyes. "I ain't gettin' in the middle of this. You just behave yourself, Mr. Abe. I got extra starch, and I know how to use it!"

"I'll be on my best behavior, Miz Taylor, if only to please you." He grinned. "Emma, shall we return to our guests?"

The two returned to the room, and Emma was still seething. She handed Chuck his wine. Before she could have a word with him, Abe spoke up.

"So, Chuck, I take it you're going to Tulane?"

"Yes, sir. I graduate this year."

"Congratulations. I've heard so *little* about you." His glance at Emma went unnoticed by Chuck. "What are you studying? What are you planning to do?"

"I'm a business major. I plan to get into banking."

Abe's eyes twinkled. *Wait for it...*

Chuck grinned sheepishly. "Any contacts you may have in the business would be appreciated, sir." He drank more of his wine.

George coughed. *Jews and banking—oh, Chuck! How many stereotypes can you hit in one night?*

Abe nodded thoughtfully. "If I hear of anything, I'll let you know. Enjoying the wine?"

"Oh, yes, sir. It's great."

"I'm glad you like it. Allow me to top off your glass."

DINNER WAS LEG OF LAMB with pepper jelly, scalloped potatoes, and asparagus. As he sat down, Bingley smiled warmly at the glowing tapers and pulled something out of his jacket pocket. To everyone's amazement, it was a yarmulke.

"Wow, this looks great, but I'm a little surprised," he said as he placed the yarmulke on his head.

"What do you mean, Chuck?" asked Abe.

"I must say I expected something more like gefilte fish, matzo ball soup—stuff like that."

"Why would you think that?"

"I did some research about Jewish traditions on the Internet." Chuck then noticed none of the others had on a yarmulke. "Umm, did I get it wrong? Should I take this off?"

"Not really, but we aren't so traditional here. Keep the yarmulke on, though. It looks good on you. Very becoming."

"Papa!" Emma thought she was going to die. She touched Chuck's hand. "I'm sorry you misunderstood, Chuck. It was really sweet of you, though."

An abashed Chuck Bingley looked at his plate. "It's okay, Emma. Mr. Weinberg, please accept my apologies. I hope I didn't, I don't know, offend you."

"Of course not, Chuck. We appreciate the effort. Eat up. Top you off?"

George started to eat, a little ashamed that he didn't take the effort to warn Chuck. He didn't like the way Abe was teasing the young man, who was now looking a little pale.

"So, tell me more about yourself, Chuck. Where're you from? Where did you go to school?"

"Baton Rouge. I went to Catholic High."

"Who are your folks? Any brothers or sisters?"

"My mom's Catherine Bingley. I have a sister, Carrie, at LSU." He took a gulp of his wine. "Just us."

"I see. Catherine Bingley—I don't think I know her. What does she do?"

"She's retired. She doesn't have to work, 'cause of the settlement." Four glasses of wine on top of his nervousness was starting to have an effect on him.

"Settlement?"

"Yeah, 'cause of my dad's death." Chuck babbled as he drank more wine. "My dad was an insurance agent—life, health, that sort of stuff. Anyway, he was driving along the River Road about eight years ago when he was hit by a tanker truck from one of the chemical plants. Thing just blew up. Between all of the insurance Dad had bought and Mom suing the hell out of the chemical company, she was able to retire from her paralegal job and move to the Country

Club of Louisiana, a real fancy subdivision outside of town. Dad had also set up education plans for my sister and me. So Mom lives in the lap of luxury, Carrie and I get the college ride of our choice, and I lost my dad."

"Interesting story, Chuck."

Emma flashed daggers at her father before turning to Chuck. "Chuck, I'm so sorry. Were you close to your father?"

"Yeah, kinda. Dad always meant well, you know, about spending time with us, but he worked real hard and kept long hours." The wine was making Chuck maudlin. "I wish he didn't, you know, work so hard. I wish I'd seen him more."

"At least you've got your mom," she said. George flinched; he was acquainted with some of the abusive phone calls Chuck had received at the AI house from his mother.

"Yeah, I guess that's something."

Emma's eyes filled with tears. Dinner was going down in flames. George tried a change of subject. "So, Abe!" he asked. "How's the golf game?"

Emma held her face in her hands. *How much worse can it get?*

"WILL HE BE OKAY?" EMMA asked George as he stood in the doorway of the bathroom, after the sounds of retching finally ceased.

George turned his head. "Chuck's gonna be fine. I guess the wine and rich food didn't agree with him." He turned to his fraternity brother. "How're you doing there? Want some help up, Chuck?" More sounds of retching.

Bingley groaned. "I thought I was gonna die. Aww, Em, I'm sooo sorry...Aww jeez." He doubled over with dry heaves. It was a few more minutes before George could help his inebriated friend up and help him wash his face. He walked Chuck to the main room, supporting him with an arm around his shoulders. Emma trailed behind.

"Mr. Weinberg, I'm sorry for ruining dinner," Chuck managed.

"That's quite all right, Chuck." Abe tried to stand upwind of his sick guest.

"I just got over a stomach bug…I guess I should've canceled, but I didn't want to disappoint Emma. I think I ought to go home, now."

"You'll feel better in the morning, young man."

"Em, God, I'm sorry. Oh, but I'm sorry."

Emma wanted to hug him, but the smell was too much. "I know, Chuck." She turned to George. "You'll see him safely home?"

George nodded with a small smile. Soon they were out the door, Chuck still moaning his apologies.

Emma turned daggers to her father. "Papa—"

"Now, princess, just wait one minute."

"No, I will not! I am ashamed of you!"

"Ashamed of *me*? What did I do?" He pointed towards the door. "*He's* the one who almost vomited on our dinner table!"

"His name is Chuck Bingley, Papa!"

"I know what his name is, Emma. Believe me, I know."

"And what do you mean by *that*?" She asked dangerously.

"Let him bring his Manischewitz wine and yarmulke all he wants, but he'll never…" His voice broke. "He'll never be good enough for you."

"I was right. This is about Chuck being a gentile, isn't it? That's why you had Doctor George here! Papa, this is my life!"

Abe's heated retort died in his throat as Mrs. Taylor came into the room. "Before I leave," she scolded, "I thought y'all should know I can hear y'all in the kitchen." Both Emma and Abe looked like kids caught doing something naughty. "Miz Emma, you shouldn't talk to your daddy that way. And Mr. Abe, I *told* you to behave yourself!" She wagged her finger. "My, my! What would Miz Ruth have to say 'bout you two if she was here!" She huffed as she pulled on the coat she carried. "I'm goin' now. I'll finish cleaning up in the mornin'. An' if I was you two, I'd get me some sleep before y'all say something y'all will regret for the rest of your lives." She turned on her heels and marched back into the kitchen.

Abe and Emma eyed each other warily. "I suppose she's right, Emma."

"This isn't over. We'll talk about this in the morning." With that, she fled upstairs while Abe Weinberg sat alone in his Chippendale-furnished dining room.

Uptown

"I AM SUCH A FUCK-UP…I am such a fuck-up!"

George Katz drove his used Lexus through the streets of Uptown with a sickly drunk Charles Bingley chastening himself in the passenger seat. Chuck's red Jeep Cherokee remained parked in front of the Weinberg home.

George was not pleased with himself. He had known for years how mischievous Abe Weinberg could be and did nothing to give Chuck a heads-up.

Why did I keep my mouth shut? Am I jealous? Of what? Of Chuck with Emma? No, I can't be. I've known her since she was a child! She's like a sister to me.

Isn't she?

"I am such a fuck-up…I am such a fuck-up."

"Hang in there, buddy. We're almost home."

Saturday, November 21: Garden District

EMMA ENTERED THE KITCHEN THE next morning and found her father, as usual, at the breakfast table, drinking coffee over the Saturday *Times-Picayune*.

"Good morning, princess."

Emma said nothing as she poured her own cup. She took a chair across from him and began.

"We need to finish last night's discussion. I want to do this now before Miz Taylor gets here and I go over to the NCJW." Abe nodded.

Emma fiddled with the handle of her cup. "Papa, what happened last night hurt me. Chuck is my boyfriend"—Abe flinched at the word—"and you embarrassed me. You have no right to treat a nice person like Chuck that way."

"I know, and I am sorry," Abe said sincerely. "I do hope he's feeling better."

"I wouldn't be surprised if he never wanted to see me again."

Abe took a sip. "That might be for the best."

"What is with you? Why are you so set against Chuck? Don't tell me it's because of the wine and the yarmulke. You invited Doctor George over before you even met Chuck. You made up your mind before you laid eyes on him. Why? Is it because he's not a Jew?"

Abe sighed. "Yes."

"I don't believe this! We're not observant. We hardly go to synagogue more than twice a year! Papa, Irene married a gentile! Do you feel this way about Tyler?"

Abe turned away to gather his thoughts. "Tyler's a good man...a very good man. He loves your sister very much—"

"But he's still a *goy*. Is that it?"

Abe nodded sadly. "Yes, he's still a *goy*." As Emma prepared to explode, Abe continued, "Emma, please, you must understand. We are Jews—"

"I know that!"

"Listen, please! We are what we are. All over the world, we're hated and mistrusted. Insulted and slighted. Killed and expelled. Even in Europe, we aren't completely safe or accepted. Only in America and Israel do we control our own destiny.

"In Israel we have been at war for over fifty years—longer! Our people, my people, *your* people are under constant attack! The others...they do not want peace. They want to drive us into the sea. They want us dead! They want to finish the work begun by Hitler and the czars!

"But here, in America, *we* are the enemy. We're destroying ourselves from the inside by intermarriage, by assimilation. The Jew comes from the maternal line—you know this. But so many of us who have married outside the faith don't raise their children as Jews. They treat our heritage like an ethnic group. But being Jewish is more than that. You must remember what your mother taught you, Emma!

"Tyler and Irene—they will not send my grandchildren to Hebrew school. They'll be lost to us, not join in the long line of Jews who fought for generations to preserve what your sister has thrown away. As much as I love Irene—as much as I like Tyler—this is a hole in my heart. I cannot let you go down that road—not without talking to you to see if this is what you *really* want."

Emma sat amazed as she listened to her father's speech. "I didn't know you felt this way, Papa."

"I know we haven't been as observant as we should've been. Your mother, of blessed memory"—he paused as a small smile crossed his lips—"she was always after me about attending, but there was always something else to do. A game, a trip—something. When she left us, I...I just couldn't go without her.

"But that doesn't mean I'm not a Jew in *here*." Abe thumped his chest. "That I don't feel as a Jew. Thousands of years, we've been here, Emma. I don't want us to be the generation that fails all the others who came before us. Too much blood has been shed, too many souls lost."

Abe reached over to take his daughter's hand. "It is a great responsibility, being a Jewish woman." He sighed and let a quiet moment pass. "So, what about this Charles Bingley of yours? Do you love him?"

"I don't know. He is my friend, and I like him a great deal. But I'm still getting to know him. I haven't thought that far down the road."

"I am sure he's a good man. A bit too earnest for my liking, but I know he means well. But, Emma, can you not find a good man who's Jewish, too? One you can love and respect and who loves and respects you in return?"

"It's not like I've gone out and looked for one. My friends are my friends. I'm sure there are plenty good Jewish men out there."

"There was one in our house last night."

Emma was flabbergasted. "Doctor George? He's old enough to be my...my older brother!"

"What is age if two loving people come together?"

"Papa, be serious! Me and Doctor George? That's too weird!"

Abe smiled. "Perhaps, but as you see, there are good Jewish men out there. Is it not as easy to fall in love with a Jew as any other?

Besides, think of how easy the wedding would be. No strange non-denominational ceremony where everyone is standing on a beach somewhere reciting bad poetry. And think of all the banking contacts!"

"Papa!" she giggled in spite of herself.

Abe smiled and squeezed her hand. "Emma, my not-so-little princess, I only want what's best for my girls. Your mother always wanted you both to meet nice Jewish boys who would make you happy and give her lots of fat grandchildren. Can you try? Can you not do this for me? For your mother—for our people?"

For the first time in her life, Emma felt the pressure of being a Jewish woman—the responsibility. She felt overwhelmed. Bewildered, yet proud.

"I don't know, Papa. Let me think about it."

Tears glistened in Abe's eyes. "No matter what you choose, know that I love you. I love Irene, and I will love you, no matter who you marry. And I will love all of my grandchildren."

"I know, Papa, I know."

They sat quietly, not knowing what to say next.

Emma broke the silence. "I have a lot to think about. But I won't give up Chuck just because you want me to. I won't let you hurt him again, either."

Abe lowered his head sadly, knowing he had lost. "I see. Do you want me to call him and apologize?"

"No, I think enough's been said about last night. I'll see what Chuck thinks, though. He may think he still needs to apologize to you."

"No, he doesn't."

Emma shook her head. "I agree, but that's the way it is with Chuck. He's a very nice person. That's why I like him. That's why he's my friend."

Abe nodded.

She reached over and squeezed her father's hand. "But I will think about what you've said, okay?"

"Okay."

Emma gazed into her father's face before looking at the clock on the wall. "I've gotta go. I'll be back by dinner time."

She got up and kissed the top of Abe's bowed head. With a lingering glance, she let herself out the kitchen door.

Abe was still at the table, staring at his coffee cup, a half hour later when Mrs. Taylor arrived to clean up.

Chapter 6

Later that Saturday morning, Emma parked her Saab in the parking lot of the NCJW and entered through the front door. She made her way in well-remembered steps towards a large room in the rear.

She stood in the doorway, looking around the room. She watched the women, some three generations of the same family, move about as they did their work. Emma recalled the times her mother, Ruth, brought her and Irene with her as she did her volunteer work. She could hear her voice as she cheerfully did what she could to make the world a better place. She could smell the same odors—disinfectant, perfume, doughnuts, and coffee.

An all-enveloping sense of *belonging* engulfed her. It warmed her and chilled her.

"Emma! Are you here to work, dear?" asked Mrs. Rosen.

Emma opened her eyes. "Yes. This is my place."

NOVEMBER 26 (AP): THE TULANE Green Wave gave its fans an unforgettable Thanksgiving present, walloping the Louisiana Tech Bulldogs 63 to 30 and going undefeated for the first time in the school's history. The Wave, by beating Houston the week before, guaranteed it would go to the Liberty Bowl as Conference USA's champions to face the Western Athletic Conference's BYU Cougars. But by going undefeated and cracking the BCS Top Ten, there are those who would claim Tulane deserves a shot at one of the bigger bowls.

December 2 (Times-Picayune): After months of speculation, the bad news fell on the Tulane Football program today as Head Coach Tommy Bowden announced he had accepted the head coaching job at Clemson University effective immediately.

Thursday, December 3

EMMA AND CHUCK WALKED SLOWLY along the running path in Audubon Park on a bright, chilly afternoon, neither looking at the other. Emma had spent several days in contemplation and prayer, trying to decide what to do.

Her father's words at breakfast after the horrendous dinner party had affected her in ways she could not have predicted. They had touched something deep inside, something her mother had planted in her heart years ago. She had always taken her Jewish roots for granted, and now she faced a Rubicon of sorts. A choice had to be made. And, as painful as it was, Emma felt she had chosen the right one for her.

"I'm sorry, Chuck...Oh my God, I'm sorry I've hurt you, but I have to do this."

"Emma, please, I'm sorry about what happened at your house. I was an idiot."

"No. You have nothing to apologize for. There's nothing wrong with you."

"Then why are you breaking up with me?"

"Because of me, because of what I am. I've thought a long time about this, and I've come to realize that being a Jew is very important to me."

"But what does that have to do with anything? That wouldn't make any difference to me!"

"It's not that easy. You don't understand, Chuck. I've made the choice only to date Jewish men. I want my husband to share my faith, not just tolerate it."

"But Emma—"

"Let's sit down." After they had seated themselves on a park bench, Emma asked, "Chuck, when you think about who you are —what you are—the principles that shaped you, the traditions you hold dear, can you see yourself as anything but Catholic?"

"Emma, I go to Mass maybe twice a year."

"But you still consider yourself Catholic, don't you?"

"Yes."

"It's the same with me, only I've begun to feel the need to become more involved in Judaism." She then told Chuck about how she had been reevaluating her life and what she wanted out of it. She tried to have him see her dawning desire to fully embrace her faith. How it was becoming part of her.

With tears in her eyes, she looked at him. "You've been such a good friend to me. I don't want to lose that. Please say you understand."

Chuck put on a fake smile and said all the right things, but inside he was torn up. *This is Jennifer all over again. Why? Why does this keep happening to me? I try to be a good guy. But I keep getting shit on!*

Emma reached for him. "Chuck."

He stood, Emma following him. "Look, Emma, it didn't work out. I wish you well. I hope you find happiness."

"Chuck, you're too good."

Yeah, I'm such a nice guy—everybody says so. So how's that workin' out for ya, Chuckie-boy? "See you later, Emma."

Chuck walked back to the Tulane campus, fighting his own tears, and leaving a weeping Emma standing alone in the autumn afternoon sun.

Wednesday, December 9

THE PRACTICE ROOM WAS FILLED with the sound of voices accompanied by a lone piano.

> *O come, O come, Emmanuel*
> *And ransom captive Israel…*

The Loyola Christmas Choir was practicing for their upcoming concert. Marianne Dashwood tried to keep her mind on her singing, but she was preoccupied with thoughts of John Waguespack.

Marianne was attracted to the handsome and charming Tulane business student and enjoyed being with him. He was fun, funny, and attentive. However, every time Marianne would start to contemplate taking their relationship to another level, *something* would come up. Some drama with Tommy. A weekend with his folks. Greg Wickham would pop by.

Marianne tried to be nice to Greg for John's sake. She knew he was the source of John and Tommy's marijuana, and he seemed to be John's good friend. Yet, there was something about Greg that made her uncomfortable. She felt he was watching her all the time like a beast everyone thought was tame—but wasn't.

She worked hard to banish such thoughts from her mind. It was her sheltered upbringing in Jackson, Mississippi, she reasoned. Greg was a little strange, but that was due to his drinking and smoking. Some guys like to appear dangerous, she knew, but that didn't mean they were. He was probably a teddy bear underneath. He was John's friend, so she should learn to get along with him.

But he scares me.

The conductor's voice broke in. "Come on, people! The concert's in two weeks! Let's put some effort into it!"

Marianne cleared her mind and concentrated. The result was better this time. Apparently, Marianne wasn't the only member preoccupied.

"Okay, Marianne," said the choir leader, "let's work on 'Rose.'"

Marianne moved to the front of the choir and, in her clear soprano without accompaniment, sweetly sang:

> *Lo, how a Rose e'er blooming*
> *From tender stem hath sprung!...*

Elizabeth entered the offices of the *VOICE* and tossed a computer disc on Justin Middleton's desk. "Sorry it's a little late," she began, only then noticing he wasn't paying attention to her. "Justin? Earth to Justin."

"One sec, Liz," he said, his face buried in his computer screen. "Let me finish this paragraph."

"What are you writing?"

Justin finished typing. "There! Come take a look."

Elizabeth walked around the desk and peered over her editor's shoulder. "Why New Orleans Sucks." She straightened up. "What's this all about?"

"Just writing about how backwards this place is. Great place to party, but the rest is horseshit."

Elizabeth straightened up and put her hands on her hips. "Justin, you're talking about my home! We've got our quirks, but so does every other place. There are a lot of good people here."

"Who gives a shit?" Justin scoffed. "I can't wait to wipe the crap of this stinking town off my feet. Come May, when I get my diploma, I'm outta here! I'm going to someplace civilized—New York, Boston—someplace not populated by a bunch of inbreds."

Elizabeth barely held her temper. "Why did you come to Loyola, then, anyway?"

"To party—what did you think?"

She hid her grimace. *Glad we could have been of service.* She gestured at the disc on his desk. "That's my column this week. I have to go. I've got some exams to study for."

"Right," Justin said absently as he started to type again. "See ya."

EXAMINATIONS OVER, THE GREAT UNIVERSITIES of New Orleans emptied for the Christmas season. Mostly emptied—competitive athletics did not stop for such things as holidays. For this was Sport, and the people had to be entertained, especially in football-crazy South Louisiana.

The Tulane football team ended its season 11-0 and ranked tenth in the country. As champion of Conference USA, it earned the right to play on New Years' Eve in the Liberty Bowl in Memphis. Its opponent would be the Brigham Young University Cougars.

Even though the Green Wave was undefeated, Tulane had lost its coach, and not many gave them a chance against an experienced BYU.

Tuesday, December 29: Tangipahoa Parish

ELIZABETH RELAXED IN THE FRONT passenger seat of Chris Breaux's truck. "I want to thank you guys again for coming to our rescue," she said.

"No prob, Elizabeth," said Chris as he piloted the pickup northbound on Interstate 55. "We were glad to help out. Right, Will?"

"Don't make such a big deal over it, Boudreaux," agreed William from the rear driver-side seat. "Marianne's house in Jackson isn't out of our way, and we're staying at the same hotel in Memphis. Chris certainly has room in this tank. Glad to have you on board."

"Well, you guys are certainly life-savers."

"Did John say why he had to cancel?" Chris asked carefully.

"He said something came up with his family. He was really sorry."

"How's Mari taking it?"

"Just between us, not well. She almost canceled, too. I would hate for her to miss this trip. Do me a favor, and don't bring it up, huh?"

Chris nodded. "Our lips are sealed. All we'll talk about is football."

"Yeah, you rite." Elizabeth smiled.

Darcy grinned. "I didn't know you were such a Tulane fan, Lizzy. It seems most of the folks in bayou land are Tiger fans."

She turned around, placing her arm along the seat back, eyes twinkling in mischief. "It's my contrarian nature, I guess. Everybody pulled for LSU back home, so I suppose I wanted to be different."

"So how come you went to Loyola?" William asked, mesmerized by those eyes.

Her smile faded a bit, and the twinkle went out. "Because they offered the best scholarship."

"Oh, of course." William blanched. He knew he'd stepped into it. Elizabeth turned around, so she didn't see how Darcy's shame showed on his face.

"Way to go, Will," scolded Chris. "I'm sure he didn't mean anything, Lizzy. Did you, Will?"

"Elizabeth, I'm sorry…I didn't mean anything disparaging about Loyola, believe me."

Elizabeth paused before she turned again. "It's okay, Darcy. Let's just have a good time." She turned to Chris. "Can I turn on the radio?"

William thought it would be best just to keep his mouth shut. He wondered why it bothered him so much whether Elizabeth disapproved of him.

Meanwhile, Elizabeth returned to watching the countryside roll by. She forgave William—kinda—but it was another indication of the difference between them. *I didn't have all the money in the world to go to any school I liked, Will. Rich guys like you will never understand.*

Too bad. He's really cute.

Morgan City, Louisiana

JOHN WAGUESPACK WAS NOT SITTING at home during the week between Christmas and New Year's. But instead of heading north on I-55, he was driving south on US 90 towards the coast. Greg Wickham had wanted John to pick up a package in Intracoastal City, but he didn't know when it would get there. So John's job was to sit around a third-rate, no-tell motel over the New Year holiday and await a call on his cell phone.

John had no illusions as to what was in this package. He knew he was getting in too deep, but he needed the money. Things would be tight until Tommy could return from rehab and pay his share of the rent again—*if* Tommy returned. There was no way he could go to his family for cash. That door was closed.

This was the weekend he was finally going to connect with Marianne. They had fooled around a bit before, and she was *ready*. But leave it to Greg to screw everything up.

If it wasn't for the money! he raged. *Greg is gonna owe me big time for this!*

Wednesday, December 30: Memphis, Tennessee

NEW ORLEANS HAS BOURBON STREET. Los Angeles has Rodeo Drive. Las Vegas has The Strip. Many cities have a unique street that identifies them, and Memphis is no different. Theirs is Beale Street.

An act of Congress declared Beale Street the "Home of the Blues." The accuracy of such a designation might be in doubt, but there is no argument that it is the entertainment capital of Memphis. Over thirty nightclubs, pubs, and restaurants attract people from all over the world to hear the Memphis Blues played by masters of the art. No tourist could fail to go there. It would be like missing Graceland, the home of Elvis Presley, which is also in River City.

The best way to absorb this cultural icon is to stroll slowly along the avenue, taking in the music emitting from the clubs. Unfortunately, Beale Street was not designed for the kind of cold weather that late December 1998 brought. Temperatures in the thirties with high humidity and wind gusts of twenty miles per hour would chill the hardiest Yankee or Mountain Man, much less a contingent of Cajuns from Louisiana.

But at least the clubs weren't crowded. The BYU fans, the "Saints," were not a partying bunch. True to their Mormon faith, they rejected alcohol, tobacco, and caffeine. There was no rule against going to nightclubs that served such things, but many felt uncomfortable. That left the place for the Tulane fans and the locals, and they made the best of it. What they lacked in numbers, they made up for in consumption. The purveyors were not unhappy.

Elizabeth and Marianne caught a ride with the guys to join up with their friends. It wasn't long before the group of AIs and hangers-on were ensconced in a corner booth waiting for the band to come back from a break.

"Where's Emma?" asked a flushed Chuck Bingley.

"Oh, she stayed home," answered Elizabeth, surprised at the question. She knew Emma would have been uncomfortable, thinking Chuck was still hurting.

"She should have come. She's missing a great time," Chuck responded. "She's not—she didn't stay away 'cause of me, did she?"

"No, no," Marianne lied. "She doesn't like the cold. She's a Superdome kind of girl."

"Good, 'cause I'm okay with her. She's a friend. You tell her that, okay?"

"Sure will, Chuck."

The band started up, egging on the Tulane faithful; the group was soon on the floor, Marianne with Chuck, and Elizabeth found herself with Darcy.

"Every time I go to a dance, I end up with you. How is that?" she shouted over the music.

"Unlucky, I guess." William grinned. *He* didn't feel unlucky.

Thursday, December 31

MEMPHIS'S LIBERTY BOWL IS A beautiful stadium, half set into the ground. It does not appear very large as people approach it, and they are pleasantly surprised at the size of the place once they take their seats.

Marianne and Elizabeth rode to the game with Chris and William and met up with their friends outside the gate. Entering the stadium, they passed by the concession stands selling food, drinks, and souvenirs to the faithful. The group grabbed some burgers, and Elizabeth looked at the items nearby.

"Oh, look! They've got Riptide Beanie Babies for sale!"

"Really?" asked William. Sure enough, there were small stuffed reproductions of the Tulane pelican mascot. "Hey, fella, give me one of those."

"Something to keep you warm, Darcy?" Elizabeth teased.

He smirked. "On second thought, make that two." Paying the man, he turned to Elizabeth. "For your information, Boudreaux, this is for my sister, Gina, at home."

"Right, so what's the other one for?"

He tossed it to her.

"Darcy! I can't accept this!"

"Sure you can," he said over his shoulder as he joined the others.

Elizabeth looked at the Riptide doll in her hand with surprise. *Why would he buy me something?* She shrugged, carefully placed the Beanie Baby in her purse, and ran to catch up.

The field at Liberty Bowl is aligned north-south, with the home stands oriented on the south side of the field. Therefore, the visitors' stands are usually in full sunlight, while the walls keep the home side in shadow. This is usually an advantage to the home team during the hot summer and fall in Memphis, but winters can be frigid in River City, as it was this New Year's Eve in 1998. Tulane knew all about the idiosyncrasies of the stadium. Their C-USA rival, the University of Memphis, played their games in the place, so Tulane selected the visitor's side for themselves and their fans. It was a wise choice. The temperature was easily ten degrees warmer on the Louisiana side of the field that sunny early afternoon than it was for their Utah opponents. Still, artic gear was *de rigueur* for the fans in the stands.

William's cell phone rang. "Hey, Dad—you made it."

"Yep. Cold enough for you?"

"Aww…why don't you join us here in the stands like a real fan?"

"Not me. There's a reason I worked so hard and made my money—so I can watch football games from suites with their own bar and restrooms."

"I heard that. Still, I wanted to watch this game with my buds. Your flight was okay?"

Mr. Darcy had taken the DGS jet to Memphis. *"Smooth as silk. Got in this morning and checked into the Peabody."*

"I take it Gina didn't change her mind and come along."

"No, she wanted to go to a girlfriend's house for New Year's Day. Hey, why don't you join me for an early dinner tonight?"

"Sure, but I'm here with Chris and some other friends. Can I bring them?"

"Of course. Make sure that brunette next to you comes, too. She's a looker."

"What?" He looked at Elizabeth, seated next to him. "You can see me?"

There was laughter over the connection. *"These Nikon binoculars you got me for my last birthday are good for more things than bird watching."*

"Oh, boy. I guess I better behave myself."

"Enjoy yourself, Son."

THE TULANE STUDENTS AND OTHER fans were going nuts during the final moments after the failed onside kick by BYU. *TULANE 41, BYU 27*, the scoreboard said. The team carried the Liberty Bell trophy to the student section, sharing the glory with them. Elizabeth jumped and screamed and hugged everybody in sight, and she was sure William gave her a kiss during the melee. Renditions of the Alma Mater and Fight Song were sung, and with a final Hullabaloo, the crowd filed out of the stands into the freezing evening.

The AIs laughed and sang at the top of their lungs. *"Twelve and 0! Twelve and 0! Twelve and 0!"* they chanted. In the bitter cold of a Memphis December night, life was very good.

Darcy barely heard his cell phone ring. "Hello?"

"William, can you hear me?" He could barely make out his father's voice over the noise.

"Dad! How 'bout that game! Yahoo!"

"Yes, Son, it was great. William, I need you to listen to me."

Ice water flooded William's insides. The last time his father called him "William" was when his mother died. "What is it? What's wrong?"

"I need you to meet me at the VIP gate right away."

"Why? What's up?"

"No time. Hurry, Son."

"Yes, sir." Hanging up the phone, he reached out and grabbed Chris's shoulder. "Chris, my dad just called. He wants to me to meet up with him."

"Should we wait for you?"

"No, you go on ahead."

Marianne was next to Chris. "Aren't you coming out with us?"

"Yeah, maybe...we'll see. See ya." Darcy turned on his heel and moved as quickly as he could through the crowd.

Chris watched him leave, puzzled at his friend's expression, then he was jostled. "Hey!" cried an excited Elizabeth. "Where's Darcy? We gotta party!"

Marianne answered, "He just left."

"Left? Where'd he go?"

Chris, not knowing how to answer, decided not to ruin anyone's night. "His dad just called, and Will went to meet up with him."

"You mean he ditched us for his father?"

Chris shrugged and Marianne rolled her eyes.

Elizabeth snorted. "His loss! Come on, we gotta paint this town Green and Blue!"

WILLIAM DASHED INTO HIS MOTEL room to gather his belonging. He had only a few minutes. He had tried to call Chris, but he wasn't answering his cell phone. Throwing all his gear into his duffle bag, he had time to pen a short note:

Chris, I've got to get back to New Orleans. Family business. I'll call. Have fun and I'll see you in town.

Will

William looked at the note but didn't like it. He reached for the pen again.

"William!" cried his father, "let's go!"

"Just one more minute, Dad!"

"No time! *Now!*"

William placed the note on the dresser, grabbed his duffle, and walked quickly to the waiting limo. The driver hit the gas as soon as the door closed, driving towards the airport.

"Have you gotten through to the doctor?"

"No, they're still in surgery."

"Dad, it's only her appendix."

George Darcy snapped at his son. "When *you* have children, William, we'll see if you think 'it's only her appendix.'"

William flushed with embarrassment. He hadn't gotten a dressing down like that since he 'borrowed' one of the farm's tractors when he was nine. "Sorry, Dad."

Mr. Darcy grasped his son's strong forearm. "You and Gina are all

I have in this world, Will. Family is everything—remember that."

William was mortified to see tears in his father's eyes. "I will, Dad."

Mr. Darcy gave him a weak smile and patted his arm. "I know you will. We'll be home soon. They're warming up the jet as we speak."

Within thirty minutes, they were airborne.

January 1, 1999: I-55, south of Memphis

NEW YEAR'S DAY DAWNED COLD and wet as a light rain fell on Memphis. Chris, operating on four hours sleep, made his way out of town towards Marianne's home in Jackson, Mississippi.

"You gonna be okay, Chris?" asked Marianne.

"I'm fine. We didn't party *that* hard last night. I'll get you home in no time." The windshield wipers beat out a monotonous rhythm.

"If you get tired, pull over," said Elizabeth from the back seat. "I've driven a pick-up before."

"I promise. I'll be okay if I can get a bit of rest at your house, Mari."

"Sure, that would be fine. Stay as long as you need. Mom loves company."

The plan was to drop Marianne and Elizabeth off in Jackson. The girls were to return to New Orleans in a couple of days while Chris pushed on for the city.

"Heard from Will?" Marianne asked.

"I left my cell phone charger at home. It's dead. Will left me a note in the room. Seems he flew back with his Dad last night."

Elizabeth, leaned back in her seat and mumbled, "Must be nice. Guess they didn't want to miss any New Year's Day bowl games on TV."

"He said it was family business," Chris explained.

"I'm sure." Elizabeth wondered why she felt so disappointed. She looked down at her handbag, Riptipe half hanging out.

I just can't figure out that guy.

Part Two

It has been said that a Scotchman has not seen the world until he has seen Edinburgh; and I think that I may say that an American has not seen the United States until he has seen Mardi-Gras in New Orleans.

— Mark Twain, *Letter to Pamela Moffett, March 1859*

Chapter 7

I wish everybody would quit fussing over me," complained Gina Darcy from her East Jefferson Hospital bed.

"No way, sugar pie," said her father. He sat in a chair next to the bed, patting her hand. "You just heal up, so we can take you home."

"But you missed all the Bowl games! That's no fun!" She had her new Riptide Beanie Baby grasped firmly in one hand.

"We'll get over it," said William, standing at the foot of the bed.

Just then, a lovely blond nurse came into the private room. "And how are you feeling, Miss Gina?"

"Okay, but my side still aches a bit, Nurse Jane."

She nodded and, after remarking about her gift, took Gina's temperature and blood pressure. "All your vitals are fine."

"When will she be discharged, nurse?" asked Mr. Darcy.

"That's up to the surgeon, but I wouldn't be surprised if she left us tomorrow."

George Darcy nodded. "I want to thank you and the entire staff for taking such good care of my little girl, Nurse Boudreaux."

She gave a radiant smile. "It's been a pleasure."

William stared at her. There was something about the nurse. "Are you related to the Boudreauxes from Chackbay?" he blurted out.

"I'm from Chackbay." She raised one eyebrow in a familiar manner.

"Really? Do you know Elizabeth Boudreaux?"

"She's my sister."

William's smile lit up. "Small world! I know your sister. My name's Will Darcy. I go to Tulane."

"Jane Boudreaux, senior nursing student from SLU. Nice to meet you, Will. Are you one of the AIs Elizabeth's made friends with?"

"Sure am. You have a very nice sister."

"Thank you."

"SLU—that's up in Hammond," observed Mr. Darcy. "How do you find the commute from across the lake?"

"You get used to it." She looked at her patient. "Gina tells me you flew back from Memphis two nights ago. I hope you saw the game. Elizabeth told me she had a lot of fun."

"We did, and we enjoyed it."

"A friend and I drove Elizabeth and her roommate to the game," William felt compelled to add.

"Really? It *is* a small world." She checked her watch. "I'm sorry, but I have to complete my rounds. I'll tell Elizabeth I met you, Will." She turned and bestowed a brilliant smile on Gina. "And I'll see you later, Miss Gina." With that, she left the room.

"Isn't she just an angel, Daddy?" observed Gina.

George Darcy nodded, but his attention was on his son, a small smile on his lips. *So the brunette has a name: Elizabeth Boudreaux.*

LATER, AS THE TWO MEN drove along Airline Highway towards Dansereau Plantation, Mr. Darcy turned to his son. "Tell me about Elizabeth Boudreaux."

William was surprised at the question. "What do you mean? Why are you asking about her?"

George Darcy laughed. "Son, I wiped your bottom when you were still crapping in your diaper. I *know* you. I saw your expression when you were talking about Elizabeth to her sister. She was the brunette sitting next to you at the game, right?"

"Yeah."

"You're interested in her, aren't you?"

William had no idea he had been that transparent. "Dad! No! I mean…Look, Dad, Elizabeth's a nice, pretty, smart girl. But she's a sophomore, for crying out loud!"

"So? Is she immature?"

"No, I wouldn't say that, but there's a four or five year difference in our ages."

Mr. Darcy looked at his son as though he had lost his mind. "Your mother was six years younger than I was, you know."

"That's different." The excuse sounded stupid, even to William.

George Darcy was quiet for a moment. "When was the last time you went on a date?"

"I don't know—Dad! I'm okay. I've just hit a dry spell, is all."

"Don't kid a kidder. I know what you've gone through in the last few years. I saw the kind of girls who chased after you. Take Chuck Bingley's sister—Cassie, Carol—"

"Carrie."

"That's it, Carrie. I wouldn't blame you for being off dating if all the girls were like that one. After what you *own* instead of who you *are*. But don't throw the baby out with the bathwater." He sighed. "Will, you're only young once. Enjoy yourself. I'm not asking you to get *married*, mind you—"

"Thanks." William crossed his arms and stared out the windshield. This conversation was downright uncomfortable.

"But how are you going find a girl you might marry someday if you don't date? Take a nice girl to a movie. It won't kill you. And you might find you don't know as much about people as you think you do."

William, pained, looked at his father. "You think I'm like that —judgmental?"

"You can be, Son, when you're not careful. Remember what I taught you: let people prove themselves first. Give 'em a chance."

"I try, Dad."

Mr. Darcy reached over to pat William on the shoulder. "I'm proud of you, Will. You have all the makings of a good man. That's all we can ask of ourselves in the world. I want you to enjoy yourself. Life is short. Don't waste it."

Tuesday, January 19: Uptown

A WEEK AFTER THE GIRLS returned from Jackson, the dorm room phone rang. Marianne answered.

"*Hi, is Elizabeth there?*"

"Sure, I'll—Will? Is that you?"

There was a pause. "*Yes.*"

"Hey there, good-looking! How was the plane ride back?"

"*It was good. May I speak to Elizabeth, please?*"

Elizabeth looked up from her bed. "Is that Will Darcy on the phone?"

Marianne nodded. "Sure, hang on." She held out the phone to Elizabeth. "It's for you."

"Why?"

Marianne covered the receiver with her hand. "I don't know. Wait! Maybe he wants to ask you out!"

"Yeah, right." Elizabeth took the phone. "Hello, Will?"

"*Hi, Elizabeth. Did you have a good visit at Mari's house?*"

"Yes."

"*And you had no problems coming back?*"

Elizabeth was befuddled. "Nope. We're alive, as you can tell."

"*Good, good. Look, Elizabeth, would you, umm…would you like to go catch a movie sometime?*"

Elizabeth was shocked speechless for a moment. "A movie? You're asking me to a movie?"

"*Yeah, a movie. Right.*"

Marianne jumped up and down. "I told you!" she mouthed.

Elizabeth waved her hand in an effort to stop her roommate. "Darcy, are you asking me on a *date*?"

"*Well, a movie-style date, yeah. I guess I am. Do you want to?*"

"I suppose so." She looked with wide eyes at Marianne, who was grinning for all she was worth.

"*Good, good. When?*"

"When what?"

"*When do you want to go? To the movie?*"

"Umm…whenever."

"How about this Saturday?"

"Saturday? Sure."

"Okay, good. Anything you want to see?"

Before she could answer, Marianne snatched the phone away. "Will! John and I are going to a movie this Saturday, too. Wanna double up?"

"Mari? Yeah, I guess so, if that's what Elizabeth wants to do."

Marianne put her hand on the receiver again. "Come on, Lizzy! You and Will come with us. It'll be fun!"

Elizabeth felt as though things were spinning completely out of control. "All right, if that's okay with Will."

Marianne uncovered the receiver. "Elizabeth said yes! We're going to the seven o'clock show at the Prytania. Here's Lizzy again!" She shoved the phone into Elizabeth's hands. "And tell him we'll grab pizza afterwards!"

"Will, did you hear that?"

"Yeah, it looks like the Prytania at seven on Saturday and pizza afterwards. That sounds okay to you?"

"Fine," she replied with a voice half an octave too high.

"I'll get with John to see when we'll pick y'all up. Thank you, Elizabeth. It'll be fun."

"Right. See you then."

"Bye."

Elizabeth hung up the phone. Marianne was grinning like a fool. "I *knew* it! I *knew* he liked you!"

"How long have you thought that?"

"Since forever! I could tell by the way he always looks at you."

"Yeah, right. He's just waiting for me to make a white-trash fool of myself."

"That's unfair! Why would he ask you out if he didn't like you?"

Elizabeth glanced at the Riptide Beanie Baby on her dresser. "I don't know. I'm sorry; I guess you're right. I'm surprised, that's all. I had no clue."

"Sheesh, you're the only one! Emma and I have been waiting for ages for Will to ask you out."

"No way."

"*Way.* It's obvious the way his eyes follow you around a room. He likes you, Lizzy."

"Then why hasn't he said anything before now?"

"Don't know. Why don't you ask him?"

"Yeah, right. I can just see it." Elizabeth batted her eyes and, in a singsong voice, said, "'Will, why haven't you told me before now how much you wanna jump my bones? How have you resisted my loveliness for so long?'"

Marianne frowned. "Lizzy, you can be mean sometimes." Before the open-mouthed Elizabeth could respond, Marianne continued. "Just be nice to him on Saturday, huh?"

Elizabeth tried to respond then stopped herself. *I'm scared of him! He's…he's Darcy! He's gorgeous, rich, smart, and popular. His family owns half of St. Charles Parish. I'm just a little girl from the swamps. Darcy's DGS could buy and sell Daddy's company and not miss a beat. I'm scared of getting my hopes up, thinking we could be something good just before he dumps me for someone prettier, smarter, and richer!* But she couldn't admit that to Marianne.

"I'll be good, I promise."

"WHAT WAS THAT ALL ABOUT?" asked Chris as William hung up the phone.

"Nothing. Just setting up a date for Saturday night with Elizabeth Boudreaux."

Chris's jaw dropped. "Elizabeth? The *she's-too-young-for-me* Elizabeth Boudreaux?"

"Yeah. That was a little stupid of me, wasn't it?"

"Yeah, just as stupid as that note you left me in Memphis," his roommate reminded him. "Why didn't you tell me Gina was sick?"

"Well, I did. I left you a message on your cell."

"Which I didn't get until I got home."

William shrugged. "Not my fault you forgot your charger."

"You could've put that in your note."

"Sorry, we were in a hurry. Brain wasn't working, I guess."

"No, it's that privacy thing you've got, buddy." Chris pointed a finger at William. "You know everybody else's business, but you don't tell anybody yours."

"That's not *altogether* true."

Chris crossed his arms. "Uh-huh, and why didn't I know about your birthday until three months after the fact when we were first rooming on campus?"

William looked away. "Didn't need a gift, I guess."

Chris shook his head. "That's gonna get you in trouble one of these days, partner."

William gave him a serious look. "I'd love for you to continue your diagnosis of my mental health, Dr. Breaux, but I've got to call John Waguespack to coordinate Saturday night," he said as he reached for the student directory.

Carrolton

"OKAY, WILL, SEE YOU SATURDAY," John said as he hung up.

"Who was that?" asked Greg Wickham, who sat sprawled on the couch, nursing a beer.

"Will Darcy. Mari arranged a movie double date on Saturday."

Greg took a swig. "Double date with who?"

"Her roommate, Lizzy." John took a pull from his own beer.

"Gonna cramp your style, going to the show with another couple."

"Yeah, I had other plans." John meant to bring Marianne back to his apartment.

"Too bad." Greg belched. "Since you won't be needing the place, I'll be around on Saturday. I'm gonna meet with a new customer anyway, an' I don't wanna have to come all the way across the river beforehand." He looked at John. "That is, if it's all right with you." The light tone in his voice was betrayed by the hard glint in his eye.

Shit! There goes my chance to score with Mari! "Umm, sure thing, Greg. No problem."

"Thanks, dude. When does Bertram get outta Greenleaves?"

"Next weekend."

"He's movin' back in?"

"Yeah. He's gonna get a job this semester and register for the fall term."

Greg frowned. "I don't like it. Can't trust a guy who's gone straight. Why don't you run him off?"

John almost spit out his beer. "Greg, I need the rent money!"

"So? You can get that from me, runnin' errands."

Terror flooded John's belly, but he hid it well. "Greg, I can't. I gotta go to class. I can't run errands and study. Might flunk out." He could see Greg was considering his words. "So, with Tommy here, I can keep this place and go to class."

There was a long pause. John tried to keep from sweating.

"Okay," Greg said as he took another sip of his beer. "Got any Doritos?"

John started breathing again. "Yeah, let me go grab a bag."

Saturday, January 23

"THIS IS A BAD-ASS CAR, Darcy," exclaimed John as they rode in William's BMW from John's apartment to Loyola, listening to Van Halen.

"Thanks, John."

"But your choice in music is lame!" John reached over and switched the station from classic rock to an alternative station. Nirvana came pouring out of the speakers. "Now, that's what I'm talkin' about!"

William gritted his teeth. The only thing he hated more than someone touching his radio was grunge rock.

Before long, the two men were walking into the lobby of the girls' dorm. Marianne and Elizabeth were waiting for them beside the couches. William almost stopped dead in his tracks as he beheld Elizabeth. Her green turtleneck sweater was perfect against her skin and set off her eyes, while her curls framed her face. Dark jeans and boots gave her a sophisticated yet casual look. Her clothes did not hide her figure; they set it off, and that was a great thing.

Elizabeth seemed unaware of the effect she was having on his blood pressure. She saw no admiration in his serious, dark look. William was head-to-toe in black—cashmere mock turtle-neck, slacks, and polished shoes. The only noticeable difference William could detect was that Elizabeth's nervousness seemed to have returned.

"Hi, baby." Marianne had on the same heavy coat she had worn to Memphis over her T-shirt and jeans. She gave John a kiss and then turned to the others. "Ready to go?"

"Sure, the car's waiting up front." William waved his hand. "After you."

Two hours later, the couples exited the Prytania Theater. A landmark in Uptown, it was known for art films and foreign language movies. The occasional popular film was shown; tonight it was *You've Got Mail*.

"Well, what did you think? I liked it," said an animated Elizabeth.

"That was great!" Marianne was arm-in-arm with John. "It was so romantic!"

I'm surprised you saw any of it, thought Will, *the way you and John were making out.*

"Good chick flick," judged John.

"What about you, Darcy?"

"Umm, the acting was good."

"What—didn't you like it?"

He shrugged. "We could've rented *Sleepless in Seattle*. It was basically the same movie."

The girls loudly proclaimed Darcy was *so* wrong and began to list the differences.

"All right, all right, I give up!" William laughed. "I bow to your superior knowledge of romantic comedies!"

"Good choice, Will," said John.

A few minutes later, the four were seated in a booth at a local pizza joint. New Orleans was not renowned for its pizza, but this place claimed it served "authentic New York style pizza," and its popularity with the college crowd spoke well for the product it dished out. Large pepperoni and vegetarian pies were ordered, along with a pitcher of beer.

"I didn't figure you for a veggie eater, Darcy," remarked Elizabeth. "I would have pegged you for a meat-lover's kind of guy."

"Now why would you think that, Boudreaux?" The two hours in the dark theater had restored their usual banter.

"You're such a manly man," she teased. "I'll bet you used to throw away your green beans when you were little."

"I did until I learned how good they taste. You know Cajuns, Lizzy—they'll eat *anything*." He wagged his eyebrows.

"Oh, gross! I haven't eaten yet!" said Marianne, mock disgust in her voice.

"Sorry." William turned to Elizabeth. "I tried a veggie pizza a couple of years back and liked it. Don't worry; I can still put away my share of pepperoni."

"No! You can't touch my pepperoni! It's mine," cried Mari.

"You're gonna eat a whole large one?" asked John. "What about me?"

"You should have ordered one for yourself…No! Stop! Hahaha, stop tickling me!"

"You asked for it!"

Elizabeth seemed amused until she looked at her companion. William, embarrassed by the exhibition, had turned away.

The rest of the evening passed pleasantly sharing good pizza and light conversation. It was to be an early night as Marianne was leaving the next day with the Loyola Choir on a ten-day tour. Elizabeth and William walked into the dorm lobby, giving some privacy to the other couple.

Marianne and John took advantage of it, immediately engaging in a passionate embrace. Hands and lips were everywhere, and they acted as though they were going to explode.

"God, I want you so bad," growled John.

"You can't…you can't come up—Elizabeth."

"C'mon back to my crib, baby."

"You said Greg was there."

John was desperate. "Fuck Greg! I'll throw him out."

"Oh, baby…I can't. I gotta get ready to leave."

John kissed her passionately. "Don't leave me like this!"

"John, don't make this harder than it is."

John looked at her, and then broke up laughing. It took a moment for Marianne to catch her double entendre, but when she did, she laughed with him.

Meanwhile, William and Elizabeth stood next to the couches in the lobby, waiting for the others. William was impatient. Finally, he blurted, "What's taking them so long?"

Elizabeth looked at him in wonder. "What do you think?"

William chuckled. "Probably finishing what they started in the theater."

"Darcy!" She playfully slapped his shoulder.

"C'mon! Do you think they saw any of the movie?"

Elizabeth giggled. "Probably not. But then, I'll just rent *Sleepless in Seattle* for them so they can see what they missed."

"Oooh…good one, Boudreaux."

"Well, thank you, kind sir."

William grinned. "Did you enjoy yourself tonight, Elizabeth?"

"Yeah," Elizabeth responded, not hiding the slight surprise in her voice. "It was fun."

"Yeah, it was. We'll do it again—next time without the chaperones." He jerked his thumb over his shoulder.

A slow smile appeared on Elizabeth's face. "I think that would be nice."

William took Elizabeth's hand. "I guess I ought to say good night, Elizabeth."

"Good night, William. Thank you for a lovely evening." She saw William lean in, so she offered her cheek. Just before he made contact, she heard the front door open. Instinctively, she turned towards the noise, which put her mouth right in William's path. Neither knew what surprised them more—the kiss or the electric shock both felt as their lips collided.

William jumped back, muttering apologies.

"It's…it's all right, Will," Elizabeth managed.

They still held hands. William looked at her, and then released his hold, his fingers slowly sliding across her palm. His hand fell away, breaking contact and the magic that held the pair spellbound.

"I'll call, okay?" His voice was gruff.

Elizabeth nodded. William walked towards the lobby door. Just as he reached it, Marianne came through, shoulders hunched up, distracted and rumpled. William said good-bye to her, threw one last look at Elizabeth, and left.

Marianne stabbed the elevator button. "I've got packing to do, roomie," she mumbled.

"Yeah, sure," said Elizabeth, one eye on the lobby door.

Outside, William found John leaning against the BMW, obviously in a frustrated mood. They climbed in and drove off into the night, both men thinking about their dates.

Chapter 8

Saturday, January 30: Garden District

Elizabeth and Marianne were sitting around in Emma's living room, drinking soft drinks and visiting, when Elizabeth's cell phone rang. She excused herself and took the call.

Elizabeth covered the phone. "It's my sister Jane! She's gonna get Mardi Gras off and come visit!"

The girls expressed their delight at the announcement.

"Where is she going to stay?" asked Emma.

Elizabeth laughed. "Haven't gotten that far. I guess she'll bunk in with Mari and me." Marianne nodded.

Emma made a face. "Nonsense! She can stay here. We've got plenty of room."

"Em, are you sure?"

Emma smiled. "Hold on a sec." She got up and walked towards her father's study.

Meanwhile, Elizabeth returned to her call. "Jane, hang on. We're working on something here."

Emma leaned through the door to her father's study and soon returned to her friends, flashing a thumbs-up.

"Jane," Elizabeth cried happily into the phone, "Emma, my friend from Newcomb, says you can stay at her place. ... No, it was her idea. Here, talk to her." She handed the phone to Emma.

"Jane? Hi, I'm Emma Weinberg. I want you to know my father and I would be happy to host you while you're here for Carnival. We have several spare bedrooms. ... No, it wouldn't be an imposition at all. Elizabeth's a dear friend, and I look forward to meeting you. ... Fine. ... Lizzy will send you the directions. Here's your sister." Emma returned the phone to Elizabeth.

"Jane, I'll send you an email with all the details. ... Yeah, me too. Oh, this is gonna be so much fun!"

A HISTORY OF MARDI GRAS
A series for the *Loyola VOICE* by Elizabeth Boudreaux

IT'S THAT TIME OF YEAR, gang. Time to put on silly costumes and stand by the street, killing ourselves to dive after junk we'll be throwing away in March. And drinking way too much the whole time. It's Carnival time in the Big Easy!

For the next few issues, I will be exploring just what the heck this Mardi Gras thing is all about. Like a lot of things, it has its roots in religion. Somehow, going to Loyola, you just knew I was going to bring up religion, didn't you? Well, since this place is supposed to be for higher education, just sit back and let me school you.

It all has to do with Lent, the forty days before Easter. (You Catholics out there, help me with the heathens.) During that time of introspection, one is supposed to sacrifice—a farewell of sorts to the pleasures of the flesh—and refrain from the good things in life: meat, chocolate, and booze. But we're not going to throw them away, are we? Let's use them up first!

Carnival, the time between the Feast of the Epiphany (also known as Kings' Day or Twelfth Night—you know, the "Twelve Days of Christmas") and Ash Wednesday, the first day of Lent, is celebrated throughout the Roman Catholic world. Brazil, for example, is renowned for its elaborate street parades, where dancers strut their stuff to a Latin beat. But no one does Carnival quite the way it is done here. Nobody else throws cheap trinkets from floats.

Mardi Gras, French for Fat Tuesday, is really the last day of the Carnival season. It starts in New Orleans on Twelfth Night, January

6. It continues with balls and other celebrations throughout southern Louisiana and the Gulf Coast. During the last twelve days of Carnival, hundreds of parades all across the region build up to the big day, Shrove Tuesday, when Rex, the King of Carnival, takes over the streets of the Crescent City. It's party central of the entire US of A.

It's a lot better than the whole Pancake Day stuff in Britain, Ireland, and Australia, huh?

Many are surprised to learn the first Mardi Gras celebration occurred in Mobile, Alabama in 1703. The first modern day pageant in this city was a nighttime parade by the Mystick Krewe of Comus in 1857. The daytime street parades began with the School of Design, better known as the Rex Organization, in 1872. The Zulu Social and Pleasure Club, at the time a totally black krewe, rolled for the first time in 1909.

Most Mardi Gras krewes developed from private social clubs, which had restrictive membership policies. Since all of these parade organizations are completely funded by their members, most of whom are the movers and shakers of the community, the event is called the "Greatest Free Show on Earth." And aren't we glad about that? Leaves more cash for beer.

The original purpose of Mardi Gras krewes was to parody European monarchs. Later, the themes of the parades and the maskers have been to mock politicians and current events. That was why krewe members were originally masked—so the powerful wouldn't know who was making fun of them. It might be their own brother-in-law!

The word krewe is itself a purposeful misspelling of the word "crew." It has become traditional to name krewes after figures from mythology. Secrecy is all-important in the krewes. In fact, Comus never reveals the identity of its king to the public.

Thursday, February 4: Uptown

WILLIAM WAS WORKING ON A term paper for his management course when his phone rang. He grabbed it automatically. "Will here," he said absentmindedly.

"Will, it's Lizzy. Did I catch you at a bad time?"

All thoughts of cash flows and exchange rates fled from his head. "Elizabeth! No, no…just working on a paper. It's all good. What's up?"

"Is Chris there? I would like to talk to him."

"Chris?" William repeated. *Why did she want to talk to him?* As soon as his jealousy flared, it subsided. "Yeah, he's right here. Hang on." He passed the phone to his roommate.

"Chris do you know anything about Mardi Gras in Mamou, Louisiana?"

Chris was puzzled. "The *courir*? Sure, I've ridden in it."

"Really? That's so cool. I'm writing a series about Mardi Gras, and I've never seen the Mamou courir. Do you know somebody I can interview?"

"Never seen it? Cher, that's sad. That's how we do it in Cajun country." Chris told her his father had ridden in the *courir*, and he had followed suit while in high school.

"We didn't do any of that stuff in Chackbay. Just the usual parades."

"That's the difference between you Swamp Rats and us Plains Cajuns."

"So, can I interview you?"

"I've got a better idea. Want to see it in person?"

"See it? Of course, I would love to see it! Are you serious?"

"Yeah. I was planning to go home on Lundi Gras anyway to see the folks. You can come with me. We'll put you up."

"I— sure! Let's do it! Thank you, Chris!"

"No problem, Lizzy. Here's Will again."

William took the phone. "I take it you're going to Lafayette for Mardi Gras?"

"Just Monday and Tuesday. This is so neat! I get to see a real live courir. My sister's coming in— Oh no!"

"What? What is it?"

"I forgot my sister Jane is coming in for Mardi Gras on Friday the twelfth. I can't abandon her to go to Mamou on the fifteenth! I'll have to cancel the trip."

"Why don't you take her with you? I'm sure Chris won't mind."

"But she's never seen Carnival Day in New Orleans—Rex, Zulu, all that stuff. That's why she's coming. And I wanted to introduce her to you and my friends."

William almost said he'd already met her sister when his brain kicked in. *She wants to introduce* me *to her sister. That's good, isn't it?* "It's okay, Elizabeth, she can hang out with us. You go do your research, and we'll make sure she has a nice time."

There was a slight pause. *"Really, Will? You'd do that for me?"*

You'd be amazed what I would do for you, Elizabeth. Aloud, he said, "I would be happy to, Elizabeth."

Elizabeth's voice was flustered. *"Well…that's very nice. Thank you."* There was another pause before Elizabeth teased, *"I guess she can help fend off Carrie."*

Darcy groaned. "Oh, man, is she coming in, too?"

He heard Elizabeth's laughter. *"I just assumed. My guess is she'll be there wearing as little as the weather permits and throwing herself at you!"*

"And you're going to abandon me?"

"You're a big boy. You can handle yourself." Her tone changed. *"Thank you for your offer. You're a good friend, William."*

"Anytime, Elizabeth."

"I'd better go now. Thank Chris for me, and tell him we'll firm up the time for the trip later. Bye, William."

"Goodbye, Elizabeth." William hung up the phone thoughtfully.

He and Elizabeth had met several times for coffee since their movie date. Nothing romantic—just two friends sharing java and conversation for a half hour. It was all he had time for with term papers and trips back home to spend time with Gina.

William was impressed with Elizabeth's maturity and mind. She was both smart and sharp, and he had to be on his toes to meet the challenge of her banter and opinions. He found her good-natured and fair-minded. She accepted they didn't always agree, and she was willing to reconsider her stands, assuming his arguments were on firm ground. For his part, he saw she had some viewpoints he needed to mull over, as well.

It didn't hurt that he found her prettier each time he saw her. She wasn't model-thin like most of the coeds who pursued him. Her curves made her lovely, real, and approachable; a man could spend a lifetime happily exploring that territory.

Chris broke his thoughts. "Anything wrong, buddy?"

"What? No, I'm fine. Why'd you ask?"

"You had a weird expression on your face." Chris considered a moment, then offered, "Umm…Will, are you okay with me taking Elizabeth to Lafayette?"

"Why shouldn't I be?"

"I'm just helping a friend with her research."

"Right. I know that."

"It's not like it's a date."

"No, it's not. I mean…" William frowned. "Do you want to date her?"

Chris laughed. "No, no."

"What's so funny?"

"You, buddy. You ought to see the look on your face!"

"What look?" he asked lamely.

"Don't worry, partner, I won't do anything to screw up your chances with the lovely Miss Boudreaux."

"Humph," grunted Will, unwilling to give his roommate the satisfaction of being right. "Just research, right?"

"Right."

William nodded and returned to his term paper. A wasted exercise, as he could not concentrate. His phone call with Elizabeth and subsequent conversation with Chris had opened his eyes to a new possibility.

Sweet Jesus, am I falling for her?

"So everything's taken care of?" asked Marianne.

"It looks that way," said Elizabeth. "Jane comes in on the Friday before Mardi Gras and stays at Emma's, I go to Lafayette with Chris to see Mardi Gras at Mamou, and Will and the guys will entertain Jane on Mardi Gras day."

"Wow, I wish I could see Mamou."

"You wanna come? I'm sure Chris wouldn't mind."

"Nah. John wouldn't like it."

"How're you two doing, anyway?"

Marianne sighed. "I don't know, Lizzy. Most times he's all sweet and funny and attentive; I just wanna eat him up." She looked at a photo of them she had on her nightstand. "I really like the way he kisses and holds me."

"Y'all done it yet?"

Marianne shook her head. "No. It's not like I don't want to."

"But?"

Marianne laughed. "There's always some big, hairy *but*, isn't there?" She frowned. "Every time it seems like the right time, something happens. And then, he doesn't call for days at a time. I'm starting to wonder whether...whether he doesn't see us—doesn't see *me*—as anything more than a potential roll in the hay."

Elizabeth sat on the bed. "If that's the way you feel, then maybe you shouldn't sleep with him."

"But I don't feel that way *all* the time. When I'm with him, and it's good, it feels so right. Maybe" —she paused—"maybe if we did sleep together, it would, you know, show him how good we could be."

"Mari, sex to keep a guy around never works. I know. Remember, I told you about my old boyfriend back in Thibodaux?"

"Yeah, I *know*, but it hasn't been easy on John."

Elizabeth held her hand. "Look, I like John, but I gotta say I don't like the way he treats you sometimes."

"But, guys are dense, you know."

"Sure, I know that. It could be the usual guy stupidity." Elizabeth smiled. "It's up to us to train them right. So, just go slow. If John's the one for you, he'll respect that. Then, when it's right, you'll know."

Marianne bit her lip. "You're right. No need to rush things." She sat up straighter. "John'll prove himself—just wait and see. So, how're things with you and Will?"

"What?" Marianne's knack for changing the subject always threw Elizabeth. "Umm, fine. We're friends."

"Yeah, sure." Marianne mimicked a phone call: "'Really, Will? You'd do that for me? You're a good friend, William.' Oh, yes, you're *just* friends!"

"Mari, c'mon! We've just gone out to see a movie. Once!"

"Mmm-hmm, and how many times for coffee?"

"A few times."

Marianne smirked. "You might think he's just a friend, but he might think differently."

"You're reading *way* too much into this. Trust me."

A HISTORY OF MARDI GRAS
A series for the *Loyola VOICE* by Elizabeth Boudreaux

THE OFFICIAL COLORS FOR MARDI Gras are purple, green, and gold. Yes, there are "official" colors. For something that was set up back in the day to make fun of everything, Mardi Gras has lots of rules. These colors were chosen in 1872 by the School of Design, better known as the Rex Organization. They chose these colors to stand for the following:

- Purple represents justice
- Green stands for faith
- Gold stands for power

The tradition of throwing trinkets to the crowds during Mardi Gras parades was initiated in the early 1870s by the Twelfth Night Revelers and has become a time-honored expectation. It began one year when the parade featured Santa Claus aboard a float, who dispensed small trinkets to the watching children. Exactly why they did it is lost to history. Everybody liked it, and it continues to this day.

In 1884, Rex threw the first medallions (silver-dollar-sized commemorative coins, later called doubloons) instead of the customary trinkets. Early medallions were much heavier than those minted today and were usually awarded only as ball favors. Today's doubloons are usually aluminum anodized in a variety of colors, depicting the parade theme on one side and the emblem of the particular krewe on the other. They're lighter and cheaper, which is always good. Many of these doubloons later become collectors' items. Other popular throws include long strings of pearlized beads, which girls just love, and plastic cups bearing the emblems of the krewes, great for drinking beer. Something for everybody! The traditional cry of parade-goers pleading for throws is, "Throw me something, mister!" If the maskers are tossing those long pearls, then you hear, "Show me your tits!"

The first thing tourists learn about Mardi Gras parades is that they don't go through the French Quarter. There's no room there, Gomer! Instead, there are two routes to Canal Street. The Mid Town route is Canal Street from the central part of the city to the river before turning to disband in the Convention Center. The Uptown route starts on Napoleon before turning downriver along St. Charles Avenue to Downtown and Canal.

Most tourists stay near their hotels and watch the parades with the throngs in the Central Business District. The crowds are usually twenty to thirty deep, held behind steel barricades. This is great for the local merchants, as they have a steady stream of customers. Good for pickpockets, too, but you didn't hear that from me. Can't have the tourism people mad at me.

It is also an advantage to the residents. They watch the parades from the relative quiet of the residential areas closer to the start of the parades. It is far more family-friendly—no Girls Gone Wild there. Boys, choose your poison: naked women or room to stretch out and bringing your own beer. Tough call, huh?

It takes college students a carnival season to figure this out. Everyone wants to have at least one Mardi Gras Downtown. Afterwards, they learn what the locals know: stay out of Downtown or leave town.

Sunday, February 7: Carrolton
THE SLICKLY SWEET SMELL OF marijuana filled the apartment as Greg took another toke. "Ahh…It's all good, JW."

John took a hit off his own joint. "Yeah, you rite."

"Got any plans for Mardi Gras, dude?"

"Nope, just hang out with Mari, I guess."

"You gonna get you some o' that, or you gonna keep beatin' your meat?"

"Fuck you, Greg."

"Fuck *you*, queer-boy. She's still holding out on you, ain't she?" Greg laughed. "If you weren't spankin' the monkey, your balls would fall off!"

John took a puff and then set the joint onto an ashtray. "You said it. Sometimes it's *this* close," he held two fingers about an inch apart, "and something goes wrong."

"What? She's frigid?"

"Nah, nothing like that. Just—shit happens, you know what I mean?"

"Gotcha. You need something to set the mood, dude."

"Like what? She won't do weed. Says it hurts her vocal cords."

"I can get something better than—" Before Greg could finish, the apartment door opened. "Well, look who's back—the Chicken Man! How're you doing there, Chicken Man?"

Tommy Bertram, still dressed in his Popeye's Fried Chicken uniform, closed the door behind them. "Hello, Greg. Long time no see," he said coldly.

"You didn't bring us a bucket?" Greg taunted.

"Must have slipped my mind. Can I talk to you for a moment, John?"

After the two went into Tommy's bedroom, John began, "I'm sorry, dude, he just came over—"

"Look, when I moved back in, you promised no grass, no drugs. I can't have that shit around. It's bad for my recovery."

"I know, man, I know. Give me a minute. I'll get rid of him."

Tommy nodded, and John left the bedroom. He approached Greg carefully, trying to keep his fear hidden.

"Greg, umm...you see..."

Greg looked at him with empty eyes. "You're throwing me out, Waguespack?"

John swallowed, sweat forming in the small of his back. Neither spoke.

Greg's guffaw broke the silence. "Gotcha! It's cool, man. I've got places to go, anyway. 'Sides, I guess Chicken Man's rehab buddies'll get pissed if he smells of ganja. Losers."

John's relief was visible as Greg gathered up his stuff. As he turned to go, Greg said, "See what I mean about straights. You change your mind; you call me. See you later."

After the door closed, Tommy came out of his room. He had changed out of his uniform into a T-shirt and jeans. He didn't say a word, but he walked directly to the window in the room and opened it.

"Hey!" cried John. "It's forty degrees out there!"

Tommy gave him a look. "Gotta clear the air, man." He opened the kitchen window, as well. When he returned to the living room, John was putting on a jacket.

"I'm freezing my ass off, man."

"Tough." He sat on the couch while John took the armchair. "Look, John, we'll go over this one more time. I was really, really messed up before. If it wasn't for Greenleaves, I might be dead now. Understand? *Dead.* I can't do this stuff anymore. I can't handle it."

"I'm sorry, dude."

"Lemme finish, okay? When I got out, I convinced my old man to let me move back here. We…we got real close during rehab. Worked out some issues. I really let him down, dude. He—damn, this is hard." Tommy choked back a sob. "He loves me, an' I love him. I really fucked up. But we're getting better."

Tommy stared at John. "That was the only way I was able to convince him to let me move back here. But there are some conditions." He ticked them off on his fingers. "*One*—no drugs, or access to drugs, or even the presence of drugs. *Two*—I go to NA and do my rehab. *Three*—I get a job. *Four*—I take some classes at UNO this summer. If I do all that and stay clean, I can re-enter Tulane in the fall. Meanwhile, he's helping with the bills, including the rent."

"Yeah, and I appreciate that."

"John, you promised me and my dad there wouldn't be any drugs 'round here. You gotta keep your word, man."

"It wasn't my fault. Greg came here and lit up."

"Shit, who are you kidding? I saw you with a joint!" Tommy jumped up. "Do you have *any fucking idea* how hard this is? I smell this shit, and I wanna go nuts! Do you know? Do you know I wake up every morning—*every fucking morning*—and tell myself, 'Today, I won't do drugs. Today, I'll keep clean.' Every morning, dude—maybe for the rest of my fucking life!"

He reached into his pocket, pulled out a coin, and thrust it into John's face. "See what it says on the back of this thing? '*One Day at a Time*.' That's what I gotta do.

"Look, dude, the reason I talked my dad into coming back was to help you out. You're my best friend, John. I know you need help paying for this place. I can help you, I can prove I can make it on my own, and maybe..." Tommy paused. "Maybe help you some more. Like, why don't you come with me to NA? You know, just to listen in?"

"What?" John cried. "I don't need to go to Narcotics Anonymous! There's nothing wrong with me!"

"Look, it was just a suggestion. You don't go, that's cool. It's there if you want it, man."

"Look, don't get all weird on me."

"Like I said, it's cool. But you gotta keep your word, John. You keep the drugs out; I stay and help out. Greg comes back, and best friend or not, I'm outta here. Simple as that."

"Right."

Tommy reached over and patted John once on the knee. "I'll never forget how you helped me, John. You're my pal 'til the end. But I gotta get healthy and stay healthy. We okay?"

John reached over and shook his hand. "We're okay," he told his best friend.

Tommy grinned. "Then how 'bout helping me close these windows, buddy? It's freezing in here!"

As they did, John thought furiously, *How do I explain this to Greg? Shit, I need a joint!*

Chapter 9

Friday, February 12, 1999: Garden District

It was the Friday before Mardi Gras, and all through Emma's house, it was anything but quiet.

Emma dashed through the various rooms, trying to prepare for her guest, Elizabeth's sister Jane, and all her friends who were going to use the place as their central headquarters and designated restroom for the parades. Mrs. Taylor had prepared tons of hors d'oeuvres, but they were still in the refrigerator, yet to be placed out or heated. The decorations had to be finished, the beer and wine chilled, and Papa was useless.

Just as Emma was ready to scream, the doorbell sounded. *No! Jane can't be here now! I'm not ready!* Emma brushed off her hands on her apron, ran her fingers through her hair, and answered the door.

"Doctor George! Come in; come in. I didn't know you were coming over. You're not working?"

"Abe invited me. I'm on call for Sunday, but other than that, I'm free."

"That's wonderful. Papa's in his study watching basketball. Can I get you something?"

"No, I'm okay. What's with the apron? What are you doing? Looks like you're getting ready for a—oh, Emma, Abe didn't do it again, did he?"

Emma laughed. "Oh, no. Everyone's coming by before the parade. We've got plenty—even for *you*." She looked down. "And this apron was my mother's. I wear it to remind me of her. She always wore it when she was setting up a party." It wasn't some frilly June Cleaver thing; it was white and functional with the exception of the initials "RW" in script across the lone pocket—something a real cook might wear.

George looked at all the boxes in the dining room. "Looks like you've got a lot to do."

"You don't know the half of it. I've got to get all this stuff done, Elizabeth's sister is staying here for Mardi Gras, and Miz Taylor's off for the weekend."

"Need some help?"

Emma smiled at her long-time friend. "Would you? You're such a sweetie!" She grabbed his hand. "C'mon!"

Emma concentrated on the decorations while George schlepped the heavy stuff. Emma was on a stepladder when she lost her balance, only to be steadied by George's strong arms.

"Watch it there, Em," he advised.

Thanking him, she returned to her task. However, she glanced every so often at her rescuer. She had never been aware of his strong hands or long fingers before. Now that she noticed, she could see the good doctor had a fine pair of guns on him. The idea of George working out was an intriguing notion.

He really is a good-looking guy, she considered. *I wonder why some girl hasn't snatched him up yet?*

AN HOUR LATER, THE FOOD to be heated was set out next to the oven, the beer and wine were on ice, and the dining room was decorated in Mardi Gras colors. The chips and nuts were already in their proper dishes. Steamers stretched from the chandelier to the corners of the room. Purple, green, and gold confetti was strewn over the tablecloth just so. Emma stood back to judge her efforts, one hand on her chin.

George wiped his hands with a dishtowel and watched her from the kitchen. In her all-purple outfit with the apron over it, Emma had grown to be a beautiful, sophisticated, yet domestic woman.

No one could ignore her two most prominent assets, of course, and George felt the stirrings he had experienced many times in the last few years.

One was the occasion of Emma's graduation from Newman. She wore a lovely white dress with a slightly low neckline. She was laughing for the first time since her mother's death, and she bent over slightly to retrieve her Coke; George was in prefect alignment to appreciate her décolleté. It was the most disconcerting feeling George had ever experienced.

Since then, George had unsuccessfully fought his lust for her. It was a losing cause. One of Emma's more endearing qualities was her modesty. She had absolutely no idea how gorgeous she was. Instead, she'd complain about her nose or gripe what a pain it was to wear contacts. But she wouldn't do anything about it. Emma disliked hospitals and was terrified of surgery. That was why she refused to get a nose job or LASIK surgery. As far as George was concerned, he never wanted her to change. There was something charming about her face, and her nose, long or not, suited her. It made her Emma, and Emma was lovely just as she was.

And there were other things to appreciate about her. She had a kind and generous personality. Her loyalty and devotion to her father was admirable. He knew, for all her protests to the contrary, that it was she and Mrs. Taylor who ran this household.

Damn if he wasn't falling in love with her.

George moved into the room, stopping right behind Emma. "It looks lovely, Emma. Don't change a thing."

She looked back over her shoulder at him, and he knew she missed the double meaning in his words. "You think?" She turned back to the table and sighed. "Okay, we're done."

George shifted so he was alongside her. "I remember what a wonderful hostess your mother was, Em. You do her proud."

She turned to him. "Oh, George, that's lovely. Thank you."

George fought to keep his eyes from moving south. Emma's scoop top was too darn tempting. Her brow started to wrinkle, and George tried to keep his expression neutral.

They were saved by the doorbell.

"Oh, they're here!" Emma cried as she fumbled to remove the apron. "Here—be a dear," she said as she thrust the garment into George's hands before and dashing to the door, calling for her father as she did.

George chuckled, tossed the apron onto the kitchen counter, and rejoined Emma. By then, she was welcoming in Elizabeth, Marianne, and a beautiful blonde woman carrying a suitcase. Abe had just walked out from his study.

"Welcome to Casa Weinberg! You must be Jane," Emma cried as she extended her hand.

"Yes, Jane Boudreaux. Thank you for your hospitality."

Emma looked back over her shoulder. "And here is the master of his realm, my father, Abe Weinberg. Papa, you know Marianne and Elizabeth. This is Elizabeth's sister, Jane Boudreaux."

Abe greeted her with a smile. "So, you're our guest for the next few days, hmm? Nice to meet you, Miss Jane. Let me take that bag for you."

"Oh, sir, it's quite unnecessary!"

"I know, but this is my house, and no young lady is going to carry a heavy bag here." He picked it up with a grunt. "My goodness! What do you have in here—rocks?"

Jane blushed to the roots of her hair. "Mr. Weinberg, I'm so sorry!"

"Papa!" cried Emma with a sharp look.

Abe chuckled. "Hee-hee, just my little joke. Forgive me, Miss Jane."

"Sure you don't need any help, Abe?" teased George.

"You just entertain the ladies, Doctor, while I take care of this little matter," Abe huffed. He began to walk up the stairs. "Your bedroom is the first on the left."

"Your father's very nice," said Jane.

Emma was still frowning. "Yeah, he's a riot." She turned to the man beside her with a smile. "And *this* handsome man is our friend, Dr. George Katz." She stepped closer to George and touched his arm. After exchanging introductions and greetings, the guests began to praise the decorations. "Thank you," said Emma, "but I couldn't have done it without George, here."

"Is that so?" Marianne smirked. "I didn't know you were so talented, George."

"Or so domestic," added Elizabeth with a grin.

"Bachelors can do many things, ladies."

Emma broke in: "And that's enough of that! C'mon, Jane, let me show you to your room." As the other girls went up the stairs, Emma quickly returned to George's side. Without hesitation, she kissed his cheek. "Thanks, George, for everything." She gave him a happy smile and hurried upstairs.

George watched her go, her kiss still warm on his face. He was still there when Abe came downstairs.

"Hey, George, want to catch the second half of the game?" Abe gestured towards his study.

"Sure," he said as he tore his eyes from the top of the stairs. "Who's playing?"

"LSU and Arkansas."

"Cool. Want me to grab you a beer out of the fridge?"

"I HOPE THE ROOM IS okay," Emma said after showing Jane around.

"Okay? It's lovely, Emma. Thank you so much. This was very kind of you. When is everybody coming over?"

Marianne sat on the bed. "About an hour before the parade. Wait 'til you meet them, Jane. They're real nice."

Jane nodded. "If they're anything like your boyfriend, I'm sure they will be."

There was deafening silence in the room.

"What boyfriend?" asked Emma.

Jane was clearly perplexed. "Downstairs...George. I'm sorry; did I get something wrong? I just thought—" She blushed as Marianne and Elizabeth laughed. "I said something silly, didn't I?"

"I don't know," Marianne said as she observed a red-faced Emma. "Do you have something to tell us, Em?"

"George?" Emma squeaked. "You think *George* is my boyfriend?

That's—no way! He's like a *brother* to me!"

"Well, this *is* the South, darlin'," Marianne drawled.

"Mari!" Elizabeth cried while laughing.

"You take that back, you redneck!" Emma cried as she threw a pillow at her. A short, giggle-filled pillow fight ensued.

"Emma, I'm sorry I embarrassed you," said Jane.

"No, it's okay. It's just…weird."

"He's really cute, Em," suggested Marianne.

"You could do worse," Elizabeth added.

Emma looked about the room with a shocked expression. "Me and *George*? Nah!" She jumped up—to end the strange discussion more than anything else. "Let's get your stuff put away before everybody gets here, Jane. This party's gonna be so much fun!"

"Turn up the music!" Henry Tilney cried. The familiar whistling of Professor Longhair filled the room. "Now, that's the way to start a parade!"

Emma walked through the dining room, happy to see that everyone was enjoying themselves. Abe had found a corner and was talking with George. Elizabeth had Jane in tow, introducing her to everyone. There was a jostle at her elbow.

"Oh, Em! I'm sorry," giggled Marianne. "Don't you love full-contact parties?"

"Jane is a real sweetheart, don't you think?"

"Yeah," Marianne answered. "I'll bet she doesn't have a mean bone in her body."

"Yeah, just like…"

Emma's voice trailed off as her mind began to work. In the last few months, she realized ending things with Chuck Bingley had been the right thing to do, but knowing she was right didn't make her any happier. She felt guilty over the whole episode. She had pursued Chuck, and she had broken up with him. She hurt him. A nice guy like Chuck deserved better, she felt. *He deserves someone nice.*

A slight frown graced Marianne's face. "I've seen that look before. You're planning something, Em. What is it?"

Emma only smiled and looked around. When she saw someone who could help, she grabbed Marianne's hand and dragged her towards Cathy Moreland.

"Hey, Cathy. Thanks for coming over."

"Wouldn't have missed it." Cathy's smile was a relief to Emma. Things were rough between them for a couple of weeks in the aftermath of her breakup with Chuck. Cathy was very protective of "her boys" in the frat, but a long heart-to-heart in December had patched things up between them.

"Do you know if Chuck is coming?" Emma asked.

"Yes. Will's bringing him, so he'll show. Why do you ask?" There was a suspicious tone in her voice.

"I want to do something nice for him."

"Okay." Cathy lowered her voice. "That sister of his will be coming, too."

Emma grimaced. "That's what I was afraid of. Come to the kitchen with us. I need your help."

Puzzled, Cathy joined Emma and Marianne in the kitchen. "So, what do you want me to do?"

"Distract Carrie. I'm gonna set up Chuck with Elizabeth's sister."

"What?" the others said in unison.

"Shhh, keep it down! Look, have you met Jane?"

"Yes, she's real sweet, but I don't think—"

"Oh, come on, Cathy, she'd be perfect for Chuck! Think about it. Have you met anyone as nice as Jane?"

Marianne said, "No, now that you mention it."

Cathy responded, "Emma, I've only known her for five minutes. I'm hardly in a position to judge—"

Emma waved her hands. "Trust me, Cathy. She's a female version of Chuck."

"But what's the big rush?"

Emma looked intently at her friends. "I feel real bad about how things ended between us. I want to make it up to Chuck. Jane's visiting from out of town. This might be our only chance." She knew Marianne was getting excited about the idea, so she focused on Cathy. "I just wanna introduce them and give them a chance to spend some time together. Give 'em a chance."

"Bait the field," added Marianne.

"Introduce a girl who could make Chuck real happy. What do you say?"

Cathy was convinced. "Okay, I'm in. What do you need me to do?"

The girls talked in low tones for several minutes, working out their strategy. Finally, Emma smiled at her co-conspirators. "We all set? Let's do it!"

Marianne sang, *"Matchmaker, matchmaker, make me a match."*

Cathy picked it up, *"Find me a find."*

Together, *"Catch me a catch!"*

Emma blushed. "Stop it!"

Giggling, Marianne and Cathy continued to sing as they left the kitchen, Emma tagging behind.

A HISTORY OF MARDI GRAS
A series for the *Loyola VOICE* by Elizabeth Boudreaux

THE KREWES IN NEW ORLEANS are generally all male or all female, and the so-called "old-line" organizations are mostly broken down by race. At one time, this was the law in the segregated South, but today, this is the preferred association.

It is a little-known fact that the first King of Carnival, the first Rex in 1872, was Jewish. His name was Lewis Solomon. As it turns out, he was the last Jewish King of Carnival. While there are Jewish members of the elite Mardi Gras krewes, they are not among the social tier that represents Carnival royalty. They'd take your money, but you wouldn't be king. In response to this, a group of Jews got together in the 1990s and created the Krewe du Jieux, a satirical marching club attached to the renowned French Quarter parade Krewe du Vieux. They hand out painted bagels along with the usual Mardi Gras beads and trinkets.

It's very expensive to belong to a krewe. Members are responsible for dues, a costume rental, ball tickets, a new dress for the wife, and throws—the trinkets tossed from the floats. The beads, doubloons, cups, stuffed animals, and other items are bought by the gross, and the final bill runs into the thousands of dollars—just for the right to give it all away to a bunch of strangers.

Carnival is also the end of the long and elaborate debutante season in New Orleans. White young ladies have their coming out during their sophomore year in college, whereas African-Americans debut while seniors in high school. The parties start in September and continue until the young women serve as maids, or even queens, of the various krewes to which their fathers belong. As white girls often attend out-of-town universities, many transfer back to a local college for their sophomore year to participate in their debut. It is not known how many of them transfer back after their year is done. My guess is not many.

Expenses for a New Orleans family with more than one daughter can be crippling. It's not unusual for house repairs to be put off for years while the girls go through their debuts. It is an indication that an Uptown family is finally through with the seasons for their daughters when the contractors show up to repaint the house.

JUST BEFORE HE OPENED THE door to the Weinbergs' house, Chris turned to William. "Lighten up. This is a party, not a funeral, Will."

"Yeah, yeah. Give me a beer, and I'll be all right." He was proud of himself; he hadn't given Carrie Bingley a death stare. She was wearing a cropped Danskin top and low-slung, super-tight Capri jeans, her decidedly toned abs prominently displayed. Obviously, she thought going to this parade half-naked was going to impress William. Instead, he was only embarrassed for the clueless coed.

"Yeah, you rite," said Chris and Chuck in a chorus.

Carrie rolled her eyes. The four walked into organized chaos. A second line to "Hey Pocky A-Way" was going full steam in the living room.

"I see the natives are restless," muttered Carrie.

"C'mon, Red, I know you want to do it," teased Chris.

"Do *what*?" asked Carrie in an icy tone.

"Dance. That's what you Golden Girls do, right?"

Chuck groaned. "Chris, stop picking on my sister, please, even if she does deserve it."

"What kind of brother are you?" Carrie snapped before she turned to Will, looking at him in a beseeching manner. "Are you going to let them talk about me this way?"

Emma saved William from answering. "Hi, everybody! Come make yourselves comfortable." She took a step closer to Chuck. "Chuck, thank you so much for coming."

Chuck gave a weak smile. "Thank you for inviting me."

Emma gave him an earnest look. "Chuck, I hope we will always be friends."

He took her hand. "We *are* friends, Em."

"How nice to see you again, Emma," Carrie uttered coldly, looking at her hostess with barely disguised loathing, something that did not escape anyone's notice. Carrie Bingley was a pain in Will's ass, but he knew she was fiercely loyal to the brother she loved. She obviously did not forget this was the girl who broke up with Chuck and hurt his feelings. Forgiveness would be a long time coming, if at all.

For her part, Emma responded civilly. "Nice to see you too, Carrie. Is your friend Anna coming?"

"No, her family went to Disney World this year."

"I hope she has fun. You are all welcome here for the rest of Carnival. Chuck, there is someone I'd like for you to meet. Ah! Here she is now."

Elizabeth joined them, arm-in-arm with a pretty blonde girl. The girl was familiar to William.

"I want y'all to meet my sister, Jane Boudreaux. She's a senior nursing student at Southeastern. Jane, this is Will Darcy, Chris Breaux, and Chuck Bingley from Tulane. And this is Carrie Bingley from LSU."

At that moment, Emma pulled Elizabeth away to talk privately. Meanwhile Jane took a second glance at William.

"Hi, everybody. We've met, haven't we, Will?" She blinked. "Oh! At East Jefferson! How is your sister?"

Will smiled. "She's just fine, Jane, thanks to your good care."

"What's this?" asked Chuck. "Did Jane help take care of your sister?"

"She sure did."

"William!" cried Carrie, "I didn't know Gina was in the hospital."

"Wasn't widely known, Carrie." *And really was none of your business*, he thought. "It was a minor thing, and she's all better now."

Jane smiled sweetly. "Thank you, but I didn't do much."

"I'm sure you did," Chuck said. "So, you finish up with your courses this spring?" Emma and Elizabeth had rejoined them.

"Yes, I do."

"What are you specializing in?" asked Chris.

"Pediatrics."

Chuck smiled. "Children—you must like children."

Jane's eyes grew animated as she talked about her love of caring for her young patients. Chuck stepped closer and the two fell into, for all intents and purposes, a private conversation.

While they talked, William found himself slightly behind and to one side of Elizabeth. He couldn't stop gazing at her pretty face, flushed with happiness. He felt Carrie's glare on him, but he didn't care. So what if Chuck's sharp-eyed, annoying sister suspected his interest in Elizabeth Boudreaux? He had about given up fighting his attraction for the cute sophomore.

She really is something else, he considered. *Why am I being such a horse's ass about this? I really want to know her better.* William began planning. *Okay, after Mardi Gras, I have to finish that group project. Once it's done, it'll be close to Spring Break. After that is finals, but that's no big deal. So, if her schedule isn't too bad, I can focus on Elizabeth during Spring Break. Yeah, that will work.*

"Hey, partner," Chris said to Elizabeth, breaking William's thoughts, "are you all set for Monday?"

"I sure am," she happily replied. "When are you picking me up?"

For the first time in his life, William Darcy felt a twinge of jealousy. He knew Chris had no designs on Elizabeth, but he didn't like that she was going out of town with him. *Knock it off,* he berated himself. *You're thinking like a jerk!*

Chris was still talking. "How about early—say, ten o'clock? We can pass by my folks' place in Lafayette a little after noon."

"Okay."

"What's this?" Carrie blurted to Elizabeth. "Are you leaving town for Mardi Gras?"

"Yes, Chris is taking me to the Mamou *courir.*"

"Oh, how nice." Carrie seemed notably relieved.

William almost laughed. *Won't do you any good, lady!*

Cathy walked up and took Carrie by the elbow. "You're just the person we need! Would you give us a hand in the kitchen?"

"Kitchen? Me?" Carrie sputtered. "What do you want *me* to do in the kitchen?"

Cathy wore her most innocent expression and said in a voice a bit louder than necessary, "Don't be modest. Chuck brags about your cooking all the time, doesn't he, Will?"

William had heard the exact opposite from Chuck, but a glance at Cathy told him to go along with this. "Yeah, Chuck often speaks of your talents in the kitchen." *Lack of talents, actually.* "And you know me; I always love a good home-cooked meal," he threw in for good measure.

Carrie's eyes grew wide. "Why, Cathy, I would be happy to help. I won't be long, William." With a sickly smile, she followed Cathy into the other room.

"So, is that what you're looking for, Darcy? A woman who knows her way around the kitchen?" Elizabeth teased.

"Among other rooms," William replied with an arch look, which caused Elizabeth to laugh.

A confused Chris broke in. "But really, Carrie doesn't know the first thing about cooking! Chuck says she can hardly boil water. What's going on?"

Emma took a satisfied sidelong glance at Chuck and Jane, who were so into their own world that they were unaware of anything else. "Don't you worry, handsome. Everything is just fine."

William turned to Elizabeth. "What are you so amused about, Boudreaux? You've been trying not to crack up for the last ten minutes."

"When I'm right, I'm right. You did catch that getup Carrie was in, didn't you? She would be *so* disappointed if you didn't. She obviously wore it for *you*."

William sighed. "Yeah, I did. You know, it's like a chef dressing up a hot dog when all the customer wants is a hamburger. The hot dog just won't satisfy." Chris broke up laughing.

Elizabeth blurted out, "And what would satisfy you, Darcy?" Her face went red as she realized the portent of her question.

You, his mind screamed, but he kept silent. It was too soon, and he didn't want to scare her off. "I'll know it when I see it, Boudreaux," he said, flashing his dimples.

Both Chris and Emma looked at each other with raised eyebrows, reacting to the banter.

"Folks," said George, "Abe thinks it's time to get outside. It's almost parade time."

Chapter 10

A HISTORY OF MARDI GRAS
A series for the *Loyola VOICE* by Elizabeth Boudreaux

Mardi Gras is famous for the highly decorated floats from which the masked krewe members toss throws to the spectators. What most visitors do not realize is that only a few krewes—Rex, Zulu, and the super krewes—actually own their floats. All the others rent them from float builders like Blaine Kern Enterprises. The floats are kept in several large warehouses in the area called dens and are decorated to match the krewe's theme.

Of course, this is Mardi Gras, and *decorate* is loosely defined. Most floats have some sort of large figure, usually a head. Decoration can be minimal, depending on budgets. Therefore, it wouldn't be rare for a smallish krewe whose theme was U.S. Presidents to have Abe Lincoln's head on a float for mermaids. It's Mardi Gras! Who really cares?

Now, I'm not talking about the big guys, the super krewes, or the Mardi Gras Day monsters. Those guys take float design seriously. And they have the money to make sure it's done right, all the way down to the costumes worn by the maskers.

Maskers are supposed to throw away from the street, for the safety of the revelers. However, this is loosely enforced. Police will stop a float if riders are hanging over the side or encouraging children to run alongside. Anything else is fair game. Children and young women seem to get the bulk of the throws, especially if the women are skimpily attired.

Garden District

HERMES AND LE KREWE D'ETAT were the entertainment on that Friday. The people gathered on the neutral ground in the center of St. Charles Avenue. They were safe from the streetcars; they stopped running several hours before the parade. Safety from the ladders was another question.

Several years before, some parents discovered that holding their child up on a ladder during a parade gave the child a much better view, and they caught more beads. Someone came up with a seat that could be affixed to the top of the ladder. An entrepreneur started mass-producing the seats. Before you could say "free enterprise," Mardi Gras routes everywhere were infested with ladders.

Each ladder could hold two small children. So, if a family had three kids, they needed two ladders. And one for their niece. And a couple more for their in-laws. A forest of ladders arose.

The structures ranged from eight to twelve feet high. You would think, at those heights, that the ladders could be placed away from the curb, but then you would not be making an allowance for human nature. One of the unwritten laws of parades—Mardi Gras or otherwise—is, "Get the kids as close to the action as possible. Safety is a secondary issue. Courtesy is not to be considered."

With a wall of ladders in the way, all the non-ladder folk were just out of luck if they actually wished to *see* the parade. Desperate times called for desperate measures. Those without kids got their own ladders, and a ladder "arms race" broke out. Others had to erect platforms in the yards along the parade route if they were lucky enough to *live* on the route.

The other poor slobs had to either search for "ladder-free" zones or stake out their territory hours in advance. Regardless, they had to be careful. The "ladder people" were relentless. They were known to seize sites along the route by chaining their ladders to light poles.

Of course, the city officials tried to do something about the issue. They passed ordinances mandating the ladder be the same distance from the curb as the ladder was high. This rule was immediately ignored. Police would advise people to move the structures, but they rarely enforced the law. The parents of young children tended to be locals who voted, and it would not do to cause trouble for members of the City Council. Only one law was strictly enforced; teams of city workers, armed with chain cutters, would descend upon the parade route during the night, confiscating any ladder foolishly attached to any piece of city property.

The people would bitch and moan—and buy a new ladder. The war would go on.

PARADE TIME APPROACHED, AND THE crowd ventured forth to claim its spot along St. Charles Avenue, the men carrying the supplies. Emma was exceedingly proud of herself. Jane and Chuck had not stopped talking since they were introduced.

"I see it worked," a male voice came from behind her.

"See what, George?"

"Your very obvious matchmaking between Chuck and Elizabeth's sister."

She turned to him. "Take that back. I was *not* obvious."

George laughed. "If you say so."

"Anyway, it worked. Just look at them."

"Anybody can get lucky, Em."

"Humph! Luck's got nothing to do with it. I'm just very talented at this, and I'll prove it to you. I've already scoped out my next triumph."

"Oh? Who's the victim?"

"Elizabeth and William."

George raised his eyebrows at her. "You're trying to set up Will Darcy? Good luck with that! Hope you like eating crow."

"We'll see who'll be eating crow. How do you like it: stewed or fried?"

"Whatever. Where do you want this ice chest?"

They secured a location, and the group waited for the first siren, indicating the NOPD escorts were close by. The party broke up into several loose groups: Chuck and Jane were joined by Elizabeth, William, Chris, and Carrie, who'd been released from her kitchen duties. Henry and Cathy were with a younger group of AIs and their dates. Emma stood back to take it all in, her father and George nearby. Marianne seemed to be on the outskirts, looking around.

Looking for John, thought Emma sadly. She had come to the belief that John wasn't good enough for Marianne.

"Carnival Time" was playing on the boom box. Marianne started to shout and wave. Sure enough, John ambled up with a tall, rangy companion.

"Holy—" breathed Henry. "Tommy! Hey, everybody, it's Tommy! Tommy's back!"

AS ONE, THE PARTY DESCENDED upon Tom Bertram, full of shouts and handshakes and slaps on the back. Cathy and others made sure there were a few kisses on his cheek, as well. Only Marianne and John moved away from the reunion.

"Hey, baby!" John reached for Marianne. He was happy and horny and hoped tonight was the night.

But Marianne rebuffed him. "You're late, John. Where were you?"

John was taken aback. "Umm, I had to bring Tommy. It's his fault."

Marianne held up her hands. "Enough, John. It's *always* somebody else's fault! No, don't touch me."

"Aw, c'mon, baby, don't be mad."

"I *am* mad. I've been waiting for you for over an hour. John, I'm real tired of this. If you want to be with me, you have to start keeping your word."

John blew up. "Shit! Mari, you just don't understand! Sometimes stuff just happens! I can't help it!"

"You could have called."

"But I didn't think we were running that far behind. I thought—"

"No, John. You didn't think. You didn't think of me."

"What are you talking about? I think about you all the time."
Usually in some sexual position.

Marianne stood with her arms crossed over her chest, looking daggers at John. John fought not to show the fury he was feeling. *How can this be* my *fault? I'm the victim here!* Instead, he assumed his most pitiful expression.

Ultimately, Marianne's resistance broke first with a sigh. "John, I don't wanna get into a fight tonight. Let's just enjoy the parade. But I expect you to treat me better in the future."

It sounded like an ultimatum. John did not like ultimatums.

He licked his lips and seemingly capitulated. "I'm sorry, Mari. I promise this will be the last time. I'll be on time. I'll call if something happens. That's the way it's gonna be from now on. I'll try to do better."

"All right. Let's join the others." Marianne turned and walked towards the crowd still surrounding Tommy.

Inside, John was seething. He knew his chances of sex with Marianne that night were toast. *Damn frigid bitch! Everything happens to me!*

The *tête-à-tête* went unnoticed by almost everybody in the crowd, except for one medical student.

THE WAIL OF THE POLICE sirens recalled everyone's attention to the reason they were standing in the middle of the St. Charles Avenue's neutral ground. The most important vehicle led the parade—the power company truck outfitted with a probe to check the clearance beneath the canopy of live oak limbs. As the crowd thinned out, Tommy was left alone with William and Elizabeth.

"Bertram," offered William as he shook the younger man's hand, "welcome back."

"Thanks. It's good to be back."

William nodded. "So, are you coming back to school?"

"Gonna try to next fall. Gotta work on my recovery. I'm working this term and going to NA."

"NA? That's wonderful, Tommy," responded Elizabeth.

"Where are you working?" asked William.

"Popeye's on Napoleon and Claiborne. I'm off tonight, but I gotta work through the rest of Carnival. We sell a lotta chicken over Mardi Gras, dude. Whoa!" With a grin, he bent and picked up a doubloon that had just missed his head. "Gettin' dangerous out here! Anyway, I'll be putting in twelve-hour days startin' tomorrow."

William nodded again. "You got to do what you got to do, Tommy."

"Yep."

Elizabeth touched his arm. "Well, I think you're going to be just fine, Tommy. We'll be praying for you."

"Thanks, Lizzy."

William looked Tommy right in the eye. Tommy didn't flinch. "Good luck, Tommy."

"Thanks." With nothing else to say, Tommy waved and strolled up to where the younger people stood.

"Boy's got a tough row to hoe," William said.

"But he'll make it, don't you think?"

William shook his head. "Recovery from alcohol or drug dependency is real hard. Most don't make it. Relapse rate's sky high."

"But Tommy will make it!"

"Maybe." As they talked, Carrie and Chris approached.

Elizabeth stared at Darcy with surprise. "How can you be so cynical about your fraternity brother? Don't you believe in him at all?"

"We'll see. I'll be pulling for him, but I won't get my hopes up."

"Jeez, you're a hard-ass, Darcy!"

William's response died on his lips as Carrie grabbed his arm. "Enough of this! C'mon Will, let's get back to the parade." William allowed himself to be dragged off with a searching look at Elizabeth.

Chris sidled up to Elizabeth, who was clearly pissed off. "I'd cut the boy a little slack, Elizabeth. There are things about him you just don't know, things that make him the way he is."

Chris had calmed Elizabeth down somewhat. "Ooooh, sounds like a story there. Care to dish?"

"Not my tale to tell, Liz. All I'll say is he has a real issue with substance abuse."

Elizabeth allowed a small smile. "Well, he is your best friend, so that must count for something."

Chris chuckled and rubbed the back of his head. "Yeah, well, Will can be a stick-in-the-mud, sure. But when the chips are down, there's nobody I'd trust more. One other thing: you think Will's tough on others? Maybe. But that's only because he holds everybody to the same high standard he holds for himself. If Will's a hard-ass to anyone, it's to William Darcy."

MUSIC AND MERRIMENT FILLED THE mild, nighttime air along St. Charles. The floats, pulled by small tractors, rolled sedately down the famous avenue, lit up from stem to stern with bare, electric bulbs. The maskers, in varying states of inebriation, filled the air with beads, doubloons, and other trinkets. They tended to throw toward pretty girls, and it was a testament to Alpha Iota's ability to attract good-looking ladies that the group got far more than its share, even with nobody lifting their tops.

The marching bands played everything from Mardi Gras standards to badly arranged versions of current top-forty hits. The famous live oaks of Uptown and the Garden District were festooned with stray strings of beads. It was as though the old lady that was New Orleans had put on her cheapest costume jewelry and joined in the fun.

The city's dance studios were out, too. The girls, varying in age between six and fifteen, wore their skimpy costumes and half-danced, half-marched in step behind a van or pick-up truck, blasting out hip-hop. It was something only a mother could love.

Elizabeth had retreated to the group's collection of ice chests to get a cold drink. Bored, a couple of the guys were tossing around a Nerf football. Just as Nick Patel was stumbling after a long throw, a little black girl walked out of the crowd, directly in his path.

Before Elizabeth could scream a warning, William Darcy appeared out of nowhere. He blocked the girl with his body, sending Patel to the earth. William was hit hard, but he refused to move, holding himself on his hands and knees, grimacing in pain. The child was scared stiff and stared at her savior with wide eyes.

Elizabeth finally got her legs to work and ran towards them. By that time, Chris knelt by the pair, talking to the girl in soothing tones as he turned repeatedly to his friend. A few steps away, William made a gesture that Elizabeth should look after Patel instead. He then turned his attention to Chris and the child.

Elizabeth and others were soon assured that Patel was unhurt. Her eyes flew to William, and she watched him and Chris talk gently to the frightened girl. She was obviously lost, and William slowly stood up to scan the crowd. His clear look of pain made Elizabeth gasp.

After a moment, William called the others' attention to something to their right. Elizabeth saw a large black man in the early stages of panic, walking along the back of the crowd, head whipping around, calling out to someone.

The little girl nodded, and William and Chris walked her by the hand towards the man. He gave a shout of relief and seized the child, holding her high in the air before clasping the girl to his chest, kissing her repeatedly. The man shook hands with both men. William paused to share a few words with him, one hand on his shoulder, while Chris shook hands with the happy little girl. He laughed and gave the girl the longest string of beads from around his neck.

The father and daughter disappeared into the crowd while William and Chis rejoined their friends.

"Are you all right, Will?" Elizabeth cried.

"I'll feel it in the morning, but I'll live, Boudreaux. How's Patel?"

Elizabeth reported Nick suffered no damage to anything but his pride. "He didn't know what happened at first, but he was grateful for what you did when he saw that little girl. That was her daddy, I take it?"

"Yeah. He told me she has the habit of wandering off. He was really scared."

"I'll bet he'll keep a closer eye on her from now on," Chris said.

"He told me he's going to keep her on a leash." Darcy winced.

"Man, I gotta work this out. Didn't know Patel could hit so hard. My shoulder hasn't felt this bad since high school and that last playoff game against John Curtis."

"Do you want a beer, Will?" Elizabeth offered.

"Yeah, I think it would help."

"Help him over to the folding chairs, Chris. I'll be right back." She gave William a smile and moved quickly to get his drink. When she turned to hand the brew to William, she saw Carrie had found him and was sitting on the chair next to him, rubbing his arm and expressing her horror that he had been hurt.

Something made Elizabeth take the chair on the other side of William as she handed him his beer. "Thanks, Elizabeth." His eyes seemed to plead with her to get rid of Carrie.

"Shall I get Jane to check you out?"

"No, it's all right. Let her enjoy the parade." He looked over towards the street and gestured with his beer. Jane was up on Chuck's shoulders, screaming for beads.

Elizabeth was stunned. All her life, Jane was the *good* girl of the Boudreaux family. She made the best grades; she was the most popular; she was queen of homecoming and president of her class. She casually dated but never had a serious boyfriend. Elizabeth could almost guarantee that Jane was still a virgin. Unlike the impertinent Elizabeth, sarcastic Mary, drama-queen Kit, and spoiled Lydia, Jane had never given her parents a moment's trouble.

Jane did *not* climb on top of a guy she had just met—until now.

"I think she's having fun, don't you?" William quipped.

"Umm…excuse me for a second," said Carrie as she got to her feet. "Oh, my God, Chuck has fallen in love *again*?" she mumbled as she strode directly towards her brother with the nurse on his shoulders.

Chris took the chair vacated by Carrie. "You can close your mouth now, Elizabeth."

"Wow," Elizabeth breathed. "That's *so* not like Jane." She shook her head. "But she's a big girl, and Chuck is a nice guy. So, you're right. Let her have some fun."

She took a long pull on her Diet Coke. *This had been an interesting night. Jane, Tommy…and William.* She glanced at him from the corner of her eye. *Just who are you, Mr. William Darcy? Every time I think I've got your number, you surprise me. I still can't quite figure you out.*

THE GROUP HAD BROKEN UP after the last float passed by, the large mechanical street cleaners doing their best to clear the tons of trash left behind. All agreed where they would meet tomorrow. The parades would not be on St. Charles again until Sunday. George walked the Weinbergs and their guests to the door. Abe and Jane went into the house after saying goodbye to the doctor, but Emma remained.

"Goodnight, Em. It was a lot of fun."

Emma gave him another peck on the cheek. "You gonna meet us on Canal Street tomorrow, or do you want to pass by here and come with us?"

George shook his head. "Can't. I'm on duty for the next couple of nights. No parades for me." At Emma's surprised pout, he smiled and leaned closer. "I'll come by Mardi Gras Day, okay? Bright and early."

"All right. If you'd rather hang out with a bunch of sick people than us, that's fine. We'll still let you in on Tuesday."

George grinned. "Good night, Emma. See you Tuesday."

For a moment, he paused as though he were going to move in and return the kiss—but on her mouth rather than her cheek. His eyes were on her lips, so inviting…so tempting.

Emma's eyes grew. She was rooted to the spot.

George froze there. *C'mon, meet me halfway. Show me you want this.*

The moment was only a breath long, but it seemed to last forever.

Then it was over. George straightened up and took a step back. Emma couldn't meet his eyes.

"Good night, Emma," he said again in a much lower voice before turning and going down the steps to the sidewalk for the trek to his car.

He did not see Emma thoughtfully watching him through the half-closed front door.

Chapter 11

Chris Breaux walked in an open pasture not far from his family's house. His father was an accountant, but their country house abutted a farm that raised horses as well as sugarcane. Strangely, the air was warm and sweet, not the usual cold and damp of February in Louisiana.

He knelt down to run his hand through the tall grass. *Springtime*, Chris thought, *it smells like springtime.* The sun was still low; it had to be only an hour after sunup. He gloried in the heat of the sun on his face.

A girl's sweet laughter invaded his thoughts. Turning, he saw a slim, dark-haired woman walking barefoot about fifty yards from him. Chris started walking towards her. As he grew closer, he could hear her voice, low and lovely, humming a tune. She turned her head and gave him a come-hither look over her shoulder.

It was Marianne Dashwood.

Chris could feel his heart pound as he approached the vision. Her white, lacy top, undone to show a hint of her sweet breasts, was worn over a swirling skirt of denim, her hair flying about her face. The blazing sun was jealous of the smile she gave him—a smile of pleasure and promise. Chris knew he would die if he could not have her in his arms.

Yet, he stopped a few paces away, filling his eyes and mind and soul with the splendor before him. Marianne looked at him through her lashes, biting her lip to hide the smile that danced about her mouth.

"Your home is beautiful, Chris," she said in a voice like a song.

"Not more beautiful than you, Mari," he was able to answer, his desire for her almost all consuming. "You're the most beautiful girl in the world."

"You're so sweet." She laughed. "But you didn't tell me your home was magical!"

Chris looked around. "Magical? There's no magic in this place." He turned to her again. "It only feels that way when you're here."

"Flatterer! It *is* magical—look!" She bent down. "All the creatures here are so incredibly loving—just like you are, see?" She stood up with a dark, coiled length in her arms. "Have you ever seen such a thing?"

Chris took a step back in surprise. "My God, Mari. That's a snake!"

"Of course, it's a snake—a big, beautiful king snake. Look how he loves me." The creature was moving up her arms, towards her neck.

Horror choked the breath out of Chris. "Mari, no—that's a water moccasin! It's poisonous! Get it off you!" He held himself back, fearing any sudden move might cause the serpent to strike.

Marianne was astonished at his cry. "Chris, you're wrong. He *is* a king snake. Don't you think I know a friendly snake when I see one?" She gazed at it. "I think I'll name him John. Aww, look… he wants a kiss."

The moccasin opened his cotton-white mouth, fangs gleaming in the sun.

"MARI!" Chris screamed.

Chris Breaux sat upright in his apartment bed, sweat covering his face. He looked wide-eyed about him before falling back onto his pillow.

A dream—it was all a dream. No, it was a goddamn nightmare.

Chris threw an arm over his eyes as he willed his breathing back to normal. Once he knew he could stand up without his knees giving way under him, he rolled out of bed. After a short detour to the bathroom to splash water in his face, he padded into the kitchen and fired up the coffee maker. Continuing into the den, he plopped down on the couch to wait for the coffee to finish brewing, trying to forget his nightmare.

Chris knew he had a knack of understanding people and their motivations from a young age. More than once, he found himself in the role of mediator while at school. It was then he decided to become a psychiatrist and use his gifts to help people. He well remembered how his classmates reacted when he shared his plans. Many humorously demanded to know what was wrong with *him*, given the old wives' tale of psychiatrists joining the profession to work out their own demons.

Chris laughed at their miscomprehension. Once he was in school, however, he found that, while most of the students entered the field for the same reasons he did, there were enough who needed help themselves for him to understand how the myth began.

No, Chris Breaux was about as levelheaded a person as they came. He could look at situations with as much objectivity as humanly possible—most situations. He was having a hard time with John Waguespack and Marianne Dashwood.

Chris sighed. There was no use denying it. He was falling in love with Marianne Dashwood. Sure, she was pretty, but that wasn't the main reason. There was an inner beauty he sensed in her. He saw the evidence of it in her kindness, her joy in simple things, her friendship, and her talent. He had gone to the Loyola Christmas Concert, and he was blown away. Many times he had laughed as Chuck Bingley describe this girl or that girl as "an angel," but once Chris heard Marianne's voice, he knew he had seen and heard one.

There was one problem. She was dating John Waguespack, a fraternity brother. *"Thou shall not steal a brother's girl—ever"* was a hard and fast rule.

Chris had previously believed William was wrong about John Waguespack, but ever since the dance on Halloween Night, he suspected his roommate had been correct all along. Chris knew John lied about Bertram's condition at the inquest. Tommy had done more than smoke a joint. Chris had seen all the signs. He was certain John knew what Tommy had taken. The only thing that stopped Chris from challenging John was that he couldn't prove it.

This put Chris in a delicate situation. He was interested in Marianne, and she was dating John. John was an untrustworthy bastard, but Chris couldn't prove it. John was a brother, subject to the code. Chris was a loyal Alpha Iota, and he would not break the code unless absolutely necessary. And even if he did, disparaging one suitor was no way to recommend one's self to a girl. If Chris shared with Marianne what he believed about her boyfriend, he *might* extract her from a deteriorating relationship if she believed him. But there was no guarantee she would. In fact, it might drive her to defend John more firmly out of misguided loyalty.

Chris sighed. Maybe being patient was the best course of action. Things had grown rocky between Marianne and John. Maybe she was figuring him out on her own. The best thing to do was wait and let the thing implode and then be there for her when she needed a shoulder to cry on.

"Up already?" asked a sleepy William from his bedroom door.

"Oh, hi, Will. Coffee's on."

"What time do you wanna leave to join up with the others on Canal Street?" He talked as he poured.

Chris looked over at the clock. "I guess in a couple of hours. How's the shoulder?"

"It's okay. I ate some Advil last night."

"Better living through chemicals."

"Speaking of chemicals, what are the chances of Tommy staying clean?"

Chris sat back. "Hard to say. Rehab is only effective if the addict is committed to recovery. Most need to hit bottom, first. Has Tommy done that? I don't know."

William stared at the mug wrapped in his two hands. "My uncle never did get clean and sober. He gave Daddy and my grandparents hell for thirty years. The family spent thousands cleaning up after him. Then, he goes and blows his head off. That, more than anything, caused MawMaw's heart attack."

"A lot of families have gone through that, Will."

"I know. It doesn't make it any easier."

As the two sat, drinking coffee, William looked over at his friend. "You noticed that fight between Mari and Waguespack?"

"Yeah, I did."

"Looks like trouble in paradise."

"Maybe."

"You going to do anything about it?" William chuckled at Chris's shocked expression. "Don't deny it. I've seen the way you've been eyeing her."

Chris shook his head. "You know I can't. Not now."

William nodded. He knew the code as well as Chris.

Chris decided to get his own shot in. "How 'bout you? You going to stop kidding yourself about Elizabeth? You like her, so…"

William's open expression closed up. "Since when are you so interested in my love life?"

"I can't wait to see Mr. Perfect all dopey-faced in love. So, what's the problem? She's pretty; she's smart; she's not after your money. What else are you looking for?"

William tapped a finger on the arm of his chair. "I know that. I know that." He looked down, his arms on his knees. "You think Elizabeth likes me? You know, like more than just a friend?"

"You won't know 'til you find out. But I think you've got a shot if you try. 'Course, the question is, do you *want* to try?"

"Yes, I do."

Chris didn't expect his reticent roommate to admit it. "Well, I'll be damned. Good luck, buddy!"

William finished his mug of coffee. "Let's see how the weekend goes." He stood up. "I'm going to grab a shower."

Chris sipped his coffee. "Leave me some hot water, will ya?"

William flexed his shoulder with a grin. "We'll see—hydro-therapy, you know."

Garden District

ELIZABETH AND MARIANNE RETURNED TO the Weinbergs' house just before eight. Emma let them in, and Elizabeth made her way to the guest room to visit with her sister while Marianne joined Emma in the kitchen.

"Knock, knock," Elizabeth said as she opened the door. She found Jane sitting up in bed. "Whatcha doing, sleepyhead?"

Jane greeted her sister fondly, and Elizabeth joined her on the bed. "I was enjoying a rare sleep-in. This is a really dreamy bed."

"I thought you might be still dreaming about somebody," Elizabeth teased.

"Oh, I had so much fun yesterday, Lizzy! Everybody was so nice. Mr. Weinberg and Emma are really gracious, and your friends made me feel so welcomed."

"Especially one."

Jane giggled. "Chuck is nice." Elizabeth just looked at her, with a half smile on her face. "He was a perfect gentleman. And so interesting to talk to! Why, I could talk with him for hours!"

"You did. Being handsome with strong shoulders didn't hurt, did it?"

Jane was completely embarrassed. "I don't know how it happened! One moment we were standing around, trying to catch beads; then Cathy was on her boyfriend's shoulders, calling out for us to do the same. Chuck and I exchanged a glance. And the next thing I knew, I was up there!"

Elizabeth laughed. "My big sister—love at first sight!"

"Elizabeth! Don't say that! Love! No, no, no, no! But"—she began to laugh as well—"I do like him! He's coming today, isn't he? He said he would."

"Oh, yes—and that sister of his, as well!"

"Why do you say that? Carrie is a little protective of her brother, that's all. We got along just fine."

Elizabeth smirked. "Well, she'll leave you alone today, I think. She's too busy going after Will Darcy."

"Oh, really? I didn't realize that. Are they going out?"

"No, but it's not for lack of effort on Carrie's part."

"I see. It's Will who's not interested." Jane's mouth turned down. "Poor Carrie."

Elizabeth hugged her sister. "Jane—feeling sorry for Carrie Bingley? You're the best person I know."

"Why don't you like her, Lizzy?"

"Oh, she's a big phony—all Miss Golden Girl." She threw her head back. "Look at me. Aren't I gorgeous?" she said in a breathless voice as she flipped her hand through her hair.

"It isn't because she likes Will Darcy, is it?"

Elizabeth blinked at her sister's question. "Why should I care about that?"

Just then, the bedroom door opened. "Hey, you two!" cried Emma as she and Marianne poked their heads through the doorway. "Let's get a move on! We got breakfast downstairs."

"It's king cake," added Marianne, "strawberry cream cheese."

Elizabeth gave a hoot. "C'mon, Jane, get dressed or there won't be any left for you!"

A HISTORY OF MARDI GRAS
A series for the *Loyola VOICE* by Elizabeth Boudreaux

YOU JUST KNOW THAT SINCE this is New Orleans, the food capital of the nation—sorry, New York and San Francisco—that there would be an Official Mardi Gras food. There is and its name is king cake.

You've all had it—an oval tube, tasting somewhat like a cinnamon roll, with purple, gold and green stuff on the top. But where did it come from?

The king cake has been around for a long time. Its roots, like so much in Louisiana, come from France. But if you ever ate a French king cake, you wouldn't recognize it. It's round, but the texture is flaky, a bit like a croissant. The sweetness comes from honey and nuts, and there's no icing. It's French, right? What did you expect?

The cake is served to commemorate King's Day, the Feast of

the Epiphany. Remember that? In New Orleans, it evolved into the form it has now. As we Americans like our pastries sweet, icing was added. Some bakery decided to top it with purple-, gold-, and green-tinted sugar sprinkles, which caught on in a big way. Now everybody does it or colors the icing itself.

Plain king cake definitely needs the icing, IMHO. The cake is dry and bland to my taste. That's why, when some bakery stuffed theirs with cream cheese filling, it took off like a shot. Now, king cakes are filled with everything including strawberry, lemon, blueberry, raspberry, pineapple (!), and chocolate—and even combinations thereof. If you want to get on my good side, show up with strawberry cream cheese. Yumm!

Everybody has their favorite bakery. You can get into a fight over whose is best: Gambino, Haydel, or Randazzo. Don't ask me, I'll never say.

Now the baby thing. It all started with the Twelfth Night Revelers in 1870. To this day, their official king cake has several ribbons attached to colored beans. All are silver except for one gold one. The maids of the court pull the ribbons. The lucky maid who pulls the gold bean is the queen of the ball.

The cake was so popular that everybody wanted to have king cake parties. But now a single bean was hidden. The lucky person who got the bean was to host the next party. The bean evolved to a coin and finally a baby, either porcelain or plastic. Today, the person who gets the baby is supposed to buy the next cake. So, the winner loses and the losers win. Sounds like a plan.

There is an etiquette to enjoying king cake. If you share, you must be willing to own up and cheerfully buy the next cake. It should be at least as large as the first and, if the first was filled, so should the next one. Don't get cheap and replace a large blueberry cake with a small plain one. And never try to replace the baby into an uneaten piece. Bodily harm may follow.

Mid-City

PLEDGES ARE USEFUL IN A fraternity. They are the source of new members, so the chapter can live on after the older actives graduate. They pay dues. They clean the house each weekend, which means the actives don't have to do it. And they can be counted on to "volunteer" to sit out all night and reserve a prime viewing spot along upper Canal Street for the Endymion Parade.

Just before lunch, the AIs, their dates, and friends descended upon the chosen location, still guarded by the pledges. They caught the warm-ups acts. Iris was the oldest and largest of the all-female krewes, while Tucks was one of the few co-ed organizations. Tucks took political mockery to new heights.

Everyone showed up in dribs and drabs. Emma brought Marianne and the Bennet sisters. William and Chris rode in the same car. Chuck arrived alone, as did John. Everyone was in place for Carrie's grand entrance.

"How are you feeling?" Elizabeth had just asked William about his shoulder when she caught sight of Carrie out of the corner of her eye. She could barely keep from laughing out loud. "Oh—my —gawd! She has less on than yesterday! Darcy, how will you be able to resist such a bounty before you?"

William didn't respond. He only closed his eyes and pinched the bridge of his nose.

Carrie was wearing another Danskin crop top—peach—but this time she paired it with an orange skirt so short it barely covered her ass. As a nod to decency, she had on matching dance briefs underneath. Her long, tanned legs traveled unencumbered to her scrunched-up white socks and sneakers. A chocolate purse, sunglasses, and a white scrunchie in her hair finished the outfit. Not a few of the guys started to drool.

"Hello, William," she cooed. "Been waiting long?" She turned to a red-faced Elizabeth. "Something wrong, dear?"

"No (cough), nothing at all (cough, cough)."

"You really should get that cough looked into," Carrie said seriously.

"You—you're right," Elizabeth managed as she turned away, knowing that she couldn't look at the girl a moment longer before exploding. She waved as she ran with Emma and Marianne to get some water, all smothering their giggles.

A HISTORY OF MARDI GRAS
A series for the *Loyola VOICE* by Elizabeth Boudreaux

DURING THE LATE 1960's, PEOPLE outside of the cream of New Orleans Uptown society, the ones unable to join the old-line krewes —normal people, in other words—started their own organizations. These were not the small, secret societies. These were open to everyone—white, black, Jew, newcomer—just as long as you could afford the dues. These became the Super Krewes of Endymion, Bacchus, and Orpheus. To highlight their parades, they began having celebrities as their kings or grand marshals.

You can imagine how well that went over in the early days.

The Saturday before Mardi Gras now belongs to the largest of the super krewes, Endymion, 2,000 members strong from all over the United States. They are best known for two things. One, they rejected the traditional route along St. Charles Avenue for a trek down Canal Street from Mid-City to Downtown. Second, the maids, in their elaborate gowns, ride their own small floats interspersed between the large ones filled with krewe members.

People stake out territory along Canal Street for days in preparation for this parade, arguably the locals favorite outside of Mardi Gras Day. Tents, tarps, ladders, and construction tape were used to reserve prime viewing areas. Endymion, being so large, also stepped off relatively early for its trip to the Superdome and the 10,000 to 15,000 guests at its extravaganza held there. The early start made it family-friendly if one watched it from the beginning of the route and wanted to get the kids home at a decent hour.

My only question is: With 15,000 guests at the Endymion Extravaganza, how come I can't get a date?

This year's theme is "Cooking," and world-famous, New Orleans chef Emeril Lagasse is Grand Marshal. Well, the food ought to be fantastic!

DURING A BREAK, CHRIS, LEANING against one of the ice chests, started strumming a guitar, singing Paul Simon's "Take Me to the Mardi Gras." Conversation died as everyone turned to listen. At the second chorus, Marianne, who had been sitting cross-legged on the blanket with John, joined in. Her sweet soprano blended perfectly with Chris's tenor. By the end of their impromptu duet, their friends were hooting and hollering for an encore. All but John. Chris turned them down with a good-natured wave of his hand as he set down the guitar. Marianne stared at him in surprise.

"I didn't know you could sing so well, Chris."

He gave her his best "aw-shucks" grin. "Thanks, Mari, but we all know you carried the song. You could make a frog sound good."

Marianne got on her knees. "Now that's just not true! You have a beautiful voice! How long has he been hiding it?" she asked the others.

"He's the only guy in the chapter who can sing the National Anthem and hit the high notes," revealed Chuck. "But he's better on the piano."

"Really?" Marianne turned to Chris. "What do you play?"

"Lots of stuff, but I really like jazz."

"Me too! I just adore Ella Fitzgerald!"

The two continued to talk about their favorite jazz standards while John grew more and more angry.

Envy was the beginning and end to John Waguespack. The self-assured, almost cocky attitude he showed to the world hid his insecure nature. What other people had, he longed to possess, and what was his, he held onto jealously.

John glanced at William Darcy. He couldn't believe Carrie Bingley's outfit, and he couldn't fathom William's stubborn inattention to it and to her.

Hell, if I didn't have Mari right here, I might make a run at that!

But he wasn't going to blow a half-year's effort to get Marianne into the sack. Since their argument the day before, John intended do whatever was needed to get back on track. Marianne's obvious enjoyment of Chris Breaux's company threw an unexpected twist into his plans. John sought to hide the building resentment he felt.

Look at Darcy! He's so fucking rich he can blow off a hot-to-go piece like Bingley's sister! And Breaux—that sumbitch's got money, too. So he's gotta go after my woman? Can't he buy his own? I ain't got no money! I ain't got shit!

But I'm gonna have Mari. That's gonna be my piece of ass! Bet on it!

FINALLY THE MAIN EVENT, ENDYMION, rolled by. The floats and throws were plentiful. It was as though the riders had to make up for not being worthy of joining an old-line krewe by showing they had money to burn. Some maskers tossed the beads by the gross, not even taking the trinkets out of the bags.

The girls' favorite part was watching the maids glide by. The maids were lashed securely to their mini-float. The only parts of their bodies they could move were their arms. They trusted their little pages to hand the beads to them to toss.

Parades didn't always run smoothly. In fact, delays and stops were par for the course. About a half hour into the parade, a Louisiana Army National Guard contingent halted in front of the group.

A captain, wearing his Class A green dress uniform, Mardi Gras beads hanging from his neck, cried, "At ease!" Instantly, the company assumed the classic position of legs spread and one arm behind the back, M-16s held by the other leg. The officer strolled next to a sergeant, glancing around.

"Oh, my God," whispered Carrie. "Not him!"

The captain must've heard; he looked over and suddenly grinned. "Take over, Sergeant," he ordered as he moved towards the group. Carrie started to back up.

"Well, well, well. If it isn't Carrie Bingley. You're lookin' mighty fine, lady. Those *are* clothes you're almost wearing, right? LSU ain't marching tonight?" the tall, handsome captain asked.

Elizabeth could see he had black hair and blue eyes under his hat. He looked great in his Class A uniform; she had to admit.

"What are *you* doing here?" Carrie gasped.

"What does it look like?"

She pointed at him. "That uniform! Where did you get *that*?"

He looked down at it. "This? I got it from Wal-Mart, what do you think?"

"*You're* in the Army?"

He smiled. "Army National Guard." He looked at the others. "Sorry, Carrie here has forgotten her manners. I'm Captain John Buford from Baton Rouge. In my civvies, I'm a lawyer."

"Glad to meet you, Captain," Chuck offered, extending his hand. "I'm Chuck Bingley. This is Jane and Elizabeth Boudreaux." He introduced the rest. "You know my sister?"

Buford grinned. "Yeah, I know her."

"In your dreams, John!" Carrie spat.

He leered. "Yeah, there, too. C'mon, when are you gonna admit you're crazy about me?"

Carrie lifted her chin. "Like I would waste my time with an egomaniac like you! You just go and play with your soldier boys, counselor. God help this country if we have to depend on people like you to defend her!"

The parade was getting ready to move again, and Buford grinned at Carrie. "Nice to see all of y'all—even you, Carrie. Y'all behave yourselves, now. Don't do somethin' I wouldn't do."

He returned to his soldiers, all business now. "Attention!" Rifles crashed as the troops responded. "Right shoulder—huh!" As one, the M-16s rose to the proper position. "Forward march!"

As the National Guardsmen marched off, the others turned to an embarrassed Carrie. "I met John Buford the year he was finishing law school. A bigger jerk you've never met! He thinks he's God's gift to women."

"He seems to like you," offered Chuck.

Carrie wilted. Elizabeth figured this was the last thing she wanted to happen in front of William Darcy. "The only thing he'd like is to get into my pants! Apparently, I'm the only girl not to fall for his smooth act. And it's going to stay that way!"

"Yeah, sure," Elizabeth muttered under her breath. That boy looked *way* too good in his uniform, and Elizabeth knew that Carrie thought so, too.

CARRIE BINGLEY HAD FINALLY HAD enough of the waiting and hinting.

The incident with John Buford had shaken her. She had met the conceited law school student at a party, two girls hanging all over him. It should have been a compliment to her that he shook them off to talk to her alone, but the way he talked to her, the way he looked at her, turned Carrie off. She figured he just wanted to add to his harem. Carrie Bingley wasn't having any of that! She was nobody's Number Two.

Since then, they had met repeatedly. John had always showed interest in her, and Carrie always blew him off. She wasn't going to be a notch on John Buford's bedpost, no matter how gorgeous he was. She was going to find romance on her own terms.

It was time to get this thing with William Darcy off first base. She watched and waited until William walked over alone to the ice chests. She quickly intercepted him, and while he was reaching over to grab a beer, Carrie slipped a hand inside the back pocket of his jeans.

William stood up slowly. "Carrie. Can I help you?"

Carrie curled around his body and smiled suggestively. "Will," she breathed, "why don't we blow this party? We can go to the Quarter and hit the clubs, or"—her tongue wet her lips—"we can go to your place."

William's face remained impassive as he slowly reached back and extracted Carrie's hand from his jeans. He brought her hand from around him and released it. "I think you've had enough to drink, Carrie. Shall I have Chuck drive you back to your motel?"

Carrie's eyes grew wide as she stared at him, his reaction completely undoing her. She shook as she stared into his stony face, as hard and beautiful and cold as a statue.

Then she *knew*. It was so stunningly obvious, actually, that she was amazed she'd been blind to it. Reality screamed into her mind the words she had fought so long not to hear. *He's just not into you.*

"I-I'm sorry. I…" Carrie stumbled over her words, the jolt to her ego ruining the connection between brain and tongue. "Forgive me. I-I must be—"

"Carrie, I'm sorry. It's not you. I really wouldn't be good for you. You need someone who would—"

Carrie put her hand up. "No, please, I get it. That's all right. I understand. Please, just leave me alone." She slouched down to sit on the top of a closed ice chest, fighting back mortified tears.

For years, ever since they met, Carrie thought she would fall in love with William Darcy. Her mother expected she would, and Carrie had no objection. He was good looking, he was a gentleman, and he was well off. She was sure would grow to love him. For years, she had tried.

She never thought about *Will*, though. It had never occurred to her that William wouldn't fall in love with her. She had refused to contemplate why he had resisted so long.

Now she *knew*. She had wasted years over him. She had been a fool. It was too soon to think of *why* he didn't like her. It was enough for now just to wallow in her wretchedness.

It wasn't long before Carrie had company. She wouldn't look at her brother as she wiped her face. "So, he went to get you, did he? Come to console the poor, deluded idiot? You needn't bother."

Chuck groaned. "Aw, Carrie, it's not like that. Do you want to leave?"

Her head jerked up. "No. No reason to make you leave. You're enjoying yourself." She gave him a brittle smile. "I'm sure Jane would never forgive me."

"Carrie," said Jane's soft voice behind her, "that's not true. Chuck wants to help you. I want to help you, too. Whatever you need. If you need him to take you home, then that's what Chuck should do."

For some reason, Jane's sincere kindness broke through Carrie's hastily thrown up defenses. Her eyes watered again as she glanced at the blonde nurse behind her. Jane held out her hand and Carrie took it. They sat together on the ice chest in silence, holding hands as Carrie quietly wept.

ELIZABETH STOOD A WAYS OFF with the others, sighing as she took in the sight of the Bingleys with Jane. "Nothing like a little drama to perk up a parade. Any other hearts you're planning to break tonight, Darcy?"

"Elizabeth!" admonished Marianne while restraining a giggle.

William looked down. "Elizabeth, I already feel like crap. You don't have to rub it in."

"I'm just *teasing*, Darcy," said Elizabeth defensively.

William turned and looked at her, an unreadable expression on his face. They were locked in a gaze for a moment before she turned away.

"Will, it wasn't your fault," Cathy said.

"Yeah, she kind of put herself in that situation. What else could you do?" Elizabeth asked reasonably.

William ran a hand through his hair. "I don't know. I guess you're right. I'm sorry I hurt her feelings."

Elizabeth looked back at the ice chests. "Jane'll make her feel better, just watch. She's got the gift." She took William by the hand. "C'mon, let's go watch the rest of the parade."

John, who had been watching silently, could not figure William out. *For cryin' out loud, Carrie friggin' propositioned him! What the hell was Darcy thinking passin' that up?*

AN HOUR LATER AS THE parade was breaking up, John started kissing Marianne's neck. "You wanna do somethin' tonight, Mari?"

She pushed him away. "John…"

"No, no. I didn't mean anything. I meant hittin' the Quarter or something."

Marianne yawned. "Not tonight. Why don't you come with us back to Emma's?"

John blanched. Going to a girl gabfest at the Weinbergs was not his idea of a good time. "Ah, no, Mari. I just remembered: Tommy wants to grab some grub after work. I'm gonna meet him back at the crib." He wasn't too worried if Marianne called his bluff. Getting her into the apartment was only half the battle. And if she decided to continue over to Emma's, there was always Plan B.

"Oh, okay." She gave John a quick kiss. "Tell Tommy 'hi' for me." She sighed. "I'll see you tomorrow, okay?"

"Want me to pick you up?"

Marianne smiled. "Yeah—Elizabeth can grab a ride, too."

Shit! "Okay," he said as he kissed her again. "See ya." He waved as he made his way to his car, already pulling out his cell phone to call Greg to score a little grass.

"SO WHAT ARE YOU GUYS doing?" Elizabeth asked William and Chris. "Chuck's coming over to Emma's."

"I was thinking of packing it in. How 'bout you, Chris?"

"I'm ready when you are, partner."

Meanwhile some of the group mentioned going down to the French Quarter. "Come on," said Nick Patel. "We can watch the stupid tourist gals flash their boobs for beads! It'll be great!"

Boy, that's something I wanna see, thought a morose Carrie, sitting on folding chair. *And maybe later for laughs I can pull out my wisdom teeth with a pair of pliers.*

Just then, she felt a hand on her shoulder. It was Cathy. "Carrie? You want to come?"

"I don't think so."

"Come on with us. We won't be out too late. Henry and I want to do some dancing. It'll be fun. I know how much you like to dance."

Oh, what the hell. Why not? What else can go wrong tonight? "All right, as long as it's not too late."

"You go have fun, Sis," advised Chuck, his arm around Jane.

Impulsively, Carrie stood and kissed both of them on the cheek. "Thanks for everything, Jane."

"Are you feeling better?" Jane whispered. "Remember, you don't have to have a man to prove you're worth something. You're wonderful just the way you are."

"I'm fine," she assured her. "I'll see you both tomorrow." Carrie saw Jane didn't quite believe her. In a funny way, it made Carrie like the girl even more.

The group destined for the Quarter climbed into several cars. Carrie left hers off Canal Street and drove Downtown with Cathy and Henry. They found a parking lot about ten blocks away and walked the rest of the way.

The French Quarter was jumping that warm Saturday night. Because Mardi Gras was early that year and didn't coincide with Spring Break, there were noticeably fewer college-age party people jamming it up. Unfortunately for the merchants, business was slightly off. But Carrie and the others could walk down Bourbon Street without having to squeeze their way through the inebriated throng.

Cathy suggested they head for one of the dance clubs. Carrie followed quietly. She was hurt and embarrassed—and angry for being hurt and embarrassed. There was only one cure for it: dance the night away.

That's it! I'm through throwing myself after men who don't appreciate me. I'm not going to waste any more time on Will Darcy. It's a hard lesson to learn, but Jane's right. I don't have to have a man to prove I'm worth something. I have family and friends who love me. I'm just gonna have fun. Be myself. Respect myself. Starting right now!

Look all you want, boys, she mentally declared as she walked down the street. *You're not getting any of this!*

Chapter 12

Sunday, February 14: Metairie

Carrie Bingley woke up groggy and uneasy in the pre-dawn. She was in her bed in her motel room, but something felt wrong somehow. Was it all those Zombies she drank?

Someone (Patel?) had suggested going down to the Quarter to laugh at the boys trying to get all the tourist girls to remove their tops for beads. Before she knew it, she was in some dance club, music blaring loudly, and drinks had magically appeared in her hand. It would have been rude not to sample them, wouldn't it? Now, in the wee hours of the morning, Carrie felt she had made a mistake. She had no remembrance of returning to her room last night.

Good Lord, she thought, *did I drive in this condition?* She was the daughter of an insurance agent, and the lessons he drilled into her had stuck. She put a hand to her face. *Wait a minute. I rode with Henry and Cathy to the Quarter. I don't remember going back for the car. How did I get back here? Did they bring me back?*

A strange sound told Carrie she had other, more immediate issues with which to deal. That was a snore. She had no roommate.

And there was someone in her bed.

Carrie leapt out of bed, awaking a large form lying next to her. She stumbled into the chair next to the bed and made out clothes on it—green-colored clothes.

Just then, Carrie realized she was buck-naked as the form began to rise.

"You! Who the hell are you?" she cried as she pulled the sheets off the bed in an effort to cover herself.

"Now, isn't this a disappointing way to wake up," drawled a familiar voice.

"John?"

"Hey, she remembers me," said Buford.

"What are *you* doing here?" She then noticed he had on no more clothes than she did.

"Now's that's a dumb question, even for a Golden Girl."

"Oh, my God! No, not you!" Carrie sat on the chair, memories flooding back.

"Carrie," Buford said in a gentle voice as he sat up and moved to her side of the bed, keeping as much of himself under the covers as possible. "It's okay. I didn't take advantage of you; trust me."

"Are you trying to say we didn't—?"

"Well, of *course* we did it, but it was what we both wanted. Don't you remember?"

Carrie covered her face. "I think I'm going to be sick."

"Wait!" Buford kicked off the covers and dashed towards the bathroom. In a moment, he returned with a trash can. "Here."

Carrie looked at the can. "You idiot! I don't mean *sick* sick! I mean embarrassed!"

"Oh. Well, with all those Zombies you drank…" Carrie shook with repressed laughter. "What's so funny?"

"You're naked."

"Uh, yeah. So are you, as a matter of fact."

Carrie shook her head. "I don't believe this! Will Darcy blows me off, I get drunk, and I end up in a motel room with John Buford of all people. My life sucks."

"Carrie," Buford knelt and tenderly took her hand, "if it means anything, it was real good."

Carrie snorted. "So good I don't remember any of it."

"You don't remember?"

"No, I don't," Carrie said automatically, trying to make sense of it. This kind, affectionate man was not the John Buford she knew.

Buford seemed shocked. "Are you kidding me? You don't recall running into me at the club? You seemed happy to see me." He frowned. "We got up to dance to that Britney Spears song—"

"Madonna," Carrie corrected him absentmindedly.

"Right, Madonna, and—" He caught himself and slowly smiled. "Yeah, Madonna."

Carrie saw her mistake. "Uhh, the time at the club *is* coming back to me. But I don't remember anything else!"

A twinkle replaced the concern in Buford's eye. "Really? You don't remember dirty dancing with me?" His hand softly encased one of her knees.

"I-I wouldn't call *that* dirty dancing."

"I recall you grinding your hips into me, but if you say so, I'll take your word for it. You've gotta promise to show me some *real* dirty dancing sometime, though."

Carrie swallowed nervously and put her knees together, as his now caressing hand was definitely distracting her. "Like that's going to happen."

"So…" He ran his finger along the outside of her calf. "You have no recollection of me taking you back to your motel; is that what you're saying?"

"I kinda—"

"And the front seat make-out session in the parking lot outside?"

"The night is a blur." She gasped as her face turned red. His touch was driving her mad!

"And inviting me in? And attacking me once the door was closed?" His lips descended on her knee.

Carrie shivered. Buford's attentions had succeeded in parting her knees.

He took the opportunity to softly kiss the inside of one. "You practically tore my uniform off, Carrie," he whispered as he kissed the other knee, getting in a little lick as well, "after you whipped off that pretty little top of yours. I can't believe you have no memory of *that*."

Carrie whimpered.

"Yeah," he grinned in a cocky way she found both infuriating and devastatingly attractive. "That's the sound you made waiting for me to put on the condom. Like you couldn't wait. And you say you don't remember." He rose on his knees and moved close to her face.

Carrie was breathless, but she fought to regain control of the situation. "Maybe I do, and maybe I don't. But what's done is done. You can go now. I won't hold anything against you. You don't have to worry about me making any complaints." If he left now, she would die, but she made the offer anyway.

Buford silenced her with a soft, sweet kiss, his hands cupping her cheeks.

"Why'd you do that?" she asked softly. His face was only inches away.

"'Cause I wanted to. 'Cause I liked it." He kissed her again. "I like kissing you, Carrie."

"Stop," she whispered unconvincingly.

He frowned, clearly uncertain now. "Are you sure you want me to go? I will if that's what you really want."

"Yes. No. I don't know." Her mind was unsure, unlike her traitorous body.

"Let me help you make up your mind." This time he kissed her with growing passion. Unable to stop, her hands moved on their own to his face. The next thing Carrie knew, Buford had lifted her out of the chair and was carrying her back to the bed.

"What are you doing?"

"You said you don't remember what happened last night."

"I…I remember some of it," she admitted. "All of it, actually."

"Well, that's good, but I want to make a better impression on you."

"What do you mean?"

"I'm gonna make sure you'll remember this time for the rest of your life."

A FEW HOURS LATER, as the sun peeked through the window, Carrie awoke again in a much better frame of mind. Buford's strong arms embraced her as they spooned together. Carrie felt warm, safe, and desired.

He kept his promise, she thought with a grin. *I'll never forget the second time.*

She felt him stir. "Hmm...hey, babe," he murmured.

"Hi yourself, soldier."

"Mmm, you feel nice." His hands moved over her naked form.

"Watch where your hands are going there, mister."

"Believe me"—he nuzzled her—"I know exactly where they're going."

She turned in his embrace with a bawdy smile. "Is that so? Don't you think I might have something to say about it?"

His smile faded as he looked at the clock. "Had I more time, I would be happy to explore that topic with you, pretty lady, but I've gotta meet my people at Jackson Barracks for breakfast."

"Oh." *Was this just a one-night stand?*

"Damn," he said as he rolled to the other side of the bed. "I don't want to leave."

Of course, he's leaving. I'm just what I never wanted to be—another notch on John Buford's bedpost. My life sucks.

"Hey," he exclaimed, "come with me."

More than just the room lit up in the dawn. "Come with you?" She rolled over and propped herself on one elbow.

There was Buford's devastating smile again. "Yeah. Wives and such are invited to breakfast."

"Wives and such," she repeated. "And just what am I?"

"You're my girl."

Carrie looked wide-eyed at him. "I'm your girl? Just like that?"

Buford put his hands behind his head, looking very pleased with himself. "Yep. Just like that."

A HISTORY OF MARDI GRAS
A series for the *Loyola VOICE* by Elizabeth Boudreaux

YOU CAN'T HAVE A PARADE without bands. Mardi Gras in New Orleans is no exception. In fact, Carnival attracts the best marching bands in the nation outside of the Rose Parade.

As an old band geek (my instrument was the flute), I can tell you that marching bands come in two flavors. The most popular style is the martial corps marching band. They look like robots moving in unison down the street. All the military bands are corps style, and so are most of the college and high school bands.

Having been in a corps band, I can tell you it's not as easy as it looks. You have to be in step, keep in line, and maintain your diagonal without moving your head. You use your eyes, instead. The effect is to move as one organism, concentrating on the sound. Never overpowering, you should blend properly with the rest of your bandmates. When it's right, you can *feel* the harmony. It's a rush.

There are a lot of very good corps bands out there. The US Marines are a particular favorite of mine. But I think the best college corps band, outside of the academies, is Texas A&M. Their tight formations, quick turns, and outstanding sound are what the rest of us are trying to achieve.

The other style is show band, a manner made famous by Grambling State University. Mainly adopted by inner-city high schools and historically black colleges, their high-stepping, dancing, and really big sound turn on the audience in a big way.

Show bands are either really good or really bad. There is no in-between. It is extraordinarily hard to dance as they do *and* sound good at the same time. The best just blow you away. No wonder they are so popular with the crowd.

You can start a major argument over which school has the best show band. Grambling, Southern, Florida A&M, and others all have their loyal fans. I wouldn't dream of giving my opinion. But as far as high school bands go, nobody works harder than New Orleans' own St. Augustine Catholic High School Marching 100. I have heard the football players are glad they aren't in the band —'cause the band workouts are too tough.

Lower Ninth Ward, New Orleans
CARRIE FELT VERY SELF-CONSCIOUS AS she entered the garage staging

area in Jackson Barracks hand-in-hand with Buford. He directed her over to a sergeant in camouflage, holding a little girl and standing next to a woman.

"Sergeant, report," Buford ordered.

"Everyone present and accounted for, sir." He shifted the child as he took in Buford's clothing; he was still in the Class As from the day before. "Umm, I thought we were in BDUs today."

"We are, Mack. This is my guest, Miss Carrie Bingley. Carrie, this is Sergeant Leslie MacDonald, known far and wide as 'Mack,' and his wife, Wendy. I left my change of clothes here. I'll change, and we'll grab the chow. Take care of this lady, Mack."

"Our pleasure, sir."

Buford gave Carrie a quick peck on the cheek and went into another room. Meanwhile, Carrie was mortified; she was sure *'We slept together'* was plastered all over her face.

"Hi, Carrie. I'm very glad to meet any friend of Captain Buford." Wendy MacDonald immediately tried to put her at ease.

"Thank you," Carrie answered as they shook hands.

"We've been worried about him. He never brings anybody to these gatherings."

"Really?" Carrie squeaked.

"Yes. Half of us have been trying to set him up with our relatives or friends. He's so nice, and we hate to see him lonely."

John—lonely? Carrie's mind rebelled with this intelligence. The idea that John "Master of his Universe" Buford, hotshot lawyer and reported ladies' man, was lonely was hard to accept.

"But I see we shouldn't have bothered." Wendy retrieved her daughter from her husband. "And this young lady is Brittany. Say hello, Brittany."

"Goo," was Brittany's answer, as she reached out for the newcomer.

"Ah, she likes you. Do you mind?" Before Carrie could respond, Brittany was in her arms.

"I-I haven't had a lot of experience with babies," Carrie explained as the squirming child sought her neck. "I'm afraid I'll drop her."

"Naw," said Mack. "She's got a grip of iron. Once she has you, she ain't going anywhere."

"Come on," said Wendy as she took Carrie's arm. "Let me introduce you to everybody."

Halfway through the introductions, Buford rejoined her, dressed in his starched camouflage Battle Dress Uniform. "Ah, there's a pretty picture," he greeted her.

Carrie noted he was eyeing the child in her arms. Returning Brittany to her mother, she said to Buford, "Don't get any bright ideas, soldier boy."

"Don't know why I shouldn't. You're a natural." Carrie blushed as they continued to greet the rest of the command.

Later, over bacon and eggs, Carrie leaned over to Buford. "Everyone's so *nice.*"

"You sound surprised."

She looked down at her plate. "Most of the people I meet are more standoffish, not like this."

"Well, you are the captain's girl," he joked.

Her eyes flew to his. "You're *kidding.*"

"Well, mostly. Seriously, some of the best people I've ever met are in the National Guard. Weekend warriors, volunteering to serve whenever we're needed. Taking out the bad guys or helping during a natural disaster—that's our job." He waved at the people seated around them. "Look at these people here, Carrie. Lawyers, accountants, oil field workers, secretaries, teachers, mechanics. We're not doing this for the money; believe me. I could tell you about Duty, Honor, and Country, but you wouldn't understand." He shook his head. "It's something we do because it needs to be done.

"But there's another reason, Carrie. You've got to admit you can be a bit standoffish, too. But you've been very receptive to everybody today."

"But why do I fit in here?"

"Maybe 'cause you're out of your comfort zone. You're forced to trust us, so you've dropped your defenses. You're a nice person, Carrie, when you want to be."

Carrie was taken aback. No one had called her nice before. "I haven't been very nice to you." She caught herself thinking of the night before and added, "Well, except for, you know. Yet, you never gave up. Why?"

Buford gave her a strange look. It was serious and amused at the same time. "'Cause I always knew you'd be my girl."

"*Excuse me?*" Carrie was dumbfounded. "What about all those bimbos?"

"Them? They chased me more than I chased them."

"You didn't exactly send them away."

"Carrie, my reputation in college wasn't very accurate." At her incredulous look, Buford added, "Just because those girls hung around me didn't mean I slept with them."

"You mean all at one time?" she said looking away.

Buford continued in a lower voice, "Look, I've done some things I'm not proud of, but I did a lot less than you apparently think. 'Sides, I wanted to be with you. You're pretty, you're smart, and you don't take any crap off anybody. I like that; I always have."

"Then why weren't you nicer to me?"

Buford shrugged. "In a weird way, I thought I was. Teasing you, I mean. Dumb! Just shows how much growing up I needed to do. The National Guard helped me do that." Buford set down his plate. "Look, Carrie, I admit I was a bit of a jerk at LSU, but I was serious about you. I still am. I want us to be together. I think we'll be real good together."

A lump formed in Carrie's throat as her stomach did somersaults. "I-I don't understand."

He leaned in and kissed her cheek. "Just give me time. Let me show you why I think you're wonderful."

Carrie melted as Buford's bright blue eye bore into hers. "Okay."

Mid-City

BUFORD DROVE CARRIE BACK TO her car off Canal Street. People were preparing for the parade later, and the traffic was heavy. He was able to get within a half-block by parking illegally in someone's driveway. "No problem," he claimed. "Being a lawyer has its advantages. I know people. I can get about any ticket I want waved."

"Nice ability to have there, John," Carrie said sarcastically.

Buford walked Carrie to her car. "Look," he said, "I don't have much time. I gotta get back to Jackson Barracks."

Carrie just looked at him as he dug into one pocket. He pulled out a couple of business cards and a ballpoint pen. "Here," he said as he wrote furiously on one of them, "this is my home number. My work number and cell are on the other side. Can I get your number?" He handed her the two cards and pen.

Carrie scribbled her phone numbers on the unmarked card and returned it with the pen.

"Great," Buford smiled. "I'll call. I promise."

"Any more parades?" She could think of nothing else to say. She didn't want to get her hopes up.

"No, this is our last one. Everybody's heading out afterwards to spend Mardi Gras at home." He took her hands. "Carrie, last night was unbelievable—special. You're a very special lady." He kissed her. "I *will* call. Trust me."

"I have to. I'm your girl, right?" she asked, her joking tone belying her conflicted emotions.

"Yeah, you rite." Another kiss and he was gone.

Garden District

Elizabeth, Marianne, and John met u•p with their friends along the St. Charles route on Sunday evening, parking near Emma's house. This was one of the big events of Carnival—the Bacchus Parade, the oldest of the super krewes. Many of the throng were in Star Trek costumes to honor Bacchus XIX.

As expected, Chuck was glued to Jane's side. The young nurse didn't seem dismayed by it at all. Right next to the couple was Carrie Bingley.

Elizabeth had to admit she was surprised Carrie showed, given the humiliation she had undergone the night before. But there she was, hugging and chatting with Chuck and Jane as though she had not a care in the world. She was dressed more conservatively—a white T-shirt, stone-washed jeans, and sandals.

William wandered over. "Hi, Boudreaux." He glanced over at Carrie. "Am I safe, or is she armed?"

A bright smile covered Elizabeth's face for a moment. "No, it looks like you're out of harm's way. How's your shoulder today, hero?"

William returned the smile. "A lot better, but don't expect me to pick you up."

Elizabeth laughed. "You mean like Chuck and Jane? No way! You'd tear up your back."

"I doubt it."

John Waguespack was behaving himself for a change. He had been polite to Elizabeth and attentive to Marianne and, for the first time in a long time, early for their date.

About an hour later, the sirens signaled the approach of the krewe. Soon, the crowd was cheering Bacchus XXXI, Jim Belushi. The actor and comedian, best known for taking his late brother's place in the Blues Brothers, joined a privileged list of celebrities invited to represent the God of Wine. Belushi was having the time of his life as he tossed beads and doubloons to his subjects for the night.

The masked lieutenants rode on horseback and were dressed in Romanesque armor. Huge floats, with names like Bacchasaurus, Bacchagator, and Bacchawhoppa, each holding as many as eighty riders, made their way down tree-lined St. Charles Avenue.

Elizabeth was surprised at Carrie's behavior that evening. Unlike the night before, she was polite and friendly, yet distracted. It was not puzzling that she ignored William; after last night, it was to be expected. But she didn't seem depressed either, and Elizabeth was curious as to the cause.

About a half hour later, they had their first clue. Carrie, who had been peering down the route, suddenly gave out a small squeal and began to fight her way towards the street curb.

"What's up with Carrie?" asked Emma.

Carrie was waving her arms and bouncing up and down, screaming, "Go Army! Yay! Looking good, guys! Woo hoo!"

"Okay, it's confirmed," William said in a low voice. "Carrie has lost it."

"What in the world?" Chuck managed.

Jane touched his arm. "I guess she likes soldiers."

After the camouflaged guardsmen marched by, Carrie turned towards the group and saw the expressions on their faces. "What?"

"What was *that* all about?" demanded her brother.

Her face turned as red as her hair. "Just…umm…supporting our troops."

BACCHUS WAS, AS USUAL, GENEROUS, and the throws were plentiful. Towards the end of the parade, Emma threw one arm around William's waist while doing the same around Elizabeth's neck.

"And how are two of my favorite people doing tonight?"

William winced. "All right. I've caught my share. How 'bout you, Elizabeth?"

Elizabeth saw William's expression, and she assumed he was falling back into his stick-in-the-mud routine. *Can't you lighten up for one full night, Darcy?* "Don't know if I can make it back to the car," she said, indicating the number of beads around her neck.

Emma grinned at them. "Y'all coming back to the house afterwards?"

Elizabeth spoke first. "Not tonight. I've got an early start tomorrow. Going to Lafayette with Chris, you know."

"Aw, c'mon, Elizabeth, just for a little while?" Emma whined. Elizabeth just smiled and shook her head. Emma turned to William. "You're stopping by, aren't you?"

"Maybe for a couple of minutes. I think I'll pack it in early."

Emma clearly was not happy about this turn of events. "Mari! Cathy! We all set for tomorrow?"

"Set for what?" asked John.

"We're gonna have a ladies' day out on Monday, showing Jane around while Elizabeth abandons us for Lafayette. We'll be back in time for the parade."

"Lundi Gras for the ladies!" laughed Marianne.

John didn't look overjoyed at this news, but Chuck put on a cheerful face. "That's great. I know you'll show her a good time."

"You bet, Chuck," Cathy assured him. "We're gonna do the Quarter—everything!"

"And the Riverfront!" added Emma. "Rex is supposed to meet up with the King and Queen of Zulu tomorrow at six! The mayor and everybody's gonna be there!"

"Oh, stop!" cried Elizabeth. "You're gonna make me jealous."

"Wow, sounds like fun," said Chuck. "You are coming back for Orpheus, right?"

"Wouldn't miss it, Chuck. We'll be back in time," Emma assured him.

Marianne turned to John. "You okay?" she asked in a low voice. "I guess I should have told you, but we just decided it tonight. It's just us girls. We'll be back here before parade time."

"Sure, you show Jane a good time, babe. I'll see you here tomorrow." He leaned down for Marianne's kiss on his cheek and closed his eyes so Marianne couldn't see his anger.

Lower Ninth Ward

THE YELLOW ORLEANS PARISH SCHOOL bus pulled up in the parking lot of Jackson Barracks just after 10:00 p.m. The troops of Buford's company trudged out of the bus, a little tired after their third five-mile march in as many nights, and walked into the waiting arms of their wives and husbands, girlfriends and boyfriends. First to leave the bus was Buford, and he stood next to the door, allowing his people to precede him. Not only was it the right thing to do, he knew there was no one waiting for him.

Last off the bus was Mack. They walked together towards the waiting cars. Buford intended to take his farewell of Mack's family before he retrieved his gear and began his lonely journey home to Baton Rouge. About ten feet away from Mack's minivan, Buford came to a dead stop. Standing in the headlights next to Wendy MacDonald was a tall redhead in T-shirt and jeans.

"Hi, soldier. Need a ride home?"

Buford could say nothing.

Carrie's smile faded. "I thought it was too late for you to drive all the way back to Baton Rouge," she explained.

Hesitating for another moment, he watched the normally calm and collected Carrie Bingley bite her lip as she twisted her hands together nervously. Finally, he was able to utter her name.

Carrie was perfectly baffled by Buford's reaction to her impulsive act. She felt sure he would shoot her one of his infuriatingly devastating cocky smiles. The serious look on his face was disconcerting and alarming. *Oh, my God. He doesn't want me here.*

Before Carrie could get her muscles to work and make her escape, she found Buford's strong hands on her upper arms. His bright blue eyes stared right into her green ones. Carrie felt her soul was as completely naked before him as her body had been the night before. Buford breathed out, closed his eyes, and pulled Carrie close, resting his forehead against hers.

"I didn't expect this," he said softly, his voice full of wonder.

Carrie relaxed in his embrace as the realization of his true feelings flowed through her. "Neither did I," she said as her hands touched his waist, a nervous smile trembling on her lips. "This is happening so fast."

Mack coughed before interrupting. "Well, see you later, Captain —Miss Carrie. Hope you have a good night."

Wendy grabbed his arm. "C'mon, Mack, before you make a bigger fool out of yourself." She got her family into the minivan and pulled out of the parking lot.

Carrie and Buford stood together almost alone in the lot, a couple of streetlights illuminating the scene. Carrie was the first to speak. "John, is this for real? Do you feel this...this thing between us? Is it the same for you?"

"I know I kid around a lot, but believe me when I tell you I've never felt this way before."

"Can you promise me one thing? That we'll both try as hard as we can to make this work?"

"You sound scared."

"I'm terrified, John." She managed a small smile. "I suppose you're as confident as hell."

"You suppose wrong. I'm scared too, babe. I'm almost drowning here."

"So what do we do?"

Buford leaned in and kissed her. It started hesitant and soft, but it soon grew into much more. Buford pulled back and stared at her. "I promise you, Carrie, I'll put everything I've got into this. I don't know where we're going, but I don't want to be anywhere but here. I don't want anything but you."

Carrie looked searchingly into his eyes. Seeing the conviction on his face and hearing the honesty in his voice, she smiled and wrapped her arms round his neck. This time she initiated the kiss. It was a long time before they came up for air.

"Follow me?"

"To your motel?"

She smiled. "I'm paid up through Tuesday."

"Let me grab my gear."

"You don't have to work tomorrow?"

"I'm taking the next couple of days off."

She gave him a mock serious look. "Great. Your bosses will probably fire you."

Now he gave her the cocky smile she had expected. "Me? Nah. I make too much money for them. I'm a lawyer, remember? I've practically got a license to steal." He kissed her again. "Oh, by the way—even though it's almost over, Happy Valentine's Day."

Chapter 13

Elizabeth dashed about the room as she neglected to pack the night before. Entering the shared bathroom, she opened the medicine cabinet and collected her necessities.

Toothpaste, toothbrush, cosmetics, hair spray, shampoo, conditioner, hair products. The humidity in New Orleans insured a curly-haired woman would have more than her share of bad hair days. *What else? Oh, yes, the birth control pills. Sigh. If only I could have a normal period. Haven't really needed these for much else since Thibodaux.*

Tossing the items into a zip-top plastic bag, she almost ran into her roommate as she exited the small bathroom.

"Slow down, Lizzy," Marianne advised. "Chris isn't due for over an hour."

"Can't," she returned as she filled her overnight bag with a change of clothes. "I want to grab something to eat from the cafeteria before he gets here."

"Sorry I can't join you, roomie. I'm on my way to pick up your sister."

"Oh!" Elizabeth stopped her packing. "Have a good time. Tell Jane I'll miss her. I hope it doesn't rain too much."

Marianne returned the good wishes, picked up her purse, and was out the door. Elizabeth collected her notebook and other writing materials.

Right at ten o'clock, Elizabeth's cell phone announced the arrival of her ride. Minutes later, Elizabeth jumped into Chris's truck.

"Ready to pass a good time?" asked Chris.

"You bet! Let's go!"

❧

THE GREAT ATCHAFALAYA SWAMP CUTS southern Louisiana in half, separating the swamp Cajuns of Houma and Thibodaux from the plains Cajuns of Opelousas and Lafayette. The interstate travels more than twenty miles over the swamps and bottomlands of the state's second largest river. The swamp is a national treasure, the home to alligators, crayfish, and other inhabitants of this North American rainforest. It also is home to the greatest threat to the city of New Orleans.

The fact is that the mighty Mississippi built Southeast Louisiana by moving and flooding. Eons ago, the channel was the present-day Bayou Teche near Lafayette. The uncontrollable stream meandered eastward over the millennia, the silt it carried from two-thirds of the North American continent slowly creating swamps and forestlands. By the time de Salle discovered the river for his king, it had moved as far to the east as it would ever go.

The spring floods made the land near the river both rich and dangerous. Man would solve the problem by building the largest levee system on the planet, stretching thousands of miles up the river and its two major contributories, the Missouri and Ohio. Trial, error, and technology would finally win the day, and the Mississippi would be channeled to dump its millions of tons of silt from millions of acres of farms and yards from thousands of square miles of America into the deep off the continental shelf of the Gulf of Mexico.

Yet, what man can make, nature can destroy. It was

known in the early half of the twentieth century that the Atchafalaya was siphoning more and more of the Mississippi's flow. By the middle of the century, it had reached one-third and showed no sign of stabilizing. The conclusion was inescapable: the Mississippi was moving again.

For the Mississippi to make such a change was completely natural, but in the interval since the last shift, a nation had developed, and the nation could not afford nature. The consequences of the Atchafalaya's conquest of the Mississippi would include, but not be limited to, the demise of Baton Rouge and the virtual destruction of New Orleans. With its fresh water gone, its harbor a silt bar, and its economy disconnected from inland commerce, New Orleans would die, and all the commerce along the Lower Mississippi would die with it.

In 1963, the US Army Corps of Engineers dammed the "Old River," but they couldn't kill it. The swamp was too valuable. A flow had to be allowed, and commercial travel on the Atchafalaya had to be taken into account. Therefore, the flow was maintained at thirty percent. Locks were put in place to allow traffic between the two rivers and a third one, the Red River. This construct, the Old River Control Structure, was a balancing act, preserving the Atchafalaya Swamp while protecting New Orleans.

A flood in the 1970s almost caused the structure to fail. Many say it is doomed to failure; nature cannot be stopped. Some on the extreme fringe of the environmental movement said the structure was an abomination to Gaia—Earth Mother—and should be destroyed. People had to learn to live with nature not tame it, they said. If that put Morgan City under twenty-five feet of water, so be it.

It is not difficult to imagine that this argument

had little attraction in the Bayou State or the halls of Congress. The construct's security was paramount to the citizens of Louisiana.

Never fear, said the Feds. The US Army Corps of Engineers was on the job. They'll keep you safe. Whom could you trust if you couldn't trust them?

Uptown

CHUCK'S CELL PHONE RANG. "HELLO? Yeah, I'm fine. ... What? ... You sure you're okay? ... All right, Sis. See you tomorrow. Bye."

"What's that all about?" asked Henry.

"Carrie. Says she's gonna sleep in and get some rest. So, with Jane hanging out with Mari and Em, it looks like I'm a bachelor today."

Henry chuckled. "I know. Cathy's joining them."

Chuck sat deep in thought. *Carrie's all alone. I hope she's not mooning over Will.*

Lafayette

THE BREAUXES LIVED IN A modest, three-bedroom, split-level ranch southwest of Lafayette in what used to be a cane field. Now, the barren land was spotted with houses on two- or three-acre lots and very few trees. Cajuns liked trees—just not near the house. (Might fall on your roof during a storm, don't you know?) So they planted them along the perimeter of their property. Under the power line always seemed a popular spot for live oaks.

Elizabeth and Chris entered the house through the door in the garage. It opened into the kitchen, where they found Mrs. Breaux. She was by herself as Mr. Breaux was at work. A jolly woman almost as wide as she was tall, Mrs. Breaux insisted they eat some lunch after the introductions were completed.

"Boudreaux," thought Mrs. Breaux aloud, "are your people from Breaux Bridge?"

Elizabeth swallowed her spoonful of seafood gumbo. "No, ma'am."

"St. Martinville? I know Donald Boudreaux. He married a Gaubert."

Elizabeth shook her head. "My family's been around Chackbay and Thibodaux forever, though I think we had relatives who came from the river."

"Give it up, Mom. Boudreaux's a common name. You don't know everybody."

"Just give me some time, Chris, I'll think of somebody."

Chris leaned over to Elizabeth. "It's Mom's firm opinion that everybody's related to everybody. It's just a matter of looking back far enough."

"Well, that's true, isn't it?" insisted his mother. She sighed. "Well, Elizabeth, how did you meet my Chris?"

"Umm…at a party." Elizabeth was unsure of the question.

"*And…*" she raised her eyebrows.

Chris jumped in. "*And* we're friends. *Just* friends, Mom. Sorry."

"Oh." Mrs. Breaux deflated. "Well, we're happy to have you here in any case, Elizabeth, even though that no-good son of mine is too picky for his own good!"

"Jeez, Mom, you're starting into me already?"

"Your brother's married, and he's two years younger than you."

"Mike, the auto mechanic," Chris clarified before whispering, "married two years, with a two-year-old son."

"Chris!" cried his mother.

Elizabeth giggled at Chris's embarrassment at being overheard. "That's all right, Mrs. Breaux. Will I have a chance to meet them?"

"Oh, yes, they'll be here tomorrow before we go to all the festivities. Mike is riding, too." She frowned at Chris. "Margie is a lovely girl and a wonderful mother. She works at the bank. Why you have to pick on her?"

"Not her, Mom—just Mike." He grinned. "He's the one who can't do things in the right order. Can't help but to rag him about it. Been doing it for twenty-two years."

Mrs. Breaux shook her head. "It never stops! You should have seen them as teenagers, Elizabeth! I thought they were going to be the death of me! Have you had enough gumbo? Can I get you any more? No? Well, then, let me show you to your room."

Metairie

CARRIE HAD INDEED SLEPT LATE, and she and Buford had awakened for good at about ten. But they didn't dress. Carrie had the unusual experience of spending the greater part of the day completely nude, with a man in a similar state, just talking.

It was Buford's idea. He bet Carrie she couldn't stay naked all day. Carrie took the bet with the caveat that towels were permitted to answer the door.

At first, Carrie was self-conscious. She didn't have body image issues like some of her friends, but it was still strange to sit cross-legged in bed without a stitch of clothes on talking to a buck-naked man—in particular, a gorgeous creature like John Buford. He was tan and built. He had plenty of hair where he needed it and none where he didn't. His five o'clock shadow was persistent and pleasing. At her insistence, he wore his dog tags. In return, Buford had her retain her necklace. The awkwardness soon passed, and while they never forgot the nudity of the other, it was not that big a distraction. It got to be fun since they both knew what was coming.

They talked about everything—childhood, school, common acquaintances, jobs and careers, dreams and plans. Carrie giggled as Buford told stories about his family. Buford held her hand as Carrie tearfully told him her history. They argued over who had harder workouts—the National Guard or the Golden Girls. Carrie heard about every mission Buford had been sent on. They discussed the state of the world and whether the crawfish season was going to be better than last year. Carrie, who had never talked to one guy for more than ten minutes at a stretch, conversed for hours with John.

They ordered pizza when they got hungry. Carrie could barely hold in her laughter as Buford got the door—with a towel around his waist—to pay for the pies and drinks. There was something incredibly silly and sexy about eating pizza in the nude, especially if you shared.

They made love when they got the urge. Actually, it was when Carrie got the urge. She pushed her lover back down on the bed.

"Now, Mr. Captain John Buford, Esquire, Master of the Universe—I'm gonna make you beg for mercy!"

"Pretty big talk for a dancer," he taunted back.

Carrie leered and reached down between his legs. "We'll see," was all she said as she lowered her head.

Buford seized the sheets in his fists as she pleasured him with her hands and mouth. He did all he could to hold out—he thought of work, golf scores, the last twenty-mile march with full pack—anything. When he thought he was going to go out of his mind, she ceased. She made a production out of fitting him with protection. Slowly straddling him, poised over his erection, one hand holding him steady, she halted and looked him right in the eye.

"Well?" she drawled.

"Lord, have mercy!"

French Quarter

EMMA, CATHY, MARIANNE AND JANE left the Weinbergs' house just after eleven o'clock. It took Emma some time to drive her Saab to her father's reserved downtown parking spot. The four gathered up their purses and made for Canal Street.

Minutes later, the quartet strolled through the crowds on Bourbon Street. The gray overcast skies dampened the festivities with a bit of drizzle—not enough to stop the partying. The narrow streets, turned into a pedestrian mall, were filled with people in various states of dress, almost slouching from the vast quantity of beads about their necks, moving from bar to pub to dance club to hotel. Most had a cup of something in their hands. The smell of stale beer and worse filled the air, as did the sounds of jazz, Mardi Gras standards, rock, county, Zydeco and techno-dance. Street performers were out in force as were the ever-present teams of police.

"This is nothing!" Emma advised Jane. "You ought to see Mardi Gras Day. The costumes alone are worth the hassle!"

Within a few crowded blocks, the group passed by the first of the French Quarter hotels, famous for their galleries. It was early in the afternoon, so only a few of the galleries were peopled with revelers. The kings and queens of all they surveyed, they taunted the throngs below, waving their beads as though they were precious jewels.

"Oh," said Jane wistfully, "I'd love to do that—have a balcony room on Bourbon Street."

Emma laughed. "Yeah, just reserve them at least a year in advance and be ready to pay top dollar. Corporations and tour groups grab the majority of them."

Above them, a couple of comely coeds were egging on the crowd. The chant from the street, *"Show your tits! Show your tits! Show your tits!"* filled the afternoon air. With a smile, the two complied, to an appreciative roar.

"This is so wild!" cried Jane as her companions laughed.

A group of young men, college students who were not strangers to the various dens of alcohol that lined Bourbon Street, were the most boisterous of the bunch below the balcony. "Hey baby!" cried one of them. "How do you like this?" He turned around and pulled down his shorts.

"Oh—my—gawd!" Marianne laughed.

Mooning the perky pair was not enough, it seemed. The man turned around, his pants and boxers about his knees. "Get a load of *this!*"

Just then, the scene descended into momentary chaos. Figures in blue and green swarmed the inebriated group. Marianne, Jane, and the other girls were confused and disorientated by the sudden noise and movement. A few curse words and the scrum of people broke into two groups, the blue-and-green band moving away while the remainder recovered from the shock.

"Hey! TJ! They've got TJ!" one of the college boys cried.

The second group followed after the first.

"What—what was that?" asked a shaken Jane.

"New Orleans' finest doing their jobs," answered Emma. "Let's go." The girls moved in the opposite direction.

A HISTORY OF MARDI GRAS
A series for the *Loyola VOICE* by Elizabeth Boudreaux

I KNOW YOU GUYS DON'T want to hear this next part. You've all met them. A lot of you have been hassled by them. We've read in the paper about the controversies and corruption and all the other junk. But this part is irrefutable.

The New Orleans Police Department is the best crowd control police in the United States.

Finished screaming? Okay. Now think about this, those of you from Atlanta, Pittsburgh, and Seattle—how would the cops in your town handle what happens during Carnival?

See what I mean?

The truth of the matter is that the NOPD is the reason Mardi Gras goes off as well as it does. They know how to keep tabs on what's going on and to allow the fun to happen without ruining it for all of us. We know people who have had to be detained during the festivities, and we don't feel sorry for them, do we? That's because we KNOW those fools went too far. Stay within the loose rules and everything's cool.

There are several secrets to their success.

One, the NOPD is out in force. They are everywhere. In the Quarter, they have people on almost every block. To do this, they bring in reinforcements. Louisiana State Police, sheriff deputies, and police officers from across the state team up with the local cops to patrol the party areas. They are on every block of Bourbon Street for the duration.

Second, the boys and girls in blue know what to see and what not to see. Mardi Gras is supposed to be crazy, and they know it. So the cops let things go during the last week of Carnival that they wouldn't normally overlook any other time. It's like football referees that "let 'em play" during a big playoff game rather than throw their little yellow flags everywhere. So, if the occasional top goes up, no big deal. Just follow the unofficial rules of Mardi Gras, and everything's cool.

Drink out of plastic or cans. Glass is a huge no-no. Common sense here, folks.

Girls, if you want to make the boys happy, okay. Just don't make it a habit. Too much skin, or too often, will result in a request to shut it down. Leave 'em wanting more.

Guys, life is unfair. You can't give the girls a show of your own. You try to pull down your pants, you will be busted. Trust me.

Girls, you grab *your* pants, you'll get the same result as the boys.

Everybody, keep your hands to yourself. Enjoy with your eyes. If you try to *help* someone put on a show, *you'll* be the show as you're hauled off to the lockup.

Climbing anything is a no-no. Common sense here, again.

Public urination is never okay. You pee—you pay.

If you play it cool, the cops will play it cool. Neat concept, huh?

Third, the NOPD has a not-so secret weapon...

LT. RICHARD FITZWILLIAM, DUE TO his seniority, was assigned to the afternoon shift in the Quarter for Lundi Gras. Usually a quiet time with few incidents, he could take a moment to enjoy himself —as he did now with an inebriated engineering student wearing his Georgia Tech T-shirt.

"Peeing on the street, huh? What's that all about?" The student was sitting on the curb, hands secured behind his back with zip-tie handcuffs while Richard and a state trooper were processing him. "What in the world made you think that was okay?"

"It's Mardi Gras. You know...they said..." the student mumbled, his eyes on his sneakers. They were on a side street between Bourbon and Royal, a couple of squad cars and a paddy wagon making up their command post. Revelers passed on the sidewalk across the street, taking in the impromptu entertainment.

"*They* said? *Who* said? Who said you could whip out your wiener and wiz all over *my* town? Is that what they're teaching you at Georgia Tech?" He turned to his companion. "I thought it was an institution of higher learning, didn't you?"

"Just a shame, Fitz," replied the trooper. "No manners at all."

"Is that what you do in Atlanta? Just piss right in somebody's alley? Is that how they handle things there?"

"No, but I thought—"

Fitzwilliam leaned down, his hand on his knees. "How would you like it next time I'm in Atlanta I just walk in and take a leak right in the middle of your dorm room? How'd you like that?"

Before the student could answer, the radio secured to Richard's shoulder board began squawking. Richard and the trooper listened for a couple of moments.

"Right, I copy. Ready to receive," he radioed back. He turned to his companion. "Get this guy in the wagon." He walked over to a cop in one of the cars. "Incoming," he said through the open window.

A minute later, four patrolmen, two NOPD and two sheriff's deputies from a western Louisiana parish, were frog-walking a young man around the corner, his belt undone and his beads swinging as they walked. One of the NOPD looked nervously over her shoulder.

"What we got?" asked Richard.

The female cop reported. "Drunk, trying to flash a balcony of women. Didn't take to being arrested, and neither did his buddies." Just then, a group of men about college age came around the same corner. There were six of them, all large, one wearing a Penn State sweatshirt. They were shouting and cursing.

Fitzwilliam barked an order into his radio. "Okay," he said to his companions, "back-up's coming. Get him in the wagon now." With that, he moved to the unruly group, holding up his hands. "Okay, guys, party time's over! Y'all just walk on back to the street, and everything's gonna be okay!"

"No way, dude!" cried what seemed to be the leader of the gang. "We want TJ back! He ain't done nothing!" The others agreed loudly.

The patrolmen formed a semi-circle behind Fitzwilliam, their hands on their batons, while the lieutenant tried to reason with the visitors. "Look, guys, he's under arrest for lewd behavior and public drunkenness. You can collect him at the police station in the Quarter after we get through processing him."

"Drunk? Fuck, most of the people out here are wasted. Go arrest them! Stop hassling TJ!"

"Fuckers just wanna screw with the tourists," claimed another student. "Assholes!"

Fitzwilliam stood patiently. "Guys, you *really* don't want to do this."

The students disregarded Fitzwilliam's warning, shouting and psyching themselves up to rush the officers. Fitzwilliam knew he had only moments to decide when to order batons out and defend themselves. *Any second now.*

An instant later, two mounted NOPD galloped from around the corner right at the enraged students. The massive horses, highly trained in crowd work, pinned the group against the wall of a nearby building. As planned, the shock of the huge animals took the fight out of the gang. The intimidated men began falling back towards Bourbon Street, their cries now full of fear of being trampled rather than freeing their friend.

Fitzwilliam sighed in relief before turning to his command. "All right, we're gonna let that bunch go, but I want y'all to keep an eye on them for a while. They'll calm down now. Good work, everybody."

Fitzwilliam strolled over to the mounted police. "I thought y'all would never get here."

"Sorry, Lieutenant, we were a couple of blocks away. Got here as quick as we could without trampling anybody."

Fitzwilliam didn't want to admit how close he was to ordering batons out. "Trail that bunch for me, okay?"

"You got it, Fitz."

Richard returned to the wagon and ordered it to deliver its human cargo to the station.

"Is it always this exciting, Fitz?" drawled the state trooper as the wagon pulled away.

"That? That's nothing. Sometimes we get John Goodman or Dan Aykroyd walking by. Now, *that's* exciting."

Garden District

THE HIGHLIGHT OF THE LUNDI Gras festivities, which included a feast of free live music topped off by a set at Spanish Plaza by The Iguanas, was the first-ever greeting of the king and queen of Zulu by Rex, King of Carnival. Following Rex's arrival by Coast Guard cutter at six o'clock and a fireworks display, the emcee introduced Zulu, prompting the crowd to burst into a chant, *"Zu-lu, Zu-lu, Zu-lu!"*

Rex greeted and thanked Zulu and then offered a special tribute to Louis "Satchmo" Armstrong.

"This is a great moment for Mardi Gras, a great moment for the city of New Orleans," Zulu proclaimed.

The mayor, for his part, called the occasion a "symbolic coming together." Adding to the historical aura was the fact that, as several officials duly noted, this year marked the 300th anniversary of the christening of Pointe du Mardi Gras, a plot of ground some sixty miles south of New Orleans, where a French-Canadian expedition landed on Mardi Gras Day, March 3, 1699.

Addressing his royal subjects at Spanish Plaza, Rex predicted, "Tomorrow is going to be a fabulous day for us all!"

As the music began again, the four ladies hurried to Emma's car for the trip back to the Garden District. Due to traffic, it was almost an hour before they joined the others along the parade route. Harry Connick Jr's Krewe of Orpheus was rolling by.

"Did we miss Sandra Bullock?" asked Jane.

"Afraid so," said Chuck. "But I caught a doubloon for you."

Jane accepted it with a shy smile. "Thank you, Charles."

The look on Jane's face would have sent the old Charles Bingley into orbit. But this was a wiser man—more cautious, more deliberate. He knew he liked Jane Boudreaux a lot, but he was not willing to give his heart away completely. "You're welcome. Did you have fun in the Quarter?"

Jane happily described the girls' adventures to Chuck and William while the parade passed by. Emma watched the scene with a satisfied look as John greeted Marianne.

"Hey, babe, I missed you," he said.

Marianne kissed his cheek. "Me, too. We had a blast."

"Good, I'm glad."

"Yeah, we had so much fun we're gonna have a sleepover tonight."

John did a double take. "What?"

"I'm sorry, baby, but it was Emma's idea. Jane's so excited." At John's disappointed look, she added, "It just came up. Look, we've got to keep Elizabeth's sister entertained. There's plenty of time for us tomorrow." She played with his shirt. "We've got parades all day, there's the party at the house afterwards, and we'll be together the whole time."

John gave her a smile. "Right. We got all day tomorrow. You promise, right?"

"I promise."

Yeah, until something else comes up. John's mind was made up. "Okay, you have fun tonight. Just do me one favor."

"What's that?"

He whispered in her ear. "Don't stay up too late."

"Ooh, sounds like you've got something planned."

John just grinned.

EMMA WAS LAUGHING WITH CATHY and Henry, trying to catch beads. She had backed up to catch a particularly long strand when she collided with something rather firm. Strong arms prevented her from falling.

"Are you okay, Em?"

Emma turned her head to her rescuer. "George? I thought you were working tonight!"

"No, not tonight."

"But you told me!" George helped her regain her feet before he released her. "You said so Friday."

"No, I didn't."

"Yes, you did. You said you were working at the hospital this weekend."

George smiled. "In case you forgot, today's Monday. The weekend ended last night."

Emma had her fists on her hips. "You said you would be here on Tuesday. What was I supposed to think?"

"That I was gonna be here on Tuesday. I didn't say anything about Monday."

"Right!"

"So, am I supposed to leave?"

"No! I mean—arggh, you drive me crazy!"

"I'm sorry. I just decided at the last minute. I didn't know if I was going to be tired or what."

Emma's expression changed. "How tired are you?"

"Not bad. The shootings go down for Carnival. Mostly injured drunks along with the usual mayhem."

Emma took his hand. "Well, I'm happy you're here. Can I get you a beer?"

"Sure, that would be nice."

Emma smiled as she pulled him along with her. "Well, come on with me. I have to tell you 'bout my day."

JOHN WAGUESPACK CLIMBED INTO HIS car after the parade. But instead of turning on the ignition, he used his cell phone.

"Greg? It's John."

"Yeah, whadda ya want?"

"Remember the offer you made me? Something about *setting the mood*?"

"Yeah. Changed your mind?"

"I think we gotta talk."

THE GIRLS WALKED BACK TO the house, singing "Mardi Gras Mambo" badly. They were laughing and carrying on, Abe and George following, hauling chairs and coolers.

"Think you're gonna get any sleep tonight, Abe?"

"Shoot, it gets too bad, I'll put on my robe and join them."

Emma looked over her shoulder. "Oh, no, Papa! We'll be quiet! We promise! Right girls?" That triggered another round of giggles.

Abe chuckled. "What is it that causes perfectly normal females to revert to twelve-year-olds when they get more than three together?"

"Don't know, but if you find out, you'll get rich." At Abe's direction, George placed the ice chest on the front porch.

"I'll see y'all tomorrow. 'Night Abe, ladies. Behave yourself, Emma."

Emma rolled her eyes. "Good night, *Doctor Katz*. Don't forget your Metamucil."

He grinned. "I take it every night. Later."

Emma's musing over George's unexpected appearance was interrupted by Marianne. "Hey! Do we have costumes for tomorrow?"

"I didn't bring anything," confessed Jane.

"Well, we'll just fix that!" announced Emma with a gleam in her eye.

Lafayette

ELIZABETH SCRUNCHED DOWN INTO THE covers of the Breaux's guest bed, thinking about her sister. She hoped she was having fun, but without a cell phone, she didn't want to run up a long-distance bill on the Breaux's telephone to check on her.

I'm being silly. Will and Chuck will take care of her. Hah—Chuck definitely will!

She frowned. *Things are happening awfully fast there. I hope Jane doesn't get hurt. I shouldn't worry. Chuck's a great guy, and Jane's made a friend of Carrie, of all people.*

She sighed. *Jane's got the gift, I guess. Everybody loves Jane. Still —Oh, stop it! You're not Jane's keeper. Besides, William will be there. He'll look out for her.*

That's weird. Why did I just think of Darcy?

She shivered and went to sleep.

Chapter 14

Elizabeth arose early and dressed in jeans and a T-shirt. Mrs. Breaux had a hot breakfast cooking on the stove as she entered the kitchen. She, Chris, and his dad were at the table already enjoying their coffee.

"Well, Elizabeth, how did you sleep? All right, I hope?" asked Mr. Breaux.

She nodded, and the conversation turned to the events of the day.

"After breakfast, I'll put on my costume, and then we'll go over to the assembly area," said Chris. "Once the *capitaine* determines that everyone has arrived, the riders will take off for our first stop. You'll be following in one of the trucks."

"Do you ride, Mr. Breaux?"

"Ah, that was long ago, Elizabeth. These old bones o' mine can't take that no more. The *courir* is for the young men. Me, I just sit and enjoy my beer."

"And you do a good job of that, I can tell you," teased Mrs. Breaux.

Mr. Breaux threw up his hands. "Aii-eee, listen to that! That woman would make you to think I'm a drunkard in the street! *Mas non!*" He leaned over to Elizabeth. "If she wasn't so good looking, I would have throwed her out my house and got me a twenty-year-old."

"And what makes you think you can get a twenty-year-old, old man?"

Mr. Breaux grinned and pulled his wife into his lap. "You right. It would be more trouble than it's worth. Have to break in a new wife—aw no!"

Chris chuckled and his mother swatted his father. "Why'd I marry you, anyway?"

"'Cause I'm the best dancer you ever saw." He grinned at Elizabeth. "Dat's where I met her, an' we fell in love doing the two-step."

"And they go dancing most Saturday nights to this day," added Chris.

Elizabeth looked at the open, happy faces of the Breauxs with a twinge of envy. Her own parents' marriage was not nearly as affectionate.

A HISTORY OF MARDI GRAS
A series for the *Loyola VOICE* by Lizzy Boudreaux

WE ALL KNOW MARDI GRAS or think we do. Standing on the side of the street, screaming for beads, cheering on the bands, and drinking too much—all that is correct for much of the Gulf Coast. Communities from Texas to Florida, from Belle Chase to Shreveport, hold Mardi Gras parades. Heck, even cities as far north as St. Louis try to get into the fun.

But there is nothing like the *Courir de Mardi Gras* held in south central Louisiana. Harking back to ancient Europe, when the peasants were permitted one day a year to beg food from their masters, a hundred or more riders on horseback scour the countryside to gather items for a communal feast.

I can't tell you how much fun I had witnessing this in Mamou, Louisiana. I followed along the twenty-mile route, the hundred-or-so costumed riders leading the way. The *capitaines* wore capes and cowboy hats—a curious combination, to be sure. The riders, the *Mardi Gras*, wore costumes in the traditional colors of the season, purple, gold, and green. Some, like my friend and guide, Chris, wore the traditional high-pointed conical hats called *capuchons*, while others sported the droopy three-cornered hat favored by jesters. We didn't gallop; instead, we serenely processed down the black-top roads in this rural area, the flat fields of rice and sugar cane broken up by the occasional crawfish pond.

We arrived at a farm, and after the *capitaines* received the ceremonial permission from the landowners, the fun began. The *Mardi Gras* lined up in a field, and a dozen chickens were released. The men dashed after the birds, dirt, mud, and feathers flying everywhere—more mud than anything else; it had been raining earlier. Spectators watched gleefully, some hanging from trees, as the birds were finally caught one-by-one. All Chris caught was mud. Tasks completed and hearty *merci beaucoup* later, we were on our way to our next destination.

Along the way, the group sang "La Chanson de Mardi Gras" while musicians on the trucks played along.

> *"Capitaine, Capitaine, voyage ton flag*
> (Captain, Captain, wave your flag)
> *Allons se mettre dessus le chemin.*
> (Let's take to the road.)
> *Capitaine, Capitaine, voyage ton flag*
> (Captain, Captain, wave your flag)
> *Allons aller chez l'autre voisin.*
> (Let's go to the other neighbors.)"

I'm told other towns have either mixed *courirs* or all-female versions. That's fine for the cause of equal rights, but keep me away from horses, please. A flatbed truck was just fine.

Garden District

ABE WEINBERG OPENED HIS FRONT door when he heard the doorbell. There, waiting for him, was a man in hospital garb, an over-sized plastic stethoscope about his neck, sunglasses, and a sign on his chest.

"Oh, hi, George," greeted Abe nonchalantly as though such characters showed up at his door every day. "C'mon in."

"Thanks, Abe. Everyone set for the big day?"

"You're the first here. The girls are still upstairs. They had a late night last…"

Abe's voice trailed off as he noticed George's attention was focused up the stairs. Turning around, he saw Emma gliding down. She was in a form-fitting, knee-length, low-cut, blue halter dress and heels, a short black wig, and a beret. There was a white stain on the upper part of the dress. Her smile was accented with lips painted in a color of red so shocking it could be seen a quarter-mile away.

"Hi, George," she said, pausing a couple of steps from the bottom and leaning on the banister. "You like?"

"You wore Monica Lewinski last year," he reminded her, schooling his face not to show how well he thought the tight dress looked on her.

"It's still in the news. And you're one to talk—Doctor of Love!"

George grinned as he glanced at the sign around his neck. "Oldie but goodie." He turned to Abe. "You costuming?"

"Nah, that's for you young people. I'm going to be an old fart and sit in my folding chair. You want some coffee?"

"I've never turned down a cup of coffee in my life."

"Beer, either," added Emma as she joined them.

"Best kind of beer is free beer, Em." He worked hard to stop his eyes from wandering south. Emma's cleavage was breathtaking. He was *very* glad his scrub trousers were loose fitting.

"Be back in a sec," said Abe. "Y'all wait here for the others."

George turned back to Emma and noticed something he had not seen before. "Nice necklace. New?"

Emma's hand touched the Star of David hanging from a gold chain. "It was my mother's."

George looked deeply into her eyes for a moment. "That's nice. She was a wonderful lady."

"Thank you."

"You know something? I like you with dark hair."

Emma's eyes opened wide at the comment, but before she could respond, the doorbell rang. It took her a second before she broke off the look she was sharing with George to answer it.

"Hi, guys! C'mon in!" Chuck and Will were in polo shirts and jeans. Welcomes were exchanged as they moved over to the living room. "Y'all aren't costuming today? Spoilsports!" Emma turned to George. "I'm glad *somebody* around here knows how to get into the Mardi Gras spirit!"

George smiled to hide his turbulent feelings. Emma looked so damn sexy and innocent at the same time.

"Oh, here they are!" Emma moved to the staircase. A moment later, Marianne bounded down, a Catholic girl's school skirt rolled an inch too short, knee socks, and a white blouse tied around her bare midriff. Her hair was in pigtails and there was black makeup around one eye.

"I don't get it, Mari," said Chuck.

"Britney Spears, silly!"

William grinned. "Aren't you taking *Hit Me Baby One More Time* a bit far?" He gestured at her black eye.

"Correct, Mr. Darcy! You get a gold star!"

Chuck groaned as he slapped his forehead. He suddenly froze as another person came down the stairs. She was in a light-blue leotard with white tights and tutu. White wings trimmed in silver danced at her shoulders while a silver halo floated above her blonde hair. Peeking out from her tresses were two small red horns.

Marianne laughed. "We spent all night making those wings! Doesn't Jane look great?"

Chuck's mouth fell open. "Yeah," he finally managed before getting his second wind. "I like it—a lot. You look great, Jane. You all look great," he added belatedly. Jane blushed as she glanced at a transfixed Chuck Bingley.

George gave his compliments as well, wondering whether Chuck picked up the subtle message in Jane's costume: *There's a devil underneath those wings, buddy. I think you've got the green light.*

The doorbell rang again. This time Raggedy Ann and her beau, Andy, were escorted in.

"Cathy, I *love* those!" screamed Mari.

"You look like an idiot, Tilney," teased George. If Henry colored, no one could tell from all the make-up.

"Nah," said Will, "he never looked better in his life. He certainly has the hair color for it."

"You two cut it out!" cried Emma. "At least somebody knows what Carnival Day's all about!"

"And what am I, chopped liver?" demanded George.

Emma just smiled.

THE GROUP STRAGGLED TO THEIR site along St. Charles Avenue for the parades of Mardi Gras Day; they were joined by John Waguespack and the other AIs. It would still be at least an hour before Zulu would make it there, and everyone was relaxing and watching the various walking clubs go by, waiting for the most famous of them, Pete Fountain's Half-Fast Marching Club.

William was in conversation with his friends when Cathy broke in.

"Chuck, your sister's here." The amused tone in her voice caught everyone's attention. Chuck turned around and his jaw dropped open again.

Carrie was walking hand-in-hand with a tall, dark-haired man in an LSU ball cap. Both were wearing Mardi Gras rugby shirts and jeans.

"Who's that?" asked Henry.

"He looks familiar," responded William.

Jane smiled. "Isn't he the solider Carrie was talking to Saturday?"

"No way," mumbled Chuck as he narrowed his eyes. "Is it?"

Carrie seemed more than a little apprehensive as she and Buford joined the crowd, and the look on her brother's face wasn't helping matters. She made the introductions and stood back, observing the interaction between her one-time obsession, Will Darcy, and her —*whatever* the hell he was—John Buford.

Buford eyed his erstwhile competition. *He's tall—maybe he's got an inch on me—and lean, probably cut. Played ball, obviously. Sharp dresser, got money. I can see why Carrie was interested in him.* Buford stood a little taller. *Well, you had your chance, loser. She's mine.*

Darcy could feel the challenge emanating from the newcomer. He saw a tall, broadly built man, with a full face and light blue eyes. There was something familiar about him. His body said he was an athlete, and his frank gaze spoke of his confidence in his own abilities. His body language told him that he considered Carrie his property. *And you're welcome to her, partner.* Yet, William's ego would not allow him to back down, and he returned the gaze steadily.

William shook Buford's hand, their grips just a bit strong, proving themselves to each other. "Welcome to the party, John."

"Thanks, William." There was a pause. "Play any ball?"

"Quarterback and center field in high school. You?"

"Linebacker and first base. Did some wrestling, too."

"Anything in college?"

"Tried to walk-on with the Tigers, but it didn't work out. Played golf, though."

William smiled. "*That's* where I know you. I was on the Tulane golf team."

Buford smiled in return. "I know. You were damned good."

"I did all right."

Now that the pissing contest was done, the two fell into a relaxed discussion over Baton Rouge area golf courses.

Carrie stood on the outer edges of the conversation, watching. She could not help comparing the two men. Each was very good looking and comfortable in his own skin. Buford was the more gregarious of the two, Darcy saying only a little bit more than what would be considered polite at first. As he warmed to his companion, he relaxed. Still, he was more a listener than a talker. Darcy's eyes were dark while Buford's were light. Darcy's dimples were on either side of his mouth, but were rarely seen. Buford's was right in the middle of his chin for the entire world to see.

Carrie was not an especially intuitive person, but she had a revelation that morning. Darcy was a BMW—finely built and honed, expensive but worth the money, mysterious and deep, yet open to the person willing to put forth the effort to learn how it worked. Buford was a Corvette—plenty of power and polish, everything right in front of you, no tricks, no drama. Take it or leave it.

And he likes me—a lot, she realized. *I think it's time for me to drive domestic for a while.*

Later, after the men exhausted their discussion as to the quality of the local golf establishments, Carrie had a quiet moment with Buford by the ice chest.

"You know," he said as he dug through the offerings, "we should've brought some Cokes and beer. Don't feel right just helping myself." He handed her a Diet Coke.

Carrie shook her head. "Emma would've had your head. Chuck told me not to bring anything; that's her way. She loves entertaining." She changed the subject. "John, could we leave early, say after Rex?"

"Sure," he said. His face showed concern. "You feeling okay?"

"Mmm-hmm, just a little tired. It's time to go home." *And see if this thing can survive without the magic of Mardi Gras.*

He smiled. "Yeah, I wanna get you back on our home turf. How 'bout dinner Saturday night?"

"I'd like that."

"Okay, it's a date." Carrie barked with laughter. "I say something funny?"

"Oh, John," she said, torn between humor and mortification, "after everything that's happened this weekend, it will be our *first date*." She brought her hands to her face to wipe away the tears that had appeared.

Buford wrapped an arm around her dancer's waist. "The first of many, Carrie. Remember, you're my girl."

She bit her lip. "You promise?"

"I promise," he returned softy just before he kissed her.

Ten feet away, Jane saw Chuck's mouth fall open yet again.

ZULU IS SUPPOSED TO ROLL at 8:00 a.m. sharp, but it's usually late. In earlier years, it was intentional as part of Zulu's mission is to parody Mardi Gras itself. Now, as tradition-bound as any other krewe, it just seemed a jinxed organization. It certainly had more than its share of mechanical breakdowns and flat tires.

But Zulu was worth the wait. As the Big Shot rolled into view, the waiting crowd went nuts. Soon the floats and bands were upon them, and the party really began.

All members of Zulu were in blackface—jet-black makeup with exaggerated white lips. It was an intentional jest as almost all members of Zulu are African-American. The politically correct need not apply.

Both Zulu and his queen ride, usually on separate floats, followed by their faithful Soulful Warriors and the rest of the all-male krewe. Zulu also got the lion share of the show bands, which really got the blood going. And of course, there were the coconuts. It was what everybody wanted and hardly anybody got. That didn't stop everyone from trying.

Unlike everyone else, William did not have his hands up, screaming for coconuts. He was concentrating.

Sixth float, left side. Sixth float, left side. Sixth float, left side.

After the fifth float rolled by, William worked his way to the curb. He bided his time, waiting for a high school band to march by, his eyes never leaving the approaching float. Finally, he took a step onto the street and raised his arms. He scanned the riders in black face.

A minute passed by before one of them, a plastic cigar between his teeth, shouted, *"Will Darcy!"*

William waved harder. "Leon!"

Leon Anderson, Assistant Vice President of DGS, pulled the cigar out of his mouth before reaching down for something. A moment later, he lowered a black object wrapped in a plastic bag. As a teenager made a grab for it, he jerked it up again. "No, man, that's for my bud there!" He lowered the precious hand-made Zulu coconut, the Holy Grail of Carnival, into William's waiting hands.

"Thanks, Leon!" William cried as he saluted him.

Anderson smiled wildly. "Party on, William! Mardi Gras!" He waved before he began throwing beads again.

William was soon among his friends again and received a few congratulatory slaps on the back.

"Wow," smiled Jane, "a real Zulu coconut! May I see it?"

William gave a wink to Chuck. "I don't see why not." He handed the prized object to the angel. "It's yours."

It took a moment for William's words to register. Jane blinked and looked up in shock. "Mine? You're giving this to me?"

"We promised your sister we'd show you a good time, Nurse Boudreaux. I hope we gave satisfaction."

Jane gave a most un-Jane-like squeal and kissed Chuck. She then recalled who gave her the coconut and gave William a kiss, too—a much more sedate one. "Thank you, Will! I don't know what to say!"

William rubbed his cheek. "I think you've just said it. Don't you think so, Chuck?"

Chuck just smiled stupidly while Jane, realizing what she had done, blushed prettily.

Emma glanced at George. "Am I good or what?"

"You win, Em."

THE HIGHLIGHT OF MARDI GRAS Day was Rex. The King of Carnival glided along the parade route, regal and imperial, acknowledging his enthusiastic subjects with a wave of his scepter. His two young pages tossed doubloons to the crowd. Float after float followed in his wake, each more elaborate than the prior one, showering the assembled with a booty of throws.

Standing next to Marianne and helping her catch throws, John Waguespack was on his best behavior. "The day turned out pretty good, huh?" he shouted in her ear. "The rain is still holding off."

Marianne was talking to him about one of the bands when John's cell phone rang. "Excuse me a sec, babe." John moved off to the far side of the neutral ground. "Greg?"

"Yeah. What time does everything get started again?"

"The party at the AI House starts after the truck parades, but it won't get really cranked up 'til eight tonight."

"Right."

John glanced around. "You got the stuff?"

"Sure. Don't worry 'bout it. Got it covered. I should be there about ten. Be cool, JW."

"I owe you for this, man."

"Hey, anything for my main man. Later."

John pocketed the cell phone. When he returned to Mari, she asked, "Who was that?"

"Greg. He was checking on when the party at the house gets started."

"He ought to be out here."

"Not his thing, babe."

"But he's missing out on all the fun!" Marianne pouted. "I don't know why you hang out with him. He's so gloomy."

John chuckled. "Greg's the kind of guy that brings joy wherever he goes."

Lafayette

THERE WERE HORDES OF MEDIA attending the Mamou *Courir de Mardi Gras*, and Elizabeth found herself sitting in one of the large tents next to a long-haired young man sporting a goatee.

"Hi, I'm Elizabeth Boudreaux." She extended her hand.

"Hello. My name is Kurt Wanger," he said in a strong German accent.

"Where're you from, Kurt?"

"From Berlin. I write freelance for newspapers there."

"Have you been to America before?"

"Yes, but not to Louisiana." He smiled. "Is very crazy, is it not?"

"Yes it is! Are you enjoying yourself?"

"Yes! Food, music—all very good. Beer—not so good." He held up a Coors.

Elizabeth laughed. "You ought to know about that. So what do you think about all this?"

Kurt looked around. "We have Carnival in Germany—parades, floats. Much like your Mardi Gras in New Orleans. But not like this. Riding horses, gathering food from farmers. Chasing chickens." He laughed. "But it made little sense to me. Why? Why do this? But I have an idea, now. The people were very poor long ago, yes?"

"Yes, that's true."

"And these French people received much prejudice from the English, yes? So this is reenacting a time long ago when the people hid their identities and stole food from the landlords to feed their villages. A protest against the oligarchy, I think."

Elizabeth was agog. "A protest against the oligarchy? What are you talking about? It's just a tradition—like Halloween. You know, trick-or-treating?"

"You mean when American children dress up in costumes to extort candies from their neighbors?"

Elizabeth shook her head. "That's not quite it. Look, have you ever participated in a scavenger hunt?"

"I have heard of this, yes."

She waved her hand at the costumed riders. "That's what this is. They've gathered food for a communal meal, a big pot of gumbo. Everybody's invited, including the people who provided the food. You do know that the *capitaines* get permission before stepping onto private property. Everybody's in on it."

"I knew this, but—"

Elizabeth cut him off. "But you don't get it."

"It is difficult."

"Do you speak French?"

"I have a little French."

She indicated the dancers. "Listen to them. Listen to the words of the song the band is playing. Do you understand it?"

Kurt narrowed his eyes in concentration. "It…it is hard. I do not understand many of the words."

"It's Cajun French. It's a dialect, corrupted over time. You have to understand, we're not French if what you mean is that we have a loyalty to Paris and France and all things French. We're Cajuns, the descendants of the French Acadians who were forced out of Eastern Canada two hundred years ago. We're proud of our French heritage, but that's as far as it goes. We didn't return to France when we were exiled because France didn't want us! Most of the Acadians ended up here, and here we formed our own heritage, our own food, and our own music. Our own view of life, as well."

She looked at the dancers moving about the floor. "They look happy, don't they? But the words to the song are sad. Most Cajun music is depressing ballads about lost loves, unfaithful spouses, and hard luck."

"Like American country music," suggested Kurt.

Elizabeth laughed. "Right! But Cajuns aren't sad. We're not cynics or stoics. We're a basically happy people. Our *joie de vie* is real. We say *laissez les bon temps roule,* 'let the good times roll' because tomorrow we may die. All those people out on the dance floor know that. A storm could come and wipe out all they own. Sickness may strike their families. The car could break down. The bank loan may not come through. So what? Enjoy today! Enjoy the now! You're here, your loved ones are here—what could be better?

"People say that Cajuns are insular, closed, guarded. That's true, but not for the reasons you think. Family is all-important to us. Family is *everything.* Look around at the tables. All those groups are people related to each other. We all have our friends, but we hang out with our family. Marriage between distant cousins is expected. Makes the holidays easier; you don't have to go to more than one Thanksgiving dinner."

She gave the German writer a look. "And before you say anything, just know that marriage between *first* cousins is illegal in Louisiana. Unlike other states, say…" she finished with a grin, "New York."

Garden District

AFTER REX CAME THE ELKS Orleans and Crescent City truck parades, the democratic expression of Mardi Gras in the Big Easy. Huge tractor-trailers, three hundred or more, made their way down St. Charles Avenue. A few of the trucks were as elaborate as any super krewe float. Most, however, were definitely of the backyard variety, built by families and friends, which only added to their charm. Small children tossed beads to teenagers and senior citizens as the trucks rolled ponderously under the oaks. Air horns made their own unique music. It was the mark of the true die-hard Mardi Gras fan to watch each and every one of them.

It would be mid-afternoon before the last truck passed by and the avenue belonged to the street cleaning vehicles. A much-diminished group of revelers made their way to the Weinberg house. Marianne had returned to her dorm, so besides the Weinbergs, only William, Chuck, and George joined Jane in the living room.

"Emma, I'm going upstairs to change and pack," Jane told her host. "I'll be down in a few minutes. Are you going to the party at the AI House?"

"No, I don't think so. But you go ahead."

"Okay, I'll take my own car, then. Be right back!" The now slightly bedraggled angel made her way upstairs.

"You know, I'm going to change, too," announced Emma. "Papa, can I trust you to entertain these fine gents in the meantime?"

"I think I can handle that, princess."

"Oh, you can handle it. I just want you to behave yourself." With a firm look, she followed Jane out of the room.

"Man, I'm beat," complained George.

"Can't take it anymore, old man?" asked Chuck. "You coming to the house?"

George ran a hand threw his thinning hair. "Naw, I think I'll just hang around here." He turned to Abe. "If that's okay with you."

"George, you're always welcome here," Abe assured him. "You, too, Chuck."

Chuck nodded. "Thanks, Mr. Weinberg."

Baton Rouge

BUFORD FOLLOWED CARRIE BACK TO Baton Rouge along I-10. They took her exit and parked on the shoulder just before the entrance to the County Club of Louisiana. Carrie lowered her window as he walked up.

"Thank you for a lovely weekend, John," she told him as he leaned on the car.

Buford knew she wanted to take her leave of him here. They had talked of many things on Monday, including Carrie's complicated relationship with her mother. "Dinner on Saturday—I'll call."

She nodded as they kissed. "Just let me know where to meet you."

"Okay. Any preferences?"

"I can't think right now, John."

"I'm sorry."

"Don't be." Impulsively she added, "Kiss me."

He did and it was more than the sweet peck the first one had been.

"John, I'm scared."

He smiled, but his expression was earnest. "Carrie, just trust me." His smile widened. "Besides, you've got no choice. You're *doomed*. So get the deer-in-the-headlights look off your face."

"How?" she demanded. "How do you *know*?"

He lightly touched her cheek. "Because I'm doomed, too."

Another kiss, a quick one, and he returned to his car. With gravel flying and a toot on the horn, he pulled his Mustang back onto the frontage road towards the nearby Interstate. Carrie watched him until he was out of sight.

A few minutes later, she had parked her Sentra in her driveway and gone into the house through the garage door. Her mother was on the couch in the great room.

"Carrie, is that you?"

"Yeah, Mom, I'm back."

Catherine Bingley rose and kissed her only daughter. "And did you have a nice time?"

Carrie smiled to herself. "I did, Mom."

"Oh, good. I take it William Darcy was there. Any movement on that front?"

"It's the same. No change." Carrie's expression was neutral.

The Widow Bingley frowned. "I'm not one to tell you how to run your life, but for the life of me, I don't understand why you are so hesitant in securing that Darcy boy. I know he's Chuck's best friend and all, but he won't be available forever. You have to exert yourself if you want to get him."

She continued for some time along this vein, and Carrie, with years of experience, knew the best way to deal with it was to stand and pretend to listen.

Finally, after exhausting the subject, Catherine spoke of her son. "How is Chuck, dear?"

It took Carrie a moment to realize her mother had changed the topic of her inquisition. "He's fine, Mom."

"Is he happy, or is he still moping over that Weinberg girl?"

Carrie thought back to her last sight of her brother, laughing with Jane Boudreaux on his shoulders crying out for beads. "He's good. I think he's over Emma."

"Oh, good. That was just a bad situation waiting for him, Carrie. I know it's fashionable to be tolerant and all that, but mark my words: mixed marriages never work, especially between our kind and Jews."

Carrie was almost temped to ask what *our kind* was but held her tongue, knowing it would just lead to another fight. She had not approved of the relationship between Chuck and Emma but not for the crude reasons her mother had. She just didn't think they were suited to each other enough to withstand Catherine Bingley's disapproval. She could write a book on the number of things Catherine Bingley disapproved of.

Mrs. Bingley was still holding court about interracial and interreligious marriages when Carrie's endurance for her mother's hypocrisy ran out. "Mom, excuse me, but I'm awfully tired. I'm going to lie down for a while."

Thus excused, Carrie and her suitcase were soon in her bedroom. She lay down on her bed, hugging a pillow. Her mother's ranting had dredged up her most dreadful memory.

It was mid-morning of a winter's day during her freshman year in high school. She had gotten sick to her stomach and had gone to the nurse's office, but there was no answer at home. Her father was on the road, as usual, so he was out of pocket. Chuck got permission to drive his sister home and return. As they lived on a corner lot in their modest neighborhood, Chuck dropped off his sister at the corner and hurried back to school. The street was deserted save for a Buick parked across the street from their three-bedroom, two-story house.

Carrie was puzzled. The open garage door clearly showed her mother's car. Yet the front door and garage door were locked. Sighing, Carrie dug her key out of her purse and let herself in. Once in the hallway, Carrie called for her mother, announcing herself. She pulled off her coat and placed her book bag in the dining room, her usual place to do homework, and was about to go in search for her mother when she heard a door slam. Catherine Bingley dashed down the stairs in a bathrobe, hair in disarray, calling out for Carrie.

Carrie explained she had come home sick from school and said Chuck had to drive as there was no answer at home. Mrs. Bingley told her she had laid down for a nap and had not heard the phone. Fully apologetic, she escorted her daughter to her room and instructed her to lie quietly and rest. She would check on her soon. She gave her a kiss and closed her door.

Carrie got a glass of water from the Jack-and-Jill bathroom she shared with Chuck and sat down on her bed, drinking it. Her room was directly over the front door, so she heard it close a minute later. She would never know why she felt compelled to stand up and look out her front window. She observed a man she had never seen before walk quickly across the front lawn and cross the street, climb into the Buick, and take off down the road.

She stood stock-still as the implications of what she had just seen became apparent. Carrie may have been just fourteen, but she knew about such things. She knew what this meant.

She barely made it to the bathroom before throwing up the remains of her breakfast into the toilet.

Carrie gripped the pillow tightly to her chest as she tried to drive the images from long ago from her mind. She had told no one of what she saw. Less than a month later, her world was turned upside down again when her father was killed. Carrie had to be the strong one as Chuck was shocked into numbness and her mother fell to pieces. It was on Carrie's shoulder that Catherine cried. For three days, Carrie practically carried her mother through the funeral procedures. Chuck was useless. He could barely function himself.

Catherine soon recovered and sued everybody in sight. She quit her job and moved the family into their present house with the settle-ment money. Carrie never saw the stranger again, and it would be over a year before her mother would date, and then only sporadically. Doctors, lawyers, businessmen, but never *that* man. Her mother never remarried or had a steady boyfriend. It was as though, with the house, Catherine Bingley had gotten all she had ever desired.

She became her mother's confidante, very much against Carrie's wishes. It just wasn't right to hear the things Catherine shared with her about her father. Nothing blatant, just implied: workaholic, distant, unable to fulfill a spouse's needs. Enough was suggested to make Carrie very uncomfortable. Her father was dead. Did her mother have to belittle him?

Tears flowed down Carrie's face as she considered her warring emotions about her mother. How was it possible to love and loathe someone at the same time?

She got out of bed and retrieved her cell phone and Buford's business card out of her purse.

"John? It's Carrie."

"Hey, pretty lady! I was just thinking about you. What's up?"

"Nothing." She had an irresistible urge to hear Buford's voice. "Are you home yet?" She could hear road noises.

"Almost. I've got a few blocks to go."

"I…I want to thank you again for the weekend, and I'm looking forward to Saturday."

There was a sight pause. *"Thank you, Carrie. I can't wait to see you."* Carrie felt a chill run through her as she noted the desire in his voice. *"Decide where you want to go yet?"*

"Any place is fine."

"Japanese?"

"Oh, John, I could just die for some sushi."

"That's my girl. I'll make the reservations and call you later."

"Okay. Call me on the cell phone, all right?"

"Right, got it. 'Til later, babe."

"Bye, Johnny." As she hung up, she smiled at herself. *This must be serious. I'm giving him nicknames, now.*

Chapter 15

Uptown

The after-parade party was in full swing at the chapter house, and a slow song played on the sound system. William leaned against the bar with a bottle of water watching Henry and Cathy dancing in each other's arms to Celine Dion. There was a new sparkle in the frat's Sweetheart's eyes that matched the new accessory on her finger. Cathy's head was on Henry's shoulder, gazing at the diamond engagement ring she had received just an hour before.

No one in the chapter was surprised at the news of their engagement. The two had been inseparable for over a year and a half. Henry and Cathy—it was hard to think of one without the other.

William took a sip of water, suddenly wishing it were something harder. He felt a longing for the kind of deep relationship with another person his parents had, the type Henry and Cathy apparently enjoyed. Something real and strong. Strong enough to last a lifetime.

Had he found her? Was she a beautiful Cajun with the most intriguing eyes he had ever seen? Was it time to stop holding back and find out?

Next week, he promised himself yet again. *I'll start next week.*

Lafayette

It was after nine in the evening before Chris and Elizabeth made their farewells and pulled out of the Breaux's driveway. Elizabeth immediately cracked her seat back to get some sleep.

"Tired, Elizabeth?"

"You betcha. We've been going since six this morning. I'm wasted. But thanks, I've got some great stuff." She looked over. "Oh, wait—how are you? Are you okay? Can you make it?"

Chris grinned. "Sure. I've gotten used to pulling long hours. No problem."

"You get tired, you pull over, all right?"

Chris nodded. "I hope you enjoyed yourself."

Elizabeth smiled, her eyes closed. "Oh, yeah. Your family's great. Though I think they were disappointed I wasn't your girlfriend."

"*C'est la vie.* They should be used to frustration by now."

"Why? How come a great guy like you doesn't have a girlfriend—if you don't mind me asking?"

There was a slight pause. "No, I don't mind, as long as you tell me why *you're* not dating."

"Hey! I'm the reporter! I ask the questions around here!" Both laughed it off before Elizabeth continued. "I'm sorry, Chris, I'm sure it's none of my business."

Chris sighed. "Nah, it's all right. Medical school isn't exactly conducive to romance. The hours suck. Girls don't like being in second place to an organic chemistry text, y'know?"

"Shallow girls might feel that way. I'm sure not all the girls are like that."

Chris said nothing for a moment. "It seems the good ones are taken."

"No, they're not. Just look around." A thought jumped into her mind. *Damn, if it weren't for John, Chris would be perfect for Mari.*

"Maybe," Chris allowed. "How 'bout you? What's your excuse?"

Elizabeth glanced at him and then looked out the passenger window. "I don't know. I'm through with *boys.* I had my fill of them back home. I guess I haven't found a man who's nice and smart and solid yet."

"Hmm...*that* sounds like somebody I know."

"Yeah, who? Besides you." She grinned.

"Me?"

"Yeah, you're definitely an all-around, upright guy."

"It's useful being upright when doing rounds. Hard to see a patient lying down."

Elizabeth playfully slapped his shoulder. "Really, who were you thinking about?"

"William."

Elizabeth was taken aback. "William? Will Darcy?"

Chris chuckled. "If you think *I'm* upright, Will's the paragon of righteous dudes."

She waved him off. "Oh, c'mon! Can you see it? Me and *Darcy*? I seriously doubt I live up to his standards!"

"What do you mean by that?"

Elizabeth hoped the darkness of the cab prevented Chris from seeing the embarrassment on her face. "Let's get real! He's Mr. Tulane! He practically runs the damn school! He does what he wants, when he wants. He can have any woman he wants. Look how he had to fight off Carrie Bingley."

Chris wore a confused frown. "I thought y'all were friends."

"We *are*, it's just—" She sighed. "Chris, you're sweet, but there's no way. Will and I are just friends. And that's the way we like it."

"If you say so."

Elizabeth was relieved the conversation ended. But the damage was done. A pair of devastating dimples floated in her mind's eye as the Silverado hurtled eastward in the night through the Atchafalaya Swamp.

Uptown

MARIANNE WAS USUALLY A HAPPY person, but tonight she was downright giddy. Romance did that to her. Cathy and Henry's announcement had touched her right in her heart. An engagement during Mardi Gras! How romantic!

Marianne's happier outlook also improved her opinion of her own boyfriend. He had done everything she asked. He had been thoughtful, on time, and considerate. He didn't even blink at Marianne's last-minute change of plans the night before. She was in a very forgiving mood, Elizabeth wouldn't be home until after midnight, and John was looking *real* cute.

"Hot, babe?" John asked as they were dancing.

"Oh, yeah." *In more ways than one.* "Let's get something to drink."

The pair left the dance floor for the kitchen, where they ran into Greg Wickham.

"You look like you could use a drink, Mari."

She ignored the slight leer in Greg's voice. Her mind was more agreeably focused on John.

Greg smiled. "I'll getcha something if I can get a dance."

She glanced at John, who just shrugged. "It's a deal," she said.

John walked Marianne to a couch. "You hang out here. I'll be right back." He then followed Greg into a back room while she sat waiting.

"Okay, dude, she'll be ready for you in about ten minutes. Just be cool."

"I can't calm down, man. You sure this will work? It ain't gonna hurt her, right?" John was a nervous wreck.

"Nah, just loosens the inhibitions, dude." He dug something out of his pocket. "Here, go take the edge off."

John took the joint gratefully. "See you in a few, dude." John left out the rear door.

A few moments later, Greg handed a fruity cocktail to Mari. "Here ya go—enjoy."

Marianne took a sip. "Mmm, this is good! What is it?"

"Secret recipe from my bartending days."

"Where's John?"

"He had to take a leak. Wanna dance?"

"Just a minute." Marianne tossed back the remainder of the drink. "There! Let's go."

George and Emma did not go to the party at the AI House. Instead, they spent the evening with Abe, watching TV and unwinding. George was still in his scrubs, but Emma had changed into a T-shirt and jeans.

It was just as well, for George and Emma were reevaluating their relationship—if it could be called one. George found he had fallen into a teasing banter with Emma, and she seemed to like it. He knew he had become more and more attracted to her, and his resistance to her was nearly zero. The last thing he needed was for her still to be in that form-fitting dress.

George sat on one end of the couch, the end nearest Abe in his La-Z-Boy. He tried to keep his attention on the television, but he kept glancing at the attractive girl lounging on the other end of the sofa. Emma leaned against the far armrest, hugging a pillow, her legs drawn up on the couch, her bare toes nearly touching George.

Throughout the evening, George's eyes drank in her lovely, full lips and her tousled, blonde hair. Her Star of David pendant gleamed in the limited light, drawing his gaze to her full breasts, barely contained by her T-shirt. The more he looked at her, the more he realized that somehow Little Em had grown into a beautiful woman. A woman he wanted to know and hold and kiss and—

George shook his head and turned back to the TV.

What George didn't know was that Emma was furtively observing him, too. She had not really noticed what an attractive man her dear friend was until that weekend. She had dismissed the almost kiss of Friday night as her hyperactive imagination, until George showed up unexpectedly Monday evening. New, exciting, and frightening thoughts now invaded her consciousness. She wondered how his kiss would taste, how his arms would feel about her, his hands gliding over her body.

Very un-sisterly thoughts, indeed.

But could she risk their life-long friendship? George had always been there for her: as she was growing up, when her mother died, when her sister married. He was like an older brother. Yet...

But we're not so much brother and sister, are we? No, we aren't —not at all.

Neither was aware of the other's intense interest, and as for Abe, he was oblivious.

JOHN WAS ONE FRUSTRATED GUY. He intended to smoke the joint in the backyard, but he didn't count on Chuck and Elizabeth's sister using the swinging bench to sit and talk. Giving up and returning to the house was out of the question. He was too tense to be any good for Marianne when Greg's little helper kicked in. He needed to level out, and there was nothing like a joint for it. He had to find a new place.

What's there to worry about? She wants to do it. Greg's just helping things along. That stuff ain't going to hurt her. It'll be great. I just gotta relax.

Unfortunately, the street was filled with late night revelers. John walked one block and then another, but was unable to find a quiet place. He was about to chance using somebody's backyard to light up when he saw his opportunity.

Two minutes later, John Waguespack, sophomore marketing major at Tulane University, one of the finest institutions of higher learning in the United States, was crouched down in the rear alley behind a convenience store, hidden from sight by an overflowing, stinking garbage dumpster, nervously smoking marijuana.

ABOUT HALFWAY THROUGH THE DANCE, Greg could see that his concoction was taking effect. Moving quickly before anyone else could notice, he took Marianne by the elbow and maneuvered her into the back hallway. It was momentarily deserted, Greg was happy to see. But John was missing. Greg didn't have time to wonder where the stupid pothead had disappeared. He had only minutes before the girl would be almost unable to walk.

Greg opened the first bedroom door he found. Luck was with him; the room was empty. He got Marianne inside and closed the door. She barely made it to the bed before she passed out, falling face up half on the bed, her feet on the floor.

Greg smiled. Everything was working to plan—except John wasn't there.

Where is he? It don't take that long to take a couple hits off a joint. Shit, fucker's probably smoking the whole damn thing!

He turned to leave and find his missing partner, and his hand was on the doorknob, when he hesitated. He looked over his shoulder at the helpless coed, her short skirt bunched up high on her thighs.

Damn, she's fine! Them legs seem to go on forever! He felt himself getting excited. *I could use a little of that myself.*

People who knew Greg Wickham soon learned there was something *off* about him. They had no idea just how *off* he really was. Absent from his basic make-up were thoughts and feelings most people took for granted—feelings like love, mercy, and compassion. The truth of the matter was that Gregory Anthony Wickham lacked most of his humanity. His urges were animalistic, and his self-control was nil. He saw something he wanted, he took it and dealt with the consequences later. In many ways, people did not exist in his world. They were simply *others—clients—enemies—victims.* He had been that way all his life.

Learned experts argued endlessly about whether people like Wickham were psychopaths or sociopaths. Was it nurture or nature that made such monsters? It was a meaningless exercise. Whatever they were, they were dangerous individuals to be around a young woman when they got horny.

A feral grin formed Greg's features as he stared at Marianne. *Sure, why not? Consider it payment for services rendered.* He locked the door as he reached for the front of his jeans. *She's a little flat on top, but ya don't screw tits. John's fault he gets sloppy seconds. He should've been here.*

AFTER THE TEN O'CLOCK LOCAL news, Abe Weinberg switched the TV set over to the local PBS station and one of the great traditions of Mardi Gras—the Meeting of the Courts.

To the classic sounds of *If Ever I Cease to Love*, the official theme of Carnival, the silver-clad King of Comus and his consort approached the royal dais where Rex and the Queen of Carnival, dressed in gold, awaited them on their thrones. The masked Comus and his un-masked queen paid homage then took their place beside them on their own thrones. Then all four, Rex with his scepter, Comus with his goblet, and their consorts, rose and acknowledged the combined krewes before the dancing commenced. The entire ceremony took about fifteen minutes.

As the broadcast ended, George arose to go home. He took his leave of Abe, who remained seated, but Emma insisted on walking him to the door.

At the threshold, George turned to Emma. "Goodnight, Em."

"'Night, George. Drive safe."

George hesitated, and then turned to open the door. He was halted by Emma's hand on his arm. Turning, he received a peck on his cheek.

"I...I hope you had—"

Emma's words were cut off as George returned her kiss, softly, on her lips. He drew back, his eyes concerned that he had stepped over the line. Emma touched her lips with her fingers, looking at George in wonder.

"Em, I—"

His apology was cut off. Emma reached up and returned the kiss, and the pair savored the moment.

"Emma," George managed, his hands now holding her face, "you know this can change everything."

"Yes."

"Is this what you want?"

"I don't know. Maybe. Do you?"

"I don't want to hurt you."

"Then don't."

George blinked. "Don't what?"

Emma's lips quirked up. "Don't hurt me."

George paused for a moment as he tried to work out Emma's logic. He then smiled. "Only you, Em—only you could have put it that way." He kissed her again, deeper this time. "Don't worry. I'll never hurt you. Never."

JOHN FINISHED HIS JOINT AND got to his feet, the world seeming so much better now. He crept out of his hiding place and walked back to the chapter house, knowing Marianne was waiting for him. He took the front steps two at a time and entered the house, looking for Greg and Marianne. The smile on his face faded as he saw no sign of either.

Confusion was the first emotion that registered, one that was quickly replaced by another—*dread*. Something had happened. Something unplanned. Something *bad*.

John was searching the chapter room for Marianne when he saw a disheveled Greg come out from the back hallway. John quickly cornered him.

"Where were you?" he demanded. "Where's Mari?"

"Waitin' for ya, dude," Greg grinned. "All primed. 'Course, you get leftovers."

John was horrified. "What did you do?"

Greg indicated with his head and led the way down the hallway. John found Marianne passed out on a bed, her clothes in disarray.

"What the fuck?"

"Roofies, dude. Works every time." Greg waved at the girl. "She's ready."

John was furious. Greg had said his concoction would loosen her inhibitions, not knock her out. And he had never said anything about participating! This behavior was something John had never seen before. Greg wasn't defensive or ashamed; he was proud of his crime. He was acting as if he had given John a great gift rather than abusing and raping his girlfriend.

An enraged John intended to begin by cursing out his companion, but the words died in his throat as he saw something far more frightening than Marianne's condition. Greg's eyes were empty; they were cold like a shark. His smile had no humor in it.

John's anger disappeared, replaced by a cold fear that grew rapidly into horror. For the first time, he realized Greg was truly dangerous. Instinctively, he knew his next statement would determine whether he survived the night.

"Ah, thanks, Greg. But I think I ought to get her home." John barked out a fake laugh. "I'm not into necrophilia."

Greg blinked. "Suit yourself, dude."

Swallowing the bile of terror, John carefully pulled up Marianne's panties and repaired her clothing, all under the seamlessly careless gaze of Wickham. John thought furiously. In Greg's mind, he had done his friend a favor. Should Greg become aware that John felt differently, he would be insulted. It was not good for one's health to insult Greg Wickham.

John picked up the unconscious girl. Wordlessly, Greg held the door open for him. John quickly moved down the hallway towards the back door. He had almost reached it when it was opened by William Darcy.

"Hey, John!" Darcy's friendly greeting became an accusation. "John, what's going on? What's wrong with Marianne?"

Waguespack went white as he began stuttering an excuse.

"Marianne needs a doctor!" Darcy declared. "I'm calling for an ambulance."

"No! I mean, thanks, Will, but I've got it handled," John cried. "She's just a little wasted, is all."

Darcy put his arm on John. "Not this time, John! Come on; let's get her into a room."

"Hey!" interjected Wickham. "Don't you listen good? He's got it handled. Get lost, asshole."

Darcy turned on Wickham. "*You* get lost. This isn't your house. Get the hell out of here."

"Fuck you, rich boy! Nobody tells me to get lost!" shouted Wickham. He moved to shove Darcy out of the way. A mistake. Wickham found himself pinned face first against the wall, one arm twisted behind him, Darcy's strong forearm hard against the back of his neck.

"Like I said, this isn't your house," spat Darcy from between his teeth. "Shut your mouth."

John saw his opportunity and fled out the door, carrying Marianne and disregarding Darcy's cries to stop. He kept going to his car, stopping for nothing. In his panic, all he could think of was to get Marianne back to her dorm.

"ALL RIGHT, HE'S GONE," CRIED Wickham. "Lemme go!"

"Not just yet," growled William. "What the hell's going on? What's wrong with Mari?"

The yelling had attracted company. The hallway started to fill up.

"I'll *kill* you, you fucker!" screamed Wickham.

"Will! What's going on?" Henry fought his way through the crowd.

William kept his eyes on the struggling, spiky-haired intruder as he answered. "Something's wrong with Marianne. John just carried her out of here. Wickham here knows something about it."

"John carried her out?"

Before William could answer Henry, Chuck came in through the back door, Jane Boudreaux close behind. "Do y'all know what's wrong with Mari? Will, what the hell is this?"

"Ask Wickham here."

"I'm telling you nothing!" Wickham raged. "I'll let my Glock do my talking!"

William shoved hard, yanking Wickham's arm tighter. "Threaten me again and I'll break your arm," he said in a cold, unemotional tone. His cousin Richard's lessons in self-defense had come in handy.

Chuck grabbed William's shoulder. "Let him go, Will."

William hesitated before releasing Wickham. The blond-haired man twisted around, eying the crowd.

"You got anything to say, Greg?" asked Chuck.

"Nothin'—'cept you'll be seeing me again, rich boy!" He pointed at William.

William crossed his arms, unafraid. "I'm sure my cousin on the NOPD will like to know that, Wickham."

"Yeah, right! Who do you know on the police, asshole?"

"Lt. Fitzwilliam—narcotics."

Wickham blinked, and his entire manner changed. "Look, you just stay outta my way, and I'll stay outta yours." With that, he squeezed between the wall and Chuck and fled the house.

Chuck turned to the others. "Now, will somebody tell me what's going on?"

WICKHAM SLAMMED THE DOOR OF his Camaro, his arm still aching and his mind still steaming. For a moment, he thought about his gun, hidden beneath his car seat.

I'll get my nine and show 'em what happens when you disrespect G-Daddy! Yeah, just light that place up! Watch rich boy crap his drawers afore I bust a cap into him!

A moment's sanity flared like a light in darkness. *'Cept there's a crowd. I can't kill em all. Five-O'll be on my ass before I get five blocks. Maybe later? Wait and jump Darcy some other time?*

Think, asshole! Too many witnesses saw you! Darcy goes down, Fitzwilliam comes after me! Darcy's his cuz? Shit, Fitzwilliam would kill my ass for sure!

As much as he hated it, he had to retreat. Too much business was at stake. His life was at stake.

Okay, so rich boy gets lucky. I'll find some other way of ta-kin' him down.

JOHN MANAGED TO MANEUVER A barely conscious Marianne from his car to her dorm lobby. It was after eleven on Mardi Gras night, so the residents and guests in the lobby barely registered that another coed had over-indulged. No one stopped or even questioned the pair, and John made it to the elevator undisturbed. Minutes later, they were at Marianne's room door.

"Mari, Mari, can you hear me? I need your key. Mari?" John asked.

The girl only mumbled incoherently. With a sigh, John propped Marianne against the wall and looked through her fanny pack. It took only a moment to find her key and another moment to open the door. He half dragged the girl into the room and let her fall onto her bed.

John tossed the key onto a desk and thought of what to do next. An image of her with Greg flashed through his mind, and he wanted to throw up. All thought of making love to Marianne was gone. He *couldn't*, not now, not after what Greg had done.

With a mumbled curse, John reached down and removed Mari-anne's shoes. He positioned her fully on the bed and placed the covers over her. After tucking her in, he almost kissed her forehead before thinking better of it. With a last glance, he let himself out of the room.

PATEL SHOWED CHUCK THE STATE of his room. "I can't believe he used my room! Look at my bed!" The pillows were on the floor and the sheets were twisted and crumpled.

"Who did you say was in the room?"

"John's girlfriend, Marianne, that Wickham character, and John."

Chuck rubbed his tired eyes, his head fuzzy. He wished Darcy was still there, but he had left a few minutes earlier. *Damn, I could use his advice.* "John was in here with Greg and Mari?"

Patel's eyes went wide. "No, I'm wrong!" he remembered. "I saw him in the chapter room most of the party. He must have come in here for only a few minutes before he left with Mari." He looked around. "I gotta clean up this mess."

Chuck sighed. This night had ruined his first real date with Jane Boudreaux. She had left for Hammond right after Wickham disappeared. "Yeah, go ahead. I'm gonna get some sleep. We'll talk more in the morning."

"ALL RIGHT," SAID THE CHIEF of Police as he watched the seconds count down to midnight. "NOW! Start them up!"

A hand signal was made, and the sirens blared as three patrol cars in echelon formation began to move down Bourbon Street. Crews had already removed the barricades that would have prevented this maneuver. The chief and dozens of his people walked behind the cars, Richard Fitzwilliam among them. The chief raised a bullhorn.

"EVERYONE, MARDI GRAS IS OVER. CLEAR THE STREETS. MARDI GRAS IS OVER FOR 1999! PLEASE CLEAR THE STREETS. THE CITY OF NEW ORLEANS THANKS YOU FOR VISITING US. WE HOPE YOU ENJOYED YOUR-SELVES, AND WE HOPE YOU WILL RETURN VERY SOON. CLEAR THE STREETS. MARDI GRAS IS OVER."

Again and again, the chief repeated the request. Behind him, the street cleaners had already begun the process of reclaiming the French Quarter. Fitzwilliam always loved this part—the look on the tourists' faces as they realized the party was over. No more acting the fool in the street. After all, it was midnight.

It was now Ash Wednesday. Lent had begun.

Part Three

Everyone in this good city enjoys the full right to pursue his own inclinations in all reasonable and unreasonable ways.

—*The Daily Picayune*, New Orleans, March 5, 1851

There is a house in New Orleans
they call the Rising Sun.
And it's been the ruin of many a poor boy.
And God, I know I'm one.

"The House of the Rising Sun," traditional folk song

Chapter 16

Elizabeth had gotten up early the next morning to race to Mass. It was Ash Wednesday, the day faithful Catholics received ashes on their forehead as a reminder that the forty days of Lent had just begun. She had gotten in after midnight the night before from Lafayette and was surprised Marianne had beaten her home. So, like a good roomie should, she quietly undressed and went to bed.

She got out of bed early the next morning, showered, dressed quietly so as not to awaken her roommate, and left for Mass. Now it was time for breakfast, and Elizabeth returned to see whether Marianne was up yet. She opened the door to the sight of her, wrapped in a towel and still wet from her shower, sitting on the bed with her head in her hands.

"Rough night, roomie?"

Marianne groaned. "I…I don't feel so good."

Elizabeth started to giggle until she noticed how pale Marianne was. She moved to her side. "Are you all right?"

"I don't know."

Elizabeth felt her damp, cool forehead. "No fever. What happened last night?"

Marianne covered her eyes. "I don't remember." At Elizabeth's exclamation of concern, Marianne continued. "I really didn't have much to drink. Only some soda and punch. The last thing I remember, I was at the AI house, dancing…then, nothing. I got up a few minutes ago. I thought a shower would help, but I don't feel any better."

"How did you get home?"

Marianne shook her head. "I don't remember."

Elizabeth's eyes grew wide. "Oh, Mari, this is bad. Do you think —did somebody slip something in your drink?"

"I don't know," she whispered.

"Oh, my God! We've got to get you to a doctor!"

Marianne picked up her head. "Elizabeth, don't. I'm all right. Nothing happened. I don't need to see anybody."

"Mari, don't be silly—"

"Elizabeth, I mean it." Marianne insisted. "I'm all right."

"But if you've been assaulted—"

Elizabeth was cut off by the telephone. "Hello?"

"Elizabeth? It's John. Is Mari there?"

"Yes, she is. John, what happened last night?"

"Nothing. Let me talk to her."

"Nothing?" Elizabeth cried, anger in her voice. "John, did you hurt her?"

"No, I swear!"

"Is that John?" asked Marianne weakly.

Elizabeth covered the receiver. "Yes." She paused. Her instincts told her Marianne talking to John was a bad idea.

"Let me talk to him." Marianne held out her hand. Against her better judgment, Elizabeth handed over the handset. "John?"

"Mari, how're you feeling?"

"Not so good. I'm real light-headed. And my stomach's upset."

"Aww, man. Did you sleep okay?"

"John, I don't remember much."

"There was some real strong punch at the house last night. I guess it got to you. Just get some sleep. Classes are off today, right?"

"You brought me home?"

"Yeah. I had to dig in your fanny pack to get your key. I tucked you in."

Marianne glanced at Elizabeth's concerned face. "John, Elizabeth thinks there may have been something in my drink. Do you think that's true?"

"No way! AIs don't do that sort of stuff." Marianne remained silent. *"You still there, Mari?"*

"Yes. Thank you, John."

"No problem. You gonna get some rest?"

"Yes, I'm going to stay in today."

"Good. That's the best thing."

"Are you going to come by?"

"Umm, I'm a little busy—"

"Oh."

"Look, babe, I'll be by real soon. I'll call, okay?"

"Okay, John."

"You get some rest. Next time we won't party so hard. Later, babe."

"Bye, John," she said to the dial tone.

"Well?" demanded Elizabeth.

Marianne turned away from her and crawled back into bed. "John said the punch was real strong, and it hit me hard, so he brought me back to the dorm. Look, I'm tired, and I want to go back to sleep, Elizabeth."

"But, you should be checked out by a doctor."

"Elizabeth, I'm okay. Just leave me alone." She pulled the covers over her head.

Elizabeth could do nothing. She left the room for the cafeteria and breakfast, dialing Emma's number as she walked.

Mid-City

WILLIAM HAD JOINED RICHARD, HIS wife, Olivia, and their daughter for Mass at the Fitzwilliam's church and later went to his cousin's house for breakfast. Given Richard's hours the night before, this was more like dinner to the policeman.

"Had a good Mardi Gras, Cuz?" asked Richard.

"It was okay," William admitted, "until last night. We had a situation at the fraternity house."

"What happened?"

William gestured with his head at the women. "Things got a little out of hand, but it's okay."

"Mardi Gras and fraternities—a match made in heaven," was Olivia's sarcastic observation.

"Yeah, I suppose so. We just have to keep non-members out of the house."

"Outsiders causing trouble?" Richard drank his coffee.

"Yeah." William felt a need to unload. As they ate a breakfast of lost bread[2], William continued, "There's this guy in the frat. He's popular with a lot of the younger members, but I have my doubts about him. He keeps bring this Wickham guy around. He's nothing but trouble if you ask me."

Richard nearly spit out his coffee.

"Honey?" cried Olivia, "are you all right?"

"Daddy, are you sick?" asked his daughter, Megan.

Richard coughed into his napkin as William pounded him on the back. "Thanks, Will," he finally managed. "Coffee went down the wrong way. Did you say 'Wickham'?"

"Yeah. Greg Wickham. Do you know him?"

Richard's eyes went wide. "I do. Was he your *situation* last night?"

"He was part of it. I had to throw him out of the house."

Richard turned toward Megan and changed the subject. William picked up on it and played along. Whatever the story was, it was not for a little girl's ears. Once breakfast was done, Megan happily scampered into the den to watch Nick Jr. on TV while the adults continued their previous conversation.

"Tell me what happened last night." Richard's low tone made the hairs on William's neck stand up.

William recounted the events in the back hallway of the AI house from the night before, leaving Marianne's name out. Olivia was a nurse, and her training kicked in.

"Describe how the young lady was behaving."

"She was really out of it—disoriented. I don't think she knew where she was."

"Did she appear drunk?"

William thought for a moment. "No. It seemed different, somehow."

---

2 French toast

Richard looked at his wife. "Rohypnol?"

"It could be."

William felt his concern rising. "What's Rohypnol?"

Richard answered. "It's a date-rape drug, known on the street as Roofies." William went pale as his cousin continued, "Did she go to the hospital?"

"No, John took her home."

"John—he's the frat brother you were talking about? Wickham's friend?"

"Yes, he's also the girl's boyfriend."

Olivia shook her head. "If she took Rohypnol, she has to be examined soon. The drug only lasts in the system for seventy-two hours, at most."

"Yeah, that's one problem," Richard said. "The other is Wickham. You said you roughed him up?"

"I had to defend myself," William pointed out.

"Roofies...Wickham...Greg Wickham..." he mused. "Damn, I should have known it!" He slammed his hand on the table. "Wickham's G-Daddy! Why didn't I see that?" He turned to his cousin. "Will, this Wickham is a bad character. He's a drug dealer. I busted him a few years ago for selling to high school kids. Now he's out working the college crowd. The SOB's dangerous."

"How dangerous?" asked William.

Richard looked into William's eyes. "He might come after you."

"I didn't hit him, Fitz. I only restrained him."

"That won't cut you any slack." Richard ran his hand through his hair. "Okay, I can talk to my captain, beef up patrols. We can always offer you protection."

William protested. "C'mon! You're overreacting."

"Will," Richard shot back, "you may know all this fancy college shit, but I'm the one with a graduate degree in what happens on the street. Guys like Wickham won't come after you with fists. They use guns. It'll be a drive-by shooting. You need protection. If you won't use us, call your dad."

William wasn't usually frightened by anything, but his cousin's words had truly scared him. "All right, I'll call Dad right away."

"What about the girl?" asked Olivia.

William sighed. "I'll try to talk her, try to find out what happened. And if it's what I think, I'll try to convince her to get checked out." At the others' concerned expressions, he continued. "No, I'm not telling you her name. This will be her decision."

Uptown

AN HOUR LATER, WILLIAM WALKED into the lobby of Loyola's Buddig Hall. After talking to his father and agreeing to have an armed guard meet him at his apartment later, William tried to get into touch with Marianne, but there was no answer on her phone. Thinking she might be asleep, he made up his mind to go see her.

After getting their room number from an R.A. on duty, he knocked on their door. It was opened by Emma Weinberg.

"Emma! I didn't expect to see you here." William was taken aback. "Is Mari in?"

"Yes, but she's sleeping."

"Is there any way I can talk to her?"

Emma shook her head, then unlocked the door and stepped into the hallway. "Look, Will, she's in no condition to talk to anybody."

"What do you mean? Is she all right?"

Emma hesitated. "She's sleeping, so I guess that's best for now."

"What's wrong with her?"

"She's just tired."

A little frustrated, William asked, "Is Elizabeth here?"

"She's out." Emma was unusually cold.

William was going to suggest Marianne go to a doctor, but the look on Emma's face told him his advice would not be well received. "Em, can you tell Mari after she wakes up that I came over and wanted to look in on her? And tell her if—if she wants to tell me anything, I'll be happy to come back, or talk to her on the phone, or whatever."

"All right, William. Thanks for coming by." With that, Emma let herself back into the room, closing the door in William's face.

"WILL CAME BY," EMMA SAID softly as Elizabeth let herself into the room.

"He did? What did he say?" Elizabeth tried to hide her warring emotions.

"He wanted to know how Mari was doing."

"I'll bet. What did you tell him?"

"Nothing, like we agreed. He also said that if Mari wanted to say anything about what happened last night, he wanted to know."

"That's why he came over. He's covering the fraternity's ass. If something happened last night, the *last* people Mari should talk to would be anybody in Alpha Iota."

"Yes, I suppose so." Emma was clearly uncomfortable. "Lizzy, are you sure we're doing the right thing? Will's a great guy. I can't believe he'd have anything to do with hurting somebody."

"I don't believe it, either, but…" Elizabeth was reminded of her ex-boyfriend in Thibodaux. He was a great guy, too—until he cheated on her. "Look, this has to be Marianne's decision."

"I suppose you're right." Emma dropped her voice to a whisper. "Still, you don't think *John* did anything, do you?"

Elizabeth looked at their sleeping friend, worry clearly shown on her face. "Lord, I hope not."

"WICKHAM'S A DRUG DEALER? SHIT, I should have known!" cried Chuck as he slid down in his chair. His bedroom in the AI house was filled with the other chapter officers and Darcy. Many of the others were still woozy from drinking the night before.

"Do you think he gave something to Mari?" asked one of the others.

"Roofies or GHB, probably," answered another.

"Knock off the speculation, guys," advised Henry. "Let's deal with the facts here."

"Yeah, the fact that the university is gonna shut us down!" claimed the second man.

"Nobody is going to shut down Alpha Iota, not if we keep our heads." William rejected the idea. "We've got a mess, and we have to clean it up—starting with Waguespack. He's gotta go."

"Will's right," said Chuck with unexpected force. "I gave that sumbitch one chance too many. He's history!"

"But John didn't rape Mari, did he?" asked the first man.

"Don't say that!" barked William. "There was *no rape*—not unless Mari says otherwise! Don't you guys get it? If the story gets out that Mari was attacked last night, true or not, everybody is going to be jumping on her. The school, the press, the cops, lawyers—the whole town. It will make her life a living hell."

"Yeah, and it wouldn't be too good for us, either," said the sergeant-at-arms.

"Right, it's bad for both parties, but that's not what's important." William looked each man in the eye. "Unless Marianne says otherwise, nothing happened. We have to be solid on this. No wild stories, no gossiping, no speculation. Now, if Mari does come forward and says something happened, we cooperate fully without reservation. Let the cards fall where they may. Until then, we protect Mari."

"And the frat," added the sergeant-at-arms.

Henry was clearly troubled. "Will, why not talk to the dean of student affairs? It sounds like it was Wickham, not John, who may have done something."

William thought for a moment. "Normally, I would agree with you, Henry, but my cousin warned me that Wickham's a vindictive bastard. If we turn him in without proof, the cops can't hold him. Nobody can protect us if he comes after us."

"That's why the big goon is in the chapter room?" asked Chuck.

"Yeah, he's my bodyguard. My dad hired him just in case Wickham wants to get even for the way I manhandled him in the back hall."

The others looked at one another as the seriousness of the situation sunk in.

Chuck grew grim. "Okay, I'm calling an emergency chapter meeting tomorrow night—pledges and actives. We'll take care of Waguespack then. We'll also go over the new rules about outsiders at AI parties. They'll be forbidden until further notice."

There was further discussion over the strategy for the meeting in two days' time before the group broke up. As everyone was leaving, Henry had a last word with Chuck.

"I think we're making a big mistake about this, Chuck," he said. "We ought to go to the dean."

Chuck patted his vice-president on the shoulder. "Henry, trust William. He's never let us down before."

Gretna

THAT EVENING, GREG WICKHAM WAS awakened by his cell phone. Glancing at the caller ID first, he answered, "Go ahead."

"Fitz has been talking about you in the squad room. He's after you bad."

A chill ran down Greg's spine. "What's he sayin'?"

"He's figured out your handle. He knows it's you in Green Wave country."

Greg shot up from his bed. "Shit! You were supposed to protect me!"

"I did what I could. I'm callin' you, ain't I—givin' you a heads-up?"

"How'd he find out?"

"Don't know, but I heard somethin' about his cousin gettin' a bodyguard."

"Fuck." Obviously, Darcy *was* Fitzwilliam's cousin and they talked. *Rich boy's got a bodyguard? That didn't take long. Scared of ol' G-Daddy, huh?* "Okay. Thanks. I owe you. The usual at the usual place?"

"That'll do." The line went dead.

Wickham sat and thought. Having a mole in the NOPD Second District was his greatest asset. A little coke went a long way to protecting his operation. The mole had planted misinformation, protecting his identity. They didn't know whether cell phones could be tapped or traced, so they always talked without using names or places.

Now it had paid off again. Five-O was on to him. Time to fold up this operation, at least for a while. *Maybe not—maybe get some*

new go-betweens? Cut into the profit margin, but it would be safer.
I'll think about it.

Meanwhile, how am I gonna get even with rich boy?

Carrolton

"SLOW DOWN!" CRIED TOMMY. HE had come back home after working the day shift at Popeye's to find his roommate filling suitcases.

"No, man. I gotta get outta here," John said as he threw clothes into a duffle bag.

"Tell me what the hell is going on."

John took a breath. "I've got a...situation."

"With Greg?"

John nodded.

"Really bad?"

"Yeah."

Tommy's eyes were wide. "*Jail* bad?"

John nodded again.

"John, go to the police. Cooperate. They'll get Wickham off the street."

"I can't! They'll put me away."

"What the hell did you do?"

"It-it wasn't supposed to hurt anybody! I was just easing my way with Mari."

To John's surprise, Tommy slammed him against the wall. "John, did you hurt Mari?"

"It wasn't me; it was Greg!" He struggled to break Tommy's grip.

A million thoughts went through Tommy's mind, but he asked the most important question. "Is Mari all right?"

"I think so, yeah. I got her back to her room, an' I talked to her this morning. She's okay."

Tommy took a breath. "Did Greg rape her?" As John began weeping, Tommy shook his shirtfront. "Answer me!"

"I don't know! I don't know!"

"All right," he released his friend, "tell me everything."

And so he did, from Greg's offer of *help,* to Marianne's new resistance to John's charms, to the events of the previous night. All the while, Tommy grew more and more depressed and disappointed with his friend. Finally, drained, John sat on his bed.

"Is that *all*?" Tommy asked. "Anything else happen?"

"That's all I know. I swear." John held his face in his hands.

Tommy shook his head. "Dopin' a girl just to get laid? Shit, that's low, John. I really thought better of you."

"I know, I know. I feel real bad about it. I'd make it up to her if I could."

"Then why are you leaving?"

"I'm scared, man. What Greg did—that's against the law. But if I tell the police anything, they'll lock me up 'cause he was doing it for me. And if they don't, Greg'll come after me. You know how crazy he is. He'll kill me."

"The police can offer you protection, John. C'mon, do the right thing."

"No, not yet. I gotta get outta town—gotta think things over."

Tommy, with the newfound insight he gained from being sober, had suspected John was a weak man, but he hadn't realized just how pathetic his friend truly was. Maybe later, when John calmed down, he would listen to reason. "All right. Where're you going?"

"Not to my dad's," John spat. "I gotta aunt in Hattiesburg. She'll put me up."

Tommy got to his feet. There was nothing he could do for now. "All right. Look, I gotta get to my NA meeting. Call me when you get to Hattiesburg."

"Sure. Sure thing, Tommy." He looked up, tears still in his eyes. "You're the best friend I've ever had, Tommy."

"Yeah." He patted his best friend on the shoulder. "I'll always be here for you, dude."

Uptown

MARIANNE WOKE UP WITH A start. Looking around, she saw Elizabeth sleeping in her bed. The clock showed it was after 10:00 p.m.

The pain of the morning was fading, but she still felt sick to her stomach. Grabbing a granola bar on her bedstead, she tore off the wrapper and began to munch her first food of the day. She began to feel a little better until her eyes fell on the pile of clothes on the floor.

Dirty, her mind screamed. *They're dirty!*

Driven by something she barely understood, Marianne got up quietly and placed the items into her laundry basket. She retrieved her purse and keys, made sure her laundry supplies were in the basket, and silently let herself out of the room.

She went to the dorm's laundry room and started the washing machine.

Chapter 17

William and Elizabeth were sitting at a small table in a dark and cozy music club. It was a modern place, a combination of steel and dark wood, very different from the usual, decrepit jazz joint. A single candle illuminated their wine glasses as they listened to the combo on the well-lit stage and watched the figures on the dance floor. William's dark suit paired nicely with the simple black dress that hugged Elizabeth's curves, her neckline just on the naughty side of daring. He was jealous of the pendant that teased her cleavage. Her wavy hair was swept up off her neck, giving her a sophisticated look and allowing her earrings to catch the light. His fingers grazed her hand, and she smiled at the attention, her eyes never leaving the stage.

"Will you dance with me?" he whispered.

She turned her lovely face to his, her smile catching the candlelight. William rose and extended his hand towards the lady. She gently took it and allowed herself to be led to the dance floor, joining three other couples. Without a word, William took her into his arms, and they moved together, slowly swaying to a bluesy saxophone.

As they danced, Elizabeth laid her head upon William's shoulder. William smiled as he breathed in the scent of her—a soft mix of flowers and something he couldn't quite place in her perfume. He could feel the warmth of her body through her thin dress. He ached for her, so he gave into temptation to place a light kiss behind her ear. He felt, more than heard, her chuckle of approval.

She lifted her head to gaze into his face. The multi-colored lights of the stage danced on her soft skin. "How is it," she asked softly with a heart-stopping smile, "that I always seem to be dancing with you?"

"I don't know. I can't speak for you, but as for me, I don't want to dance with anybody else."

Her eyes moved to his lips before returning to look up into his. "Neither do I." Her lips parted as her arms pulled him closer.

As he lowered his mouth to hers, she closed her eyes and tilted her chin.

"And now, back to the Radio Gawds!" blared his clock radio.

William groaned and pounded the pillow as he turned over. This was not his first dream about the lovely Miss Boudreaux, but this one had great potential—and an embarrassing effect upon his anatomy. *Damn, just when it gets to the good part!* William switched off the radio and got out of bed reluctantly to start his day.

Fifteen minutes later, William was well into his morning mile run through Audubon Park. Today was a little different—there was a six-foot, five-inch black man running beside him, a nine-millimeter pistol tucked inside his sweats.

"You do this every morning?" the bodyguard asked as he kept a steady pace.

"Yeah, a mile every day unless it rains."

"Good warm-up, Mr. Darcy," the bodyguard judged.

"Warm up?"

The other man laughed. "Sir, I usually do three miles, but I can take it easy on you."

William glanced at him. "Retired military?"

"Yes, sir. Ten years in the Marine Corps."

"How come you're not a cop?"

"I was a military police officer in the Corps. After I got out, I was given this opportunity. There's more money in the security business if you've got a brain in your head."

"What else do you do, besides protect people?"

"Our firm handles all sectors of security, sir. Investigations, reviewing plant and office security, supply chain and inventory, cargo handling, systems and threats—outside and inside. We've gotten into computer security in a big way, and we're looking at identity theft. Lots of bad guys out there. It keeps us busy."

"I'm surprised Dad was able to hire you on such short notice."

"Sir, DGS is one of our bigger clients. Our firm's been on retainer for years."

William blinked. He realized, for all his studies, there was still a lot about DGS he didn't know. At least business school had taught him that learning was a life-long process. Business changed too quickly for anyone to get comfortable. There was always something new on the horizon—new opportunities and new threats. Learning to deal with the constant change that was international business was the difference between success and failure.

In May, I get my MBA. Then my real advanced studies begin.

ELIZABETH AWOKE AND ROLLED OUT of bed, preparing to dress for class, when she almost tripped on a large object between the two beds.

"Mari, you left your laundry basket in the middle of the floor again," she said automatically before her brain kicked in.

Marianne groaned and turned over. "Huh? What's that?" She saw the basket. "That's funny. I don't remember putting that there."

Elizabeth started. "What do you mean you don't remember? What did you do last night? Don't you remember?"

"No." Marianne's eyes grew wide as she fully came awake. "No, I-I must have done my laundry, Elizabeth, but I just don't remember." She sat up and held her head in her hands. "I don't remember *anything* at all about last night! Oh my God, what's happened to me?"

Elizabeth crossed the room to console her scared roommate. "Have you ever blacked out like this before? Have you ever had trouble remembering?"

"I don't know!" Marianne cried before calming down a bit. "I always remember stuff. This has never happened to me before. I...I don't sleepwalk, do I?"

"No. Marianne, I'm very worried about you. Please, I really think you need to see a doctor."

"I…I guess so."

"Marianne, no more stalling. We're going to the hospital—now."

Garden District

EMMA MET THEM AT THE emergency room at Touro Infirmary. Once admitted, Marianne and her friends were placed in an examination room. The attending physician soon appeared and asked a few questions. Once she heard about Marianne's lack of memory, she shooed the other two girls out of the room and began her examination.

A half hour later, the doctor found Elizabeth and Emma in the waiting room.

"I have to let you both know that I've contacted the police. That's standard procedure in cases like this."

"What did you find?" asked Elizabeth.

The doctor motioned the two to follow her. Outside of Marianne's exam room, she asked the girls to wait while she received Marianne's permission to discuss her case. Marianne agreed, Elizabeth and Emma were invited inside, and the doctor looked at the chart.

"Not much. There was some bruising and definite evidence of sexual activity. No tearing or other damage, though." She sighed. "What raises our concern is Miss Dashwood's lack of memory about what happened Tuesday night. We've taken a blood sample for testing."

"Testing for what?" asked Elizabeth, fearing the answer.

"Rohypnol or GHB. Those are the most common ones."

"You mean date-rape drugs?"

"Yes."

"No, I can't believe it," said Emma. "Nobody at the AI House would use something like that."

"You'd be surprised at what I've seen, miss," responded the doctor dryly. "I wish you had gotten here sooner, Miss Dashwood. The more quickly we see things like this, the better. The police will send someone down to take your statement. I ask you to think carefully about what happened that night. Tell them everything. You never know what will help them."

CHRIS BREAUX HUNG UP THE phone after getting no answer at Marianne's. He couldn't understand how somebody in this day and age didn't own an answering machine, but there wasn't anything he could do about it.

His first impulse when he had heard about the incident at the AI House was to go find John Waguespack and beat him to a pulp. Chris was not a violent man, preferring reason to rage, but when it came to Marianne Dashwood, reason went out the window. His next thought was to go right over to her dorm room, but William convinced him that Emma or Elizabeth would call if there were any news. It took all the self-control he had, but he waited a day before phoning.

Figuring Marianne hadn't answered the phone because she was in class, Chris tried to think the whole thing through. Surely, Marianne wouldn't be in class if anything serious had happened. Therefore, it was reasonable to conclude that, while she may have been intoxicated at the house, it might have been nothing more than that. Still, for Waguespack to get a sweet girl like Marianne so drunk she couldn't walk was too much for Chris.

The knowledge that Waguespack's buddy, Wickham, was a drug dealer deeply troubled Chris, as it raised the possibility that Marianne had gotten intoxicated on something other than wine coolers.

Chris was going to be very interested in tonight's meeting of Alpha Iota. Maybe someone had information about what really happened to Marianne that would allow him to sleep at night. And Waguespack would finally get his.

THE NOPD OFFICER RETURNED TO her Second District office and threw down her note pad. "Well, *that* was a waste of time," she sighed as she sat down.

"False alarm?" asked her partner.

She shook her head. "A Loyola coed's in the emergency room at

Touro, claiming to be a rape victim. Only she's not the one complaining—it's her friends. They're doing all the talking while she just sits there, hardly saying anything. And there's no evidence at all."

"Nothing?"

She opened her notebook. "Blood work—nothing. Clothes —washed. Physical evidence—not much except for some bruising on the insides of her thighs. Could be thumb marks. Signs of sexual intercourse but no tearing. Apparently, the vic's showered since the incident. Witnesses—zip."

She closed the pad. "A big fat nothing. Except the girl has no memory of what happened. She's very sincere about that. She's not acting like somebody who's making this up—somebody who slept with a strange guy and is having second thoughts the next day. She's confused and scared. So, it could be Roofies or something like it."

"Blood work is negative?" her partner asked again.

"Yeah, the initial test was. They're going to run some more. But the way that stuff leaves the system, I don't have much hope." The officer rubbed her eyes. "Her friends ripped me a new one."

"No call for that."

"This brunette gal—her roommate, I think—was all in my face, demanding I search the AI House at Tulane. Like I can get a search warrant with *this*." She gestured at her pad.

"What do her friends say happened?"

"*They* say she was at a Mardi Gras party at the frat house, and *they* say somebody slipped something in her drink. But neither girl was there. Their word is all horseshit."

"Where did you leave it with them?"

"The usual—gave 'em my card and told them to contact me in case she remembers something more later. But unless the vic makes a complaint, I can't do anything without more evidence."

The male officer glanced at the wall clock. "It's lunchtime—wanna grab a po'boy?"

"Give me fifteen minutes to type up this report first."

ELIZABETH WAS STILL STEAMED BY the time the girls got back to the dorm. "Can you *believe* that cop? 'Protect and Serve'—hah! Protect who—the rapists?"

Marianne lay in her bed, holding her head. "Lizzy, please. I've got a headache."

Elizabeth ranted on, heedless of her roommate's plea. "How are we going to protect ourselves if the police won't help us?"

Emma glanced at Mari. "Elizabeth…" She gestured at the girl. "I'm sorry, Mari. Can I get you something? A Coke? Would that make you feel better?"

"No, just some quiet, please." She reached up to take Elizabeth's hand. "I appreciate everything you've done, but I just want to rest for now. Can we talk about something else?"

The other two agreed and sat down to chat softly about upcoming class work. However, Elizabeth's anger was only on hiatus. She planned to visit a certain fraternity house that night.

William and Chuck—they'll tell me what's going on. They'll fill me in. In a couple of hours, I'll know who's behind this!

DARKNESS HAD FALLEN ON BROADWAY on this cold Thursday evening. Everything looked normal at the Alpha Iota House except for a large man sitting in a chair on the porch, looking up and down the street. Inside the building, it was anything but ordinary.

The chairs again were set in a large circle in the chapter room, but there were more people this time. The pledges had joined their active brothers, and what they heard chilled them. Brother Tommy Bertram, inactive, was relaying his conversation of Wednesday with John Waguespack.

"…and by the time I got back from my NA meeting, John had left. I got a call on the answering machine from him last night, saying he was in Mississippi. That's the last I heard from him."

Charles Bingley leaned forward. "Thanks, Tommy. I appreciate your honesty. I know this was hard for you." As there were pledges present, the meeting was held in an informal manner.

Tommy sighed. "For all his faults, John has been a good friend to me."

Henry spoke up. "Has anyone heard from Marianne?" There was no answer.

"So we still don't know for sure," Chuck pointed out. "But it does look bad. Well, it's time to bring up what to do about Waguespack."

William rose from his chair. "Chuck, may I have the floor?" Chuck waved his permission. William walked to the center of the circle as though he owned the building. He planted his feet and slowly scanned the room.

"Brothers," he began, "this is no ordinary incident. This is a crisis, one that must be handled carefully and honestly. Last Tuesday, one of our brothers, John Waguespack, betrayed everything this chapter stands for: honor, brotherhood, and respect for women. He has lied to us, brought a worthless outsider into our house, and at the very least, treated a young lady in a despicable manner. We do not know what happened in Nick's room that night. We suspect, but we do not know.

"However, at the very least, Waguespack has acted in a manner unbecoming a member of Alpha Iota Fraternity. He has violated his initiation oath. We know that the purpose of tonight's meeting is to decide whether to expel John Waguespack from our brotherhood—a heavy decision but one that must be carried out for the good of all."

He looked around again. "I know you will all put aside your personal feeling and do what is right. I have no fears there. Alpha Iota has taught all of you well. You pledges, only weeks from your initiation into this fraternity, now know what I mean. You know how important AI is to all of us. As a doctor cuts off a gangrenous limb to save the body, so must we forever disassociate ourselves from anyone who so betrays our core values.

"But let me make myself perfectly clear: this chapter can go to hell if we betray the friendship and trust of a wonderful young lady!"

The room was completely silent as William stalked the floor. Every eye was on him. George Katz, in his position as alumni advisor, sat next to Chris Breaux and marveled at how William held the room in the palm of his hand. He could easily see his friend take command of a corporate boardroom or the floor of Congress if he so decided. *My God, he could be President if he ever went into politics!*

William continued. "We all know the state of the media these days—scandal upon scandal. The facts mean nothing, only how salacious the rumors are. People's lives are destroyed every day.

"Now, if you're thinking I'm talking about *our* reputation, about *our* lives, you're wrong. We have a duty, as members of Alpha Iota, to honor our guests, especially our female guests."

William pointed to the chapter's charter, hanging on the wall. "It's in our motto: *'God First, Then the Ladies.'* Guys, this is not a joke. This is who we are. If we can't live up to the standards set by the honored founders of our brotherhood, then we are not worthy to call ourselves Alpha Iotas! Not a brick of this house should remain standing if it comes at the expense of Marianne Dashwood's reputation!"

"Do we have a tape recorder?" Elizabeth asked her editor.

Justin was lounging at his computer console. "Yeah, right in that storage cabinet." As Elizabeth retrieved it, he asked, "Got a hot story?"

"I think so," she said as she checked the batteries, "and I want to get it on the record."

"What's the story?"

"A friend of mine was assaulted at a fraternity house on Mardi Gras."

Justin sat up straight. "Whoa! Which one?"

"AI at Tulane."

"You're going over there now?"

"Yes."

Justin scrambled to his feet. "I'll grab a camera and go with you."

For fifteen minutes, William held the members of Alpha Iota spellbound as he laid out his reasons for suppressing rumors about the events of Mardi Gras night. Finally finished, there was only one member not persuaded.

"Will," said Henry, "you make some very good points. But I don't see why we shouldn't bring this to the dean of students' attention."

William nodded sadly at his friend. "I wish we could, Henry —that we could trust in the system. Look, if this were an internal Tulane issue, I would agree with you. I know the administration would investigate effectively and respect everyone's rights and privacy. But this goes beyond the walls of the university. Marianne's from Loyola, and Wickham's not a student at all. That means not only will Loyola be involved but so will the NOPD. Can we count on them to keep it quiet? Can we take the chance that Marianne's name wouldn't end up on the front page of the newspaper?"

"Wouldn't the NOPD be called in if Mari was from here, with Wickham being involved?"

"I spoke carelessly. I'm sure the police would handle this professionally. It's the situation between Tulane and Loyola that concerns me. They are two separate institutions. Everything is done at arms' length. That's just the way it is. I don't believe this matter could be handled in any way but publicly."

"Do you have anything else, Will?" asked Chuck.

"No. Thank you, Chuck." William took his seat.

"Does anyone else have anything to add to the discussion? No? Very well, we'll begin." Chuck addressed the room. "We will all be voting on this. Pledges, as you are not yet full members of the fraternity, you will be taken to the back to vote while the actives will vote according to the laws of Alpha Iota. Your vote, like ours, will be by secret ballot. Please go with the sergeant-at-arms." Chuck looked at the man. "Take them to my room."

There was a knock on the door. The sergeant-at-arms gave Chuck a glance before going to answer it. Everyone in the room kept silent until he returned a moment later.

"Will," he said, "your bodyguard says there's somebody here to see you."

"You go ahead," said Chuck. "Alumni can't vote anyway. You either, Tommy—you're still inactive. Pledges, you're dismissed."

William walked through the front hall and opened the door. The bodyguard was right next to it, the bulge from his shoulder holster apparent under his half-unzipped bomber jacket. "What is it?"

He gestured with his head. "This lady wants to talk to you."

William looked over and saw Elizabeth Boudreaux standing in the front yard with a young man. "Okay, I'll handle this," William told the guard. Carefully closing the door behind him, he approached the two, the guard close behind him.

Elizabeth spoke angrily before he could descend the stairs. "Will, I want to know what's going on around here."

William looked over at the stranger. "We're kind of busy at the moment. Can I talk to you later, Elizabeth?"

"No! I want answers now." The scene was filled with the flash of Justin's camera.

"What the hell?" cried William. "What is this?"

"Darcy, what happened here Tuesday night? Tell me!"

William felt his temper rise. "Are you asking me as a friend or as a reporter?"

"Both!"

"C'mon, Darcy, spill," the photographer added, "or are you gonna hide behind your armed guard? Why do you need him? Is he giving the chapter time to dispose of the evidence?"

"Who the hell are you?" William barked.

"Justin Middleton, editor of the *Loyola VOICE*." He took another picture.

There was a low voice from behind William's shoulder. "Want me to take care of this?"

"No," William answered the guard. He grimly returned his attention to the two in front of him. If they wanted to play this formally, so be it. "We have nothing to say to the press at this time. If, at any time in the future we have something to announce, we will be sure to send you a press release." William stared intently at Elizabeth, trying to speak with his eyes. *Elizabeth, please trust me!*

"I see you passed your corporate Cover-Your-Ass class, Darcy," taunted Justin. It was obvious he was going to use every trick he knew to get William to drop his defenses and say something printable. He had no way of knowing that was the least effective way of dealing with the man before him. When William became offended or uncomfortable, he became less talkative, not more.

William's face lost all expression as he pulled himself to his full height. "You are on private property. I must ask you to leave—now." He turned and walked up the steps to the house.

"Darcy!" cried Elizabeth.

He paused. Her voice was accusatory. William turned and tried to control the raging emotions flaring within him. Affection warred with disappointment. *Damn it, Elizabeth, trust me!* His face betrayed him, showing only his anger, not his confusion.

The guard stepped forward. "Okay, folks, time to go."

"Or what—you'll shoot us?" Justin jeered.

The guard sighed and pulled out a cell phone. "You can leave now, or you can have campus police escort you away."

"Freedom of the press!" cried Justin.

The bodyguard flipped open the phone. "Want to tell that to the cops?"

Elizabeth grabbed her editor's arm. "C'mon, Justin, we're not going to get any answers here." The two got into Middleton's car and drove away. She never saw William's hard expression collapse into melancholy.

A THOUGHTFUL AND DEPRESSED WILLIAM returned to the emptying chapter room. Chris reported that the meeting was over. They had ejected Waguespack and agreed to follow William's plan of action. He then asked who was at the door.

"Elizabeth and the editor from that online paper she writes for."

Chris whistled. "What did you say?"

"What *could* I say? We've got to talk with Chuck."

A few minutes later, the two of them met with Chuck in his bedroom with Henry and George Katz. William briefed them on the events outside.

"Oh, man," groaned Chuck, "we may end up in the paper anyway."

William shook his head. "No, I gave them nothing."

Henry snorted. "Nobody reads that online joke, anyway."

Chris asked, "Did Elizabeth say anything about Mari?"

"No, I didn't want to ask about her, either, not in front of that Middleton character."

"You know, I disagreed with you on this secrecy bit," admitted Henry, "but now it's decided, we've got to stick with it."

"You're right," agreed George. "This isn't the way I would've handled it, but we've got to show a united front."

William turned to Chuck. "Did Patel wash his sheets?"

"Nope, not yet. He still has 'em in his closet."

"Keep 'em there for a while, just in case."

"In case what?"

William closed his eyes. "In case we're wrong."

"He blew you off?" cried Emma. "I don't believe it."

Elizabeth shot back, "He did, Emma. I thought I knew Darcy, but it turns out I didn't." She glanced around the dorm lobby, making sure no one could overhear. "We've got to think the worst. Alpha Iota is hiding something. They know what happened to Marianne. I can feel it. I've got to find out what it is. I'm not going to let them get away with this."

"But, they're our friends!"

"This is more important than friendship. We've got to put everything aside. This is for Marianne, and justice for all women who have been victims. Are you with me?"

Emma bit her lip. "I'll help you any way I can."

Carrolton

Tommy parked his car in front of his apartment. As he locked his car door, he heard somebody call his name.

"What do you want, Greg?"

Wickham was leaning on the side of the building, smoking a cigarette. "I'm lookin' for JW. You know where I can find him?"

"John's not here." Tommy was both pissed at and scared of the drug dealer.

"I *know* that—I'm askin' ya where he *is*. He ain't answerin' his cell."

"I don't know. He took off."

Wickham cocked his head. "Why'd he do that?"

"Why do you think? Look, I don't know what happened on Tuesday night, but John's in a world of trouble. Hell, he's just got kicked out of AI. He's left town, and he didn't tell me where he was going. That's all I know."

"Shit." Wickham dropped the butt on the sidewalk. "Look, you hear from him, tell him I'm lookin' for him, okay?"

"I'll pass it along," Tommy said in a neutral voice. He watched Wickham return to his Camaro and drive away. Tommy then let himself into his apartment. He noticed the answering machine blinking. As he hoped, John had left his aunt's phone number.

"John? It's Tommy."

"Thanks for calling me, man. How are things?"

"Not good. John, I hate to tell you this. The chapter met tonight and—"

"And they kicked me out?"

"Yeah. I'm real sorry, man."

"Shit. Can't say I'm surprised. Anything else? Anything from Marianne?"

"No, but Wickham stopped by."

"Oh crap."

"Don't worry, I didn't tell him anything."

"Thanks, buddy. You watch out for him, you hear me? He's crazy."

"I know. John, when are you coming back?"

"I don't know. I haven't decided yet."

"You can go to the police."

"Yeah, maybe. Like I said, I'll think about it."

"What about the rent?"

"Oh, yeah. Umm…we're paid up through March, I think."

"Yeah." As usual, John was blowing off something important. "John, look, if you're not coming back soon, I gotta do something about the apartment."

"Uh, can't you sublet?"

"No, the lease says we can't. But I've got another idea. I've met some people through NA who might come through—stay here for a while."

"Female?"

Tommy tried to hide a smile. "Yeah."

John laughed. *"Go for it, dude."*

"It's not like that, John." But Tommy knew it could be. Sarah was like nobody he had ever met. Having gone through the same hell, they knew each other almost immediately. They were friends, and maybe, someday, they would be more. *One day at a time.*

"Sure it ain't. Umm...I gotta go. I'll call ya soon. Maybe get down there an' meet your new lady-friend, okay?"

"Okay. Take care, John."

"You too, buddy."

Tommy sighed as he hung up. John wasn't fooling anybody. He wasn't coming back, at least while Greg was still in the picture. John was terrified of him, and Tommy couldn't blame him. Until Wickham was taken care of, John would never return and face his demons.

Tommy only wished he knew how to help.

Chapter 18

Friday, February 19: Uptown

Emma was uneasy as she walked across the quad in the center of the Tulane campus on her way to her morning class. She was still mulling over the events of the day before and couldn't decide what troubled her more: the interview with the police officer or Elizabeth's anger after her confrontation with William.

Lost in thought, she didn't hear her name being called at first. She turned and saw a spiky-haired young man half running toward her.

"Emma! Emma, wait up!"

She stopped and waited impatiently for Wickham to reach her.

"What is it, Greg?" The last thing she needed was to talk to John's stupid stoner buddy.

"Hey, there. On your way to class?"

"Yes, can I help you?"

"Umm…do you know where I can find Elizabeth?"

Emma rolled her eyes. "Greg, Elizabeth's a Loyola student." She pointed over his shoulder. "Loyola's thataway."

Greg chuckled. "My bad. I knew that. I've been lookin' for her. Got somethin' to tell her."

Emma's look brightened. Maybe he had some information about Tuesday night. "She usually hangs out at the library." She paused. "Is it important?"

Greg winked. "Oh, yeah."

It took almost a half hour for Greg to find the Loyola library. Once inside, it didn't take long to spot the brunette, sitting by herself at a table and scribbling on a notepad. Greg made sure Elizabeth was alone before he approached her.

"Hey, Lizzy."

Elizabeth looked up. "Greg? What are you doing here?"

"I was looking for you. You work for some newspaper, don't cha?"

"Yes."

"Good. I've got something important to tell you." He looked around, beginning his rehearsed routine.

"What? What do you have to tell me?"

"Umm…can we go somewhere quiet-like? Don't want the wrong people to overhear." As he expected, that got her attention.

"Okay, there are some small meeting rooms over there. We can go grab one." She got up and led the way. Greg closed the door behind him and took a seat across the small table from her.

"Okay, Greg, what's so important?"

Greg looked at his hands. "You know the AIs kicked John Waguespack out?"

"No. Why did they do that?" She pulled out a piece of paper.

"Wait, Liz, this has gotta be off the record."

"Why?"

"You'll see why after I tell ya. You can't use my name, okay?" Greg was channeling every stupid newspaper movie he had ever seen.

"You sound like you're scared."

"I am scared."

Elizabeth's eyes grew wide. "Why?"

"First your promise—you don't use my name."

"All right, I'll keep my source confidential. Now, tell me, why was John kicked out of AI?"

"'Cause they're using him as a scapegoat 'cause of what happened to your friend Marianne."

"What happened to Marianne?"

Greg looked around as though someone could overhear. "Look, I heard somethin' got slipped into her drink, an' some of the guys had fun with her in one o' the back bedrooms." He allowed his statement to sink in before continuing, "An' it ain't the first time somethin' like that happened over there, if you know what I mean."

"Who? Who did this?"

"I don't know, but I know it wasn't JW."

"How do you know that?"

He expected she would ask this question and was ready for it. "Uhh, you see, he was—you're gonna keep this quiet, right?"

She nodded.

"He was smokin' a joint with me at the time." Greg's phony guilt sounded dumb, but he hoped Elizabeth would buy it.

"Then why did they throw John out?"

"You know Will Darcy, right?" he said in a low voice.

"Yes, I do." She frowned. "You're not saying William attacked Marianne, are you? Because if you are, I don't believe for a—"

Greg held up his hands. "Wait, wait. I ain't sayin' Darcy did it. I'm sayin' Darcy's the one who's coverin' it up."

"Why would he do that?"

"Look, he's supposed to be a big wig at his daddy's firm once he gets outta college, right? Well, he can't have some scandal screw that up. Maybe prevent him from gettin' the job. So he an' his daddy are puttin' a blanket on this. That's the way it is with these rich boys. Party hard an' have somebody else clean up the mess. You know his daddy got him some muscle?"

"Muscle? You mean the bodyguard?" she said in a shaky voice. "I've seen him."

Greg laughed. He had seen Darcy jogging in the park with some big black dude and made a guess. "Yeah, they call 'em bodyguards sometimes. Cleanup crew is what they really are. Make sure little things like this are swept under the rug, an' *convince* everybody to keep quiet about it."

"How do you know all this?"

"'Cause I was there." He needed a bit of truth for bait so the dumb skirt would buy the story. He had to be careful now.

"You said you weren't."

"JW an' me got there after it was all over with. John freaked out when he saw Mari all by herself in a bedroom. He picked her up to get her outta there, but as we were leaving, Darcy tried to stop us. I had to mix it up a little with him so John could get her out. Darcy didn't like that."

"Why would William want to stop John from leaving with Mari?"

"Somethin' about lettin' them handle things, but JW wasn't havin' any of it. That's why they got rid o' him. I hear they were gonna get JW kicked outta Tulane, too. That's why he took off. He don't trust them not to make him the patsy for the chapter."

Elizabeth seemed shaken. "What did they put in Marianne's drink?"

Greg laughed. "Who knows? Frat houses are fulla shit like that."

"How do you know?"

"My dealer does a lot o' business at Tulane."

"Greg, I know a lot of the guys in the frat. I'm having a hard time believing they would do anything like this."

Greg nodded as he prepared to administer the *coup de grâce*. "Like I said, maybe some o' the guys there wouldn't do that sorta shit, but that brotherhood stuff is like all powerful, ya know? You gotta do what's best for the frat. Everybody else is outsiders. If a guy gives 'em too much trouble, they handle it inside. Ya never hear about it. Girl gets into trouble, too bad. She should've been more careful. Got to keep up the image.

"An' don't forget, a lot of these guys wanna get into politics. You think they want somethin' like this hangin' around to screw them twenty years from now? How are they gonna make their money then? Babe, you gotta understand, it's all about the Benjamins. These guys could make millions, and their folks know it. You think they're gonna let a little thing like this get in their way? That's why Darcy's old man is after me."

Greg knew he had done all he could do. So, in a final act of theater, he got to his feet. "Remember, keep my name outta this or, well, it could get real ugly for me."

"You don't mean William would—!"

Wickham successfully hid the glee he was feeling. "Nah, it's his old man I'm worried about." He lowered his voice to a near whisper. "You don't think anybody involved in the docks ain't got some Mafia connections, do ya? You look at 'em funny, they'll break your legs. They don't play games at the docks, Lizzy."

Elizabeth's big, wide eyes told Greg she had believed every lie he uttered. "Don't worry, Greg, I'll protect you."

"Thanks, Lizzy." He tapped her notepad. "You go get 'em, huh?" With that, he left the room.

Once Wickham exited the library, he dropped his fearful act and strode confidently across campus towards his parked car.

Damn, I really did a number on rich boy! That stupid cow swallowed what I fed her like a twenty-dollar whore. Now, if that bitch does her job, Darcy's ass will be in a crack, an' there's nothin' Fitzwilliam can do about it. That'll teach him to fuck with G-Daddy!

Hell, maybe JW will be able to come back and bird dog for me again. Ha! I'm fuckin' king of th' world!

ELIZABETH RETURNED TO HER DORM room, planning to call her advisor. Greg's story had greatly disturbed her, and she wanted her opinion. As she was looking through her campus directory for Dr. Jennings's number, the phone rang. To her surprise, it was John Waguespack, asking for Marianne.

"John! Where are you?"

"I can't say right now, Elizabeth. Is Mari there?"

"No, she's at class. John, look, I've talked to Greg, and he told me about Tuesday night. Is what he said true?"

There was a pause. *"What did Greg say?"*

Elizabeth gave him a condensed version of Wickham's story. "Were you and Greg outside smoking while Mari was in the house?"

"Yeah, I was doing some weed outside."

"And when you found Mari, how…how did you find her?"

"Her clothes were, you know, messed up."

"And when you were leaving, did anything happen?"

"Umm…Will and a couple of guys tried to stop me. Greg ran interference."

The world dropped from under Elizabeth's feet. "Why can't you tell me where you are? Why don't you come forward and say what you know?"

"Elizabeth, did Marianne say anything?"

"She's having a hard time remembering. You can help!"

"Elizabeth, I wish I could, but it might be best that I don't."

"Why? The AIs can't do anything else to you! Didn't they expel you?"

"Yeah, they did. I heard that last night. But, it might be bad for my health, you know?"

"My God, John! Has someone threatened you?"

"No! Look, forget I said that. I'll try to come back as soon as I can."

Elizabeth could hear the fear in his voice. "When?"

"Soon."

"John, please tell me where you are. At least, give me your phone number."

"I'll call. Trust me; this is best. This is safest. Give Mari my love, okay?"

"I will. Goodbye." Elizabeth looked at the handset as she set it down.

John was definitely scared. Terrified. Of what? Darcy's bodyguard? Of course! He's been told to be quiet! I can't believe I've been so wrong about Darcy. He's ruthless—or at least his father is if what Greg said was true. It must be! I've got to stop him!

Elizabeth reached for the phone again.

Hattiesburg, Mississippi

JOHN WAGUESPACK TOSSED THE HANDSET on the bed beside him and put his hands behind his head. He looked up at the ceiling fan in his aunt's guest bedroom, trying to decide his next move.

The phone call with Elizabeth was both good news and bad. Marianne apparently had no memory of what happened at the AI house. That was good. If she suffered no damage, there would be no police involved. Greg couldn't get mad at him. He was safe—for now.

But hearing Greg had been in contact with Elizabeth made John very nervous. He shouldn't have admitted he was scared of Greg, and he hoped Elizabeth would forget about it. Elizabeth might become an unwitting source of information for Wickham. John couldn't take the chance that Wickham might track him down through her. By bailing on the drug dealer, he had broken a promise. Greg would get pissed off, but John hoped that was the end of it. No sense taking chances, though. John planned to have a long and prosperous life.

That meant his time in New Orleans was over. Time to start again. He sighed as he picked up the University of Southern Mississippi handbook his aunt had acquired for him and began to look over the course listings.

Fortunately for him, his aunt believed his story of witnessing a crime by some members of the NOPD. She had been biased against the Crescent City for as long as he had known her and had no hesitation in thinking the worst of that "den of sin." She had promised to support him in school now that his father had effectively disowned him. His mom tried to intercede, but Dad made it clear that the bank was closed.

Auntie never did like Dad, he thought. It was easy to play one against the other.

He would miss Marianne, of course, but there was no way he could ever move forward with her now, even if something eventually happened to Wickham. It was way too dangerous. She might start remembering. Best to write that off as bad luck.

Damn, everything happens to me!

He turned his attention back to the course listings. *Hmm, casino management? That sounds cool.*

Uptown

ELIZABETH SAT DOWN WITH JUSTIN Middleton and her faculty advisor, Dr. Jennings. "I know when I took the assignment I was supposed to write an article about co-ed safety in the Uptown area."

"That's correct, Elizabeth," said Dr. Jennings.

"Well, I've got a story that speaks to that." She handed each an outline. Both read with increasing interest.

"You've got witnesses to this?" asked the professor.

"Yes, ma'am."

"Dr. Jennings," injected Justin, "I was with Elizabeth last night at the AI house. I've got photos."

"Very good. Elizabeth, when can you have a story ready?"

"I can have it to you by five," she said as she got to her feet.

"Good. This is excellent, Elizabeth. It's terrible what happened to this girl, of course, but it gives us a great chance to prove what New Journalism can do."

After Elizabeth left the room, the professor turned to Middleton. "Justin, I want to see the story as soon as it gets here."

"Yes, professor. May I ask why?"

She gestured to the outline. "If her story is as big as her outline indicates, it's our chance to really make a splash. I've got some friends at the *Pontchartrain Guardian* who would be very interested in this."

"You want to run this in the *Guardian*?"

"Yes, special from the *VOICE*. This is the story I've been waiting for—the kind of story that will put us on the map!"

Justin's eyes gleamed. This might just be the item on his resume that would get him a job in New York! "I'll get it to you right away!"

MARDI GRAS MYSTERY
What Happened at the Tulane AI House Tuesday Evening?
by Elizabeth Boudreaux

FOR YEARS, WOMEN AT UNIVERSITIES across the nation have been warned about violence and sexual assault. Some studies say as many as one woman in four will be a victim of unwanted sexual attention during her time on campus. We have been told to know the people we are with, to avoid strangers, and to stay with others, especially our female friends.

But what happens if you do all that and it doesn't keep you safe?

If we have been victimized, we have been told how to react during and after the encounter. When to fight back. When not to. To tell someone. To get medical attention. Not to be silent.

But what do you do when technology conspires against you?

The rise of "date rape" drugs has placed women in the greatest danger they have ever faced. These chemicals make people disoriented and unable to defend themselves, rob their victims of the ability to remember, and leave the body at a rapid rate. They are the perfect weapon for the rapist.

We've heard about all these things. We've seen reports on TV and read stories in the newspapers. But it doesn't hit home until it happens to someone close to you.

I have a friend, whom I'll call F. She could be your study partner, your roommate, your sister, or your lover. She did everything right. She only hung out with friends of long standing. She had a steady boyfriend, whom she had known for months. She attended a party at a place she had frequented many times in the past with people she trusted.

And she was assaulted. On Mardi Gras night. At the Alpha Iota House at Tulane University.

F's boyfriend, who I'll call M, brought her to a party at his fraternity. They were having a great time. He stepped away with a friend for a few minutes—no more than half an hour. When he returned, he expected to find his girlfriend dancing in the chapter room. Instead, he discovered her insensible in a bedroom.

Witnesses tell me M carried F out of the house. But, instead of receiving help from his "brothers," they tried to prevent F from leaving. A confrontation ensued before M was able to escape with his girlfriend. Later, when F was seen by a doctor, it was revealed that she had been sexually assaulted.

F made some mistakes that did not help her. She waited over 24 hours before going to the emergency room. She did not keep much evidence; her only proof was the bruises on her body.

Unfortunately, that was not enough for the New Orleans Police. The officer who questioned her was only interested in what would make her job easier. She could not be bothered with questioning the perpetrators.

Which brings us to the Alpha Iotas. This fraternity has been on the Tulane campus for over 80 years. Many politicians, judges, and leaders of industry claim membership in this chapter. Its ranks are filled with the best and brightest Tulane has to offer. These "Princes of Broadway" are assured success in their future lives, and they will do whatever is necessary to make sure their bright futures are not endangered.

One would think these men would protect themselves by living upright lives, acting in an honorable fashion, and not tolerating the presence of Neanderthals and other misogynist throwbacks in their ranks. But that would not live up to the *Animal House* reputation fraternities strive for. College is the time to party. They can't be worried about the occasional girl who might be attacked. She'll get over it. After all, wasn't she asking for it by coming to the house in the first place?

Besides, Daddy will clean it up.

Brotherhood is the glue that holds fraternities together. My sources tell me it is the most important characteristic of these organizations—so much so that they are willing to destroy anyone or anything that threatens the brotherhood.

Looking for answers, I went to the AI House. I was not met with concern for a friend or outrage over a violation of their supposed rules. What greeted me were stonewalling and an armed guard. It is apparent that AI knows something happened, but their only interest is to cover it up. To keep it quiet. Future careers are at stake, don't you know?

I have learned that M is the chosen scapegoat. He has been ejected from the hallowed ranks of AI. And why, do you ask? Because he wanted to go public. M is now in fear that AI is setting him up to take the fall should there be an investigation. It's one against 40. It is no wonder he quakes at those odds.

In fact, M and F have more than 40 enemies. There are the fathers of these "men" who see their enormous investment in the education of their offspring threatened. Hence, the armed guard.

Drugs are certainly no stranger to fraternity row. It would not be hard to spike a lone female's drink and have some "fun" if assaulting an unconscious woman is one's idea of a good time.

Of course, Alpha Iota may be innocent, but if that is so, why the stonewalling? Is the legendary secrecy of the fraternity system more important than finding the truth?

We cannot stand by and allow business as usual to continue. We must call out for justice. We must demand that the NOPD and officials from Tulane fully investigate the events of February 15.

Or more of our sisters will be victimized.

"Excellent, Elizabeth!" cried Dr. Jennings.

"Yeah," agreed Justin, "you really let those AI bastards have it between the eyes."

Elizabeth nodded. "As long as it spurs an investigation, I'm happy. That's what I want."

"Oh, it will. You can depend on it," Dr. Jennings assured her.

"Professor, I can add my photos to this," Justin suggested.

"Fine. See what will work, and we'll run with it." She rose and moved over to Elizabeth. "You look tired. Why don't you go get some rest?"

"I think I will."

"Good." She patted Elizabeth on the back as she walked her out the door. "I'll call tomorrow to see how you're doing. Meanwhile, we'll post your story tonight. Good night, Elizabeth. Have a good weekend."

When the professor returned to the table, she saw Justin was frowning. "She left out the details of the confrontation with that Darcy guy last night."

Dr. Jennings's ears pricked up. "Darcy? Is he one of the Delta Global Shipping Darcys?"

"Oh, yeah, his old man runs it. He's the one I've got pictures of."

"Really? Justin, that will make the story even bigger." She nodded. "Add what you know, and get me a final draft within the hour. I've got a phone call to make."

She pulled out an address book from her briefcase as she took a seat by a telephone. She quickly dialed a telephone number at the

Pontchartrain Guardian.

"Elton, darling! It's Harriet Jennings. How are you? Listen, I've got a bit of a scoop for you. It involves a certain uptown fraternity and a large shipping company. Oh, and sexual assault. Interested?"

St. Charles Parish

WILLIAM SLUMPED DOWN IN AN easy chair in his father's study at Dansereau Plantation, gratefully taking the beer offered to him. The bodyguard had made himself comfortable in the den.

"You really think Gina's going to buy the story you concocted about Goliath in there?" he asked as he took his first sip.

His father shrugged. "Why not? He *is* a security consultant. I just said he's here to check out our systems. The best way to do that is to spend a couple nights—see how the regular routine goes. Make recommendations." He chuckled. "Maybe she'll ask him a few questions about his work, but she'll get bored soon enough."

"Good. I don't want to scare her."

"Any sign of this Wickham character?"

"Nope."

George Darcy sighed. "I hope this is all an overreaction, but Richard doesn't panic. We'll keep the guard on the payroll for a week or so, and then we'll reevaluate."

"Dad, I'm real sorry about all this. This must be costing you a fortune."

Mr. Darcy snorted. "The hell with the money. Keeping you safe is what counts. Don't give it another thought."

"Can't help it."

"I know. Any update about the young lady?"

William shook his head. "We haven't heard anything, so I guess that's good." He was feeling better as time went by, feeling certain he would have heard something by now from Marianne if there had been an assault. "But we didn't wait around doing nothing. We tossed her worthless sack of a boyfriend out of the chapter. We never should've pledged the son of a bitch in the first place."

"Good. Somebody like that can bring down the whole chapter.

So, on a new subject, when do you want to start at DGS?"

"I thought right after graduation."

"You sure? No last vacation beforehand?"

William smiled. "What do you have in mind?"

"Gina's been after me to take her to Disney World again. So I was thinking I could rent one of those three-bedroom condos for a week. Ride the rides; get some golf in. You interested?"

"Interested? Sure. When?"

"Early June, right after school lets out. You can start at the office when we get back." He looked slyly at William. "You know, those condos will hold a bunch of people. Want to invite somebody? Gina already has begged me to take her friend, Margaret."

"Sure. I can ask Chuck or Chris."

"How about Elizabeth?"

William started. "Huh?"

"Elizabeth—the brunette. You've been seeing her, right?"

"Yeah, a little."

"You like her?"

"Yeah, I like her. But, you know, it's not serious." Their confrontation from the night before flashed in his mind.

"I hope not! I can bunk with you, leaving a private room for her."

"Keeping an eye on me, Dad?"

His father chuckled. "I trust you," he patted his knee, "but not *that* much. I was young once myself."

William smiled. "Let me think about it, okay?"

"Sure. Take your time."

He and his father talked for a while about local happenings before he switched on a basketball game. As they watched, William thought about his father's offer.

Elizabeth was pretty put out that I wouldn't talk to her last night, but what choice did I have? I'll call her up, explain things, smooth everything over. I don't usually get that pissed off, but that photographer really got to me!

So, then, would Elizabeth be interested in going on vacation with us? I don't want to scare her off. We've only been on one real date. But this might be the spark I need to see if she is interested in me.

William thought back on their history—the meetings over coffee, the teasing back and forth, the conversations, the trip to Memphis, the dances, and the kiss after the movie. They were friends, good friends, but William knew he wanted a lot more. Chris and his father were right. Elizabeth was a treasure he would be a fool not to pursue.

Not that it would be much of a pursuit, he judged with a grin. Elizabeth's reaction to the incident during the parade when he protected the little girl was telling. She was scared for *him*. She was worried *he* was hurt. When she brought Jane to town, she entrusted her to *him*—and Chuck, of course.

During their conversations, even when they disagreed, they always seemed to find common ground. He could tell from her smile that she enjoyed their talks as much as he did.

What am I worried about? Of course, she's interested. The pleasant vision of sitting around a swimming pool in Florida with Elizabeth in a little bitty bikini brought a smile to his face. *I'll call her tonight about Dad's offer. It will at least give me a good reason to—Oh, hell! I should've called her already and explained last night! Damn, where is my head these days? I should have her number in my address book… which is sitting on my desk back in the apartment! Oh, crap!*

He took another pull on his Abita. *This Waguespack/Wickham thing has screwed me up! I could call Chris to get her number. Nah, it can wait until I get back Sunday. I'll call her by Monday night—maybe set up a date. Yeah, that's what I'll do, and I'll surprise her with Dad's offer.* He chuckled. *Maybe set up Mari with Chris. Yeah, that will fix him! Waguespack's a gone pecan. The Code ain't in effect now, Chris!*

His father saw the slight grin on his face. "Good thoughts, Will?"

"The best, Dad."

Uptown

AT ELEVEN O'CLOCK THAT EVENING, Justin Middleton sent a command to the server in the closet in the *VOICE's* office. Elizabeth's edited story was now live.

291

Chapter 19

Ringggg! Ringggg!

Elizabeth struggled to grab the telephone, wondering who could be calling at that hour of the morning. "Hello?"

"Elizabeth? It's Professor Jennings. I need you to get down to the VOICE office as soon as you can."

"What? What's wrong?"

"Nothing, dear—except your big chance! Hurry!"

Marianne looked a question at Elizabeth, who only shrugged her shoulders as she reached for her jeans.

ELIZABETH WALKED INTO THE OFFICE to find Dr. Jennings and Justin talking to a third person—a slightly overweight, middle-aged man.

"Elizabeth, this is Elton Rank, a very good friend of mine and an editor for the *Pontchartrain Guardian*," Jennings informed her with a self-satisfied smile.

Elizabeth was confused. The *Pontchartrain Guardian* was an alternative weekly newspaper trying to make a reputation for investigative journalism. Up to now, they were best known for the seedy personal ads on its back page. Dr. Jennings had gotten her out of bed on a Saturday for this? "How do you do?" she said as she shook hands with Rank.

"I'm very happy to meet you, Miss Boudreaux. You write very well."

"You've read my stuff?"

Jennings broke in. "He's read *this* story at least, my dear." She handed Elizabeth a printout of her story about the AIs. "He wants to run it in the *Guardian*." Jennings almost laughed.

"Yes," said Rank. "We usually print on Thursday evening for sale on Friday, but I was just telling Harriet…er, Dr. Jennings that this story is so big, we can run a special edition for Monday."

"You hear that, Elizabeth?" cried Justin. "They're gonna run the whole thing—special from the *VOICE*!"

Dr. Jennings smiled widely. "We'll finally be famous, dear, thanks to you."

Elizabeth glanced at the printout. A photo with a caption caught her eye. She frowned as she saw it was William. The caption read:

"William Darcy, son of DGS CEO George Darcy and member of AI, deflecting reporters' questions about the attack. Photo by Justin Middleton."

Elizabeth turned to the photographer. "You added the photo?"

Justin's smile faded a bit. "Well, yeah, we felt it needed a little punching up."

Elizabeth turned her attention to the body of the story. New text had been added:

"Looking for answers, a photographer and I went to the AI House. We were not met with concern for a friend or outrage over a violation of their supposed rules. What greeted us was stonewalling by a very powerful member of the fraternity. William Darcy, MBA student and son of George Darcy, the CEO of Delta Global Shipping. Darcy, together with an armed guard, refused to answer my questions and threatened us if we did not leave. It is apparent he knows something happened, but his only interest is to cover it up. To keep it quiet. A future career is at stake, don't you know?"

A second photo, one of the large African American bodyguard raising his hands to ward off the reporters, was captioned, *"An armed guard at the AI house, ejecting the reporters. Photo by Justin Middleton."*

The story continued:

"In fact, M and F have more than forty enemies. There are the fathers

of these 'men' who see their enormous investment in the education of their offspring threatened. For example, George Darcy, the head of Delta Global Shipping, is one of the city's most prestigious business owners. The potential damage to the reputation of his company and the value of the company's shares cannot be underestimated. Broken heads are not unusual to those who work the docks. Hence, the armed guards."

Elizabeth looked up. "I didn't write this stuff about the Darcys."

"Justin did," Dr. Jennings admitted. "The additions were from his experience."

Justin crossed his arms. "It's perfectly normal for an editor to amend a story. That's my job."

Elizabeth shook her head. "But, this is my story, my byline."

"Elizabeth," said Dr. Jennings, "this is a bigger story than you think." She tapped the page. *"This* is what will get attention for your subject."

"Miss Boudreaux, do you stand by the story?" asked Rank.

Elizabeth felt excited and confused. She hesitated. "Why isn't Justin sharing the byline?"

"I could," Justin claimed, "but you can have it."

"Miss Boudreaux?" asked the man from the *Guardian* again.

Elizabeth thought about it. Nothing in the story was untrue, but it changed the focus of the piece. Elizabeth's aim was to start an investigation of Alpha Iota. Now the story seemed more about the Darcys.

But wouldn't that attract more attention? Isn't this all about justice for Mari? I can't be concerned for the Darcys' feelings, she thought. Elizabeth nodded.

"We finally get one over on the *Times-Picayune.* I'm sure the AP will be interested in this, too, but we're going to need more." Rank pulled out a notebook. "First, what is the name of the student who was attacked?"

Elizabeth sat down. "Is that necessary?"

"Yes, we have to protect ourselves. Don't worry, we won't release her name."

Elizabeth swallowed hard. "Marianne Dashwood."

"And how do you know her?"

"She's my roommate."

"Is she the source of all this?"

"No. I talked to her boyfriend…and others."

"I'll need their names."

Elizabeth looked down. "I can give you the name of the boyfriend, but the rest"—she looked up—"are confidential."

"Why?"

"I promised."

"All right. This is going to be huge, young lady. Congratulations."

ABOUT AN HOUR LATER, AFTER Elizabeth left to return to her dorm, Dr. Jennings spoke to her colleague. "Well, Elton, what do you think?"

Rank smiled. "We'll run a special edition on Monday, front page. But I've a request. We'd like an exclusive on this." As Justin began to protest, he continued. "We'll give full credit to the *VOICE*, don't worry. But if the AP picks this up, I want it from us. So, I'd like you to take this down from your web site."

"Dr. Jennings—" Justin began, only to be cut off by a wave of her hand.

"Done, Elton, as long as we get front page."

"You've got it."

Dr. Jennings smiled. "Justin, pull the story."

ELIZABETH RETURNED TO HER DORM room to find Marianne still in bed.

She sat next to her, stoking her hair. "Hey, roomie, how goes it?"

"Okay." Marianne's voice was listless.

Elizabeth had to fight back the tears that threatened to spill from her eyes as she looked upon her friend, once so bubbly and outgoing, now withdrawn and depressed. Any second thoughts that were gnawing at her conscience were quickly silenced.

Oh, my dear friend, I will get justice for you—no matter what it costs!

HENRY FIRED UP HIS COMPUTER and used a search engine to find the site for the *VOICE*.

"Anything?" asked Nick Patel.

Henry scanned the page. "Nope. Go tell Chuck."

"He's not here."

Henry turned to him. "Where'd he go?"

"Don't know. Ain't my day to keep track of him."

"Watch it, pledge, you're not initiated yet."

THE NEXT FEW DAYS PASSED quietly. It was a wet weekend, so William stayed inside and spent most of his time with his sister and father. As expected, Gina soon grew bored with questioning the "security consultant" and spent a great deal of time on the phone with her friends. Mr. Darcy began making reservations at Walt Disney World, and William finished up a couple of chapters in his management book. Gina convinced William to stay over Sunday night as she wouldn't see him again until spring break.

George was on call, so Emma invited Elizabeth and Marianne over for an overnighter to watch "My Best Friend's Wedding," and Marianne seemed to come out of her shell for a while. Abe Weinberg watched a basketball game in his den.

Chris, after trying unsuccessfully to call about Marianne again, finished a term paper. Richard Fitzwilliam had the weekend off, but he was reminded by his wife of his "honey-do" list, so he spent a great deal of time, and not a small amount of his paycheck, at Home Depot.

Chuck finally showed up at the fraternity house on Sunday afternoon. His only response to questions about where he had been was that he had been conducting "medical research." No amount of ribbing would get him to say more.

Carrie Bingley thoroughly enjoyed her sushi date, but she enjoyed her "dessert" with John Buford more. Cathy Moreland made Henry Tilney look at *Modern Bride* magazines until he thought he would puke. Tommy Bertram showed his new friend, Sarah, around his apartment, and she agreed to take John Waguespack's old room.

No one could know the extent of the storm that was brewing.

Monday, February 22: St. Charles Parish
WILLIAM AWOKE EARLY ON MONDAY as he had to drive back to Tulane for classes. Grabbing a cup of coffee for the road, he skipped his usual breakfast and jumped into the car, his bodyguard riding shotgun. He honked at his father, strolling out of the house to collect the morning paper. William was almost on the interstate when his cell phone rang.

"Yeah, Dad?"

"William, what the hell is going on?"

"What? Dad, what's wrong?"

"I just got a phone call from Leon. There's a story on the front page of the Pontchartrain Guardian about a girl being attacked at the AI house! I'm reading it right now from their web site."

"What?"

"It's worse than that. There's some bullshit about the Darcy family being involved!"

"Us! Who wrote that?"

There was a pause. *"Elizabeth Boudreaux."*

IT WAS THE WORST DRIVE in William's life. Fighting early rush-hour traffic with one ear glued to his cell phone, William grew angrier and angrier as his father read the story to him. It was bad enough that he and his fraternity were being attacked, but to have his father—his family—dragged through the mud was intolerable. And knowing the person responsible was the girl he was falling in love with was too much for him to bear.

Once he reached Kenner, William pulled into a gas station for a copy of the *Guardian*. The bodyguard took over driving duties as William read the article for himself. His father had told him to go directly to class and let him handle things, but William disregarded the advice.

I can't believe it! Why would Elizabeth say those things? She knows me! Why didn't she trust me? Lies, it's all lies. She was lied to—of course, she was lied to! Waguespack! He must have done it! I've got to see her. Get her to retract this. She'll believe me. She's got to!

"Park someplace close to Loyola," he told the bodyguard. "I've got to see about this."

They found a parking spot on the Tulane campus not far from Loyola. The two wasted no time but ran toward the neighboring school, William's phone ringing again.

"What?" he shouted as he ran.

"It's Chris. I was gonna ask if you heard the news, but I guess you did."

"I'll handle it!" He hung up as he turned the corner. They found themselves between the dorms and the cafeteria. Deciding the best place to start was Elizabeth's room, William trotted towards Buddig Hall, the guard following. He had gotten halfway there when he noticed a brunette exiting the cafeteria.

"Elizabeth!"

She heard her name and whirled around. She looked shocked to see William Darcy and his bodyguard running towards her, a grim and angry expression on William's flushed face, but she stood her ground.

"Elizabeth, what is this?" Darcy cried as he grew near her, waving the newspaper at her.

"Exactly what it looks like," she spat back as she crossed her arms, obviously offended at his accusatory tone.

Darcy's intentions of reasoning with her flew out the window. "How could you write this? None of this is true, trust me!"

"I'm sorry, Darcy, but I've got witnesses. You'll have to do better than that."

"What witnesses? Waguespack? That lying sack of shit?"

The bodyguard stepped up. "Mr. Darcy, you may want to keep your voice down. You're attracting a crowd."

William looked around to see at least two dozen people staring at the confrontation. "Elizabeth, let's take this somewhere private," he suggested in a commanding voice.

"No, we can talk right here. I'm going nowhere with you or your *persuader* there." She looked at the guard.

William glanced at the man behind him. "Elizabeth, you don't understand. My dad hired him—"

"Oh, yes, I know *exactly* why ol' Daddy hired him. Tell me, is he going to try to break into the *VOICE's* offices later? Don't bother; all of our notes are safe!"

"Elizabeth, why are you doing this?"

"I might ask you why you're trying to cover up the fact that one of your precious 'brothers' attacked a girl in your fraternity house!"

"Nobody attacked anybody!" William was losing what was left of his temper. "Did Mar—did anybody say different?"

"Oh, yes! I've got the goods on you now! We've got all the evidence we need. Now the police will *have* to get to the bottom of what went on, and there's nothing you or your father can do to stop it!"

"Who are you to bring my father into this?"

"Didn't Daddy hire your shadow over there?" She pointed at the guard. "Your clean-up specialist?" She spoke directly to him. "Tell me, do you work for the Gambino family or for Carlos Marcello?"

Darcy was furious. "Who's telling you these lies? What's the matter with you? You're smarter than this!"

"You're damn right I'm smart! Smart enough to know when somebody's been assaulted and smart enough to know when somebody's trying to keep it quiet!"

"Of course, I'm trying to keep it quiet, you little idiot! Don't you see what you've done?"

"Yes I do!" Elizabeth screamed back. "I'm going to make sure you bastards never hurt another girl again!"

"We didn't do anything!" Darcy shouted back. "Waguespack did!"

"Nice try, Darcy, but he's got an alibi! But it's too late to tell me now. You'll be telling it to the judge next!"

"Folks, you're causing a scene here!" pleaded the guard, but nobody was listening.

"Elizabeth, believe me, these are nothing but lies! Lies, goddammit! You've got to retract this; you've *got* to!"

"Retract the story? For what reason? *Your* word?"

"Yes, my word! You can trust me!"

"Why?"

"Because I'm in— I'm your friend!"

"My *friend*? Is it a *friend* who dismisses another friend when she comes for answers? Is it a *friend* who's a rotten, controlling bastard? A *friend* who says nothing, doesn't call for days, and yet demands total loyalty and trust? Is it a *friend* who allows a friend to be raped? I don't know what *your* definition of friend is, but it sure ain't mine!"

The guard had finally had enough. "Mr. Darcy, this is solving nothing." He took William by the arm. "It's time to leave."

William shook off the guard and looked at Elizabeth. Even through her rage, she must have seen he was no longer angry. It was worse; he was devastated.

"I don't understand. How could you do this? How could you believe this? You think I had something to do with Mari?" In a near whisper, he said, "You do! Oh my God, you do!"

Elizabeth began crying. "What else am I supposed to think, Darcy? It's the truth, damn you."

"The truth? What the hell do you know about the truth?" He threw the now-crumpled paper at her feet. "You call *this* the truth? Why didn't you come to us and get the truth?"

"I did! You wouldn't talk to me!"

"In front of that asshole of a photographer? Do I look that stupid? I thought you would trust me! I was *trying* to protect Marianne!"

Elizabeth threw up her hands. "Great! Why not tell everybody her name?"

"Haven't you just done it with *that*?" He pointed at the paper. "Do you really think her name isn't going to get out? Do you know what a hell you've just turned her life into? Does she even *know* what you've done?"

Darcy took a breath. "I didn't call you. *Well, excuse me*—I'm sorry! We were a little more worried about Mari than your feelings! Did you even tell her I came by—that we were worried about her? No, don't answer. I already know. You didn't!

"This isn't about *her*. This isn't about *me*! This is all about *you* getting your name in the paper! On the fucking front page! Are you proud of yourself?"

"No! That's not true!" Elizabeth protested.

"Oh, yeah? Then why didn't you call us before you wrote that pack of lies? You can't pick up a phone?"

A flash of guilt spread over Elizabeth's face at that.

"And that stuff about my father. How dare you say anything about the finest man I've ever known! Where the hell do you get off saying that stuff? You've never even *met* the man!

"But, I'm sure that crap helped sell the article, didn't it, *Elizabeth*? Why not go for broke, huh? You could say my little sister sells dope at Destrehan High! Wait, I've got something better! An exposé on my mother—the Russian Mafia Princess! And no worries about getting sued—*she's dead!* But maybe you could say that my father killed her! *Why the fuck not if it sells papers?*"

Elizabeth stepped back as though she had been struck.

William turned to the guard. "Do you know what I was going to do today? I was going to ask this *bitch* if she would come on a family vacation with me this summer. Why, may you ask? So that a girl I really liked would get to know my family." He turned back to Elizabeth. "But, see? I don't have to. She already knows *everything* about my family, don't you?"

Darcy was numb. "I dreamed about you, Elizabeth. I thought I liked you, maybe…maybe even *loved* you, but it's clear I really don't know you. I don't know who the hell you are."

His face darkened. "But *whoever* that is, I don't want *anything* to do with her!" With that, he spun on his heel and walked away.

The bodyguard hesitated a moment. To Elizabeth he said, "Lady, I don't know what the hell you think you're doing, but I'd watch with the innuendoes if I were you."

Elizabeth tried to control her emotions. "Or what? I'm not scared of you."

"You will be of my lawyer, 'cause he'll sue the shit out of you for libel. Good day." He then followed Will.

AFTER THE CONFRONTATION, ELIZABETH COULDN'T go to class

without calming down first. She returned to her dorm room to find Marianne, a pale expression on her face.

Elizabeth rushed to her in concern. "Mari, are you feeling all right?"

"Why?"

Elizabeth asked her roommate what she meant. Marianne repeated her one-word question while handing something to her; it was a copy of the *Guardian*. Elizabeth blushed and began stammering her reasons, but she was interrupted.

"Elizabeth, why didn't you talk to me before you did this?"

"I'm trying to get to the bottom of what happened."

"But...but maybe I don't have to know every detail. Maybe I don't want to know. What about how *I* feel?"

"Oh, sweetie, you have to see. It *is* about you—how to get this behind you—how to get justice for you."

Marianne put her hand on Elizabeth's arm. "Elizabeth, I don't remember *anything*! But I'm messed up, and I'm stressed out, so I'm going to get help. I'm going to be all right." She turned away. "But now, after this article—everybody's going to be looking at me, wondering if I'm lying—if I'm after money." She closed her eyes. "Oh, Elizabeth, you shouldn't have done this—you really shouldn't have!"

Elizabeth turned pale as Marianne's words mirrored Darcy's. "Oh, Mari, believe me, I was trying to help—really, I was!"

"Help who, Elizabeth? If you wanted to help me, why didn't you ask? Did you think I was too weak to know what I wanted?" She looked down. "Emma called. While we were talking, she mentioned Will had come by on Wednesday and asked about me, but you two had decided to keep it from me." She sighed. "You really don't think much of me, do you?"

Elizabeth was shocked. "But...but we were trying to protect you!"

Marianne stood up. "Enough, Elizabeth. I've got to go to class. Don't meet me for lunch. I don't think it would be a good idea to be seen with you."

The words cut Elizabeth like a knife.

"In fact," Marianne continued as she picked up her backpack, "we may need to change our living arrangements."

"Mari!"

"We'll talk later." With that, Marianne exited the room, leaving a shaken Elizabeth behind her. She looked around, trying to understand what was happening to her world when her eyes fell on the Riptide Beanie Baby sitting on her desk—the one Darcy had given her in Memphis.

With a cry of anger, she seized the stuffed figure and flung it into the wastepaper basket.

Somehow, Elizabeth got through the rest of the day. She received elated congratulations from Dr. Jennings, of course. The reaction of her fellow students was varied. Some, mainly females, came up to her to offer their own congratulations, but others, mostly guys in Loyola fraternities, eyed her with suspicion and hostility.

She missed her usual lunch with Mari, but as the day went on, she could understand her reasons. Many would suspect Marianne was "F," especially if her roommate was unable to hide the haunted look she had seen on her face that morning. Unable to concentrate enough to study at the library, Elizabeth returned to her dorm. She was sitting before her computer, trying to concentrate on a term paper, when Marianne returned.

"Lizzy," Marianne said in a low voice as she dropped her bag on her bed.

Elizabeth lowered her eyes. "You were right this morning. I'm very sorry for what I did and what I kept from you." Marianne nodded as she sat on her bed, her eyes red.

"You're my best friend, aside from sister. I was *so* angry, Mari. I wanted to hurt them like they hurt you. I'm afraid my desire for revenge made me act in a very thoughtless way." She gulped. "I've never been that angry at anyone before in my life. I didn't know I was capable of it. I guess I didn't really know myself."

She finally turned to Mari, the tears flowing freely. "I *was* trying to help! I really was trying to get the people who hurt you. But I should have talked to you, first. I treated you with little respect, I know, but never think I don't think much of you! I love you like a sister!

"I know I've let you down, and if you want me to move out, then I'll do it." Elizabeth could say no more as her voice cracked in regret.

Marianne reached to her friend with tears of her own. Wordlessly, they hugged and cried together. After a few minutes, Elizabeth pulled away and wiped her eyes. "What do you want me to do?" she asked.

Marianne rubbed her eyes with the palms of her hands. "What can we do? The cat's out of the bag, now."

"You don't want me to move out?"

"No"—she managed a trembling grin—"who else would put up with you?" Their hugging and crying resumed. Finally, they pulled away, wiping their eyes. "I guess we're stuck with each other."

Elizabeth grasped her friend's hand. "We'll see it through together. And don't worry. There's no reason to think your name will ever get out."

But Darcy's words came back to haunt Elizabeth: *Do you really think her name isn't going to get out? Do you know what a hell you've just turned her life into?* She began to wonder if she could keep her promise to Marianne as she reached for the phone to call Emma.

Marianne's eyes then caught a bizarre sight—Elizabeth's Riptide Beanie Baby sitting in the wastepaper basket. Quietly, she retrieved the doll.

Soon, all the AIs became aware of the article in the *Guardian*. Cell phones were ringing all over campus. Charles had to leave in the middle of a banking class to handle the crisis. Parents were called, or calls were received from them. By nightfall, an emergency meeting had been scheduled. Present were Mr. George Darcy and his top attorney.

Behind locked doors, the entire incident was revisited. Mr. Darcy and his counselor listened without making a sound, save for the lawyer's pen as he took copious notes.

Stories told, Mr. Darcy looked at the young men before him, his hands cupping his chin. He turned to his son.

"Will, this confrontation with the reporter happened when?"

"Thursday night while the chapter was meeting."

George Darcy rubbed his eyes. "And you didn't think this was important enough to mention?"

William looked down in shame but raised his face again as he answered. "Not at the time, no."

"Do you think you may have underestimated this Miss Boudreaux?"

William's face was stone. "Apparently, sir, I don't know Miss Boudreaux at all."

Mr. Darcy looked hard into his son's eyes and saw the pain of betrayal behind the anger. "All right, I think it's safe to say we've got quite the problem here. Mr. Tilney was correct. You should have gone to the dean. But that's water under the bridge. The chapter is now in survival mode, gentlemen."

Mr. Darcy's attorney agreed.

"Very well," continued Mr. Darcy. "I hereby offer the use of my legal team to any of you whose parents choose not to retain their own legal counsel. Those of you who have your own lawyers should have them call my people to coordinate our response. And gentlemen," he looked at them, "a response will be required. My people say this story has already been picked up by the AP."

He was interrupted by a knock on the door. A moment later, it was opened by the Darcy security detail.

"Mr. Darcy, there's a TV truck pulling up outside."

"And so it begins," Mr. Darcy breathed. "Gentlemen, I believe they call this crisis management in the real world. Please listen carefully to my lawyer as we discuss what we're going to do."

Chapter 20

Universities, like any large organization, are unwieldy by design. It takes time for anything to be done. Procedures and protocol must be followed. The dean of students received the first call about the *Guardian* article by mid-day. After a summary investigation, which consisted of a couple of telephone calls and a perusal of the article, a letter was mailed to the Tulane chapter of Alpha Iota Fraternity, requesting an explanation of the issues raised in the story.

By late Monday afternoon, it was apparent that the response to date had been inadequate. This fact was driven home by the third phone call from a TV news outlet. The dean made another phone call, this time to the president of the AI chapter, requesting a face-to-face meeting the next day. The AI member who took the call promised to forward the message.

It was curious that the original story appeared in an on-line publication that belonged to Loyola as it concerned Tulane students. The university planned to ask about that when the AI president met with them.

The phone call from campus security, reporting TV trucks parked along Broadway, sent a charge through the bureaucracy of the academy. The lights stayed on late as meetings were held and plans were made. Additional phone calls to AI went unanswered. Action was needed.

On Tuesday morning, the dean, escorted by Tulane security,

walked through the phalanx of cameras and correspondents to the front steps of the Alpha Iota House. There, the delegation realized they had been too slow; the lawyers had already arrived. Like flies to a rotting carcass, they swarmed with their annoying briefs and unfortunate insistence on search warrants. There was nothing for it but to retreat and call in the university's own legal eagles. The action now belonged to the attorneys.

A telephone call to the neighboring campus was made, and it was learned that Loyola had absolutely no idea what was going on. A second investigation was launched, which ran right into the Free Speech and First Amendment claims of the very-tenured Dr. Harriet Jennings. A second, seemingly irresistible, force ran into a mostly immovable object.

Wednesday, February 24

"HURRY UP!" CRIED THE TELEVISION reporter over the sound of chanting and drums. "The rally's started."

"Hold your damn horses," said the cameraman under his breath. The talent was always pushing him around, and it was his job to make them look good. There was so much he could do to sabotage the shot, and the reporters were often too stupid to realize it.

In this case, the cameraman had decided discretion was the better part of valor and dutifully prepared for the set-up shot. The reporter assumed a neutral expression and began.

"We're here today outside the Alpha Iota House at Tulane University where a coalition of activists is protesting the pace of the investigation into the events of Mardi Gras night."

The cameraman moved closer to the action as about two dozen protestors, mostly women, carried placards and chanted. One protestor beat a drum. Signs held proclaimed, JAIL AI—NOT WOMEN and NO JUSTICE, NO PEACE.

"Make sure you get what they're saying," advised the reporter.

No fuckin' kidding, thought the cameraman as he adjusted the microphone.

"WHAT DO WE WANT? *JUSTICE!* WHEN DO WE WANT

IT? *NOW!* WHAT DO WE WANT? *JUSTICE!* WHEN DO WE WANT IT? *NOW!*"

"Man," complained the reporter, "they *always* chant that. You'd think college students would think of something more original."

The cameraman pulled in tight. If the crowd looked bigger, there was a better chance of making the broadcast. Maybe the footage would be picked up by the network. One could always hope.

THE PROTEST WAS THE LEAD on the six o'clock news. "At least they spelled the words right," joked Chris.

William didn't laugh. He sat staring moodily at the screen, thinking, *how did it come to this?*

Friday, February 26

THE PUBLICITY WAS FELT ALL the way downtown at the inner offices of the New Orleans Police Department. Pressure was placed upon the Second District to move on this case at the cost of anything else. The word, it was whispered, had come down from the mayor's office. It took several days for the NOPD to arrange a formal interview with Marianne Dashwood. She met with the original interviewing officer and another woman, an assistant prosecutor with the district attorney's office. The interview went on for some time as both women tried every method at their disposal to help the Loyola coed recall the events of February 16. Two hours went by before they gave up, adding almost nothing to what they had before.

The police officer glanced at her notes one more time. "Miss Dashwood, there is one last thing we would like you to do. Are you up to it?"

Marianne held her head in her hands. "Let's just get it over with," she said resignedly.

A phone call was made, and after a short wait, a male police officer entered the interview room, a manila folder under his arm.

"Miss Dashwood, my name is Lt. Fitzwilliam. I'm with the narcotics division."

Marianne glanced at the ADA, who shrugged her shoulders.

"What can I do for you?"

He placed the folder before her and opened it. "Would you look at these photos, please?"

Before her were five photographs, all mug shots of young white men. She gasped at the fourth one.

"Do you know this man?" asked Fitzwilliam.

"That's Greg—Greg Wickham. Has he done something wrong?"

"Miss Dashwood, this is very important. Can you tell us anything about this man?"

"He's a friend of my boyfriend—*ex*-boyfriend—John. I've seen him around John's apartment and the fraternity house. He's a student at Tulane, I believe."

"Anything else?"

"No."

"Was he at the party?"

Marianne tried to concentrate. "I…I suppose so. He was supposed to come. John said so. But, I just don't remember if I saw him or not. Why are you asking so many questions about Greg?"

Fitzwilliam sat down, clearly disappointed. "Just part of our investigation."

The ADA asked, "Do you remember drinking anything that night?"

Marianne held her head again. "I…I don't know."

"Did anyone give you a drink? Please try to remember."

"I'm trying as hard as I can! I just don't remember!" Marianne broke down.

The others looked at each other and shook their heads.

THE LAWYERS MADE SURE THERE was only one admission ticket for outsiders to the Alpha Iota House. It was called a search warrant. Armed with the precious piece of paper, investigators fanned out throughout the house. At the advice of counsel, no members volunteered any information or answered any but the most basic of questions, and those got a terse "yes" or "no."

Henry Tilney stood next to Nick Patel as a policeman moved

into Nick's bedroom. "Where are your sheets?" the cop asked Nick.

"What's not on the bed is in the closet," Nick answered.

The officer turned to him. "These are all laundered. Any used sheets?"

"Just what's on my bed."

Henry had to stop himself from spurting in surprise. He waited until the cop's attention was drawn away before taking Nick by the arm and forcing him into the restroom for a private conversation.

"What the hell?" Henry said between his teeth. "I thought Chuck told you not to wash those sheets!"

Nick wouldn't look at his pledge director. "Look, you're using Mr. Darcy's attorney, but my dad got me my own lawyer. We're doing what we've got to do to protect ourselves."

Henry was amazed. "He told you to do that? That's...that's destroying evidence! Interfering with a criminal investigation! You could go to jail! I can't believe he told you to do that!"

"Who said my lawyer told me anything? I didn't say that," Nick said in an emotionless voice.

"Pat—"

"We know what we're doing. My dad—Shit, just leave me alone!" He tried to leave, but Henry's hand on his arm stopped him.

"Nick, I understand, but I *really* disagree with what they told you to do."

"Nobody told me to do anything!"

"Right." The two looked into each other's eyes for a moment before nodding. Nick made his way out of the bathroom while Henry leaned against the counter, running his hands over his face.

This goddamn thing's gonna pull the chapter apart!

Friday, March 5: Downtown

THE CHIEF ASSISTANT DISTRICT ATTORNEY sat behind his desk, allowing his assistant to have her say. She finished her presentation, and he glanced at the notes again.

"So, you're telling me"—he fingered the report—"we should move forward with this case."

"Yes, sir," she said. "I believe there is probable cause for a rape investigation."

"And how do you get that? There's nothing here."

"Sir, if you had listened to the victim—"

"*Alleged* victim," he corrected her.

The ADA was flustered and began again when she was interrupted.

"That's enough," the chief assistant district attorney stated. "If all you've got is your gut, then we're through here. Shut it down."

"Sir! You can't!"

"Can't I?" he said dangerously. "I thought I was in charge here."

"I'm sorry, sir, but I really must protest!"

"Your passion is duly noted but rejected." He stood up. "In case you've forgotten, there is a murder a day in the city. We've got twelve —count 'em, twelve—capital cases we're handling right now. We don't have the manpower to run down every case that's thrown at us. The people want results not efforts. We can't waste our time with this."

She tried one last challenge. "Can I go to the DA on this?"

"Be my guest, but I should let you know that the order comes down from him." He walked around the desk. "We'll tell the press the investigation is ongoing, but as far as you're concerned, this case is closed." He sat on his desk. "Look, I know you're new to the office, so let me give you some advice. Passion is good, but it'll burn you out. We play to win, and that means we don't take every case. That's just the way it is. If you can't take it, then maybe you need a new line of work."

"Maybe I do."

He sighed. "Think it over. If you do decide to leave, I'll give you a glowing recommendation. Now, get back to work."

Wednesday, March 10: Uptown

ELIZABETH LAY ON THE BED in her dorm room, her mind in a whirl. Campus security had just changed their phone number for the second time since the article came out. Their original number was changed to a private one as a precaution, and it was to be kept secret, yet someone had leaked the new number, and they had been receiving calls from newspapers across the country.

It had to be somebody in security or administration. Probably a student worker. Were they bribed? Is there no honor anymore?

Elizabeth tossed her body onto her side in frustration. She looked up to see Riptide on Marianne's desk. She knew Marianne had retrieved it from the trashcan, but neither said a word about it. Elizabeth tried to ignore it. Sometimes she succeeded in noticing it only twice a day.

She sat up, starring at the doll. It was painful because it reminded her of William, and that reminded her of the awful confrontation they had. Why had she said the things she did? Why didn't she tell him it was Justin, not her, who put the stuff about Darcy and his father in her piece? Why was she so angry with him?

Elizabeth knew the investigation was going nowhere. Already, the story had disappeared off the pages of the paper and the TV screens, replaced by the latest scandal out of Hollywood. Marianne could remember nothing. There was no evidence.

Could I have been wrong? No! Something happened. Greg and John said so. It's the AIs. They must have gotten rid of the evidence. Of course, that's it. And the police aren't trying hard enough.

But as she lifted her eyes to Riptide, she remembered the man who gave it to her. She could not draw on the anger that previously fueled her resolve. She was only left with the whisper of nagging doubts.

How could William fool me so completely? How could the guy who gave it to me allow anyone to hurt Marianne?

Not for the first time, Elizabeth cried in frustration.

Friday, March 19: Garden District

ABE ANSWERED THE DOOR WHEN George rang and let the young doctor in. "Emma's getting dinner ready," he explained.

"Emma?" asked George. "*She* made dinner?"

"Heavens, no! Miz Taylor made the gumbo. Emma's just heating it up. Emma cooking? I wouldn't do that to you. Wouldn't want you to get food poisoning, now would I?

"I heard that!" came a shout from the kitchen.

"You hungry, George?"

"You bet. Tell you what, Abe: I'll go help Emma. You just sit yourself at the table."

"I knew I liked you. You're a sensible man, George."

George saw Abe to the dining room table before continuing to the kitchen. It had been a while since he had seen Emma—with his work, her classes, and the scandal sitting over everything—so their only contact had been telephone calls. It would be safe to say the surprise was complete.

George entered the kitchen. "Hey, Emma, it's…" His voice died as he saw the beautiful dark-haired lady in a green floral halter dress and heels.

"Emma?"

She turned with a big smile on her face. "Hello, George."

"You…you colored your hair."

"Did I? Oh, yes, I did." She ran her fingers through her tresses. "I got tired of keeping up the blonde look, so I returned to a more natural color. You like?"

"Uhh, yeah. It looks good." *Real good.*

Emma's smile grew.

"I guess I ought to help you serve the food."

"Sure." She walked over to him, passing a bit closer than necessary, to open a drawer. "Here's the tableware." She set out what was needed. "Would you be a dear and bring this out to the table?"

George nodded and moved to gather the items. Emma didn't move, forcing him to reach close to her body to get the utensils. George had to move around her to get to the door.

"Abe," he asked the older man when he reached the dining room, "when did Emma dye her hair?"

"Oh, that. After Mardi Gras. Guess I got used to it. Looks good on her, don't it?"

When George returned to the kitchen, Emma was ladling the gumbo into a tureen.

"Want me to grab that?"

Emma looked over her shoulder. "No, I've got it." She put the lid on and moved to the oven. "Got to get the French bread. Oh, there's a salad in the fridge," she pointed as she bent over.

George got the bowl out of the Sub-Zero, trying to keep his eyes off Emma.

Is she intentionally teasing me? Because if she is, it's working.

He placed it on the counter as Emma set the bread on a butcher block cutting board. She quickly sliced it and placed it on a serving plate.

"I'll just bring these in," she said as she took the salad bowl in her other hand. Moving towards the door, she brushed against George. Her light, flowery perfume invaded his nostrils. The view down her top was breathtaking. "Oh, excuse me." She wore a knowing smile as she sauntered out.

George tried to make sense of it all. *She's driving me nuts! That hair, that dress! I've got to control myself.* He readjusted his trousers.

Emma came back into the kitchen. Again, with all the room available, she brushed up against him, her breasts brushing across his chest.

What happened next was unplanned by George. He felt as detached as though he were watching a movie. He saw a hand grab Emma by her forearm. He remotely realized it was his. Emma turned towards him, never losing her slight, teasing smile. Then her back was against the counter, and two hands pinned her there. She made no move to resist as he grew closer. This kiss was like no other they had shared. Being gentle was the last thing on George's mind. Hungrily, he devoured her lips, driving his body against hers. He loved feeling the softness of her generous breasts against his chest.

George released Emma's arms to hold her ever tighter, and her arms pulled him closer as she returned his passion. He buried his tongue in her mouth, and she began to moan. He moved his hand between their bodies, creeping up her ribs, aching to touch her—

"Hey!" came Abe's voice from the dining room, "where's the chow?"

The two broke apart, gasping for breath. Emma cried out, "Just a minute, Papa! I'm getting the rice!"

George looked sheepishly at her, but Emma would not have any of it. She grabbed him by the back of his neck and gave him a quick, hard, sloppy kiss before pushing him away.

"That will have to hold you 'til later," she whispered, her eyes alight with mischief. She gave him a naughty grin and returned to the stove.

George leaned against the counter, trying to control himself. He was sure that, if Abe had not been there, he would have been unable to stop. He would have taken Emma right there on the kitchen floor.

"You going to get the gumbo?" she asked.

"Emma!" he hissed. "I can't go back out there like this!"

She giggled. "Get yourself together. We'll be waiting." She exaggerated the sway of her hips as she walked to the dining room.

With a groan, George adjusted himself again and picked up the tureen. *I hope Abe's attention is on the food!*

EMMA WAS EXCITED BY HER success. Her hair and dress were all part of her plan to drive George into action. What was surprising was the violence of George's reaction and her desperation to learn how far she could push him. When they kissed, she couldn't move; she didn't want to move. The feel of his body against hers was exhilarating. She felt small and sensual and all the things she'd never felt with him before. She grew dizzy recalling it, the blood rushing through her ears.

She was relieved that her father seemed to be unaware of what had transpired in his kitchen. Dinner proceeded without further incident, and Miz Taylor's shrimp and okra gumbo was judged to be excellent. Of course, Emma was careful not to let her father see the teasing looks she was throwing at George. And George managed not to cough up his soup when he felt a bare foot caress his shin. She had to bite her lip to keep from giggling.

They had bread pudding in the living room: Emma on the couch, the men in armchairs to either side. Most of the time she pretended to be attentive to her father's conversation, but every few minutes she would throw a smoky gaze at George.

Finally Abe rose. "I'm gonna watch some TV."

"Papa, I thought George and I could look though some old photo albums—you know, reminisce for a while." She smiled weakly. It was something she knew would bore her father to tears. It worked, and he left them alone.

Abe looked at her and then at George. A slow grin spread over Abe's face. "Oh…right. Okay, I'll just be in the study. Have a good time *reminiscing*." He chuckled.

After Abe left the room, George said, "Well, I guess we're—"

He couldn't say anything more as Emma decided it was a good time to pick up where they'd left off in the kitchen. She pulled him onto the sofa and pressed her lips to his. He fell back, and she climbed half on top of him, doing her best to crawl into his skin. The blare of the basketball broadcast from the den was the only sound in the room.

"Em…Em, for God's sake. Do you know what you're doing to me?" George finally managed to whisper in her ear.

This was not the response Emma expected. "I *thought* you would be enjoying this!" she shot back in a low voice.

"Enjoying this? Want me to show you how much I'm enjoying this?" He gasped. "I should—if your father wasn't in the next room!" He raised his hips slightly as an exclamation.

Emma got the point. "Did I do *that* to you?" She wiggled slightly.

George groaned. "All right—you asked for it." He pulled her tightly against him and turned over. Before Emma realized it, they had switched positions, George's solid weight comfortably against her body. She smiled wickedly—a smile that faded as he grazed a finger along the bottom of her breast.

"You've got this coming," he growled. He slowly worked his fingertips to the center, as his lips caressed her neck. She wore no bra under the halter, and her excitement grew. His kisses to her throat and neck burned against her skin as his fingers had their way with her breast, first drawing lazy circles around the tip before gently squeezing the nipple between two fingers. Fire flowed through Emma's body, and she could not help but arch into his touch.

All too soon, George pulled away. "There, you've got some of your own back. I ought to finish the job and compromise you good, except Abe would probably get his shotgun and pepper my backside."

"He wouldn't. He doesn't have a shotgun."

George rolled his eyes. "He'd hit me with a golf club, then."

She laughed. "Not from his new set." They sat up, much closer together than before.

"An old one, then." George sighed. "Emma, what the hell are we doing?" George had a serious look on his face. "Look, we're getting close to a point of no return. Don't get me wrong. I like this—a lot. Too much, maybe. But, Em, if we go much further, there's no going back. If this doesn't work out, I…I don't know. But we can't go back to the way we were before."

Emma looked at him with big eyes. "You don't want me?"

George kissed her hand. "All I'm saying is we've got to know what we're getting into."

"What do *you* want?"

"Em, that's unfair. You're the one at risk. You've got your whole life in front of you. It's got to be what you want."

Emma looked deeply at him and spoke from her heart. "I want to be with you." She leaned in and kissed him.

"Me, too. Okay, we'll do this." He pulled her close. "Oh God, Emma. I feel like I just won the Powerball. A gorgeous, funny, sweet young woman just told me she wants to be with me rather than somebody a whole lot more handsome, richer, younger, or—"

"Or still has his hair." She couldn't resist teasing him one last time.

George threw back his head and laughed. Emma joined in, and then they were kissing again—until they heard the unmistakable sounds of a man getting out of a recliner. Desperately they arranged themselves, Emma grabbing a photo album from the coffee table and opening it to a random page before running her fingers though her hair.

"What's so funny?" asked Abe from the doorway.

Emma glanced down to see she had opened the photo album to a picture of her mother. She shut the book, thinking hard. "Remember the trip to Biloxi where we…where we—" she faked a giggle, imploring George with her eyes to go along.

He caught on. "Yeah, and then you went into the water, and Irene said—what was it she said, Abe?"

Abe was nonplused. "I don't have the faintest idea what you're talking about."

"Oh, well, I guess you had to be there," George said with a straight face. Emma cracked up.

"You two have lost your minds," Abe observed. He waved dismissively at the two laughing figures on the couch and returned to his basketball game.

"That was brilliant, George," Emma whispered. "He'll leave us alone for the rest of the night."

"Yeah, the old boy can dish it out, but he can't take it." George let out a breath. "I'm not too sorry for the interruption, though. Things were getting a little out of hand in here."

Emma felt her cheeks redden. "You're right. So what do we do now?"

He pulled her close. "We should talk. It's been a while since we talked. I've missed you. How've you been doing at school?"

Emma loved leaning into George's embrace. "School's okay, except for—you know."

"Yeah, I understand."

Remembering the scandal cooled Emma's passion. "George, I know I asked you before, but please, can't you tell me what's going on? How did things get this way?"

George sighed. "I really shouldn't say—Aw, shit. Everything's already gone to hell because of all this secrecy. What do you want to know?"

Secrecy? Was Lizzy right? "What really happened at the AI House?"

George shrugged. "That's just it, Emma. We don't know."

Emma sat up. "But Mari was attacked—"

"Was she? By whom?" Emma started to turn away, but George stopped her. "Wait a minute, Em. I'm spilling my guts here. You have to give up what you know, too. Did Mari actually say she was assaulted?"

"She doesn't remember."

"Then, where did Elizabeth get her information? Who's the source?"

"I don't know."

"It wasn't Waguespack? We thought that son of a bitch might be the guy lying to her."

Emma shook her head. "I don't think it was John. What happened to him?"

"He dropped out of school after we threw his sorry butt out of the chapter. Our lawyers say he's staying at his aunt's house in Mississippi."

That made no sense to Emma. "Why did you expel John if nobody thinks anything happened?"

He sighed. "*Something* happened, but John wouldn't tell us. Half the house saw John practically carrying Mari out the back door with that drug-dealing Wickham at his heels."

Emma's ears pricked up. "What's that about Greg?"

"Greg Wickham is a drug dealer, hanging around the university area. 'Course, we found out *after* Mardi Gras. He's not a Tulane student or a member of Alpha Iota. If anything happened, I'll bet it was at the hands of those two. We threw John out for bringing a guy like Wickham into the house."

Immediately, Emma remembered her encounter with Greg Wickham on campus. "Oh my God, George! A few days after it happened, I ran into Greg on the common. He was looking for Elizabeth, and I directed him to Loyola."

George sucked in a breath. "Holy shit. He must've been Elizabeth's source."

"He lied to her," she said as much to herself as to George.

"Of course, he did. Son of a bitch!" George ran his hand though his hair. "Em, we didn't know! We didn't know if Mari had been hurt. We suspected something, but we didn't know for sure. We took what steps we thought were right at the time, and then that article appeared. Then all hell broke loose, and there were attorneys running all over the place, telling us to keep our mouths shut. I really shouldn't even be telling this to you."

A knot of fear arose in Emma's chest. "Are you going to get into trouble?"

He kissed her forehead. "I *am* in trouble. I'm the chapter's alumni advisor and an employee of Tulane University Medical Center. I have some responsibility for—"

"You didn't tell them not to talk to Elizabeth, did you?"

"Things were not handled the way I suggested they should. But I have to be honest; when Elizabeth showed up at the house with that photographer, nobody was going to talk to her."

"Your armed guard made that clear," she pointed out.

George looked at her curiously. "Emma, he was Will's bodyguard."

"Why does Will need a bodyguard?"

"That night, when they were trying to carry Mari out of the house, Will got into a tussle with Wickham. Wickham's dangerous, and he might come after Will for roughing him up."

The totality of the misunderstandings hit Emma with some force. "Oh, no." She started to cry. "*Everything's* wrong. Marianne's hurting, Elizabeth got it wrong, and Will's in danger." Wide-eyed, she grasped George's shoulders. "George! Your job! What about your job?"

"Shush, don't worry. My position's not in jeopardy; I'm fairly sure. The police and the university are investigating, and we're cooperating through our attorneys. Everything will come out right in the end."

"Not everything. What about Marianne?"

"I don't know. How's she doing?"

"Scared, confused. She knows something happened, and everybody's pushing her to remember. The stress is eating her up."

"I thought her name wasn't being used by the press."

"It's not, thank God, or it would be worse. But the DA's office, both colleges, and the police want something—anything. It's awful. And Elizabeth—Elizabeth's so mad at William right now, and William's mad at Elizabeth. They're so right for each other, and now they hate each other. I can't stand it." She sobbed. "It's my fault. My matchmaking—setting up Elizabeth and William. If I hadn't done it, then maybe they wouldn't have taken this thing so personally."

George let out a short chuckle. "Em, you can stop beating yourself up over that. You couldn't set up Will Darcy with a free steak dinner if he didn't want it. Things happen. Will and Lizzy are going to have to sort out things themselves if it's possible."

"I don't think it *is* possible," she moaned.

"Maybe not." He looked at his watch and hugged her tighter. "Em, I gotta go. I've got early duty tomorrow. Let's say good night to your dad."

Emma was disappointed that Abe decided to see George to the door. The doctor took his leave of the older man and then turned to Emma. "Don't worry, Emma; everything will be all right," he assured her again as he stoked her cheek with his thumb.

"Drive safe."

"I'll call," he said before giving her a light kiss. He looked up to see Abe's amused expression.

"Umm…"

Emma looked sideways at her father. It was time to tell the truth. "Papa, George and I are dating."

"I hope so." The two men mumbled congratulations and thanks to each other as they stiffly exchanged handshakes.

After George left, Emma turned to her father. "Well?"

"He's a good man, Emma. You make me very happy."

Emma kissed her father's cheek, excused herself, and went to her bedroom. She undressed and prepared for bed, promising herself that she would talk to Elizabeth the next day. Slipping under the covers, she forgot all about scandals, controversy, and friends angry at each other. Her mind was on one thing—George.

She looked down as one of her hands moved across her breast, copying George's caresses. She recalled the sensations, the quickening of her breath, and the tightening in her belly. She had been touched that way before, but she had never experienced such an intense reaction to it.

It's because, this time, it was George.

The girls at Newman playfully teased Emma about her reticence with the boys while in high school. Her nickname was Sister Emma; some, she supposed, half expected her to convert and join a convent. It wasn't as though she didn't like boys. She just didn't feel the need to go much further than kissing and hugging. She had made out with guys countless times, but that was about it. She knew she wasn't the only virgin in college. She wanted her first time to be special with a special man, and she hadn't found him yet.

Until now.

Chapter 21

Saturday, March 20: Uptown

Tommy Bertram pulled into the parking lot of the Second District and leaned over to his passenger. "You stay here, Sarah. I'll be right back."

She gave him a kiss on his cheek. "You're doing the right thing, Tommy."

He smiled as he got out of the car. Within moments, he was standing before the front desk. "I'd like to see Lt. Fitzwilliam, please."

The desk sergeant checked his screen. "He's not in right now. Can somebody else help you?"

"Umm…I was told to see the lieutenant. Can I leave a message for him?"

The desk sergeant had almost twenty years' experience and was eighteen months from retirement. His goal in life, after almost two decades on the beat, watching other men and women get the promotions he felt he deserved, was to do as little as possible. Taking messages from some scummy informer for Narcotics was not something he enjoyed. Grumbling, he reached for a pad when he spotted someone in the squad room.

"Hey, Jonesy! Got one for ya!"

The female detective approached the desk. "What's up?" she said as she glanced at the visitor.

"Fella here to see Fitz. You wanna handle it?"

"Sure." She turned to Tommy. "I'm Officer Jones. I work with

Lt. Fitzwilliam. Can I help you?"

"You're his partner?"

"Yes, you could say that."

Tommy figured that was good enough. "I've got something for him. Can we talk somewhere?"

"Sure, just come with me." She led the way into a conference room as the desk sergeant went back to his *Field and Stream*. He was supposed to sign in the visitor, but he blew it off, figuring Jones would make note of it.

The two sat down. "Now, what can I do for you?"

Tommy took a breath. "This is about that thing at Tulane. You know—the AI house?"

"Yes. That's not really our department."

"I know, but see, I think I know who did it, and he's definitely somebody *you're* looking for."

"Okay, who?"

"You're going after the wrong guy. It wasn't John Waguespack. It was Greg Wickham."

Jones's eyes widened. "You've got proof?"

"Yeah. Let me tell ya 'bout my conversation with John."

JONES SAW TOMMY BACK TO his car. "Thank you for coming forward, sir. I'll pass this along to Lt. Fitzwilliam and the people working the Tulane case. Can we get in touch with you at this number?" she indicated on the form.

"Yeah," Tommy said as he stood by his car.

Jones looked in. "Hi! Are you with Tommy?"

"My name's Sarah," the thin, dirty-blond haired girl said, shaking her hand thought the open car window.

"Your boyfriend's very brave."

Sarah smiled. "Yes, he is."

Jones straightened up. "Thank you again, Tommy. We'll be in touch." Tommy nodded as he got into his car.

Jones watched as they drove off. Once they were out of sight, she moved directly to her personal vehicle, file still in hand, and drove down the block. She pulled into a convenience store parking lot beside a pay phone. She quickly dialed a number.

"Yeah?"

"Somebody was snitchin' on you today," she told G-Daddy.

"Fuck! Who was it?"

"Gonna cost you double."

There was a pause. *"Okay."*

"Name's Bertram. Mean anything to you?"

"Yeah, I know him. What'd he say?"

"It was you at the AI House. Says you attacked that girl."

"Fuck! How'd he know?"

Jones read Bertram's statement.

"So, whatcha gonna do with that report?"

"Depends. How're you gonna handle this?"

"I'll take care of Chicken Man, don't worry."

"Look, I don't wanna get involved in any of—"

"Too late to crawfish now with all the nose powder you've scored. You're in too deep. Don't worry. You just work your end, and I'll take care of mine. Now, what about the file?"

"I'll get rid of it. Fitz'll never know he was here."

"Good. Oh, don't get any fancy ideas about turning on me. I've got evidence stashed away. Real nice photos. You can even see the zit on your chin."

Jones sighed. She was afraid of that. One day, she would have to kill Wickham if he didn't kill her first. "Regular place, right?"

"Right." The phone went dead.

Garden District

EMMA KNEW SHE COULDN'T HAVE that conversation with Elizabeth over the phone, so she had her friend over to the house Saturday night. After a grilled chicken salad, the girls retreated to Emma's bedroom.

They sat on the bed. Emma, agitated, was wringing her hands while talking about inconsequential topics, trying to think of a way to begin.

Elizabeth reached out to quiet her hands. "You obviously have something to tell me." She gave her friend a comforting smile. "Why don't you just tell me what it is?"

There was a flash of guilt on Emma's face.

"It can't be all *that* bad," Elizabeth teased.

"Yes, it is." Finally, Emma threw up her hands. "Lizzy, I know what happened to Marianne, and oh, we were so wrong!"

Uptown

ELIZABETH SLAMMED THE DOOR OF her dorm room and threw herself on her bed, scaring Marianne.

"Lizzy? What's wrong?" Her roommate could not answer, her body shaking as she wept. Marianne could only sit next to her, stroking her shoulder. Finally, Elizabeth gained control of her tears and haltingly repeated what Emma had just shared with her.

"Lizzy, please don't be so upset. I understand. I do! Yes, you made a mistake, but you meant well. You were lied to. What is this really all about?"

Elizabeth couldn't answer Marianne's question as her attention was drawn to her Riptide Beanie Baby. Obeying an impulse she could barely understand, she took the doll into her trembling hands, and her fingers began caressing it. She remembered how surprised she was when William gave it to her—surprised and pleased.

Memories, well submerged, came flooding back to her.

The warmth of a summer's night on the AI porch. The smell of pecan waffles. The rattle of a streetcar as she walked along St. Charles Avenue. The fear she felt when a friend used his body to shield a little girl from harm. The satisfying warmth of good coffee and better conversation. Dancing to the sounds of a blues band. A movie and pizza. The thrill and excitement of a cold December afternoon. A lonely bed in Lafayette. An accidental kiss that sent shivers down her spine.

All these lovely memories had only one common denominator: William Darcy.

"Lizzy?"

Elizabeth began shaking her head. "Oh my God...oh my God!"

She gripped the doll in her fist so tightly that Marianne was certain it would burst.

"Lizzy, what is it?" Marianne cried, before recoiling from the raw pain in her friend's face.

"Mari, I love him! What have I done?"

Sunday, March 21: Hammond

IT WAS AMAZING ELIZABETH COULD drive her Civic in a straight line as her mind was jumbled with stabbing regret and self-incrimination. She was able to navigate the early Sunday morning traffic on I-10 past the airport safely before opening it up on the Bonnet Carré Spillway. At Laplace, she turned north on I-55 and traveled the next twenty-two miles on the elevated roadway, fifty feet above the cypress swamps which separated Lake Pontchartrain from Lake Maurepas. She reached ground level again just south of Ponchatoula, the Strawberry Capital of Louisiana, but that was not her destination. It lay some dozen miles further north in Hammond.

She took the University Avenue exit off I-55 inside of Tangipahoa Parish's largest city. Five minutes later, she pulled into the parking lot of a small apartment building. Her eyes looked for one sight: Jane's car. Luckily, Elizabeth was able to park near it. She made her way to her sister's second-floor apartment and rang the doorbell. A minute later, it was answered by a disheveled blonde, one hand holding a rose-colored robe closed tightly against her neck.

"Elizabeth? What are you doing here?" Jane asked.

"May I come in?"

"It's…it's not a good time. Elizabeth, what's wrong? You've been crying!" She pulled the door wide open to allow her sister entry.

"I've been such a fool! I hope you understand…I needed to talk to you." They made their way to the kitchen. Jane cleared the plates and wine glasses from the table, and the two sat down.

"Oh, Jane, what am I going to do?"

"What's troubling you? What is so urgent you couldn't call first?" She put one hand to her lips. "Oh, my God! Is it Mom or Dad?"

"No, no!" Elizabeth immediately assured her. "Everybody at

home is fine as far as I know. I didn't call because I needed to see you. I guess I didn't think it through first. Oh, Jane! I haven't been thinking well at all lately!"

Jane held her hand. "All right, tell me about it."

And she did. Elizabeth unburdened herself by repeating everything she had learned in the last few days from Emma and Marianne.

"I was wrong, Jane. Completely wrong. Everything Wickham told me was a lie. And I believed it all! I've always prided myself on my intelligence and discernment, but Greg Wickham played me like he owned me. I've caused so many people so much trouble. All my friends. How could I do that to them?"

Jane squeezed her hand. "I'm sure you didn't mean to hurt them. You weren't trying to do anything but uncover what happened to Marianne."

"But I went off half-cocked because I let my anger and pride get the best of me. And now William…" her voice trailed off.

"What about William?"

Elizabeth started crying again. "Jane, I think I love him."

Jane's eyes grew wide. "When did this happen?"

"I don't know! I was so shocked when he confronted me; I said some things, terrible things. I didn't mean them. But I felt so disappointed in him. I was angry and hurt, and I wanted to hurt him.

"But later, I couldn't get how he looked at me out of my head. That desperate look when he said he loved me, and he didn't want to see again. It took me weeks to realize I couldn't bear it. That's when I knew…that's when I realized *why* I was so angry, so disappointed in him. It was because I loved him! I couldn't believe he would keep something from me, that he wouldn't trust me."

"Then why did you say the things you said about him and his father in the article?"

She lowered her head. "I didn't; Justin added it."

"*What?* He added something to your article?"

"Jane, wait—you don't understand. As my editor, he has the right to do that, especially since he was there at the house."

They sat quietly until Elizabeth's tears stopped. "Have you talked to William yet?"

"No. I don't know what to say."

"Tell him the truth," Jane urged.

"He's so angry. What if he won't listen? What if he won't take my call?"

"Hey, Jane, you got any more shampoo?" a male voice came from behind them.

Elizabeth whipped around and beheld a half-naked Chuck Bingley. He had strolled out of Jane's bedroom with a towel around his waist. He froze in place, like something from a French farce, when he realized they had company. Elizabeth, her eyes as wide as saucers, turned to her red-faced sister.

"I *told* you it was a bad time," Jane murmured.

"Umm, hello, Elizabeth," managed Chuck. "I-I guess, umm…I'm gonna get dressed now, all right?" Without waiting for a response, he fled back into the bedroom.

Elizabeth turned to Jane. "How long has—"

"Charles and I have been dating since Mardi Gras. He comes up here most weekends."

"Oh, Jane! I'm so—ha-ha-ha!" All the tension in the room was broken by Elizabeth's slightly hysterical laugher. It was only a moment before she was joined by her sister. The two held hands as they laughed until they cried.

They had begun to catch their breath when they were rejoined by an abashed Chuck. One look at him and the two girls were lost to laughter again. They quieted down when Chuck joined them at the table.

"Sorry, Chuck." Jane gave him a kiss on the cheek.

"That's all right. I must have looked like a raving lunatic." His smile disappeared as he greeted Elizabeth politely.

Elizabeth stared at the table. "Chuck, I know you won't believe this, and I wouldn't blame you if you never talked to me again, but I was so wrong about you and Alpha Iota, and I am *so* sorry about this. About everything." She began crying again.

Chuck let her cry for a moment before quietly saying her name.

After he said it a second time, Elizabeth raised her eyes. Instead of anger, she saw only seriousness. "Why?" was his only question.

Elizabeth gulped. "Because I was lied to. And I believed it."

He lightly sighed. "Tell me, Elizabeth. Tell me everything."

And so she did. For fifteen minutes, Elizabeth told him everything she had told Jane. Once she was done, Chuck stood up and paced about the room, running his hands though his hair. After a minute, he spoke.

"Aww, Lizzy…aww, crap! What do we do now?"

"You believe me?"

"Of course, I believe you. I only wish—aw, why go into that, huh?" He sat down and allowed Jane to take one of his hands in hers. "What are you going to do?"

"I'm going to write a retraction."

"Good. Will the newspaper print it?"

Elizabeth blinked. She had not thought of anything beyond the retraction. "I don't see why not."

Chuck gave Elizabeth a lopsided grin. "Hah. I'll believe it when I see it. Printing your retraction, I mean. For whatever it's worth, Lizzy, I forgive you." He reached for her across the table, and Elizabeth grasped his hand. "But, I can't say the same for the chapter, you understand."

She hung her head. "They probably hate me."

"I can't lie to you. Some do."

"I can't imagine how much money you guys or your families must have laid out for lawyers," said Elizabeth sadly. Chuck only nodded. "Oh, Chuck, how about you? I wish I could reimburse you!"

"Don't worry, Lizzy; I'm cool."

"But, you can't afford a lawyer!"

"I didn't have to. Mr. Darcy took care of me."

Elizabeth's hand went to her mouth. "William's father? He paid for your attorney?"

"More than that—his legal team represented me."

"I can't understand how you believed that stuff about Mr. Darcy," said Jane. "He's a wonderful, kind man."

Elizabeth was surprised. "You sound as though you know him?"

"I met him in January when he visited his daughter. That's when I met William."

Elizabeth's jaw dropped. "What? Visited his daughter? What are you talking about? You've known Will since January? Why didn't you tell me?"

"Didn't I tell you? Miss Darcy was in East Jefferson over New Year's, and I was assigned to her room. That's when I met them." She frowned. "I was sure I told you."

"New Year's?" She recalled William leaving Memphis abruptly. "Was she sick New Year's Eve?"

"Yes, she had an emergency appendectomy."

Elizabeth covered her eyes. "Oh, I am *such* a fool! That's why Will flew back from Memphis! And I thought he just ditched us. I immediately thought the worst of him. How despicable of me!"

"Lizzy," said Chuck kindly, "Will can be pretty closemouthed when it comes to his family. We didn't know about Gina until after we got back."

"It doesn't matter! I'm supposed to have some discernment! Now, it seems I don't have a clue! I don't know myself at all."

Jane took her hand. "Is there anything we can do?"

"No, this is a mess I have to fix by myself." She turned again to Chuck. "I will never forget what you've said to me. I want you to know I'll make this up to you if it's the last thing I ever do. Now, I've got to get to work."

Monday, March 22: Uptown
CHRIS PARKED HIS SILVERADO IN the lot of the riverside park behind Audubon Zoo and walked towards the slim figure sitting in the grass halfway down the riverbank. He got very close before speaking.

"Hello, Marianne."

Marianne turned to him, a slight smile on her lips. "Hi, Chris."

"May I sit here?" She nodded, and he took a seat, not too close to her. "Thanks for meeting with me. It's been hard to get in touch with you."

Marianne looked out at the moving water. "We've changed our phone number twice. The first time, right after Mardi Gras. We had to change it again when somebody from the university leaked it to the press and we started getting calls from reporters."

"Aw, that's cold."

She shrugged. "I think it bothered Lizzy the most. She's pretty disillusioned. Everything she'd believed in has turned ugly."

"That's generous of you, considering everything."

"She's my friend. She explained why she did what she did. In her mind, she was trying to help." She turned to Chris. "I know it's been tough on you guys, but can you, maybe, forgive Lizzy?"

"I won't know until I talk to her. But, Mari, I asked to see you to find out how *you're* doing, not Lizzy."

Marianne looked out at the river again. "Good. It's taken a while, but I'm good." Marianne half turned to him, her eyes on his knees. "I've been talking to someone. Touro set me up with a counselor. She's helping me see that some victims never remember anything and it could be a blessing that I don't remember. We're talking it through, and I'm gonna be okay."

"No repressed memory exercises?"

"No, she said it could cause more harm than good."

"She sounds like she knows her stuff. And school?"

Marianne looked down. "That's not so good. Nobody's supposed to know it was me in those stories, but they know." She sighed. "Some people stare at me as if I've grown a third eye. Other people won't even look at me as if I'm going to accuse them of something. I've had people actually come up and *congratulate* me as if I've done some great thing for women's rights or something. It's stupid. Mostly, people avoid me, even my fellow choir members. It's like they don't know what to say to me, so they stay away and say nothing."

Chris frowned. "It sounds lonely, Mari."

"It is."

"I'm really sorry." Chris winced. There was nothing he could say that would sufficiently express the pain he felt for Marianne and not embarrass her.

"Thank you, Chris." She looked at him. "And you? How are you doing?"

"I'm fine," he said, knowing he was lying. "Being in medical school has put a buffer between me and all the crazy stuff."

Marianne nodded. The two then talked about how their classes were going before settling down to watch the busy river.

Chris tried not to look at Marianne, for his feelings were far from calm. He had fallen in love with her, and he was royally torn up about what had happened. Initially, it had been a constant struggle between what he *wanted* to do—destroy John Waguespack—and what he *should* do—give Marianne space and time to deal with what had happened to her. He knew from Emma that Marianne had been getting help. Despite his training, stepping back and allowing the healing process to proceed without interference was the hardest thing he had ever done.

They were content to sit quietly in the sun, enjoying the fragrance of freshly cut grass and clover as the freighters and tugboats sailed up and down the Big Muddy. The cheerful shouts of playing children danced over deep rumbling boat engines, occasionally interrupted by the blare of ships' horns.

Marianne abruptly broke the peace. "Chris, how is Will?"

Chris leaned back on one elbow. "Not good. He's angry and hurt. I've never seen him like this." He shook his head. "I know it sounds trite after everything that's happened to you—"

"Please don't say that. What about Will?"

"It's like something in him died. A light has gone out in him."

Marianne drew up her knees to rest her chin as she hugged her shins. "Lizzy hurt him that bad?"

"Yeah."

"She loves him, you know."

"Yeah, I figured that out during our trip to Lafayette. Will must've felt the same; otherwise, he wouldn't have felt so betrayed."

She turned to him. "Will loves her?"

"Yeah, well, he did."

"And now?"

He shook his head. "I don't know if he hates her now or hates himself for caring. Whatever it is, it's bad."

Tears flowed down Marianne's lovely face. "What a disaster! They should be together."

Chris looked out at the river. "That ship has sailed."

A ship's horn sounded right at that moment. Marianne stared at Chris, hardly believing what she had heard. A giggle escaped from her pursed lips, which was answered by a sardonic grin on his face. "Sorry, bad joke."

Marianne reached out for his hand. "No, it's okay. What else can we do? We either laugh or cry. I prefer laughing. Thank you, Chris; you've been a good friend." At Chris's frown she asked, "What's wrong?"

"Nothing."

"No, really, tell me."

He looked deeply into her eyes, trying to judge her vulnerability, before turning away. "Now's not a good time for you, Mari. We'll talk some other time." He sighed. "But I am your friend, and I always will be."

Marianne must have realized what he had left unsaid. She looked away.

"Mari, I'm sorry. I shouldn't have said that. Don't let that bother you, please."

"It doesn't, Chris. I'm glad you told me," she managed. "I'm just surprised. I had no idea."

"Mari, I'm sorry."

"I can't handle something like that now."

"I know, I know. I just want to help. Be here for you. I'm not expecting anything else."

She turned to him. "That's not fair to you."

"This is not about me. Don't worry about me. I know what I'm doing."

"Do you? These are your feelings we're talking about."

"The risk is on me. Please don't concern yourself about that. No matter what, you're important to me—as a friend. I want you to get better. Trust me; that's all I want."

"That's all you want for now. Is that enough?"

"If I'm truly your friend, it will be."

She looked at him, her eyes watery. "If…if I could feel more for you, I would. You believe that, don't you?"

He nodded sadly. "If friendship's all we ever have together, that's enough for me."

She nodded and turned back towards the river. Together they watched the sunset.

Wednesday, March 24

TWO DAYS LATER IN THE offices of the *Loyola VOICE*, Justin looked at the copy Elizabeth had just handed him. "What's this?"

"It's my follow-up on the Alpha Iota story," said Elizabeth coldly. She knew a fight was coming, and she was ready.

"Follow-up? What the hell? This looks like a retraction!"

"If a clarification of the facts of the story changes the original story, then I guess it could be called a retraction."

"I can't run this!" Justin cried.

"Why not?"

"It makes us look like idiots!"

"Don't we have a responsibility to tell the truth?"

"Yeah, but…Elizabeth, I ain't running this 'til I talk to Jennings!"

AN HOUR LATER, DR. JENNINGS had finished reading Elizabeth's new story. She looked up and her expression was not friendly.

"Do you stand by the facts in *this* story, Elizabeth?" she asked in a dangerous voice.

"Yes, ma'am. Since writing my original story, it's come to light that one of my sources had been, to put it mildly, dishonest with me."

"That's this Wickham person?"

"Yes, ma'am. I've learned he's a felon and not associated with either Tulane or Alpha Iota. He lied to me, Professor."

"But the cover-up—"

Elizabeth cut her off. "Pardon me, but cover-up of what? Even the *Pontchartrain Guardian* says there is no physical evidence of an assault. The only thing we know is John Waguespack carried an unconscious female out of the AI House while his guest, Greg Wickham, got into a scuffle with William Darcy. All of this in front of a dozen witnesses. We don't know what caused the girl's condition, and we must assume the AI members are innocent of inappropriate behavior until proven otherwise. The AIs were not forthcoming with us, but they do have a right not to speak to the press."

Dr. Jennings crossed her arms. "You know this throws your original story into question."

"If that's the case, so be it."

"Who got to you? The Darcys?" Justin sneered.

Elizabeth became furious but tried to hold her temper. "I'm sorry to disappoint you, Justin, but no one 'got to' me. I'm reporting the facts." Her cold tone left him in no doubt of how she felt about his accusation.

"*His* facts," Justin shot back.

Elizabeth didn't back down. "*The* facts, Justin. There's no other way to look at this, no matter how much some people may want to. Besides, William Darcy hates the very air I breathe."

"This might make it up to him," Dr. Jennings suggested.

Elizabeth looked at her mentor in amazement. "I can't believe you said that."

Dr. Jennings tried to stare down Elizabeth and failed. She turned to Justin. "Take this and draw up something for this week's *VOICE* —" She was cut off by Elizabeth clearing her throat. "Yes?"

"I'm requesting you print that verbatim, Professor," Elizabeth said.

"That's an editorial decision."

"I only ask," Elizabeth continued, "because I've sent a copy to Mr. Rank at the *Pontchartrain Guardian*, and I don't want to embarrass the *VOICE*."

The professor was flabbergasted. "You...you sent *this*?" Her face darkened. "You bitch! How dare you embarrass me?"

Elizabeth was shocked. "Embarrass you? I'm sorry, but this isn't about you. Innocent people have been harmed, and I'm trying to do right by—"

"Bullshit! You're covering your ass! You got the story wrong, and you're trying to save yourself from a libel suit by the Darcys!" The woman was ranting. "I put my credibility with the *Guardian* on the line for this story, and this is how you repay me? By making a fool out of me? I won't stand for it!" She tossed the story back at Elizabeth. "All right, Miss Boudreaux, we'll run your retraction, but don't bother coming to my class any longer this semester! You've flunked."

Elizabeth was shaken at the venomous attack, and even Justin was taken aback.

"You're going to fail me based on one assignment? That's not fair!" Some of Elizabeth's bravado faded.

"Get out of here, Boudreaux. You're fired from the *VOICE*," Dr. Jennings snapped.

"All right, I'll withdraw from the course—"

"I won't sign the withdrawal form. You're toast."

Elizabeth gasped. "But, you can't! I'll lose my scholarship!"

Dr. Jennings was unmoved. "You should have thought of that before writing libelous stories."

Elizabeth grew dizzy over the unfairness of it all. "I'll go to the dean."

"That's your right, but see if it does you any good. Get out of my sight. Now!"

Elizabeth turned and left the room without a response. Dr. Jennings then turned to Justin. "You have anything to say about this?"

"No, ma'am," Justin managed. He needed the credits in Jennings's course to finish his degree, and he wasn't going to blow his graduation.

Friday, March 26

CHRIS WALKED INTO WILLIAM'S BEDROOM. "Will, take a look at this!" He handed his sleepy roommate a copy of the *Guardian*. "Elizabeth's recanted her story! Isn't that great?"

William scanned the story before putting it aside, his stoic expression never changing.

"Aren't you happy about this?"

William turned to his friend. "I'm glad the truth is out, but this doesn't change anything."

"What do you mean? This guarantees the end of the police investigation."

"But not the university's." William sat up in his bed, his feet on the floor. "I've been doing a lot of thinking. This is my fault. I screwed up. I gave the chapter some really bad advice. Henry was right: we should've gone to the dean. Now, it's too late."

Chris didn't know where William was going with his reasoning. "That's not what the lawyers are saying."

William waved him off. "Screw that! Dad and everybody else have spent way too much money trying to fix what I did. It's time to end this."

"How are you going to do that?" A sense of dread grew in Chris.

William gave his friend a meaningful look before reaching for the phone to call his father.

Warehouse District

A STUNNED GEORGE DARCY SAT back in his office chair, telephone receiver still to his ear, as the implications of William's intentions became clear. "Son, are you *sure* this is what you want to do?"

"It's what I have to do."

"But the retraction in the *Guardian* —wasn't it you who talked sense to Miss Boudreaux?"

There was a pause. *"I haven't talked to her since the first story came out."*

"Oh. I thought you were her source. Y'all having been friends and all."

"Were friends, Dad. Past tense. That's over."

"This is over, too, now."

"You know *the university is not finished with us. But I can end it for good."*

George Darcy shifted in his chair, his voice rising. "William, listen to me! Being noble is all fine and good, but there's a point at which a person can veer into self-pity and even self-destruction! Sacrificing yourself for your fraternity—"

"Dad, don't you see? It's my fault."

"You did nothing wrong."

"It was my bad advice."

"Bad advice is not the same as doing bad!"

"You taught me to be a man, to own up to what I've done. Because of my bad advice, a lot of money is being spent on lawyers and stuff. If I can stop it and help a lot of people put this thing behind them, why should I not? Wouldn't you do the same in my place?"

George Darcy knew he was losing this argument. "William, there's a big difference between owning up and shouldering more than your share of the blame."

"I know. I've thought this through, believe me, and this is the right thing to do."

George Darcy recognized that tone of voice. He had raised his son to think for himself, and this was the result. He knew William's mind was made up, and nothing he could say would turn his son from his intended course of action. He was proud of and afraid for Will at the same time. His son's ironclad sense of honor made him an outstanding young man, but it was also his greatest vulnerability.

Be careful what you teach your children; they may learn it, he thought. He sighed as he ran his hand over his face. "All right. I'll call our lawyer on Monday."

Friday, April 16: Uptown

JUSTICE MOVED SLOWLY IN THE hallowed halls of academia. After weeks of negotiations between the lawyers, a closed-door meeting broke the logjam, and an agreement was made.

The AIs were called before the dean in April after spring break. Chuck and Henry represented the chapter. George Katz attended as alumni advisor, and William Darcy was present, too.

The AIs stood before the dean's desk. Sitting beside the dean was a representative of Alpha Iota's National Office. After pleasantries were exchanged, the officials got down to business.

The dean read from a statement recounting the events and violations of campus rules.

"Now before I continue, I must thank Mr. Darcy for the extraordinary cooperation shown by his legal team," he said to William. The other AIs looked at their friend in surprise, but William did not lose the grim expression on his face as he acknowledged the compliment.

"Gentlemen, it is the finding of the university that the Tulane Chapter of Alpha Iota engaged in the following violations of the rules regarding fraternities. One, having alcoholic or other forbidden substances on the premises of the fraternity house. We have taken into account that the chapter was unaware of this violation, but we find that the chapter should have taken greater care in preventing such an occurrence by exercising greater control over guests in the house. Two, that the chapter failed to report the incident of February 16 to this office in a timely fashion. We have taken into account the affidavit provided by Mr. Darcy and have adjusted our decision accordingly." He held up a paper.

"Therefore, it is the decision of the university that the Tulane Chapter of Alpha Iota be on probation effective immediately for a period ending no sooner than the end of the 1999-2000 academic year. Alpha Iota will not be allowed to participate in any rush activities during this time, will not pledge or initiate any new members into the fraternity, or make any formal or informal agreements to do so after this period of probation is lifted. The only exception from this last requirement is that the chapter shall be allowed to initiate the current pledge class. Otherwise, there shall be no parties or any other events in the house, unless requested by the fraternity's National Office. Regular meetings of the fraternity will be allowed.

"In addition, we require the following steps be taken. Charles Bingley shall turn over the office of president to the president-elect, Henry Tilney, effective immediately. The entire chapter shall take sensitivity courses on women's issues and campus safety and shall volunteer at a local women's shelter, putting in no less than twenty-five service hours per member. Mr. Tilney shall make monthly reports to this office on the progress the chapter is making on these items. The university shall have full access to the financial records of the chapter during this probationary period."

At his nod, the fraternity official then spoke. "The National Office of Alpha Iota fully supports the findings of the university, and we concur with the conditions during this probationary period. The chapter shall be on probation from national. We will be closely monitoring things, and there will be reports to turn in, as well. We add two other requirements. First, that Alumni Brother Dr. George Katz resigns as alumni advisor to the chapter and agrees not to seek this position for a period of five years."

George nodded. "I expected that, and I have my resignation right here."

"Thank you, Brother Katz. Second, that Alumni Brother William Darcy disassociates himself from the chapter effective immediately. He shall not attend any functions of the chapter, official or unofficial, and shall absent himself from the house grounds for a period of no less than five years."

The assembled murmured at this, but William's stony expression did not change.

The dean looked at William. "Mr. Darcy, in his affidavit, takes full and total responsibility for advising the chapter to act as it did in this matter. He goes on for some length on how he, and he alone, convinced and bullied the members of the chapter—"

"That's not true!" cried Chuck.

"Shut up, Charles," William said through clenched teeth.

The dean looked at William. "Mr. Darcy, do you stand by this affidavit?"

"I do, sir. The fault is mine and mine alone. I'm ready to face the consequences."

"Will, don't do this," Henry pleaded. George had a look of horror on his face while Chuck shook his head.

William would not look at any of them. "Sir, let's get this over with."

The two officials looked at each other and shrugged. "It's your funeral, Mr. Darcy. Very well. William Darcy, due to the poor judgment and leadership you displayed in this matter, you are hereby dismissed from Beta Gamma Sigma, the honorary business scholastic fraternity. You are required to resign your office in student government immediately. Your grade-point average shall stand, and you will be allowed to participate in graduation, but you will not be allowed to present the graduate students' remarks at the Freeman School's graduation."

William had closed his eyes during the dean's recitation. His friends were visibly distraught over the sentence. The dean leaned over the desk, a form in his hand.

"Mr. Darcy, there is still time to recant," the dean reminded him kindly.

William opened his eyes. "No, sir. Where to I sign?"

Friday, April 23: Carrolton

THE PATROLMAN KNOCKED ON THE door of the apartment building and cooled his heels until the manager opened it. "About time ya got 'ere," he said.

"Yeah, well, I'm here now." The officer stood impatiently. "Let's get it over with. Where's the place?"

The manager retrieved his keys, and the two of them walked up the stairs to the second-floor apartment. "Dey only a month behind on da rent, but—I dunno, dere's something's funny about dis." With the NOPD as witness, the manager opened the apartment. The smell of rotten food hit them.

"Aw, for da love of gawd!"

The cop moved in quickly. The place had obviously been tossed, and uneaten food was on the kitchen counter. Flies were all over the place. The officer quickly searched the place.

"Did you know there was a lady here?" The cop came out of the bathroom with a bra in his hand.

"Yeah, da other guy moved out a couple-three months ago." The manger moaned. "Dey stiffed me?"

"No, too much personal stuff left here. It looks like these people were surprised and taken out of here abruptly, probably right as they were fixing dinner. Look at the uncooked chicken over there."

"I don't need ta; it stinks like shit! Thank gawd da owner built dis place like a tank, or all da neighbors would've been on my ass! How long have dey been gone?"

"At least a month. Any drug activity around here?"

"You kiddin' me? Shit, I run off junkies all da time 'round 'ere."

The officer shook his head. "No, I meant in this apartment."

The man scratched his head. "In 'ere? No, I've never had no trouble from dese folks. Dat's why I called ya."

"Right. I'll file a missing persons report. Give me the tenant's name."

"Umm." The manger held up a rental contract. "Tommy Bertram."

Chapter 22

Wednesday, April 28: Uptown

Elizabeth heard the connection ring once, and then came the dreaded three-tone alert.

"I'm sorry. The number you have reached has been disconnected or is no longer in service. If you believe you have reached this recording in error, please hang up and dial the operator."

She hung up the phone in frustration. Apparently, William didn't just change his phone number; he had the service disconnected. Had he moved? It made sense. Why stay in New Orleans with all the publicity going on when he could simply return home and commute in? The number to Dansereau Plantation was unlisted. She sighed. Chuck Bingley may have forgiven her, but he wasn't going to give her that number or the one to William's cell.

Chris offered no solution. He was still in the apartment, and he would answer his cell phone, but he refused to give up William's number. None of the other AIs would speak to her.

Elizabeth groaned. How was she going to apologize to William if she couldn't get in touch with him? Wait for him outside the business school building as he exited class? No, she didn't know his schedule. Besides, she couldn't take the chance he would refuse to talk to her. Her wounded ego could not stand it.

There was only one solution. Words had gotten her into trouble; therefore, she would use words to get her out of it. She looked at her computer but changed her mind. An email would be too impersonal. Something this important had to be handwritten. William deserved nothing less.

She reached for a legal pad and began drafting her letter.

MORE THAN AN HOUR LATER, Elizabeth leaned back to review her effort.

Dear William,

Thank you for reading this letter of apology. I want to start by admitting that what I wrote in my article was wrong, and what I said to you during our argument was wrong.

The terrible things implied about your father in the story were despicable. I can only say in my defense that I did not write the part about you and your family. Others did. But I cowardly allowed it to be added to the article. For that, I take full blame.

I hope you had the chance to read my retraction. It was too long in coming, but I hope you can appreciate that I did realize my error and have tried to make amends. I make no excuses for what I did, but I hope you will give me the opportunity to explain what happened and why I allowed myself to hurt someone whom I had seen as a friend. You have been a friend to me, William, and I am truly sorry for the pain I caused you and your family.

Marianne is like a sister to me. When I realized someone had hurt her, I became livid. My one thought was revenge. I know that feeling was wrong. I was taught better by my family and my faith. I allowed my anger to blind me.

When I went to the AI House that Thursday night, I was not thinking critically. I wanted answers and, in my arrogance, thought I deserved them. I should have trusted my friends. I did not. That was wrong.

Why did I listen to Greg Wickham and believe his story? I could say he was very convincing with his half-truths and outright lies. And while that would be accurate, it wouldn't be the truth.

William, I must admit that I was angry with you. During the months I had gotten to know you, I grew to believe you were an honorable person. I trusted you and held you to an impossibly high standard. I felt my friends and I were safe with you. Irrationally, when Mari was hurt, I blamed you for not protecting her. I felt you personally had let down my friends and me.

Yes, I know this is unreasonable; in fact, it's almost insane. It has taken me a very long time to realize I even felt this way. Once I did know it, I had to think even longer to determine why. It is because I respect you so much. I know that sounds funny after what I said and what I wrote, but it is the truth. When Mari was hurt and you wouldn't talk to me, I felt betrayed.

I don't know why you wouldn't talk with me that night at the AI house. I wish you had, but I guess you had your reasons. Perhaps you knew I wouldn't listen to you. I like to think I would have, but maybe you'd have been right, given the events that followed.

Our argument hurt me very much for two reasons. First, because much of what you said about me was true. Not about my ambition —I care nothing about having my byline in the paper. But my desire for revenge was all I could think of.

Second, because of the feelings you admitted to me. I was surprised because I had no idea you felt that way about me. Now that I can reflect upon it, I'm even more disgusted with myself. I can only imagine the pain I caused you, a person I care about more than I knew.

William, I must admit you have sometimes intimidated me. It is not your fault. Your confidence, your intelligence, and your success are to be admired. But deep inside, I thought I wasn't good enough for you, and that rankled. I don't blame you; this is totally on me. You had always been a gentleman and a friend until I attacked you. I didn't know how special you were until you were gone.

I'm not telling you I care about you to earn your forgiveness. I don't deserve it. But as you were honest with me, I must be honest with you. You were once one of my dearest friends, and whether you can forgive me or not, you will always remain a friend in my heart.

My one wish is to deliver this apology in person to you and your family. But if that is impossible, I offer this letter as a poor *substitute. If you choose to end our acquaintance, I will certainly understand and respect your wishes. I will only add that I wish you only happiness in the future.*

God bless you,
Elizabeth Boudreaux

Elizabeth wiped away a tear as she bent to address an envelope.

Tuesday, May 4
"I PICKED UP YOUR MAIL," Marianne announced as Elizabeth walked through the door.

Elizabeth looked at the stack. She paused at the third one. It was her letter to William, and it was marked *Return to Sender.*

She sat down. *Now what?* She glanced at the Loyola calendar on the wall. The word *graduation* caught her attention.

Elizabeth moved to her computer and pulled up the Tulane calendar off the Internet.

Saturday, May 8: Baton Rouge
CARRIE BINGLEY SAT ON THE couch in the front room of John Buford's condo, her feet tucked underneath her, snuggling with her boyfriend. He had one arm wrapped around her and the TV remote in his hand. The LSU Tiger baseball team was on the tube. A big bowl of popcorn was on the table, and there were beers within reach. She couldn't think of a better way to spend a warm Saturday afternoon.

"Aw, come on, ump, are you blind? That wasn't a strike!" complained Carrie. A big baseball fan, she wore an LSU T-shirt commemorating the four NCAA championships the Tigers had won in the 1990s.

Buford shook his head in agreement just as the doorbell rang. "Hang on, babe, I'll get it," he said as he got to his feet. Carrie said nothing, her concentration on the game before her.

"Where is she? Where's my daughter?" came a woman's voice from the foyer.

Carrie's eyes snapped wide open. She leapt to her feet, her heart in her stomach, as Catherine Bingley swept into the room, followed by Buford.

"Mom! What are you doing here?"

"I might ask the same of you, Caroline Ann Bingley! This certainly isn't Anna Elliot's dorm room. I don't know what kind of finals you're studying for, but it doesn't look like Public Policy!" She had her hands on her hips.

Carrie blanched. She had decided to keep her relationship with John Buford secret from her mother for the present. Knowing the woman's obsession with her marrying well, particularly with William Darcy, Carrie wanted to put off the inevitable confrontation. In the weeks that passed, Carrie had delayed and procrastinated. Now the day of reckoning was upon them.

Still, Carrie was not one to back down. "Mom, let me introduce you to my boyfriend, John."

"John Taylor Buford, Jr. at your service, ma'am." He extended his hand with a smile.

Catherine Bingley ignored the gesture. "We'll see about that. I wish to speak to my daughter for a few minutes—*alone*."

Buford took the insult without a blink. "Of course. Make yourself at home. I'll be in the kitchen." He gave Carrie a quick wink and left the room.

"Mother, you have no—"

"Don't you take that tone of voice with me, young lady! Just what do you think you're doing?"

"I'm watching a baseball game with my boyfriend, Mom."

"Your boyfriend!" The older woman pointed at the kitchen. "*That's* your boyfriend? And just when were you going to tell me?" She didn't allow Carrie to answer. "Never, I suppose. If it weren't for Gloria Van de Snoot telling me she's seen you in this neighborhood —Ah! You didn't know she lives just down the block, did you? She tells me you've been spending a great deal of time here!"

"You had me followed?"

"Don't be so dramatic! I just had lunch with Gloria. That's when she told me."

"So, you came looking for me. Why didn't you just call?"

"Why, so you could lie? No, I wanted to see for myself."

Carrie sighed. "Very well, you've met John. I suppose you're wondering why I didn't tell you before. It's because I knew you'd react just like this."

Catherine's voice went up a notch. "And just how am I reacting?"

"*Over*-reacting, Mother. You're overreacting. I knew you'd be disappointed."

"And why shouldn't I be?" she cried. "You're throwing away your chance of landing William Darcy!"

Carrie had had enough. "Stop it! I'm not landing *anybody*, especially William Darcy! You are so intent on me making this great catch, you've forgotten about how I feel—about what I want."

Catherine sneered. "How would you know what you want? You're too young to know what you want!"

"I'm almost twenty-two."

"Twenty-two—and you think you know everything! Let me tell you, missy, if I knew what I know now when I was twenty-two—"

"Mother, I *don't* want to talk about Daddy!"

"Very well, then. Get your things. We're leaving right now."

She was now sure her mother had lost her mind. "Leaving? I'm not leaving!"

"Yes, you are! You are not going to throw your life away, not while you're living under my roof!"

Before Carrie could respond, Buford strolled out of the kitchen with a polite smile on his face. "Pardon me, ladies, but I couldn't help but overhear your conversation. I think everybody ought to settle down so we can talk about this like adults."

Catherine Bingley turned on him. "You're intruding on a private conversation! Leave us immediately!"

Buford's smile disappeared from his face. "Pardon me, again, Mrs. Bingley, but you are sadly mistaken about something. This is *my* house, and no one dismisses me from one of *my* rooms. I would suggest you sit down—right there." He pointed at a chair. "And then we'll continue our conversation."

"How dare you!"

"Sit. Down. Ma'am."

Buford's posture could not be called threatening; he was barely in the room. His voice was low and controlled. But his eyes blazed with a righteous blue fire. Mrs. Bingley must have felt the force of his personality because, with a small gasp, she half-fell into the chair indicated. Carrie couldn't deny his power any more than her mother and, a moment later, found herself seated even though her boyfriend's command was directed at Mrs. Bingley.

Buford's expression changed immediately. "Thank you, Mrs. Bingley," he said calmly. "I'm sure we've got a lot to talk about, but I think we ought to find out a couple things first."

He turned to Carrie and gently asked, "Carrie, do you want to leave?"

Carrie's eyes started to fill. "I think it's best that Mother and I—"

"Carrie. Do *you* want to leave?"

The pair stared into each other's eyes. Buford's blue eyes blazed again, but not in anger this time. Carrie felt the same exposed sensation she had experienced in February in a Metairie motel room. She knew John could see into her soul.

"No."

Buford smiled. "Good. I don't want you to leave, either."

Catherine Bingley was heard from again. "Well, *I'm* not going to sit around here!"

Without taking his eyes off Carrie or losing his smile, Buford said, "Mrs. Bingley, we're not finished yet." The statement sounded like a command. He blinked as he seemed to gather his thoughts. "Carrie, this might be a little soon, but I think it's time we made it clear how things stand between us and where we're going."

With that, he got on one knee before her.

"Caroline Ann Bingley, you are the most important person in my life. I love knowing you, I love being with you, and I cannot image spending my life with anyone else in this world. I love you with all my heart, with all my strength, and with all my soul. Please make my life complete by saying you feel the same, that you will live with me, be with me, and grow old with me. Carrie, my dearest love, will you marry me?"

"Oh, my God!" gasped Mrs. Bingley.

For her part, Carrie could say nothing. In fact, she could hardly believe what she had just heard. Only Buford's intense, loving, and nervous gaze convinced her she wasn't dreaming. Still, she could only manage to nod her head as her hands flew to her lips, at first gently, and then with far more enthusiasm as a smile grew on her face. Finally, like a bubble bursting forth, she cried though her fingers, "*Yes*! Oh my God, yes!"

Buford reached into his jeans pocket. "Here, this is for you. I bought it a little while ago, not planning to give it so soon. But I just got it from my bedroom, seeing how it might come in handy." He handed her the small box.

"Oh, give me a break," came Catherine's voice from behind him.

"Quiet, Mother," said Carrie absently as she opened the box. Glittering inside was a small diamond set in a gold band. She giggled slightly as she wiped a tear from her eye.

"It's not that big, I know," Buford was saying. "Just call it a down payment on what you deserve."

"Hush up, you lovely man," she said happily. She allowed Buford to take the ring out of the box and slip it on her ring finger. It fit perfectly. "I love it, Johnny. Oh, I love you so much," she said as she leaned in to share a kiss. "How did you know my size?"

He whispered in her ear, "I tried on one of your rings a few weeks back. It was the same size as my pinkie."

"When did you do that?" she whispered back.

"While you were sleeping."

Carrie definitely didn't want her mother to know about that! "Thank you, sweetie," she said in a normal voice.

They shared a look of deep understanding. "I *told* you that you were doomed."

"Yes, you did." She lightly stroked his face.

Buford grinned and got to his feet after kissing the ring and the finger it now graced. He turned to his future mother-in-law.

"Mrs. Bingley, I'm afraid we got off on the wrong foot. Now that everyone understands how things are, I hope we can make it up over dinner tonight. Why don't you take a seat on the couch next to Carrie? I'm sure you've got a lot of planning to do for the wedding." He turned his head towards his intended. "When, babe? Next year—the summer after you graduate?"

"That sounds fine, Johnny." Her head was still in a whirl.

"It's your call, sweetheart." He turned back to Mrs. Bingley. "Whatever *Carrie* wants," he warned her.

Oh, my God! He's standing up to Mom! Can I love him any more?

He held out his hand. "Can I get you something? We've got beer and soft drinks. How about some coffee?"

The intimidated woman allowed herself to be helped to the sofa. "C-coffee would be fine."

"I'll put a pot on right now. How about you, Carrie?"

"I think I need another beer."

"Comin' right up," he said as Mrs. Bingley sat down next to her daughter. "We'll grab some dinner in a little while." He disappeared into the kitchen.

Carrie gazed at her ring. *Johnny, you are so going to get laid tonight!*

Her mother broke in breathlessly. "He's…he's a bit forceful, isn't he?"

Carrie didn't take her eyes off her hand. "Haven't noticed, Mom."

Catherine Bingley seemed to catch her second wind. "Well, I hope you're happy! I wash my hands of you. You made your bed. You can just sleep in it."

Carrie blushed as she realized she and her mother had the same thought for different reasons.

"Oh, hush, Mom." Knowing what would interest her mother, she added, "Johnny's part of the most prestigious law firm in Baton Rouge. He'll make partner before you know it. Just look at this place! You think it came cheap? I think he can afford me. Now, don't you think my ring's pretty?"

Uptown

In the weeks leading up to finals, Elizabeth met separately with George Katz and Chris Breaux. George claimed no apology was necessary and assured her his position at Tulane Medical School was safe.

Like Chuck Bingley, Chris graciously accepted Elizabeth's apology. Marianne had accompanied her that day, and after prodding from both girls, Chris admitted he had seen very little of William. He was commuting from St. Charles Parish to class more days than not. Chris had moved to a new apartment, and William sometimes used the sofa bed. He also revealed the details of William's affidavit to the administration and his punishment.

"Give up his honors?" Elizabeth cried. "No, no, no! That's not fair! This is all my fault!"

"We tried to talk Will out of falling on his sword over this, but we might as well have been talking to a wall." Chris gave Elizabeth a hug. "He was determined, Lizzy, and nothing was going to sway him."

Elizabeth began to cry. "He must really hate me now."

"I don't know. He does feel really badly about this whole situation."

"Well, he's not the only one who's suffered!" Marianne's eyes flashed. "Lizzy lost her scholarship."

Chris expressed his concern, but Elizabeth waved him off as she dried her eyes. "I didn't really lose it. I'm giving it up. I talked to the dean, and she allowed me to drop Dr. Jennings's class. So I'll earn only fifteen hours this semester instead of nineteen, and I'm going to leave Loyola and change my major."

"Really? I though you wanted to be a journalist?"

"Not anymore. This whole experience has left a bad taste in my mouth. I need a new start, so I'm transferring to Nicholls State back home. They'll take my credits. I'm changing my major to communications. Writing and talking are what I'm good at. That is, as long as I know what the hell I'm talking about first instead of just shooting off my mouth." Elizabeth did not try to hide her bitterness.

Chris patted her shoulder. "Life is a series of hard lessons, Liz. It's how we deal with them that matters." He spoke to Elizabeth, but his eyes flicked to Marianne, who nodded in understanding. "What happened to the *VOICE*?"

"I was told they won't be funded next semester, so it's gone." Elizabeth changed the subject. "I need to talk to William. Can you help me?"

"Lizzy, I've tried, but I guess he's not ready yet." Chris was pained. "He's still in a bad place. Give him time."

"I'm afraid to wait. It might take too long. It might be too late if I do."

"Too late for what?"

Elizabeth didn't answer that question. "When does the business school graduation start?"

"It's next Saturday, about ten in the morning. Why?"

She reached over to pick up the returned letter. "Because I'm going to hand him this."

Saturday, May 15: Uptown

ELIZABETH WOKE UP BRIGHT AND early. The previous week was finals week, and both girls bore down on their studies, forsaking espressos and television. The night before, Marianne and Elizabeth shared a quiet meal together downtown and spent a long time talking before returning to their room to sleep.

It was a Saturday, and usually a casual day for Elizabeth, but today she wanted to look her best. She showered and fussed over her outfit before deciding on a grey suit with a chartreuse shell. She thought about her hair. Putting it up seemed too formal, while keeping it down too casual. She compromised by fixing it in a ponytail.

"What do you think?" she asked her sleepy roommate.

"You look like you're going to a job interview," Marianne mumbled. "What time is it?"

"Almost 8:30. I gotta go! Wish me luck!" She grabbed the envelope with William's letter as she let herself out.

Marianne sat up, rubbing her eyes. Thinking it was still too early to get up, she reached for the remote and turned on the TV. She wanted to get the local weather, so she turned on Channel 15's rebroadcast of last night's ten o'clock news. She snuggled into the covers as a commercial ended.

Thirty seconds past 8:30, people outside her door could hear her scream. *"No! No! Oh God, no!"*

IT WAS A FINE, SUNNY May morning. The temperature was already nearing eighty, but the humidity was reasonable. Elizabeth would have enjoyed the walk to the Freeman School Graduation except for her anxiety over what was to come.

Her plan was simple. William was certainly going to attend his graduation, and surely, his family would be there, as well. In a way, he was a captive audience. All that was necessary was to approach him before or after the event and apologize if given the opportunity, or hand him his letter if he would not speak to her. If allowed, she would personally apologize to Mr. Darcy, too. Getting a ticket to the ceremony proved to be easy. Chuck Bingley had already invited Jane, and his extra ticket was available.

The only flaw in her plan was the unpredictability of William's reaction. It was conceivable he would refuse to speak with her. Chris assured her he was going as William's guest, so she put her trust in him to prevent William from totally dismissing her until she at least delivered the letter. The candidates for Bachelors and Masters degrees usually congregated in front of the hall until the time to line up for the procession, so Elizabeth thought it best to see William then. To be honest, she wasn't sure her nerves could bear to sit through the ceremony, waiting to deliver her message afterwards. It was not a perfect plan, but it was the best she could devise.

Elizabeth turned the corner and beheld the throng waiting outside the auditorium. She took a deep breath, screwed up her courage, and continued onward. The candidates were in black robes and mortarboards, with green-and-white tassels. The MBA graduates wore light brown stoles at their throats. Elizabeth noticed some of the candidates had the white cords signifying the honors they had earned, and her conscience ached a bit, knowing what William had sacrificed.

Her cell phone buzzed in her purse, but she ignored it.

She walked closer, slowly scanning the crowd. She did not see William or Chris, but she did notice Jane and Chuck with a group of people. She waved at them as she approached, hoping they would know where William was. She saw Chuck's sister, Carrie, was there with a tall, dark-haired man and an older woman she took to be Mrs. Bingley. No one noticed her, so she called out.

"Hey, everybody! Great day for a graduation, huh?"

The shocked expressions on their faces surprised Elizabeth. "Umm, you knew I was coming, right? Did Chuck forget to tell you? What a rat! Hi, Jane, Carrie." She stuck out her hand to the older woman. "Hello, I'm Elizabeth Boudreaux, Jane's sister."

The woman shook Elizabeth's hand limply. "Catherine Bingley, Charles's mother." She looked at Chuck helplessly.

Jane leaned in. "Elizabeth, didn't you hear? Don't you know what happened?"

Elizabeth realized both Jane and Carrie had been crying. "Jane! What's wrong? What happened?" Jane tried to speak, but could say nothing.

A red-eyed Chuck croaked, "It's…it's Will."

"Oh, my God!" Fear seized Elizabeth's heart. "Will? Has something happened to Will?"

"Will's okay! But his dad—it was all over the news last night."

Elizabeth held her breath as dread overcame her.

"George Darcy was killed in an automobile accident yesterday."

Chapter 23

Tuesday, May 18

Ad in other news tonight, the New Orleans business, educational, and political establishment gathered today at St. Louis Cathedral to say goodbye to one of the community's giants, George Darcy, CEO of Delta Global Shipping. Mr. Darcy, a businessman and philanthropist, was killed in a two-car collision last Friday afternoon on River Road near his home in St. Charles Parish. Survived by a son and daughter, Mr. Darcy was interned in the family crypt in Destrehan after a funeral Mass, presided over by the archbishop. Business and political leaders from across the state were in attendance.

Questions are being raised about the driver of the other car in the accident. Richard Musgrove of River Ridge, who also died, had his driver's license suspended late last year due to a third DWI conviction, but did not serve the minimum mandatory thirty days in jail. The Jefferson Parish judge involved in the case has refused comment."

June: Uptown

LIFE MOVED ON IN THE academic world as in all other worlds. Elizabeth and Marianne completed their studies as the Darcy tragedy hung over them like a persistent cloud. Their roles reversed, and it was Marianne who offered consolation to a devastated Elizabeth, helping her come to grips with what had befallen a mutual friend to whom they had no opportunity to offer comfort. They could not impose themselves on the family's grief at the funeral, and the small contributions to the Tulane Scholarship Fund, in lieu of flowers, just didn't seem enough.

But time healed all wounds—or at least covered them with scabs—even the deepest. The semester was done, and it was time to turn another page.

Elizabeth sat on her bed, stripped of its sheets, among her packed and boxed possessions, watching Marianne finish her packing.

"I wish you weren't transferring so far away," Elizabeth groaned.

"We've been through this. It's for the best. I get to start over again, and Centenary College has a wonderful Vocal Music program."

"But Shreveport? Mari, that's almost in Texas!"

"Yes. But it's not the wilderness, you know. They have running water and electricity and everything. I hear they're even gonna get *telephones* next month," she teased.

"Okay, okay, I'm sorry, but I'm still going to miss you."

"You could come up and visit."

"Five hours away," she pouted.

Marianne laughed. "The way you drive? More like four!"

"You're going to try out for the choir this summer?"

"Mmm-hmm. If I get in, I'll be traveling all over. They perform at the White House most years."

"Wow. The famous Centenary College Choir. That's a great opportunity."

Marianne walked over and gave her a hug. "I will miss you, you rat."

At that moment, Chris walked into the room. "All set, Mari?"

She and Elizabeth broke apart. "Hi, Chris. Yeah, just—" She was interrupted by the telephone ringing. "I'll get it. It's probably Mom." She picked up the receiver as Chris turned to Elizabeth.

"You shipping out today, too?" Chris eyed Elizabeth's belongings. "Need any help schlepping this stuff to your car?"

Elizabeth shook her head. "Thanks for the offer, Chris, but—"

"She's got *us*!" cried Emma as she and George entered the already crowded room. "Look, Liz! I've brought help! He's not too smart, but he's as strong as a mule!"

"You betcha, Miz Emma," drawled the good doctor.

"Good to see you, buddy," Chris said as he shook George's hand. "We'll all pitch in, and we can knock this out in no time."

"Sounds good. Where do we start? Jeeze, you gals can collect some stuff!"

Emma patted George on the shoulder. "All in the name of beauty, George. We do it all for you."

"Yeah, right. Hi, Mari," he said as Marianne hung up the phone. He got a hug for an answer.

"I'm gonna miss you guys!" she cried.

Despite Chris's optimistic prediction, the group had to take a breather an hour later in the lobby, the job three-quarters done. The guys sat in armchairs while the girls searched for soft drinks.

"Got Henry and Cathy's present, yet?" Chris asked George.

"Yeah, got them a place setting in their china. You?"

"Haven't bought anything yet. Got time, though. The wedding's not 'til August. You going?"

George shook his head. "With me dating Emma now, nah."

Soon after the blow-up of the scandal, Emma and Cathy had a discussion. While polite, it was clear Cathy demanded that Emma choose between Elizabeth and the chapter. Emma admired Cathy's loyalty to *her boys* and hoped Cathy understood *her* loyalty to her friend. The two women hadn't exchanged ten words since. It was a foregone conclusion that Emma would not receive an invitation to the Morland/Tilney wedding.

Chris nodded in understanding before bringing up another casualty. "You heard that Nick Patel dropped out of the chapter before initiation?"

"No, I didn't hear that. Damn, he was a good guy."

"He's transferring to Duke. His family's idea, I think."

"Is he the only drop-out?"

"So far."

"How's Henry doing?"

"It's gonna be a tough year, but if anybody can keep the chapter afloat, it's Henry."

The men changed the subject at the return of the ladies.

IT WAS DECIDED TO CONCENTRATE on the rest of Marianne's belongings as she had the furthest to drive and, therefore, should leave the earliest. Thirty minutes later, the Toyota fully packed, Marianne walked out of Buddig Hall for the last time.

"Well, the phone call's been made to Dashwood Central Control, so I'm on the clock. If I don't get home in two and a half hours, Mom'll have the whole Mississippi Highway Patrol on full alert. So, give me a hug, big guy," Marianne said as she put her arms around George. "Take care of Em, okay?" she said for George's ears only.

"Count on it."

Marianne turned to Chris. Their embrace was less comfortable because the emotions were more intense. "Chris, I…" Marianne's eyes watered.

"I know, Mari, I know."

"You better email—you promised. Or I'll drive down here and kick your ass."

"Hmm, sounds like a threat."

"It sure is, Cajun-man."

Chris leaned back a bit. "You ain't got rid of me yet, gal. Drive safe." Marianne's answer was a peck on the cheek.

The guys backed off to give the girls a bit of privacy. Marianne said farewell to Emma first. "I can't call you a bimbo anymore, not with that dark hair."

Emma laughed. "Get out of here, you redneck. You got my email address?"

"Locked and loaded." They embraced. "I'm so happy for you."

Emma wept. "Thank you, Marianne. Damn, I'm going to miss you."

Marianne nodded and turned to Elizabeth. They said nothing; they just looked each other in the eye, having said everything for days before. Both were crying as they hugged goodbye.

"I'm so sor—" Elizabeth began before Marianne cut her off.

"Don't say it. Everything's gonna be good, roomie. I got a referral for a real good therapist in Shreveport, and I'm looking forward to the fresh start. So don't you dare start blaming yourself again. The only way I can be sad is if I don't see you and the vixen here at least three times a semester. Drag her ass to S'port, y'hear?"

"I will."

"How are you doing?"

"I'll be okay. I've done everything I can."

After Elizabeth heard the news about William's father and realized he was going to be absent from his graduation, she entrusted her letter to Chuck Bingley, who swore to put in into William's hands when the time was right. There was nothing else to do.

"I'm actually looking forward to Nicholls State and my new major. I'm going to build things up, rather than tear things down."

"But you lost your scholarship. How is your family taking that?"

"They're fine. I know I screwed up, but they're supporting me. I think they prefer me staying at home while I go to school, anyway." Elizabeth smiled. "Anyhow, everybody's waiting for Chuck to pop the question to Jane. You will come down for the wedding, won't you?"

"And miss the chance of seeing you in one of those horrible bridesmaid dresses? You bet I'll be there, roomie, even if I have to walk!" They hugged again. "Take care, huh?"

"I will. I'll call. 'Bye, Mari."

Marianne wiped her eyes with the palms of her hands, climbed into her packed Toyota, and fired it up. She lowered her window. "Have a great summer, everybody!" she exclaimed as she drove off.

Emma and George walked back into the dorm to get the last of Elizabeth's stuff while Elizabeth and Chris stood in the sun, watching the car disappear from sight down the tree-shaded street.

July: St. Charles Parish

WILLIAM OPENED ONE OF THE boxes from his old apartment, hunting for his HP 12C calculator. Before he could start digging, he noticed the letter sitting on top, his name, *William Darcy,* on the front. The letter from Elizabeth was hand delivered by Chuck a few days after the graduation he missed. William didn't remember where he had tossed the thing, unopened. Now there it was before him again.

He gingerly picked it up, his eyes running over the light blue envelope. Elizabeth had written *I'm so sorry about your father—EB* on the back in a fine, flowing female hand. It was thick; apparently, Elizabeth had written at length. William assumed it was some sort of an apology from what Chuck said when he handed it over.

"*I know this is something you don't want to hear, but Elizabeth's real torn up about all this. About your dad, about what happened, and what she wrote. She's really sorry, and she wants to apologize. You may not be ready to read this letter yet, but please don't just toss it. Do yourself a favor, and wait until you can read it objectively. That's all she wants. Be fair to her—and yourself. You need to put this behind you some day. Take your time. All right, buddy?*"

William closed his eyes. Remembering the letter just put that damn article back in his head. The unjust attack on his father. The pain of her betrayal. The guilt of his bad advice to the chapter. The look of disappointment on his father's face. No, he couldn't read it. He shoved it into his desk drawer. He didn't know if he ever could.

As he slammed the drawer shut, there was a knock on his door. "Will?" came a soft voice as the door opened. It was his sister, Gina, and she was upset.

"Hey, what's up?" William got his emotions under control.

"Do we have to move to New Orleans?"

William sighed. This was the third time they had discussed this. Drawing on his last reserves of gentleness, he took her hands in his. "Gina, I hate the idea as much as you. But, it's just you and me now. I've got to work at the company, and I want to spend as much time with you as I can. It's best that we move into the condo in town and that you go to Sacred Heart."

"But all my friends are here at Destrehan High!"

"I know, sweetie, but I'm going to travel out of town a whole lot, too. You would be by yourself here. In New Orleans, we're going to get Mrs. Annesley to be with you after school and when

I'm not there."

"But why can't I stay here? Mrs. Reynolds can—"

"Gina, no. Mrs. Reynolds has her own family. She can't do what needs to be done." He stroked her hair. "We've got the rest of the summer for you to be with your friends, and we can come back to Dansereau for weekends and holidays. Hey, you know you can invite your friends to the condo for shopping trips and sleepovers and stuff."

"You'll let me have my friends stay over?"

"Sure. Not too much, though. I got to get *some* sleep, squirt."

Gina's smile was tenuous and didn't last long. "Oh, Will, why did Daddy have to die?" she cried as the tears returned.

William drew his sister into his arms, wishing he could find release in tears as well. "I don't know, Gina. I don't know."

August: St. John the Baptist Parish

LOUISIANA HAS THREE SEASONS. AROUND October, the leaves turn brown and the grass goes dormant. For the next few months, the temperature varies from the eighties to the twenties. The rest of the county calls it autumn and winter, but here it is "not summer."

In February, the flowers begin to bloom, climaxing in an explosion of camellias, azaleas, and dogwoods. This is the glorious time of spring in the South. By the time Easter rolls around, summer has already begun.

Summer is high temperatures and higher humidity—humidity so thick it could be cut with a knife. From April to October, day after day, the tedium is broken by the occasional torrential thunderstorm. Much of Louisiana is too far inland for coastal breezes to moderate the anguish. Too many days the state becomes a gigantic sauna. Summer is not lived through in Louisiana; it is endured.

On such a day, a navy blue Ford pulled off Old US Highway 51 south of Manchac and the Tangipahoa Parish line. Two men in suits climbed out and made their way through a jungle of police cars and emergency vehicles, red and blue flashing lights competing with the bright noonday sun. Traffic noise from the elevated

Interstate 55/US 51 less than hundred yards away was ever-present.

One of the suits wiped his brow with a handkerchief. "Crap, it's hot, Fitz."

Richard Fitzwilliam did not reply to his companion, a detective from the NOPD Second District homicide unit. Of course, it was hot in August. Summer was no time to make unnecessary conversation or move quickly. The two policemen sauntered up to a black state trooper and a middle-aged white man in a sport coat.

"Sheriff, Captain," Fitzwilliam greeted the two as he introduced his companion.

"Hot enough for you, podna?" asked the white sheriff, who was using his cowboy hat as an impromptu fan.

"Yes, sir," he answered. "What do we have, Captain?" Regulations put the state police in command.

"Two bodies were discovered last night, a male and a female." The captain, a tall African-American in a navy blue uniform and Smoky Bear hat, led the way into the thick underbrush twenty feet from the roadside. Deputies, troopers, and others were swarming all over the place, along with the insects.

"Yeah," added the sheriff, as he replaced the cowboy hat on his head. "This old boy was bull-lightin'—poaching swamp deer, most likely—when he comes across this. Scared the crap outta him." The state police might be in charge, but he was going to get his two cents in.

Two long, black bags were before them. At the detective's nod, they were zippered open. The experienced lawmen still flinched from the stench of death that filled the air. Two bodies, male and female. Caucasian, maybe, but it was hard to tell. The elements had not been kind.

The homicide detective waved, and the coroner's people closed up the bags again. "Okay. So why call us?" he asked.

"It was a professional hit, not robbery or personal," reported the captain. "One shot each in the back of the head. Don't know yet if it was done here or if this was a body dump. ID from New Orleans was in the male's back pocket."

The two NOPD officers put on latex gloves and took the offered driver's license. "Thomas Bertram. Uptown address. Yeah, he's been on the Missing Persons list for a couple months. And the woman?"

"No ID, but there was this." He handed Fitzwilliam a necklace. The heart-shaped charm read: *S. Our love will guide us through life One Step at a Time. T.*

"Sarah Smith was reported missing about the same time," said Fitzwilliam.

"We got her dental records back in the city," reported the homicide investigator. "How long they been here?"

"It's early, but we think it's been four or five months."

The investigator checked his notes. "Yeah, that fits."

Fitzwilliam spoke up. "But why call in Narcotics?"

"We found this in the vic's wallet." Inside a plastic bag was a NOPD business card. "Is it genuine?"

Fitzwilliam took one look at it and his hands started to shake. "Yeah, it's one of ours."

"Was Bertram one of your informants?"

"No, he wasn't." When Bertram was reported missing, the Second District did a routine check of its records. It came up blank.

"Maybe he picked it up somewhere, or somebody gave it to 'im," offered the sheriff helpfully. "Maybe you got another rat inside, hmm?"

"Don't know, Sheriff," Fitzwilliam answered. But inside he did know. "Little close in here. If y'all excuse me, I'm gonna get some air." He walked off a ways, still holding the bag with the card.

Looking at the treetops, Fitzwilliam gathered his thoughts. Back in December, his captain confided that the Second District had been compromised. There was a mole in place. For eight months, Fitzwilliam had kept his eyes open, hoping the rumors were groundless. But it was a false hope; the proof was in his hand.

Jones doesn't give out her card to just anyone. Only three ways Bertram could have gotten it. Jones gave it to him, Bertram picked it up off her desk, or somebody is setting up Jones. There's no record of Bertram being in the precinct, not from Jones or anybody else. No official record, that is—but records can be changed or destroyed.

Any way you look at it, there's a rotten apple in the Second District. Either somebody's covering his tracks by pointing at Jones, or—

The rest of the thought was too painful to consider. One of his team, his people, had gone bad. A traitor and an accessory to murder. Or worse.

Fitzwilliam wiped away the sweat on his forehead as he baked in the summer heat, the air stifling and stinking. The buzzing of insects and the chirping of birds competed with the noise of traffic and the squawking of police radios. The heat built up on the inside as his anger grew.

There was only one thread that linked a mole, Narcotics, Bertram, and professional hits, and his name was Gregory "G-Daddy" Wickham. In his ten years on the force, Lt. Richard Fitzwilliam had learned to trust his gut, and that trust had broken cases and kept him alive. Now his gut was telling him that Wickham was behind this. For some reason, Wickham saw Bertram as a threat and either killed him or had him killed.

The latter was more likely. It made sense, given Wickham's record and recent changes in the drug trade. A violent gang from Treme had moved in on Uptown. Was a piece of his drug trade the price Wickham paid? He would have to find out.

Fitzwilliam sighed. The first thing to do was to have a secret talk with the Public Integrity Division. It wouldn't be hard. The PID was purposely not located in NOPD headquarters. No one but PID would know he had spoken to them. Nobody would get spooked.

It galled Fitzwilliam to rat out a fellow cop. There was little black or white in the NOPD; they were all brothers and sisters in blue. Jones might be an innocent victim after all. But Fitz could not allow his loyalty to his fellow officers to override the necessity of rooting out any cancer within the force.

He would leave the mole to the PID. Wickham he reserved for himself. That monster had destroyed a young couple trying to turn their lives around, threatened his cousin, was probably involved in an attack on a coed, and had perhaps corrupted a fellow cop. It was time for G-Daddy to go down hard. It might take him years, but Fitzwilliam was patient. He had at least ten years before retirement.

I'm going to get that son of a bitch, if it's the last thing I ever do.

The mocking cries of the birds in the trees were his only answer.

Grimly, Fitzwilliam returned to work. There was a crime scene to process.

END OF VOLUME ONE

To be continued in

Elysian Dreams

Volume Two of
CRESCENT CITY

Appreciation

When taking on a project of this scope, an author cannot do it alone. I am fortunate to have a number of wonderful ladies who serve as my **Beta Babes**, reading and correcting my gross errors. If the story you have just read speaks at all to you, it is because of these ladies' dedication to this thankless task.

Debbie Styne and **Ellen Pickels,** along with my wife, are the major editors of this work.

Sarah Hunt, Bonnie Carasso, Amy Robinson, Nicole Newchurch, and **Mary Anne Mushatt** helped make the original manuscript sing.

Ladies, thank you so much.

Thanks go to my fellow members of "The Six-Pack"—**Linnea Eileen, June, Susan, Shelby,** and **Meg**—who whined for me to write a modern. If it weren't for you ladies, *CRESCENT CITY* wouldn't have happened.

And to my #1 Beta Babe, **my lovely wife, Barbara**, who encouraged me to write this story and supported me while I relived the agony. I love you, my dear.

Bibliography, Sources, and Suggested Readings

Austen, Jane. *Emma.*
—. *Pride and Prejudice.*
—. *Sense and Sensibility.*

Caldwell, Jack. *The Plains of Chalmette: a Story of Crescent City.* Venice: White Soup Press, 2015.
—. *Elysian Dreams: Volume Two of Crescent City.* Venice: White Soup Press, 2015.
—. *Ruin and Renewal: Volume Three of Crescent City.* Venice: White Soup Press, 2015.

Dufour, Charles M. *Ten Flags in the Wind: The Story of Louisiana.* New York: Harper & Row, 1967 (out of print).

The National Hurricane Center website archives.

The New Orleans Times-Picayune archives.

Remini, Robert V. *The Battle of New Orleans: Andrew Jackson and America's First Military Victory.* New York: Viking, 1999.

Rose, Chris. *1 Dead in Attic.* New Orleans: Chris Rose Books, 2005.

Definitions

It should be noted that New Orleans and Southern Louisiana are not part of what is commonly called the American South. They have a different culture and do not have the southern drawl common to Northern Louisiana and the rest of the Southern United States.

BANQUETTE: The sidewalk.

BAYOU: A slow moving stream or river. The term, used primarily in the Southern US, is thought to be derived from the Choctaw word "bayuk."

CAJUNS: The Acadians, the original French settlers in the maritime provinces of Canada. After the British expelled the Acadians from their homes (*Le Grand Dérangement, 1755-1764*), most ended up in Louisiana. The name *Acadian* became corrupted over time to *Cajun*, which is used to describe the country folk of Southern Louisiana, their culture, language, and style of cooking.

CHER or CHERE: Sweet, sweetheart, a Cajun term of endearment to a loved one.

COKE: A cola, a soft drink. Really, any soft drink.

COONASS: A controversial term in the Cajun lexicon. The word originated in Southern Louisiana and is derived from the belief that Cajuns frequently ate raccoons. To some Cajuns, it is regarded as the supreme ethnic slur, meaning "ignorant, backwards Cajun." To others, the term is a badge of pride. In Southern Louisiana, for example, one can often see bumper stickers reading "RCA: Registered Coonass American."

CRAWFISH: Sometimes spelled "crayfish," they resemble lobsters but are much smaller. Locally, they are known as "mudbugs" because they live and grow in the mud of freshwater bayous. They can be served many ways: in étouffée, jambalaya, gumbos, or simply boiled.

CREOLE: The term "Creole" has long generated confusion and controversy. The word invites debate because it possesses several meanings, some of which concern the innately sensitive subjects of race and ethnicity. In its broadest sense, Creole means "native" or, in the context of Louisiana history, "native to Louisiana." In a narrower sense, however, it has historically referred to black, white, and mixed-raced persons who are native to Louisiana. In short, the word means different things to different people, and more than one ethnic group arguably has a claim to the term. The term has expanded and now embraces a type of cuisine and a style of architecture.

DIRTY RICE: Pan-fried leftover cooked rice sautéed with green peppers, onion, celery, stock, liver, giblets and many other ingredients.

DRESSED: Adding mayonnaise, lettuce, tomatoes, and pickles to a sandwich.

FAUBOURG: A French term for a neighborhood.

GALLERIES: An outdoor balcony, supported by posts or columns anchored to the ground. Technically, the "balconies" in the French Quarter are really galleries.

LAISSEZ LES BON TEMPS ROULER: "Let the good times roll."

LAGNIAPPE: Pronounced "LAN-yap" A little something extra.

MAKING GROCERIES: To go grocery shopping, visiting the market.

NEUTRAL GROUND: The grassy or cement strip (medians) in the middle of a divided street and boulevards. In the early 1800's, a grassy strip along Canal Street between the *Faubourg St. Marie* (where the Americans lived) and the *Vieux Carré* (home of the Creole aristocracy) was designated as a place where merchants and politicians could meet in peace. It was called the Neutral Ground, and the name stuck. The terms "median" and/or "island" are never used in New Orleans.

NEW ORLEANS: How the name of the major city of Louisiana is pronounced has caused great consternation among the locals. New Orleans may be pronounced "nu OR-le-ons," "nu OR-lens," or "NAW-lens." It is never pronounced "nu OR-leeens." Yet, the parish where the city is located is pronounced like its French namesake, "OR-leeens." Confusing, isn't it?

PARISH: A county, a political subdivision of the state.

PASS BY YOUR MAMA'S: Go to your mother's house.

PECAN: Pronounced "pa-KAWN," not "PEE-can."

PO'BOY or POOR BOY: A sandwich made with French bread, stuffed with almost anything.

PODNA: "Partner." A form of address for men, usually for ones with whom one is not acquainted.

PRALINE: A sugary Creole candy, invented in New Orleans (not the same as the French culinary/confectionery term "praline" or "praliné"). The classic version is made with sugar, brown sugar, butter, vanilla and pecans, and is a flat sugary pecan-filled disk. Pronounced "PRAH-leen," not "pray-LEEN."

SHOTGUN: Usually part of a "double." A single row house in which all rooms on one side are connected by a long hallway. Supposedly, one can open the front door and shoot a gun straight through the back door without hitting a single wall.

SNOWBALL or SNO-BALL: A snow cone—shaved ice covered with favored syrup. It's something you eat, not something you throw.

STOOP: The front steps of a house.

SHOW: The movie theater.

UPTOWN SIDE, DOWNTOWN SIDE, LAKESIDE, RIVERSIDE: The four cardinal points of the New Orleanian compass. "North, south, east, west" do not work in New Orleans.

VIEUX CARRÉ: French for "old square." It refers to the original settlement of *La Nouvelle-Orléans* (New Orleans). The district is now known as the French Quarter.

WHERE Y'AT!: The traditional working class New Orleanian greeting, and the source for the term "Yat", often used (primarily by non-New Orleanians, it is said) to describe New Orleanians with the telltale accent. The proper response is, "Awrite."

Y'ALL: The plural form of the second person verb, "you all." It's NOT pronounced as they would in the south, though—no twang, no drawl. Just "y'all."

YAMS: Sweet potatoes. They are not real yams.

YAT: A New Orleanian of working class roots.

YEAH, YOU RITE: An emphatic statement of agreement and affirmation, sometimes used as a general exclamation of happiness. The accent is on the first word, and it's spoken as one word.

About the Author

Jack Caldwell is an author, amateur historian, professional economic developer, playwright, and like many Cajuns, a darn good cook. Born and raised in the Bayou County of Louisiana, Jack and his wife, Barbara, are Hurricane Katrina victims who now make the Suncoast of Florida their home.

Jack is the author of four Jane Austen-themed books. PEMBERLEY RANCH is a retelling of *Pride & Prejudice* set in Reconstruction Texas. THE THREE COLONELS: JANE AUSTEN'S FIGHTING MEN is a sequel to *Pride & Prejudice* and *Sense & Sensibility*. MR. DARCY CAME TO DINNER and THE COMPANION OF HIS FUTURE LIFE are *Pride & Prejudice*-flavored farces.

In 2015, he released the first four of a series of historical novels about New Orleans, titled THE CRESCENT CITY SERIES. THE PLAINS OF CHALMETTE begins the series, commemorating the Bicentennial of the Battle of New Orleans. He marked the tenth anniversary of Hurricane Katrina with three modern novels: BOURBON STREET NIGHTS, ELYSIAN DREAMS, and RUIN AND RENEWAL.

When not writing or traveling with Barbara, Jack attempts to play golf. A devout convert to Roman Catholicism, Jack is married with three grown sons. Jack's blog postings — **The Cajun Cheesehead Chronicles** — appear regularly at **Austen Variations**.

Web site: **Rambling of a Cajun in Exile**:
  https://cajuncheesehead.com
  Austen Variations: http://austenvariations.com/

Facebook: https://www.facebook.com/pages/Jack-Caldwell-author/132047236805555

Twitter: @JCaldwell25

The Crescent City Series:

All available from White Soup Press

THE PLAINS OF CHALMETTE: a Story of Crescent City

BOURBON STREET NIGHTS: Volume One of Crescent City

ELYSIAN DREAMS: Volume Two of Crescent City

RUIN AND RENEWAL: Volume Three of Crescent City

Other Novels by Jack Caldwell:

Available from Sourcebooks Landmark:

PEMBERLEY RANCH

THE THREE COLONELS: Jane Austen's Fighting Men

Available from White Soup Press:

MR. DARCY CAME TO DINNER: a Jane Austen farce

THE COMPANION OF HIS FUTURE LIFE